TURQUOISE

El Colibrí de Turquesa

蜂鸟

BY

ROCKY BARILLA

ROSQUETE PRESS

 This is a work of fiction. Names, characters, places, and events are either the product of the author's imagination or are used fictitiously, and any resemblance to actual persons, living or dead, events, or locales is entirely coincidental.

Book 2 of the Little Gems series

Book Art by Rocky Barilla © 2023

Library of Congress Control Number: 2023907483

ISBN: 979-8-9882301-0-6

OTHER WORKS BY ROCKY BARILLA

A TASTE OF CHOCOLATE
Gold Medal Winner of the 2024 International Latino Book Awards
Rudolfo Anaya Best Latino Focused Fiction

LA PERLA NEGRA – The Black Pearl
First Place Winner of the 2023 International Latino Book Awards for Best Novel - Historical Fiction

SHATTERED DREAMS
Award Winner of the 2023 Latino Literary Now's Latino Books into Movies Awards for Romance
Honorable Mention Winner of the 2022 International Latino Book Awards for the Rodolfo Anaya Best Latino Focused Fiction Book

SANCTUARY
Award Winner of the 2023 Latino Literary Now's Latino Books into Movies Awards for Romance
Honorable Mention Winner of the 2021 International Latino Book Awards for the Rodolfo Anaya Best Latino Focused Fiction Book

STARS
Honorable Mention Winner of the 2020 International Latino Book Awards for Best Novel - Romance

Esmeralda
First Place Winner of the 2019 International Latino Book Awards for Best Novel - Fantasy Fiction

Harmony of Colors
Second Place Winner of the 2018 International Latino Book Awards for Best Novel - Latino-Focused Fiction

Ay to Zi
Award Winner of the 2018 Latino Literary Now's Latino Books into Movies Awards for Romance
Second Place Winner of the 2017 International Latino Book Awards for Best Novel – Romance

The Devil's Disciple
Award Winner of the 2018 Latino Literary Now's Latino Books into Movies Awards for Suspense/Mystery
Second Place Winner of the 2016 International Latino Book Awards for Best Novel – Mystery

A Taste of Honey
First Place Winner of the 2015 Latino Literary Now's Latino Books into Movies Awards for Fantasy Fiction
Second Place Winner of the 2015 International Latino Book Awards for Best Novel - Fantasy Fiction

All works are published by Rosquete Press. All works are or will be available as Kindle or CreateSpace editions on Amazon.com

DEDICATION

This book is dedicated to my compadres, Yesenia and Hector, who live in Zihuatanejo, Mexico (think Shawshank Redemption). They share their children (Emilio and Hectorín) with us.

Hector is an entrepreneur who owns a chain of small businesses and a mango farm (!). Yum!

Yesenia is an accomplished food and beverage expert. She is a renowned maestra mezcalera and wine sommelier in Mexico.

Looking forward to a future wine tasting trip with them to the Valle de Guadalupe, Mexico.

TABLE OF CONTENTS

ACKNOWLEDGEMENTS

One of the two story lines of this novel is about the Chinese migration to Mexico. The other thread is the Mexican-Chinese communities in Mexico. Chino Latinos! Like most of my books, this story is a mélange of truth and fiction. Why did I write about this subject? Several people acted as inspirations for this narration.

My neighbors, Don and Geri, do daily walks up and down our street. It's a steep hill so they often stop by to chat. Don has told me about how his father migrated from China and became a prominent professor through perseverance and hard work. Isn't this the same story for Mexicans and Central Americans, the Irish, the Southern and Eastern Europeans, et al.?

Added to this, is the fact that I was born in Chinatown in Los Angeles (albeit at the French Hospital. Go figure.). My suegro lived in Mexicali where there is a sizable Mexican-Chinese population and great Chinese food. My mother worked at Castelar Elementary School which is located in Los Angeles' Chinatown. These facts reflect the Mexican-Chinese connection. Some of my chapters share personal anecdotes about this bond.

Migration has been happening since the Garden of Eden. Over the centuries geographic borders have changed, wars have been waged, and people have migrated.

Ethnic communities have been the backbone of every country. They provide economic security but attract racism and hatred.

Aren't we all descended from Adam and Eve? Aren't we all brothers and sisters? How come indigenous peoples always seem to get screwed? These are philosophical questions that have no clear answers.

My personal belief is: while it is good to respect and appreciate similarities and differences, the bottom line is that people should treat people like they themselves want to be treated. Love thy neighbor as thyself.

Coexistence can be a beautiful thing!

PROLOGUE

The circumnavigator Ferdinand Magellan called the huge body of water that stretched from Mexico to China, the Pacific Ocean. It's been anything but peaceful! Spanish and Portuguese were the first colonial explorers Their exploits led to the forced religious proselytization of Asia, the unquenchable thirst for spices and gold, and the commerce of slave trade.

Specifically concerning the Chinese, the pejorative term "Coolie trade" espoused the notion that Asian emigrants could contract themselves to work for several years in the New World to earn money and to settle down. However, a significant number of Chinese were kidnapped or deceived into becoming laborers in the New World. Chinese were being sold like pigs "mai jui jai" (the sale of pigs). Most indentured contracts with the Chinese were never honored and there were no legal means to enforce them.

Historically, for Mexico and the New World, there was an ever-increasing need for cheap labor. African slavery was diminished as the United States became involved in slave revolts and the Civil War. In fact, one of the main purposes of the Second Amendment of the U.S. Constitution was to allow slave owners to use arms to crush slave rebellions.

The first wave of Chinese immigration to Mexico began in the 1870's. Famine, disease, and warfare had left China in shambles. Concurrently, Mexican President Porfirio Diaz wanted to modernize Mexico to emulate its European counterparts. Railroads had to be built, and immigrant labor needed to be imported. But imported Europeans workers did not like northern Mexico because of its hot desert climate. Instead, Chinese immigrants were brought in to work on the railroads and in the mines under undesirable conditions.

Mexico had been exposed to slavery by the Portuguese traders from the Orient. Along with silk and spices, the Portuguese ships also brought in all manner of Asian slaves to be sold or bartered. From all parts of Asia, these immigrants were called "Chinos," even though they were from all parts of Asia.

Chinese immigration was formally institutionalized in 1893 by the bilateral Treaty of Amity, Commerce and Navigation, which granted the Chinese immigrants to Mexico the same legal rights as Mexican nationals. Some Chinese had arrived prior to 1893 and had already established small colonies in Guaymas and Ensenada, Mexico.

But over time, Mexico became further embroiled in a political quandary. The U.S. and Europe invested in oil, mining, and cash crops e.g., cotton. Everybody had their own interests to protect. Chinese labor increased while Mexican labor decreased. The Mexican Revolution forced entities to choose sides.

It is within this context that the legacy of Chan Toy, Ana, and the turquoise hummingbird begins.

PART I – PROFESSOR REYNOSO

CHAPTER 1 – THE VISIT

Friday, March 15, 2019
Guadalajara

Juanita Gutierrez's plump little body swayed from side to side as she strolled into Professor Francisco Reynoso's office at the University of Guadalajara's History Department. Her silver-grey bob hairdo, offset by the powder blue business suit, affirmed that she was an institutional fixture at the college. The higher-up administrators had wanted Juanita to retire so that they could bring in new blood, or perhaps a relative, but she was adamant about "training" new faculty and "managing" existing professors. Everybody gave her a wide berth. She handled the department's expenses that could be reimbursed judiciously (or not).

Juanita gave a cursory knock on Reynoso's open office door with her arthritic knuckles. She had to be in her seventies, but nobody knew for sure.

"Professor, your two o'clock appointment is here," she advised him in her customary officious manner. She stared at him for a moment.

Professor Reynoso looked up from his computer and smiled at Juanita. The 5'11" academician had olive skin and was of medium build. Since moving from the San Francisco Bay Area to Guadalajara, he had exchanged his three-day growth beard for a pencil moustache at the special request of his new wife. His wife, Alex had, told him it was more Mexican. He wore guayaberas instead of a shirt and tie but was still professorial.

The 48-year-old professor's newer workplace was stark compared to his old office at Stanford University. This office was cramped and could only accommodate one large pre-Columbian painting on each wall. Back in Palo Alto, it was floor-to-ceiling plaques, photos, and prints. He had the framed certificate of his Ph.D. in Latin-American Studies earned at the University of Southern California in 1997. There was also a group photo with a youthful, long haired, Zapata-moustached version of himself standing next to César Chávez and other UFW supporters during the table grape boycott. And then there were some small 8 by 10-inch print copies of colorful artwork that included Alejandro Rangel Hidalgo, Amado Peña, and Frida Kahlo. Oh well, *así es la vida.*

Francisco was born in the Mount Washington area of Los Angeles in 1971. His Spanish growing up was pocho. After surviving twelve years of strict Catholic schools, he went over to the west side of town and earned his bachelor's degree in Spanish at UCLA. He was fortunate to do his junior year abroad in Barcelona, where he fell in love with the Spanish part of his Latino heritage.

After graduation, he moved to West Los Angeles and enrolled at UCLA's cross-town rival, USC. It took him four grueling years to earn his doctorate in Latin-American studies. His Ph.D. thesis was entitled "Mexico: Benito Juarez and French Imperialism." This controversial work was printed by the University of California Press, and it placed him in the limelight of academic debates and in the center of Latino community protests. Stanford University snatched up this gutsy academician and hired him for its Latin-American Studies Department.

Francisco was now in the middle of his first semester at the University of Guadalajara teaching as part of a special exchange program with Stanford University. Dean Dorothy Chandler and Stanford University were very excited about the potential global benefits from this Mexico-U.S. program. At least once a month he had to make a public relations appearance in front of a Mexican alumni group, community organization, or high school in order to promote the program. The more exposure of the Stanford program, the more potential funding for it in the future.

Between these guest appearances and his teaching, Francisco was improving his Spanish. No more "pochismos." He was a quick study in picking up on the local idioms.

"Just give me a moment," Francisco said in Spanish to Juanita.

Francisco started to clear off the top of his old oak desk that had been pristine two months before he began his academic assignment. His desk calendar was now filled with notes, scribbles, and scratch outs. He gathered up the pile of the Stanford files that was on his right and twisted around in his chair to stuff the materials in the credenza behind him. He moved the photo of his recent bride, Alex, with her hair tressed in green, white and red ribbons, to fill the now vacant space on the desk.

The Latin-American History course materials were another story. Placing an Aztec pyramid paperweight on top of the stack would have to suffice. Dean Miranda Ríos (his wife's comadre) had inundated him with dozens of books, articles, and journals to enhance his classes. Most were in Spanish. He literally studied them one to two hours per night when his wife Alex was working late at the hospital. She worked there as an endocrinologist.

A minute later Juanita escorted two people into the professor's office. One was a short middle-aged man wearing a robin's egg blue guayabera. His skin was dark and the hair on his head was thinned out. His brown eyes were almond-shaped. He had a long, scraggly goatee. He looked to be in his early 40's.

The first guest stepped forward quickly and extended his hand.

"Thank you, Professor Reynoso, for agreeing to see us," he gave a slight bow and extended his hand. "I'm Hao Chin Martín," he spoke in Spanish with a Mexican accent.

He handed Professor Reynoso a business card. Hao Chin Martín was a District Manager for Canada SinoMex Mining, Ltd, in Vancouver, B.C. The two men shook hands.

"And this is my colleague, Lilí Song," Hao gestured to a tall, slender woman with scarlet red lipstick and jet-black hair that extended down to the small of her back. She was sporting a long pink silk dress with a slit up to the thigh.

The young woman bowed. She looked young but was probably older she looked. He could detect the smell of cigarette smoke from her person mingled with a sweet, florid orange blossom scent. It was a bit cloying. Francisco had not expected a second visitor. His former teaching assistant, Tina Fang, from Stanford had not mentioned it in her emails.

"Please, sit down," Francisco motioned to the well-used wooden chairs. "Tina has written me and asked me to meet with you. And as you know, no one can say no to Tina."

Tina Fang had been his right-hand teaching assistant at Stanford. Tina was born in the Hong Kong/Macau region and was fluent in Cantonese, Spanish, and Portuguese. After spending the previous summer in São Paulo, she had begun her doctoral dissertation on "The Linguistic History of Early 16th Century Mexico," as a follow up to her collaborative work with Professor Reynoso on the 1527 Saavedra Mexico-Moluccas Pacific Ocean expedition. She had been transferred to an Italian Professor colleague when Francisco obtained a visiting professorship at the University of Guadalajara.

Juanita came into the room with a tray of reddish-colored cold drink, Jamaica (hibiscus) agua fresca.

"How can I help you, Mr. Martín?" the professor asked in a pleasant tone in Spanish.

"Well, as you know, Tina is a distant cousin of mine. Our families come from the same village in China," Hao was leaning forward in his chair. "Professor, may I please ask a favor? My colleague understands some Spanish and Portuguese, but she is more fluent in English."

"Sure, no problem,"

The two visitors bowed and said thanks.

"Tina spent last summer in São Paulo in the overseas program abroad," he began in English. "Rubí and Tina became good friends. Lilí is Rubí's twin sister. Tina shared her educational goals and talked about your collaborative work on Spanish-Mexican trade with the Far East."

Francisco nodded. He was listening but was confused. *What does this have to do with me? On the other hand, Tina would not have arranged this meeting if it wasn't important.* But he was feeling impatient. It was the end of the week. He wanted to escape from his office as soon as possible. He and his wife, Alex, were having dinner with Dean Ríos (Alex's comadre) and her husband Sol (Francisco's partner in crime.)

"Mr. Martín, how can I help you?" Francisco repeated, wanting to keep the conversation short and professional.

"Well, as you know, Mexico and China have had a good international relationship for almost five hundred years." He talked slowly. "I, myself, have Chinese heritage in my blood. To answer your question, we would like you to conduct a comprehensive study on the Chinese migration to Mexicali and the State of Sonora. We believe there is a vast treasure of knowledge to be had."

Francisco frowned. "This is not normally our area of expertise. UCLA Professor Roberto Chao Romero is a renowned scholar on the subject. And I think the University of Arizona might also have some interest in the subject matter. You should check them out."

Hao looked at his colleague, Lilí. Francisco had noticed that she was very attractive as soon as she had walked in with Mr. Martín. Her simple pink dress contrasted with her scarlet red lipstick. Around her neck she wore a green and red jade pendant with a small gold dragon imbedded in it and a solid jade bracelet. The pair quietly conversed with each other (in Mandarin) for a few moments.

"Sorry for that, Professor, Lilí says that her company is willing to make a modest contribution to Stanford for whatever assistance you might provide."

Francisco knew he was trapped. Dean Chandler was always looking for additional funds and Dean Ríos could certainly use the money. He had to tread lightly and be diplomatic about the request.

The professor and his two guests engaged in light negotiations.

In the end, Francisco stated that he would discuss the matter with his respective deans. He knew that the Chinese business practice would respect that.

"Mr. Martin, if I am going to submit this request, I am going to need your proposal in writing, with background documentation."

"As you wish, professor. We understand," Hao nodded.

"In terms of a contribution, how much are we talking about?" Francisco knew that would be the first question Dean Chandler would ask.

"Three million U.S. dollars," Lilí interjected.

CHAPTER 2 – COLLEGE BOUND

Friday, March 15, 2019

Guadalajara

The slender, silver-haired Esteban parked the black Lexus SUV in front of the two-story, Moorish style mansion. The cream-colored home was surrounded by a tall black wrought iron fence and was located in the upscale Colonia América of Guadalajara. Francisco got out of the vehicle.

"Thank you, Esteban," he said in a friendly, but tired, manner. "By the way, we'll be leaving for the Ríos' at about 7:30."

"Yes, sir."

Moments later, as he wearily climbed the stairs, he was greeted by his wife, Dr. Alejandra "Alex" Mora. They kissed. It was still passionate. They had been married for two months. Tonight, she was dazzling in an emerald-green dress that offset her auburn shoulder length hair. Her sparkling ebony eyes paired with the black pearl earrings and a black pearl necklace.

The 5'6" shapely Alex was born in La Paz in 1975 and was a top endocrinologist in Guadalajara. Her father had died of leukemia, so she was very cautious about her health and diet. She had been married before but was widowed after only three years of marriage.

"How was your day, mi amor?" She gave him a sweet smile.

"The same old, same old," Francisco grinned back. He always tried to downplay the ups and downs of his job. He didn't want to complain about not being 100% proficient in Spanish or about how the faculty here were so different from what he was used to. His wife was an endocrinologist who dealt with life and death situations every day; so his problems paled in comparison. They had only been married for a short period and he didn't want her to see him as a chronic complainer. Besides, he was learning: *Así es la vida.*

An hour later the couple arrived at the Ríos' two-story house in the posh Chapultepec District of Guadalajara. Francisco and Miranda's husband, Sol, began the evening by sipping margaritas in the living room and talking local sports. Alex did not imbibe much. She was nursing an iced mint tea. Socorro, a middle-aged woman wearing a white huipil with colorful embroidery, brought in a tray of queso fundido as an appetizer.

Miranda entered the salon in a long red dress with a shell necklace. "Carlos just called. He can't make it tonight." Carlos Erandi was team teaching with Francisco at the same time that he was working on his doctorate. It was part of an agreement that allowed Francisco to teach at the University of Guadalajara. Miranda had negotiated the deal, especially since Alex was the godmother of her daughter, Mirasol. The downside for Carlos was that his family lived in Guanajuato, and he drove the long-distance home on Friday mornings.

"Miranda, he really has innate teaching skills," Francisco jumped in. "The students really like him."

"I don't know what he is going to do this summer," commented Miranda, who was the dean that supervised both Francisco and Carlos. She had been recently promoted from being a Linguistics professor to the position of the Dean of the Social Sciences Department. She continued, "We are not going to have classes this summer. Budget concerns. Maybe he'll go back to being a tour guide. Either way, he is not going to see much of his family."

"When are you and comadre going to leave for your honeymoon?" asked Sol, trying to change the subject. Sol was the owner of "Los Rayos del Sol," a solar panel company and talked sports 24/7.

Francisco and Alex had gotten married on January 26 and were still debating whether to have a long summer honeymoon in southern Spain or in Sicily. Part of the problem was that Francisco had to finalize the lease of his Bay Area house. His realtor friend wanted him to sell the property, but his financial advisor told him that property prices would be rising, plus there was the issue of capital gains taxes. He also wanted to show Alex around the Stanford campus and introduce here to his friends. Right now, they were working on a visa for her.

"The end of June," Francisco answered. "Right after the end of classes."

"Oye, Francisco, when you go to Europe, rent a big villa," Sol laughed. "Miranda and I will fly over and spend a week with you. We might even bring Mirasol." Mirasol was the only child of Sol and Miranda.

For the next 45 minutes, they talked about how Miranda was handling being the new dean.

"It's quite a challenge," she stated tactfully. "The good old boys club is still going strong. But they are coming around. I leave them alone and sign off on their expenses. Everything is good. I am going to try to talk one or two of them into early retirement."

"What if they don't want to go?" asked her husband naively.

"Well, then, they might have some crappy teaching assignments and miss lunches with their cronies," Miranda gave a devilish grin. There was an uneasy laugh among the other three.

As if on cue, Mirasol waltzed into the room. She went over and gave her godmother, Alex, a kiss, and then one for Francisco.

The 17-year-old was tall and slender and had long black hair. She was wearing a blue and yellow ABBA tee shirt and indigo jeans with Adidas sneakers. She gave everyone a very white Hollywood smile.

"Mija has received three letters of acceptance so far," her father proudly announced. Everybody was anticipating where Mirasol would be attending college in the fall.

"¡Felicidades!" echoed her comadre and Francisco. "Have you made any decisions yet?"

"So far I've heard from UCLA, the University of Texas, and the University of Arizona," answered Mirasol. "I am still waiting to hear from Smith and Stanford."

"Those are all excellent schools. Are you ready for college?" asked Francisco.

"Well, yes and no," her perfect smile (thanks to braces) confidently said. "I want to explore new worlds and meet exciting people. But on the other hand, I will miss all of you."

"I think she should go to an all-girls college where there are no boys," her father added. In reality, he would have preferred a convent.

"Oh, dad!" sighed Mirasol. "Sandra (her best friend) and Erik are going to the University of Miami together. He has family there."

"That's my point!" Sol was starting to get more serious. "I bet she comes back home within a year, heartbroken and with no degree."

Miranda frowned as she gave her husband a dirty look. She didn't disagree with him, but their daughter needed to flee the nest and start making her own decisions and live with the consequences. They had raised Mirasol and trusted her.

"Dinner is served," Socorro the cook, announced, saving the day.

The green salad was served with shaved carrots, roasted pumpkin seeds, and sliced radishes. It was dressed with a few drops of a cilantro-mango salsa.

"Comadre, have you ever been to Canada?" Miranda was trying to deflect the tension in the air.

"One place that I have never been to is Vancouver," Alex took the baton. "They say it is beautiful."

"I hear their salmon is very good," Sol was now more mellow. "But their beers are very expensive and not as good as ours."

The rest of the evening went smoothly. The cochinita pibil was juicy and flavorful. After dinner, they all retired to the living room for dessert and coffee. Mirasol left the adults.

A half hour later, Alex's eyes started to droop. She had to work at the hospital the next day. They said their goodbyes.

As he kissed Miranda's cheek, Francisco suddenly became pensive about his meeting earlier that day. The conversation with Hao and his colleague had bothered Francisco. Something was not right. He softly said, "Miranda, I need to meet with you sometime this week to talk over a strange meeting I had today."

She looked at him quizzically. "No problem. A cafecito with you would be good. Let's see how you are doing."

CHAPTER 3 – TOUCHING BASES

Tuesday, March 19, 2019
University of Guadalajara

Professor Montoya retired at the end of 2018 as Dean of the Social Sciences Department at the University of Guadalajara, and was replaced by Miranda Ríos, a highly respected Linguistics professor. The good old boys grumbled and made sexist comments, but Miranda was talented and strong-willed. And she controlled the purse strings and privileges. Professor Léon was an outspoken critic of hers who was constantly complaining about this or that until his request to attend a prestigious conference (aka boondoggle) was rejected for budgetary reasons. He quickly changed his tune. She wielded a velvet glove, and her underlings were beginning to fall in line.

On the lighter side, she was able to finesse a teaching assignment for her comadre's husband, Francisco Reynoso, and recruited Carlos Erandi as an Associate Professor while the latter worked on his dissertation. She would meet with the two gentlemen every other Tuesday to review their progress. She also bounced new or innovative ideas off of them. Francisco and Carlos represented the new breed of faculty that was bold and engaging. It was Miranda who had decided to allow Francisco and Carlos to team teach the Latin-American History series. Francisco was a great mentor and Carlos was a wonderful source of information.

After Dean Ríos had a short debriefing meeting with Francisco and Carlos, the latter had to run to his dissertation class. However, that was after Alma, Dean Ríos' long-term secretary, whom she had promoted when she became dean, had fed the two men some of her homemade guayaba jelly cookies which they inhaled with their coffee. *Men are so predictable.* Dean Ríos shook her head. She and Francisco were now alone.

"Francisco, how is he doing?" she was referring to Carlos.

"Fantastic! The students really like him. His outgoing personality clicks with them."

"And Francisco, how are you doing?"

"Fine. It's a lot of hard work. The students are very tolerant of my Spanish. And Carlos helps out a lot. It's enjoyable."

“The other night you said that you wanted to talk. Is something bothering you?” Miranda was sharp.

Francisco went on to describe the unusual meeting with Hao Chin Martín and amount of money his assistant had blurted out.

“What did Tina say about her cousin?”

“I wanted to discuss this will you, before I went any further,” Francisco told a white lie. The first thing that Francisco should have done was to talk to Tina and see why she referred Hao to him. He trusted her implicitly, but he should have gotten more information.

“Since you need to talk to Tina, you might as well share the information with Dean Chandler.” Miranda and her counterpart at Stanford, Dean Dorothy Chandler, had become fast friends. They both were trying to survive academia politics in a man’s world. “This project is way beyond our expertise but getting a portion of the three million dollars would be beneficial to our institution.”

In his mind, Francisco confirmed his conviction of never becoming a university administrator. Politics and money seemed to sometimes overshadow academic excellence. *Así es la vida.*

"Yes, dean," he addressed her formally. He had made a rookie mistake of not gathering all the facts before discussing this strange proposal.

"And tell Dorothy that she needs to pay us an onsite visit," Miranda finished.

A half hour later, Francisco was back in his office. He would call Tina first. He knew that he would not be able to reach her at the Stanford campus. He could email her, but that would be too cumbersome. Besides he missed he and wanted to talk to her.

He called Tina on her cell phone but received a standard "I am not available at the moment. Please leave your name and phone number. . ." He complied, grumbling.

Crap! I need to man up and call Dean Chandler. Instead, he called his old office and his former secretary Mary Beth Smith.

"Well, buenos días, stranger," her smile could be felt across the telephone lines. "Haven't heard from you in while. How are you doing?"

They made small talk. Reynoso learned that his former office mate, Hypakia "Patty" Papadakis, had received the Daughter of Athena Award from the Greek Cultural Center.

Francisco asked Mary Beth to leave a message for Tina at Professor Segreti's office. The Italian professor had inherited

Tina when Francisco remained in Mexico. Segreti knew that he had won the lottery because Tina was super competent.

"Mary Beth, it was great talking to you. Say hi to all," Francisco was biting his tongue. "And could you transfer me to Dean Chandler please."

"No problem," she was so pleasant. "You're not in trouble, are you?"

Two minutes later, Dean Dorothy Chandler answered.

"Well, Francisco, I hope you are not going to complain about living in paradise." She liked taking the offensive and throwing people off guard.

Again, Francisco went through the spiel about his unusual meeting with Hao Chin Martín. But this time he added, "I have been trying to contact my former RA Tina Fang for corroboration and collaboration. I hope to speak to her soon and find out what she knows." Francisco knew how to cover his back.

"What does Dean Ríos have to say about this?"

"She really wants to defer to you," Francisco did not want to put Miranda in bad stead with Dean Chandler. "I believe the truth of the matter is that this sort of project might be outside the capacity and expertise of the University of Guadalajara. I know they can't do alone. In this case, they need a big brother, or should I say, a big sister."

"At first blush, neither Stanford nor Dean Ríos should be involved in such a project," Dean Chandler was trying to be circumspect. "On the other hand, three million dollars is three million dollars. There is just too much competition for institutional funding."

"How about this, dean?" Francisco was trying to put off any final decision. "Let me talk with Tina and check out her information. I will report back to you and Dean Ríos on what I find out."

"And I will also contact Dean Ríos. I really like her. It will give us an opportunity to problem solve together," the Dean added.

"Oh, I almost forgot," Francisco gasped. "She wants you to come down to Guadalajara for a site visit."

Later that night Francisco's cell phone rang. It was Tina Fang.

"Sorry, I was unavailable. My dissertation is making my hair turn grey," she was always self-deprecating. "But how are you?"

They went on with social pleasantries. And then finally, Francisco got down to business. "Tina, who is this Hao Chin Martín?"

"Oh, he is a cousin of mine. Probably a second or third level. I don't know the English equivalents. I met Rubí Song last summer in São Paolo. She is very cool. She works for China's Dragon Rare Elements Ltd. They are headquartered in Shanghai."

"Tina, I'm sorry but I'm not following what you are saying and why Hao wanted to talk to me. I didn't know how to respond properly to him."

"Professor, I'm sorry. I was just trying to help him out," Tina had always been super loyal to Professor Reynoso when she was his RA. "Did you meet Lilí Song? She is Rubí's twin sister and Hao's girlfriend."

Francisco remembered that he had picked up a strange vibe between Hao and Lilí during their meeting. Although Hao had been doing the talking, it seemed that Lilí was controlling the dialogue. *Did Tina know that Lilí was going to offer three million dollars for a Chinese project in Mexico?*

"Professor, they are trying to find a magical turquoise piece owned by Chan Toy and Ana Azuleta in the late nineteenth century. They think that conducting a study on the Chinese migration to Mexico will help them in this quest."

"Tina, did you know that they were going to offer us $3 million?"

"Aiyah! What?!"

CHAPTER 4 – MISUNDERSTANDING

Friday, March 22, 2019

University of Guadalajara

Three days later, Professor Reynoso was sifting through some of his correspondence in his office. Juanita buzzed him and said that Mr. Hao Chin Martín was on the phone and wanted urgently to speak to him.

"Please put him through, Juanita," Professor Reynoso said. From what Tina Fang had shared with him, Hao had misled him or was hiding something. He would listen to what the caller had to say.

"Hello, Mr. Martín," Francisco said politely.

"Oh, Professor Reynoso, thank you for taking my call. I talked to my cousin Tina, and she had a lot of concerns. I think there was a misunderstanding," Hao Chin Martín was talking fast and sounding nervous. *Misunderstanding, my ass!* Reynoso thought. *This guy is up to something. Should I let him talk or just hang up?*

"What kind of misunderstanding?" Francisco pressed, trying to box Hao Chin Martín in.

"Well, I could only tell you part of the story."

"Why is that?"

"My colleague and I have two different objectives," Hao Chin Martín continued. "I am interested in my Chinese culture and my family history in Mexico."

"Okay."

"But my colleague Lilí is more interested in finding turquoise," Hao Chin Martín said. "She works for Chinese Dragon Rare Elements Ltd. It's a global operation trying to acquire rare-earth elements. They are used in high tech device manufacturing."

"I don't understand, Hao," Francisco was taken off guard and was conversing more informally. "I didn't realized turquoise was a rare element." *Surely, the Chinese were not trying to corner the market on turquoise. At this point in time this mineral is not used commercially or scientifically.*

"Normally it's not," Hao Chin Martín cleared his throat. "But in this case, we are talking about some turquoise pieces that may have special properties."

Reynoso was not following but was curious. “What kind of special properties?”

“There is a legend of a turquoise colibrí (hummingbird) that acts as an aegis in offering protection.”

“Protection against what?” Reynoso continued to probe.

“Against any and all threats.”

Francisco was an expert in geopolitical matters in Latin America. This venture was a double whammy. Lilí worked for Chinese Dragon Rare Elements Ltd. It was a Chinese company. He knew that China wanted rare elements to dominate the global high-tech market. He might have to consult with several people, including the U.S. government. Should he cut Hao off now? He needed more information.

“Hao, I requested a written proposal from you,” Francisco was going to pressure Hao. “When can I expect it?”

“Professor, please forgive me. I am working on it. I have the old notes from Chan Toy. He was born in the 19th Century. The legend of the turquoise hummingbird begins with him.”

“I will need a copy of these logs. When can I get them?”

“Professor, the notes are in the Xiguan dialect of Cantonese. Very hard to translate. I don’t speak Cantonese. Lilí and her sister have been unable to decipher them. They speak Shanghainese and Mandarin.”

"So, what is your plan?" Francisco knew the notes were worthless if not translated.

"When I talked to my cousin, Tina, she said that she could translate them," Hao Chin Martín calmer now. "I probably shouldn't share this. She said she needs a new car."

They talked for about twenty more minutes. Francisco said that he needed a written proposal and an English version of the notes.

"Thank you, professor, for your understanding," Hao Chin Martín was acting humble. "We'll get you all of this as soon as possible."

"I'll be waiting," Francisco had a dozen calls to make. He would probably recommend to Dean Ríos and Dean Chandler to reject this proposal. It was too problematic.

"One more thing, professor, Lilí says that we can go as high as five million dollars. And we are paying Tina directly for the translations."

An hour later Francisco rang Tina. She picked up. "Caught you before going to happy hour, did I?" he teased.

"I wish," she said. "Just eating some noodles."

"I talked to your cousin a little while ago," Francisco wanted to get the business out of the way. "He said a lot of interesting things. More than he did the first time. Is he working for the Chinese government?"

Tina had been raised in Hong Kong and Macau. She was always leery of mainland China and its global interests.

"I don't know," Tina was thinking. "Rubí works for a high-quality gem company out of São Paulo, Brazil. So Rubí probably is not. I really don't know Lilí, so I can't say."

"I'm having trouble believing what Hao says."

"My cousin is a nice guy. He's kind of socially awkward. I think he will do whatever Lilí wants him to do. She seems to be the brains of their relationship."

Francisco then decided to drop the bomb on Tina. "I hear you need a new car."

"How did you know?" she gulped. She guessed that her cousin Hao had told the professor. Probably to make him feel sorry for her. "Yeah, I got rear-ended a couple of weeks ago. Car was totaled."

"Were you hurt?" Francisco's voice was concerned. "What happened?"

"No. Just a scratch. Somebody in a big red pickup truck didn't stop at a stop sign and plowed into me when I was stationary. The police came and gave the guy a ticket. I wouldn't have complained if they had arrested him. Now I'm wasting time talking to the insurance company, looking for a new car, and trying to scrape up some money."

"What kind of car are you looking for?"

"Probably a Prius," she replied. "I'm trying to be green. Maybe I can moonlight as a Lyft driver or Door Dash deliverer." She laughed.

"Well, I am glad that you are all right. Do your parents know?"

"Are you kidding, professor? They would have a fit!"

"So, are you really going to do the translations for Hao?"

"Well, I really must. He is a cousin," she inhaled. "And I think I may have made a terrible mistake in giving him your name and having him contact you."

"Can't he have someone else do the job? How about Lilí or her sister?"

"Not really. The sisters are not proficient in Cantonese. I have a basic understanding of Cantonese and its several dialects."

"What's the timeline for all of this?"

"About a month I would say. I didn't commit to a summer school abroad this year. I want to get my dissertation done."

"How much are they paying you for the translation?" Francisco recalled that Hao said they were paying Tina directly.

"$100 an hour."

CHAPTER 5 – TINA

Saturday, March 23, 2019

Palo Alto, California

The dawn had broken through her bedroom window. She had been awake for the last fifteen minutes. Tina did not want to get up. The bed was warm and cozy. She squeezed her eyes. Her breath seemed a little sour; nothing a little mouthwash wouldn't cure. Just a few more winks. Finally, the iPhone on her nightstand chirped. 7:30 a.m.! Time to get up. It seemed that her body and mind were allergic to sleep. She never got any. *My kingdom for a day of lounging!*

Today she put on her red tights with a matching sports bra. She hurried into the apartment's small kitchen. She squeezed a lemon into a teacup and poured in a few ounces of water. Tina nuked the drink for fifteen seconds and then gulped down the liquid. She put a slice of whole wheat bread into the toaster and went into her bathroom to finish getting dressed. Back out to the kitchen to spread almond butter and honey on toast and she was ready to go.

Normally, she would have driven to the 8:30 yoga class at the Jewish Community Center, but her car was totaled. She knew that she had to play nice with her distant cousin. She needed to earn the money for a new car. The auto insurance company was only offering a pittance for her totaled car. She still owed money on the Honda Civic. With the money Hao was going to pay her, she could buy a Prius. Maybe even a new one. She could go green.

Doing the translations for Hao was going to be a problem. She was finishing up the first draft of her dissertation at Stanford. The topic was "A Linguistic Interpretation of Early 16th Century Mexico." It was based on the scholarly research and translations she had done for Professor Francisco Reynoso the year before. She had been acknowledged in a joint academic article about the maritime attempt of Hernán Cortés to sail to the Moluccas (Spice Islands). Tina had been Professor Reynoso's research assistant until he transferred to the University of Guadalajara. Now she was the R.A. to Professor Segreti in the Italian Department.

Tina pulled her long black hair into a bun and straightened out the brown tortoise shell glasses that framed her marquis-cut emerald eyes. The weather was cool, so she put on a red fleece jacket. She grabbed her bicycle from the small living room and carried it down the one set of stairs of the apartment building.

Healthy body, healthy mind, she thought as she pedaled to her yoga class. Her dissertation and translations could wait until she got back home. Tina was a serious student. She knew that she would work through the weekend, as usual.

Tina was 24 years old. Her early upbringing in Macau had given her a British accent. When Tina was older, her family migrated to Vancouver, Canada, where she graduated with a degree in Spanish from the University of British Columbia. But she disliked the inclement weather of the Northwest. She preferred hot. During the summers of undergraduate school, she attended language schools in Antigua, Guatemala; San José, Costa Rica; and Valparaiso, Chile. Tina's passion was learning new languages while continuing to improve her Spanish. She had fallen in love with the colors and trams of Valparaiso and returned there to earn her master's degree in Spanish in 2017.

Her parents still lived in Vancouver BC. In terms of a career path, Tina was torn between finding a profession where she could be financially successful (her parents' preference), and academia (her grandmother's first choice). She could hear her maa maa's admonitions: "You don't need a man. Too needy. You study hard. Go to college. Be professor. Fortune will find a woman with an education." With her parents' blessing, she had enrolled in a doctoral program at Stanford University. It didn't hurt that her father had a third cousin who worked at the HSBC International Bank Centre in San Francisco. And her parents would have an excuse to come and visit.

Her fate was sealed when, upon arriving on campus, she saw a university posting for a research assistant position in Latin-American Studies working for a Professor Francisco Reynoso. Her language proficiencies in Cantonese, Portuguese, English, and Spanish made her a shoe-in. Professor Francisco Reynoso thought he had experienced nirvana when she applied. He subsequently brought her on as his R.A.

Tina arrived at the community center. She was a little sweaty although it had taken less than ten minutes to get there. *Happy Baby Pose, here I come!* However, her yoga class was uneventful. Tina's mind was distracted by all the work she had to do. One of her fellow participants invited her to brunch, but she politely declined. While she liked the physical training and mental and spiritual support of group exercises, she disliked distractions if they affected her schedule. She did not want to be sucked in to socializing with people she barely knew.

She was dying of hunger when she returned home. There was a large heavy cardboard box in front of the apartment door. It was marked, "Special Delivery." She initially wanted to make herself a grilled cheese sandwich and some celery and carrots with hummus for an early lunch. However, curiosity got the best of her, and she grabbed a pair of scissors to slice open the box.

There were several stacks of documents. They were written with faded Chinese characters on rice paper. The papers were moldy, smelly, and curled up at the corners. Tina sneezed as she gently scanned the documents. She was fluent in Cantonese, but these papers were in an old dialect. Very few people would be able to translate them. She was one of the few. And the fact that a distant cousin had asked her for help made it an obligation of honor.

Tina was a detail person and highly organized. How much time should she spend on her dissertation? The first draft was almost complete. She could finish it within the next two months. But she needed the money for a new car. She could divide her time fifty-fifty with the new project. She knew realistically that the Cantonese project would take twice as much time as she thought. But $100 per hour was good compensation.

There was a note in an envelope on top of the papers from her cousin, plus a check for five thousand dollars.

"Little cousin Tina, thank you for agreeing to do this translation. I found these papers in an old steamer trunk at my parents' house in Tucson. Lilí was not able to translate them. While I don't want to rush you, there will a bonus payment if you can translate these papers within a month. The information in these documents is secret and should not be shared with anyone except Professor Reynoso. Your humble cousin, Hao."

After a brief lunch, she resumed looking at the Cantonese papers. She looked at the piles. There were over 200 pages. Fortunately, it looked like it was only one author. She would try to do ten pages per day. She could have it done in three weeks.

She began the translations on to her laptop. It was slow going.

Tina had tentatively agreed to meet some friends for a Happy Hour, but she would have to cancel. She had almost no social life. Her dating had been minimal this last year since her breakup with Izzy Yoshida, a bioengineering student. He was nice, but too immature for her tastes. There was plenty of time to date after she got her Ph.D.

As she read on and on, she asked herself, "who was this Chan Toy anyway?"

PART II – CHAN TOY

CHAPTER 6 – CRISIS

Sunday, March 24, 2019

Palo Alto, California

Tina parsed through Chan Toy's notes. Her own background gave her a greater insight into the journey of Chan Toy. She knew that in the 1800's there was a high demand for foreign workers in the United States and Mexico to build railroads, mine precious metals, dig irrigation canals, and do other heavy labor. The working environment was most often in locations with the worst weather conditions. Laborers came either as indentured servants to work for approximately seven years or as credit ticket workers to work off their travel debt and expenses.

Steamships carried people from countries with overpopulation problems. Thus, the global commerce and exploitation of human labor was facilitated. No place was it truer than in China because of its high unemployment, droughts, floods, political turmoil, and battles with the British (Opium Wars). The United States and Great Britain militarily intervened into Chinese affairs in favor of more trade. The tribute practice to the Chinese emperor gave way to the one-sided economy treaty system. The United States and European countries bullied China. Discrimination and stereotypes against the Chinese were rampant.

Tina began read the papers. The backdrop of Chan Toy's story began to unfold:

1865
Guangzhou, China

At dawn, red and yellow clouds steamed up from the South China Sea that was a hundred miles away. Another day of humidity in Guangzhou pushed away the cool air. In 1856 the British and French had inserted themselves into Chinese commerce as a result of the Opium Wars. The political and economic situations in China were in flux, but Guangzhou remained the major port for foreign trade interests throughout.

Chan Toy Wu was born in a small rural village in Guangzhou, China. A small tributary of the Pearl River ran by.

The newborn was screaming. His face was red. His mother was trying to sooth him with a damp cloth. He wouldn't let his mother suckle him. The peasant mother was scrawny and couldn't have offered much nourishment, no matter how hard she tried.

Her older son (by five years) had been delivered rather easily. He had been an easy child to raise. Subsequently, Mrs. Chan had had five miscarriages.

Next to the mother, an elderly lady with long grey hair massaged the baby's feet, chanting an inaudible prayer. Tong Long was the village midwife and healer. Behind her back, people called her a witch that casted spells on friends and enemies. She was a force to be feared.

Only out of desperation had Mrs. Chan requested Madam Tong Long's assistance. She knew that the payment would be dear, but what choice did she have? Her child would die without the restorative powers of Tong Long.

"Look! He has the mark of a person caught between two worlds," the elderly woman pointed to the dark blue bird shaped birthmark on the bottom of the newborn's left foot.

"What does it mean?" the mother said weakly.

"He will travel from one place to another," the old lady said mysteriously. "The road will be filled with many stones and potholes. He will have many struggles."

"Will he live?"

"I think so," Tong Long looked pensively at the child. "You need to eat every day." Mrs. Chan was handed three pumpkin-like gourds.

Mrs. Chan nodded affirmatively.

The five-year old son, Chan Chuk Wu stared silently from the corner. He was hungry, but they would not eat their measly dinner until his father dragged himself home from the rice paddies.

"Chuk," Mrs. Chan barked to her oldest son. "Walk Madam Tong home. Carry her things for her. Come right home. Hurry up!"

The elder dipped her head in appreciation.

"Come right home, Chuk!"

"Xie xie," thanked Madam Tong.

Tong Long visited every day that week. Finally, the child had settled down and began to suckle.

One night Mr. Chan came home late. He had the smell of liquor on his breath and stunk of old stale cigarettes.

Mrs. Chan weakly lifted her head off the cushion that she slept on. The baby Chan Toy Wu was on top of her chest, sleeping quietly. “Where you been? It is very late!”

“Quiet, woman!” he yelled back. “This is your fault. You bring bad luck into this family. How is my son?”

The wife gave her husband a dirty look. *The bastard!* Then she looked lovingly down toward Toy. He was all that mattered.

The family of four struggled for five more years until a third child was born. Chan Yun Wu was so tiny when she entered this world. The pregnancy was uneventful.

However, Mrs. Chan fell into ill health. She could no longer work in the rice paddies with her husband. Instead, the eldest son, Chuk, went to work with his father. None of the children had any schooling.

The father would get drunk once a week and come home and beat his wife. The children were always afraid and would cry themselves to sleep.

The family became poorer and poorer. One day the father did not come home. Mrs. Chan told her children that Mr. Chan went off far away to work. They never saw him again. Chuk was working seven days a week to support the family.

One day, Toy saw that Madam Tong taking his sister Yun from their little house. He didn’t understand why his sister no longer lived with his family. It would be months before he would again see Madam Tong walking around the village with the little girl.

It was difficult for Toy to get a job. He was illiterate, but a hard worker. He worked with his brother on and off in the rice fields, but there was not always a lot of work.

More years passed and Mrs. Chan was stricken with tuberculosis. Madam Tong came over every day and rubbed jade shavings onto her patient's chest as she muttered some inaudible chants. Mrs. Chan's daughter, Yun, accompanied the village healer. Yun now lived with the healer.

"Need stronger medicine," Madam Tong said. "Costs much money."

The Chan family was destitute. They couldn't afford any medication and they owed Madam Tong for her services. Almost all the money that Chuk earned went to the healer. Toy had to stay home just to care for his mother

Toy had no resources to care for their mother. He was caught twice stealing winter melons and was beaten by his neighbors. In 1882 when Toy turned seventeen, his mother passed away. Toy was left to fend for himself. His brother, Chuk, left to live with his girlfriend.

It was around this time that a Yankee wandered into the village handing out flyers. Toy couldn't read, but one of his friends, Wan Tu, said that the man was looking for workers across the ocean. Toy had heard rumors about the streets in the far-off lands being paved with gold. It seemed tempting, but he had no skills. He was a weakling. He was illiterate. What work could he do?

A few days later he ran into his friend again.

"Hey, I signed up," Tu had a big grin on his round face.

"For what?" Toy's face jerked back in surprise.

"To work, dummy! Can't live in this shit hole forever."

"What will you do?"

"I don't know, and I don't care. I have to meet with Mr. Ong tomorrow. There are so many jobs in Mexicali! That's a place in Mexico. Have to make arrangements. Want to come with me?"

Toy wanted to say no. He didn't know what or where Mexico was. However, there was nothing keeping him here. He felt something between fear and despair.

"Come on. It'll be fun. Let's grab some noodles."

"I have no money."

"No worries. I pay."

The next morning Toy and Tu met down by the river. Tu looked glum. He wasn't as cheerful as the day before.

They chitchatted a bit and then Toy couldn't suppress his curiosity about Tu's meeting with the village triad chief, Beng Ong.

"Well, not so good. Mr. Ong wants 1000 yuan for papers and transportation to go abroad. I don't have that much money."

Toy sighed. He felt for his friend. He was stuck.

"He did offer me sort of a loan."

"What do you mean?" Toy asked.

"He said I could work for a Mexican company that he is in partnership with. I would have to work for them for seven years to pay off the debt. I am not sure I could do that."

The next day Toy Chan found himself in front of Beng Ong's antique shop. He walked in. There was a tall, muscular young man in front of the store.

"Yes?" said the guard gruffly.

"I would please like to see Mr. Ong. I would like to work across the ocean."

CHAPTER 7 – ENSENADA

1882

Port of Ensenada, Mexico

There were at least eighty men stuffed into a small cabin at the bow of the ship. The cramped quarters reeked of feces and renal ammonia. A handful of women isolated themselves in a corner for solitude and protection. The air ventilation was non-existent and the miasma from the Chinese passengers puking was overwhelming. It had taken Toy a whole week to recuperate from seasickness.

They got fed a rice gruel twice a day. Every other day two of the passengers were given a bucket of sea water and a mop to clean the quarters. There was no discipline among the passengers, so a few of the younger and stronger guys took charge. Nobody had anything of value, but one's food was always a worthy prize to these thugs. Anybody who opposed them was beaten.

Toy did not try to make friends or allies. He just tried to sleep and to listen to the other passengers. There was so much idle chatter among the passengers:

"I hear we're landing in San Francisco. They have lots of rich Chinese there. They will help us."

"Aiyah! The old man with the beard. He died two days ago. They took his body. Throw him into the water. His poor ancestors! No decent burial. Can't meet with the spirits!"

"They will feed you to the dogs if you try to escape."

Chan Toy was not concerned. He really didn't have a life. Anything was better than rotting in Guangzhou. Too bad Wan Tu had not come.

The passengers were not allowed to go on to the deck. They were considered valuable cargo, and the captain did not want to lose a precious commodity.

The weather fluctuated between stormy and rough to calm and humid. The ship's staff left them alone, save for an occasional kick or push.

After several weeks, there was a joyful cry from above.

"Land ahoy."

It took them almost a day to come into the crescent shaped harbor. The ship had anchored in the bay of Ensenada, Mexico.

Mexico had lost half of its territory after being invaded by the United States. The majority of Mexicans were uneducated and lived off the land. At the same time the Mexican government and the Catholic Church exploited these poor people.

Chan Toy was caught between being overjoyed at seeing the Bahia Todos Santos (Ensenada) and being afraid to leave the ship. He was filthy, stinky, and hungry. He had large dark circles under his eyes. Between malnutrition and dysentery, he was emaciated.

***

In 1542, the port of "Ensenada de Todos Santos" was established by Juan Rodriguez Cabrillo. Years later it would become a safe harbor under Sebastián Vizcaino for Spanish galleons journeying from Manila to Acapulco. It wasn't long before the Jesuits interjected themselves here.

In 1812 Mexico declared its independence from Spain. The United States saw another opportunity to acquire another portion of land like the Jefferson purchase, but Mexico refused to sell. In 1846, the United States responded by declaring war on Mexico over Texas. Mexico was soundly defeated and had to cede half of its territory to the United States. This included

Texas, California, and New Mexico. The U.S. paid Mexico $15 million as compensation.

Mexico subsequently embraced a series of reforms that established a federal system of government (rather than the existing centralized form), restricted the power and wealth of the Catholic Church, and guaranteed civil liberties.

In the 1860's, while the United States was fighting the Civil War, the Mexican President Benito Juárez drove out Maximilian and the French who were trying to rule Mexico. Most notable was the famous Battle of Puebla where General Zaragoza defeated the invincible French troops on May 5, 1867.

Starting in 1877 the dictatorship of Porfirio Díaz sought to "Europeanize" Mexico in favor of the rich at the expense of the poor. Foreign investment, modernization, and global immigration became the policy at the expense of the indigenous Mexican population. Inequality between the classes of the rich and the indigenous majority increased throughout the Diaz reign.

***

Chan Toy was caught between being overjoyed at seeing the Bahia Todos Santos (Ensenada) and being afraid to leave the ship. He was filthy, stinky, and hungry. He had large dark circles under his eyes. Between malnutrition and dysentery, he was emaciated.

Fortunately, today the bay was calm. It was late afternoon when two rowboats shuttled between the ship and the pier. Two officers of the ship and few sailors went off the ship first. They were met by a portly Mexican official with splotchy facial hair seated at a beleaguered wooden table with a huge parchment ledger in front of him.

"Buenas tardes, Señor Wilson . . . Señor Saunders," smiled the immigration/customers port representative.

The greetings were reciprocated. The lingua franca was Spanish. Documents were exchanged. A small envelope was surreptitiously slipped into the Mexican's hand.

"Everything seems in order, gentlemen," the official tipped his head for the foreigners to proceed.

For the next few hours, goods and passengers were landed onto the pier. Everyone was questioned by the Mexican official. The sailors continued to return to the ship in their rowboats for the next load.

When the Chinese passengers began to arrive, the Mexican official threw up his hands. "¡Puta madre! They smell worse than horse shit. Clean them up before they talk to me." A young boy threw buckets of salt water on them. There was a little improvement, but not much.

Chan Toy was directed to an empty spot on the pier with two other youngsters. He could tell from their accents that they came from a village near Guangzhou. Chan Toy's head was still swimming, and he had lost his sense of balance. His body seemed to be swaying to and fro. He could hear the din from the city. It was loud and seemed lively. His eyes were swollen. He seemed to be seeing bright colors all around him. His head hurt, and he closed his eyes. He wanted to sleep, but the two boys kept talking.

"Look!" said Saam, the older of the two boys. "They are taking the girls away." He was pointing to about eight girls that were being escorted into a carriage by a well-built Chinese man. Several of them were crying. The foreman, Pu-tin, yelled at them and put the fear of death into their ears.

Chan Toy wanted to vomit. He couldn't. He hadn't eaten since the previous day.

"Oh, no!" cried out the younger brother, Luk. "There are the bodies." Their middle brother Sei had died on the ship. The corpses were being piled up at the end of the pier.

"At least Sei didn't die at sea," remarked Saam. "The spirits will find him. He will be with our ancestors."

"But we are too far away," complained Luk. "What if the spirits can't cross an ocean? Where are they going to bury him?"

A devilish Mexican man with a big moustache approached the three Chinese and yelled at them in Spanish and motioned them to stand up. They didn't understand him and did not move.

A fist flew into Saam's stomach, and he yelled out.

"¡Les dije que se levanten!" Rodrigo Ramos yelled. They finally got the message. Chan Toy followed the two boys from the pier toward town. At the end, there was a staging area with several wagons and men waiting.

"You, two, go with him," Rodrigo barked. The brothers moved toward a skinny Mexican kid. "Put them on the wagon to Mexicali. They look okay enough to make the trip."

Then Rodrigo peered over to the emaciated Chan Toy. "¡Puta madre! ¡Este cabrón no vale la verga!"

Ten minutes later, Chan Toy was lying down in the back of a wagon traveling out of town. After a half hour, they approached a large adobe mansion. Chan Toy was led to the back of the main house.

"Here is your new houseboy," Rodrigo said derisively to the pregnant Soledad who was the ama de casa. Soledad was in a bad mood and yelled at a young Mexican boy to have Chan Toy bathed and be given new clothes.

Chan Toy had lost all the few possessions that he had tried to bring with him. The loose muslin pants and a similar top were welcomed.

“Back of the house!” the head housekeeper ordered in Spanish, “You are going to wash dishes starting now,”. He didn’t move.

Soledad repeated herself. “You better start learning Spanish fast. I’m not learning squawky Chinky yak.”

Over the next week, Chan Toy started to recuperate. Soledad was always scolding him and yelling at him, but she fed him three solid meals every day. He figured out that he had to wash the dishes, bring in the water, and wash the clothes. He also decided to do things he was not asked to do. Most of the time it was accepted, but sometimes not. He was not allowed to touch or wash women’s garments.

Chan Toy’s situation seemed to improve over the next few months, until one day Soledad was not around. Chan Toy was upset. She was his security. She looked after him.

Margarita, the house maid, approached Chan Toy. “Soledad has left to deliver her baby. We don’t know when she will be back.”

Chan Toy’s face looked puzzled. He had learned enough Spanish to survive, but barely had understood the maid.

"You will assume more responsibilities. I am the new ama de casa."

For the next fifteen days, Chan Toy worked from sunrise to sunset and then some. He was exhausted. He made innumerable mistakes. Sometimes he was reprimanded, other times not.

The work was challenging but Chan Toy was happy. His life was a dream compared with the nightmares he had lived in China.

CHAPTER 8 – MEXICALI ROSE

1883-92

Ensenada to Mexicali, Mexico

Another few weeks passed, and Soledad was still absent from the hacienda. Chan Toy had heard that she had delivered a little boy. Margarita, the new head housekeeper, had Chan Toy cooking, cleaning rooms, and folding clothes. He was always being scolded, but he accepted it in stride. Little by little he improved his performance.

Finally, Soledad returned with a little hairball infant named Marco. He was the star of the show with everyone cooing around him. For special events, when Soledad had greater responsibilities, Chan Toy would help babysit Marquito who was always grabbing at his queue. More than once, Chan Toy had winced when the tot pulled hard on his pigtail. Marquito thought this was funny. However, Chan Toy was later "fired" from his diaper changing duties. He left them too loose and askew. The results were stinky messes.

"¡Ay Dios mio!" Soledad remarked after she came to retrieve her son from Chan Toy.

For the next several months, Chan Toy continued to spend time with the baby. Concurrently, Chan Toy achieved a survivor's level of proficiency in Spanish. His speaking capabilities were stilted, but he understood almost everything.

Then one day Gonzalo Gonzalez arrived at the hacienda. Gonzalo worked for Hung Far who owned Chan Toy's labor contract. Gonzalo's job was to move indentured Chinese from one job to another as needed. He abruptly approached Chan Toy and barked, "Get your things. We're moving you out of here."

The household staff were sad to see him go. Margarita gave him a few loose coins and some secondhand clothes.

"We're going to miss you," Soledad's eyes were welled with tears. She held out Marquito for Chan Toy to kiss goodbye.

Early the next morning Gonzalo was driving a wagon led by two horses in an easterly direction. Chan Toy sat next to him. There were four Chinese youngsters dressed in rags who had just arrived from China. Chan Toy recalled his own dreadful experiences months before.

It took four and a half days to travel to the center of the dusty town of Mexicali. The wagon stopped in front of a combination lodging, saloon, and casino. It was called "The Mexicali Rose," and was located in the Chinesca District of Mexicali

How could so many Chinese people live here? he wondered. He would later find out that the Chinese had come as workers for an extensive irrigation project around Mexicali. Some had been recruited from China, especially from around the Canton area; and others had fled from the United States.

The Chinese who settled down in Mexicali, opened saloons and hotels, not to mention casinos, brothels, and opium dens. Chinese associations provided Chinese wives for the workers and economic and political protection from the triad gangs. The Mexican government and police turned a blind eye toward these illicit enterprises especially when money crossed hands.

Gonzalo led Chan Toy and the recent Chinese arrivals through a back door.

"Do you want to keep any of these or send them straight to the mine?" Gonzalo asked Hung Far, the obese manager of the Mexicali Rose establishment. Hung Far worked for the Ong Association, one of the Mexicali triads. "Boss says we're supposed to keep this one," Hung Far pointed his finger toward Chan Toy.

***

For the next two years, Chan Toy worked in the casino, emptying out ash trays, cleaning spittoons, wiping down tables, emptying out swap buckets, and sometimes serving drinks. The local Mexican and Chinese customers liked him, and occasionally would slip him a coin or two.

Chan Toy would report to Hung Far if he noticed someone cheating at cards or if a fight was brewing. He was unobtrusive, and nobody paid much attention to him. Chan Toy had a high sense of honesty and was very loyal to Hung Far. A few times he tried to break up a brawl. He usually received a sound beating for his efforts. Hung Far would just shake his head. "Good heart, but no brains," he would say.

Every once in a while, Chan Toy would observe some of his fellow workers stealing money from the customers or secretly snatching food from the kitchen. He did not rat out his colleagues. He was poor and knew what it was like to be hungry. In fact, Chan Toy would scavenge the leftovers from the dining room clients. Many people would leave half of a perfectly grilled steak on their plate. Waste not, want not.

As for his lodging, he shared a space in the storage room with two young Mexican boys. They helped him with his Spanish. He didn't go out much and he didn't spend any of his meager savings. However, one day he was walking in the Chinese merchant part of town and saw something that he just had to have. He bought himself a traditional Chinese black skullcap. It reminded him of Guangzhou. From that day forward he had a smile on his face when he put it on. He had made a life for himself far across the ocean.

Several more years passed. Then one day in 1889, Hung Far called Chan Toy into his office.

"I think you are almost done with contract," the manager said. "Is that right? How much time do you think you have?"

It was a trick question. Hung Far knew the exact amount of time. He reported to the Ong Association in Guangzhou.

Chan Toy shrugged his shoulders. He didn't know.

"How you like to make a little money?" Hung Far smiled. He knew that Chan Toy didn't have the slightest idea what to do after his contractual obligations were fulfilled.

Chan Toy raised his head and focused. *It would be great to make some money! I'm 27 years old! I need to do it!* Chan Toy nodded his head affirmatively.

"The job is in Cananea. It's a mining operation on Copper Mountain, but you don't have to go down into the tunnels."

It was an easy sell. The next day Chan Toy helped load the wagon and they were off. Chan Toy rode shotgun. The ride on the wagon was bumpy and hot. Hung Far drove the two-horse wagon with four new Chinese arrivals in the wagon bed amidst supplies.

They rode miles and miles through saguaro cactus and dusty trails, and only stopped for water. They survived on dried meat and fruit. At night, Hung Far kicked the boys out of the wagon and put a blanket in its bed. His pillow was a Winchester rifle. Chan Toy laid himself cramped on the wagon seat with a blanket covering him. The four Chinese passengers walked around the bushes and saguaros until they found a suitable place to sleep. The new Chinese boys had been in the back of the wagon for hours and were stiff. As the night got darker, a breeze picked up. The crickets and other critters chirped incessantly. It was getting colder. The boys had dozed off atop some creosote bushes near a bleached out fallen log. The youngsters shivered from the coldness and huddled close to each other.

The next morning Chan Toy saw one of the Chinese boys with tears in his eyes. The other boys were looking at the sole of the youth's foot. There was some type of puncture wound. The heel was swollen and reddened.

After a slight meal, the entourage resumed their journey.

Later in the day, the Chinese youngster with the infected foot started to convulse in the back of the wagon. Then his arms started to flail. At first the others tried to comfort him, but later left him alone. Hung Far said it looked like a scorpion sting. By night fall the boy was dead. They dug a shallow grave for him. The poor thing had no possessions. *Will his ancestors find his spirit?*

On the fourth day, the trail started to climb and wind through some hills. More pine trees appeared as well as different types of succulents. The ever-present buzzards flew overhead looking for their next meal. The path became rocky and one of the horses threw a shoe. Hung Far was beside himself. He was cussing as he jumped up and down. *¡Qué diablos!* The others did not dare to say anything.

Finally, Hung Far told everyone to get off the wagon. They would have to walk the rest of the way. He did not want the horse to go lame. Someone would have to pay for this unfortunate incident.

The road became narrower and narrower; steeper and steeper. The Chinese boys were all barefoot. They couldn't keep up with the wagon while going uphill. Travel was now very slow and painful. One of boys stubbed his toe and fell. He couldn't get up.

Hung Far was not happy. He was already late getting to Cananea.

"Keep walking!" barked Hung Far. "You're not riding in the wagon. Keep up or I will leave you here!"

Dawn streaked into red, orange, and yellow stripes as they arrived at a ridge above the mining camp in Cananea. Chan Toy was surprised at the dry climate of the high desert which was the opposite of his childhood in the humid Guangzhou. He was pleased and thought it was celestial.

This northern part of Mexico had been originally inhabited by indigenous peoples, such as the Yaquis and Apaches. Then the Spanish founded Cananea as a colony in 1760. Later, in 1868, Mexican General Ignacio Pesqueira discovered the abandoned Spanish mine of Cananea. It was later sold to a copper mining company. By 1889, the community had grown to be half Mexican and a quarter each of gringos and chinos.

Below them was a valley from which smoke wafted upwards. The movement of bodies could be seen appearing and disappearing from the cabin barracks to the left of the bend in the road. But what caught Chan Toy's attention was the overwhelming smell of bacon emanating from a large and long building on the other side of the road. Where there was smoke, there was food.

Twenty minutes later Hung Far was greeted by a short, stocky Mexican man who wore dark brown boots and a cowboy hat. They stared at each other.

"Git yourself inside and get yourselves cleaned up," said the mining camp boss shaking his head. "You smell like shit."

CHAPTER 9 – COPPER MOUNTAIN

1892

Cananea, Mexico

Joaquin “Chimo” Robles escorted Hung Far inside to a washroom behind the kitchen where two young Mexican girls were cutting onions and carrots. Forty-five minutes later the two men were drinking coffee in the mess hall. Hung had washed up and was wearing clean clothes.

“I thought you were supposed to bring more workers,” frowned Chimo as he glared at Hung Far. He was not happy.

“Bad joss. I lost one,” Hung was biting down on some chewy bacon, ignoring Chimo. “Scorpion bite. Got you three plus one that is supposed to work inside the house.”

Chimo nodded. “Okay. Okay.”

In the meantime, the three Chinese youngsters and Chan Toy were being processed by the head ranch hand. Kiki O'Hara had curly red hair and blue eyes. He ordered the youths to go to the company store and see the supply clerk. They would need some clothes and supplies. They didn't understand Spanish but obeyed instinctively. They had to mark their "X's" for their "purchases", i.e., new clothes, a towel, and a blanket. If they wanted something extra, all they had to do was ask for it. But since this was a company store, the costs came out of one's pay or increased the worker's indebtedness.

Afterwards, they all cleaned up at the communal washroom at the workers' barracks. There was no soap unless somebody bought some. Few did. It was considered a luxury. Finally, they were led back to the mess hall and had some breakfast. Afterwards, Chimo singled out Chan Toy and led him to the kitchen at the ranch house. He introduced him to Lee Leong who oversaw the kitchen and household staff.

"Lee Leong is your new boss, and he will tell you what to do," Chimo left him.

Throughout the next month Chan Toy did everything from fixing a clogged-up water pump to sewing pillowcases. Most of the household employees were Mexican, Yaqui, or Chinese. The common language was Spanish or to be more accurate, broken Spanish.

The ranch was in an isolated part of the Copper Mountain valley with a little stream flowing nearby. The north side of the ranch house that was opposite the courtyard was inhabited by Chimo Robles and his English wife, Charlotte. They had no children but kept Flaco the Chihuahua and Chato the beagle around as pets. The household staff resided in gender-separated dormitories at the back of the casona. Chan Toy's Spanish was now good, and he could comprehend most of what was being said. However, Chan Toy was illiterate and could not read a simple sentence. It was for this reason alone that he was not allowed to become a cook.

On the south side of the property lived the owners of the ranch, a German couple who supplied the local Cananea copper mine. Günther Heinz had immigrated from München with his wife Hilda. They had no children. They treated their workers like members of the family. The copper mine was located about a mile away. The Heinz ranch had cattle, horses, and mules, in addition to crop production and a small lumber operation in the nearby forest. The Heinz enterprise provided room and board to the Copper Mountain miners. There was a tienda de raya (company store) where the laborers could purchase anything. Life on the ranch was an idyllic situation except for the dearth of drinking water. The small stream on the property dried up often because of the high desert climate.

Most of the miners were Mexicans, Yaquis, Chinese, or displaced Southern rebels. Each group stayed close to their own kind. On Saturday nights, some of the miners wandered over to the little pueblo of Santa Clara. It had a population of almost two thousand people. There was a plazita with vendors selling corn tamales and other foods. The church was painted a raspberry color with creamy white highlights. There were small, whitewashed adobe buildings and wooden shacks within the city proper. A couple of cantinas provide alcohol, gambling, and female companionship.

The miners had to work six and a half days of the week. Most went down the deep mine shaft; others worked at the smelter where metal was extracted from its ore; and still others worked at the stamping plant where the metal was shaped into a usable form. The unfortunate consequence of the continuous mining was the need for lumber. The local supply was limited, so most of the lumber was brought in from the Tamosure Woods.

Supply wagons made several trips during the week delivering products to the railroad station or picking up supplies in Santa Clara.

Chan Toy was allowed to go into town once a week to sell wares to the townspeople. He sold inexpensive items like pots and pans or cheap clothing. He acquired the merchandise from the ranch's company store and split the profits with the proprietor. For the most part, his business flourished. He sold on credit and most of the time the customers paid up. This business practice made him popular in Santa Clara, especially among the children, who always wanted to buy his homemade kites.

On the other hand, the local merchants hated him and tried to sabotage him, but the sheriff and the mayor were his loyal clients.

A few months later, circumstances changed for Chan Toy. Lee Leong became incapacitated due to a bronchial condition and Chan Toy took over his duties. Chan Toy was placed in charge of the overall operation of the house, including the kitchen. It was during this period that he befriended Joya Azuleta, the household cook. She was a few years older than Chan Toy. He had learned that although she had dark skin and long black hair like Mexican women, she was actually a Yaqui native. Joya had been born in a little pueblo called Little Blue Rock about ten miles away. She had been married off to a Mexican who worked at various copper mines in the State of

Sonora. Her two oldest children died. The cause was believed to be from copper leeching into their drinking water. The childless couple then moved to the Cananea Mine where her husband worked. Joya was hired on as a cook's assistant for the Heinz's.

Things were better here and in 1882, Joya's daughter Ana was born. She was a healthy baby. Everybody loved her. However, a few days after the baby's third birthday, Joya's husband and two other miners died from carbon monoxide poisoning. The Heinz's felt sorry for Joya and they let the mother and daughter stay on. The German couple treated Ana as if she was their granddaughter.

***

The years flew by and suddenly Ana was ten years older. Chan Toy had grown very close to the child over the years. He tried to teach her a few Cantonese words while Ana aided him in improving his Spanish. In return for his kindness, Joya would fix him to some grilled grasshoppers with peanuts and chiles. He loved this dish.

While he was now able to speak Spanish well enough that most people understood him, Chan Toy still couldn't read or write. Joya was also unschooled, but thanks to Hilda Heinz, who spent countless hours with the child, Ana became literate.

Over time the mine started to dry up. Some of the miners left. The replacements were young and inexperienced. They didn't last very long.

One day in late 1896, a few drifters from Arkansas came into the ranch and were hired as mule skinners to run the ore to the smelter or the metal to the railroad station. They were roughnecks who worked hard all week and got drunk on Saturday nights. They hassled the Mexicans and Yaquis, calling them beaners and other derogatory names while giving them little kicks. They carried revolvers so nobody talked back. Additionally, Joya and the other household women were always being harassed by these Americanos with unwelcomed pinches and squeezes. Joya tried to make sure that Ana was not around where the gringos were.

One day Chan Toy was observing the two roughnecks mocking a young Mexican boy.

"Where's your whore mother, cabrón?" the bearded Willie Collins growled as he grabbed the kid by the front of the shirt. "She owes me a good time."

The other one laughed.

Chan Toy approached the two gringos. "Please leave boy alone," he said in broken English.

“What did you say, stinky chinky?” Willie pushed the kid away and moved toward Chan Toy. “I’ll hang your ass upside down by your ponytail. Mind you own business before you get hurt!”

Chan Toy didn’t say anything. He bowed his head and made a silent vow.

CHAPTER 10 – EXODUS

1898

Cananea, Mexico

For the next few years, Chan Toy gave Willie Collins and Bubba Abbotts a wide berth. Everybody hoped that the two rabble rousers would move on. While the drifters weren't earning much money, they had enough to enjoy the attractions of the nearby pueblo of Santa Clara on the weekends. The Heinz family "let them be" because they were good workers and would be difficult to replace. The cowboys worked hard and partied even harder.

In the meantime, Ana was developing into a chocolate-skinned beauty. Joya had to be extremely vigilant when Willie would show up at the ranch house unexpectedly. His blood shot eyes always trying to spy where her daughter was. On more than one occasions, Joya warned her daughter about how dangerous these gringos were. Chan Toy would shake his head in agreement with her.

It was the beginning of spring in 1898. This was the rainy season, but unfortunately there was very little precipitation. Bubba was bored and wanted to become a cattle herder. One day he said his goodbyes and left for Chihuahua. Willie, at first, pretended that he didn't care about being by himself. He picked more fights with the miners who tactfully backed away. Willie was intimidating. He always seemed to have his hand on his revolver. As the weeks went by, he became more aggressive with the female workers at the ranch.

When caught by Mrs. Heinz, he would simply smile, "Oh, just teasing. Ain't mean nothin' by it, ma'am. Just having some fun."

Chan Toy continued to go to Santa Clara on Saturdays. He hawked his pots, pans, and knives to the townspeople. On the latest occasion, he was returning to the ranch when he heard a piercing scream.

"¡Ayúdame!" cried a female's voice from within a nearby pine copse. It was a familiar voice. He stopped the wagon and listened. At first, he perceived nothing.

Then Chan Toy heard, "leave me alone, you pig!" He recognized that voice. He jumped out of the wagon and grabbed an iron skillet and a cleaver. He ran headlong into the grove. He looked to his right. Nothing. He looked to his left. Nothing. Then he saw a blurred vision about fifty meters in front of him. There was a rustling of leaves. Branches were swaying. Chan Toy approached without caution.

There was a big burly man. He was wrestling something. *Was it some kind of animal?* Chan Toy peered over a creosote bush. No, it was someone. He saw the long black hair. It was that of a young woman. She was being bear hugged by Willie. Chan Toy knew that the female was in deep trouble. Then another scream. The girl was Ana! Joya's daughter! Again, there was a shriek. Willie had ripped Ana's blouse off and was trying to force himself onto her!

Chan Toy's forehead broke into a sweat as he rushed toward the entangled pair.

"Leave her alone!" Chan Toy's faint threat sounded.

Willie did not react.

Chan Toy stepped forward. He raised the iron skillet overhead and swung it at Willie. It hit the cowboy between the top of the left shoulder and the head. Willie reeled around dropping the girl and growled at Chan Toy. He wasn't even fazed.

"You little chink!" Willie roared. "You're going to pay for that!"

Chan Toy took two steps back. Willie pulled out a knife. Chan Toy took another two steps back. Willie charged, swinging his knife diagonally. Chan Toy pivoted to left. He tried to swing his skillet but was too slow. Willie easily smacked Chan Toy's weapon away. Willie took another thrust at Chan Toy slashing him on the meaty part of the triceps of his left arm. Chan Toy cried out in pain.

Willie then grabbed Chan Toy and spun him around. He held Chan Toy from behind and was choking him. Chan Toy tried to scream but was cut off when Willie put his hand over Chan Toy's mouth. The air was being stifled from Chan Toy's lungs. He was panicking. His legs started to flail. Willie jerked his victim's head back and forth. Chan Toy tried to make one last effort to scream. Willie's hand clasped tighter over the Chinaman's face.

"Ya gonna die, chink!" Willie bellowed.

Suddenly, one of the two men was on the ground yelling in pain. He was holding his right hand. The stump of a missing index finger was bleeding profusely. Willie was ranting and raving. Chan's bloody mouth spit out the digit.

"I'm gonna get ya for this, chink," Willie rushed forward. Chan Toy was waiting for the lunge. He swung the skillet around and cracked it on Willie's head.

Willie was out cold. *Is he dead? Did I kill him? I can't bring him back to the ranch! They'll shoot me!*

"Chan Toy, hurry! Let's get the body into the wagon," Ana appeared out of nowhere. "We have to hide him somewhere."

Then an idea hit Chan Toy. After dragging and lifting Willie's body into the wagon, they drove around to the back of the ranch where the pig sty was situated. They dumped Willie into the backside of the pen. It was now dusk, and it was very difficult to see.

Ana and Chan Toy were both covered in blood, mud, and pig shit. Chan Toy drove the wagon back to the ranch house. He grabbed a blanket from the back of the wagon and gave it to Ana.

"You need to clean up and get out of those clothes!" he said. Ana left and rushed into the house through the back door.

Chan Toy unloaded the wagon and unhitched the two horses. He did his best to clean himself up at the trough. He washed off this mouth and the wound on his arm with the murky water. He was still bleeding. He went into the barn and salvaged some old clothing. He looked out of place in the cowboy wear.

His mind was racing. *What should I do now? Should I tell the Mr. Heinz what had happened? I could be fired. Or worse yet, turned over to the sheriff.* He knew that killing a white man, no matter how evil he was, was very seriously punishable by the authorities. *Maybe I should run away? But where can I go?*

Chan Toy snuck back into his little room and grabbed an old flour sack. His left arm was still bleeding. He loosely wrapped a towel around it. Then he packed one set of clothes and some possessions. He grabbed his leather coin purse that he had hidden under a plank and his skull cap. He closed the door and made his way outside.

He hadn't taken ten paces before he heard a hissing sound behind him. Chan Toy whirled around frightened. There were two figures hiding in the shadows.

The taller one approached him. It was Joya. Although it was now dark, he could see the tears in her eyes.

"Thank you for saving my daughter," her voice trembled. She grasped his right hand with both of hers.

Chan Toy shook his head. He was speechless.

"You must take her away from here," Joya pleaded. "She is in danger. She will always be in danger."

Chan Toy was utterly confused. *What is she saying? What does she mean?*

"Ana will take you to our pueblo," Joya anxiously whispered. "You will be safe there for a day or two. And then you must go far away and never come back." With these last words, Joya started to break down.

Chan Toy put his free hand on her shoulder. He didn't know what to do.

"Ana has my medicine bag. It will protect you. There are also a few coins."

"Señora Joya, I am so sorry all this happened to Ana and you." As a stranger in a new land, Chan Toy had been forced to become independent and not be concerned about anyone else. However, he had become attached to these two women and cared about them.

"I will take good care of her," he promised, sadness written on his face.

CHAPTER 11 – LITTLE BLUE ROCK

1898

Little Blue Rock, Mexico

The morning dawn peered over the mountain tops boasting its pink and yellow clouds. Chan Toy and Ana were tired, and their feet were killing them. The cool smell of the desert sage kept them awake. The pair hadn't eaten since the day before, and their throats gasped for water. Chan Toy was slumped over like he was about to crumble.

There was smoke wisping from a small adobe building up ahead.

"You're bleeding!" Ana noticed in the newly found light. Chan Toy's left sleeve was soaked with dark red blood.

Chan Toy's mouth was agape, but he wasn't making a sound.

"We're almost there!" Ana answered him.

Five minutes later they entered the adobe hut.

“Chi’ila!” Ana yelled out for her aunt. “It’s Ana!”

In the back corner, a bulky figure was resting on some sarapes.

“Ana, is that you, my child?” the raspy voice rang out in Yaqui. Then Aunt Teta slowly got up. She was a short, stocky woman with braided black hair, dark eyes, and a beautifully wrinkled face. She approached the pair in the small area just inside the door.

Ana ran over and hugged her aunt. She didn’t want to let go.

“What do we have here?” the aunt stared suspiciously at the bedraggled sight of a man.

“He saved my life!” Ana exclaimed. They conversed in Yaqui.

“Come. Sit,” the older woman pointed to a tree stump and a wooden chair.

As the pair did as they were directed, Chan Toy’s body fell forward. Aunt Teta noticed the seeping blood.

“Let’s take off his shirt,” she directed her niece. The two struggled to disrobe him. Ana gasped as she saw that the arm had reddened. Teta put her hand on Chan Toy’s neck. “He’s hot. We need to brew some medicine. Let’s put him over there.”

The two struggled to put him on top of some Indian blankets.

"Get my medicine bag," she pointed to the opposite corner. "And some water."

An hour later the shack smelled of Mexican epazote. Chan Toy was being forced to drink some Yaqui tea. He couldn't eat, but Ana was ravenous. She gobbled down a tortilla with beef jerky and salsa.

After finishing his tea, Chan Toy leaned back and fell asleep. He began moaning, and a few Cantonese words deliriously popped out during his sleep. He was shivering and his forehead was beaded with sweat. His clothes were soaking wet.

Two days passed. A string of pus pustules paraded across his upper arm. In the meantime, Ana and Aunt Teta spent meaningful time together. They laughed. They cried. Maybe one day Joya would return to the pueblo. Teta missed her.

Teta made daily forays into the high desert, searching for medicinal herbs and plants. She instructed Ana how to prepare them. The two women took turns rubbing Chan Toy's neck, back, and shoulder. The wound had finally stopped bleeding and the foul smell was gone. Teta applied a lemony smelling salve on the gash. The infection seemed to have dissipated. On the third day, Chan Toy became fully conscious. He weakly asked for water. He was dehydrated. His request was in Spanish. He was fed a squirrel stew with tortillas. Three times a day, Teta would rub a bird-shaped stone over Chan Toy's back. The blue rock would heat up and then vibrate, emitting a clicking sound. Then a white light would emanate from within the stone. A higher pitched clicking sound would be heard and last for about a minute. Chan Toy's left leg contorted during this healing spell.

"He has the sign of the colibrí on his foot," Teta pointed to the bottom of his foot.

During this time, Teta would speak to him in Spanish and inquired about his pain and discomfort. Chan Toy was very stoic and didn't complain. He succeeded in getting up and going outside. He found some bushes about 100 paces away to relieve himself.

Although Teta lived on the outskirts of the pueblo, near the entrance of an old, abandoned copper mine, she still kept up with the local gossip through the huarache telegraph. She heard that some gringo cowboy was trying to track down a Chinaman. There was a $25 reward for any information about the suspect. Teta knew that her pueblo was poor and that someone would give up her niece's friend sooner or later. That night she advised Ana that Chan Toy had to escape to safety, but that Ana could stay with her if she wanted to. The choice was up to. Ana, feeling indebted to Chan Toy for saving her life, decided to go with him.

By the fifth day the color was back in Chan Toy's face. His arm looked much better. His crooked tooth smile had returned. Teta informed the pair that a supply wagon was passing through Little Blue Rock on its way to Imuris. For a few coins the driver would let Chan Toy and Ana ride in the back of the wagon.

Before the pair were to depart, Teta added a few more items to the medicine bag that Ana had gotten from her mother. There were some medicinal herbs, a few small gold nuggets, and a carved turquoise colibrí.

"What's this, Chi'ila?" Ana asked her aunt inquiring about the turquoise stone amulet.

"It is tanajelah," Teta reverted to Yaqui out of Chan Toy's hearing. "It is from here. This turquoise colibrí will help you and protect you. It used to belong to your mother. She gave it to me when she moved to Cananea so I could defend myself. Now I'm giving it to you for your own safety."

Ana bowed in appreciation.

Then Teta gave her niece a knotted patterned cloth square that contained some viands for their journey.

The sun was bright as Chan Toy and Ana climbed aboard the two-horse supply wagon. The driver had a wide-brimmed sombrero that cast a shadow over his gun slinger moustache. He smelled like he had not bathed in a month. Ana was very apprehensive about sitting next to the driver, Juanito. Likewise, Chan Toy was not comfortable about making small talk. So, the two escapees sat in the wagon bed giving each other reassuring nods. From time to time Ana would inspect Chan Toy's wound. It looked okay, and Chan Toy had full range of motion.

The pace was slow. Juanito hummed corridos out of tune. The saguaro cacti were plentiful. Several types of high desert birds foraged for food, all the while squawking, singing, and trilling. Every once in a while, a jackrabbit would bounce close by.

About two hours into the journey, Juanito stopped and jumped off the wagon. He went behind some palo verde bushes to relieve himself. Ana stared at all the colorful desert flowers while Chan Toy remained silent.

Ana untied the food bundle. There were corn tamales. She gave two each to Juanito and Chan Toy who both inhaled the food. Juanito in turn shared his water bota bag with his passengers. They didn't converse much. Juanito wanted to make Imuris before nightfall.

Ten minutes later they resumed their trek. The road kept changing from muddied ruts to gravelly stretches to sandy patches. The horses didn't like their footing and would sometimes stop. Juanito alternatively cracked the whip or talked to them gently.

"Come on, chulita," he spoke softly to the chestnut-colored mare. "We have to reach the town before dusk. You will get fresh food and you can rest." The horse would whinny and after a brief pause would start up again. The other horse was just a follower.

The road leveled off and the setting was now more like a green pocked desert. There were paths that veered to the right or left. Every once in a while, a Mexican or Indian could be seen in the distance.

Chan Toy slept most of the way while Ana remained vigilant. They were almost out of harm's way.

CHAPTER 12 – HIGHWAY ROBBERY

1898

Imuris, Mexico

The morning sunbathed the chaparral valley in paint box colors. Chachalacas sprinted along the path, squawking here and there. Cool air began to morph into warm wafts. Ana rubbed her eyes. She tried to protect them from the floating dust as they bounced down the road. Chan Toy fidgeted as he tried to sleep.

The driver made a rest stop in the afternoon.

"How much further?" Ana asked the driver, her face dotted with grit and sweat.

"No mucho," Juanito was not being very conversational. *We'll get there when we get there,* he muttered to himself. *¡Pinche indita!*

An hour later there was a crossroads leading to Nogales going to the right and Imuris to the left.

"One more hour," Juanito blurted out without prompting.

Ana shook her head. She reached over and looked at Chan Toy's arm. It looked good. His right hand twitched as she touched it. Although he didn't talk about his injury, Ana wondered if he still was in pain.

The reddish clay path was now running toward two large granite boulders just up ahead. One of the horses threw its head back and snorted. Juanito pulled back the reins a bit. He knew that this passage was a little tricky to negotiate.

A few minutes later the wagon passed through safely. Juanito breathed deeply. They were almost at their destination.

Suddenly from out of nowhere, a Mexican cowboy on a horse appeared in the middle of the road. He had a gun in his hand. Juanito made an instantaneous decision. He quickly leaned forward and reached down for his rifle. Before he could lift it up, a gun shot rang out from his right. Blood spurted from Juanito's neck. He collapsed. At first the horses were spooked, and started to run away, but the cowboy blocked their way, and they slowed down to a stop in front of him.

A second rider galloped up from behind the sage brush. He was muscular and looked Apache. He wore a red bandanna around his neck.

"I didn't mean to kill him," said the Apache. "He was drawing his weapon."

"No problem," said the Mexican. "Grab the payroll box and . . ."

His voice stopped as he looked into the back of the wagon.

"This is not the payroll wagon!" he barked out. "And who are these friggin' people?" he swung his gun around. "Get out! Get out now!" Ana and Chan Toy readily complied.

The Apache made a quick search of the wagon and found a small chest underneath the driver's seat. He shot the lock off. There was less than five dollars inside. The Mexican was irate.

"Who are you?" barked the Mexican.

"We're travelers," Ana said with frightened eyes.

"Where are you going?"

"To Nogales," she really didn't know for sure.

"What about him?" the Mexican pointed with his gun.

"He is my protector."

Both the Mexican and the Apache laughed. "I'll search them. You grab some supplies. We can't take the wagon."

They unhitched the horses from the wagon and slapped their behinds. The horses took off and within minutes had disappeared.

Then the Mexican patted down Chan Toy looking for secret sewn pockets in his shirt. He found nothing. Then he ran his hand over the pants. He found one gold coin in the Chinaman's pocket. Then he went over to Ana. His hands lingered over her body as he searched or pretended to search. He found the medicine bag around her neck.

He started to remove it.

"No!" Ana cried out.

The bag began to float up from Ana's neck. Waves of blue light and sparks shot out from it. It made a shrill whistling sound. She felt pulses of heat.

"Don't touch it!" shouted out the Apache. "It's her medicine bag. We'll have bad luck if we take it from her."

The piercing noise from the medicine bag grew louder.

The Mexican pulled himself away. "Should we shoot them?"

"No, they'll probably die in the desert anyway."

Minutes later the two bandidos rode away. The noise from Ana's medicine pouch began to quiet down, little by little, until it stopped all together.

Chan Toy was not fully conscious. He didn't realize that they had almost been killed or left to die in the desert.

"They didn't find your valuables!" Ana looked at him in amazement.

Chan Toy said nothing but rolled his eyes upward, toward his skull cap.

The travelers went to check on the driver. Juanito was dead. They debated whether to search him and decided against it. The bandits had left Juanito's leather water bag. They grabbed it and their meager possessions.

"We can't stick around," Ana was taking charge. "If someone comes along, they will blame us for the robbery and murder."

Chan Toy nodded his head. He was in a foreign land, and there was a price on his head. He just wanted to escape

"Let's follow this road," she had seen the sign to Imuris a while back. "I think we have to follow the sun."

The pair started to make their way on the clay path going westward. The smell of sage permeated the air. There was a slight breeze coming from the east. Buzzards glided in the clear blue skies. They had no idea where they were. They wondered how long it was going to take them to reach their destination.

Suddenly, Ana swung her left arm out and caused Chan Toy to stop in his tracks.

"Stay here!" Ana commanded. She turned around and hurried back in the direction that they had come from. "Wait over there!" she instructed again. She pointed to a spot where there was a patch of shade from palo verde bushes.

She hung up the cloth bag that contained food on one of the branches. The other items she placed on the ground. She cleared an area where Chan Toy could sit down and rest. She took off her shawl and hung it over another branch.

Ana took a sip of water and gave one to Chan Toy. He was hungry, as was she, but neither wanted to diminish their limited food supply.

"I'm going back!" Ana got up and started walking back to the scene of the murder.

Where is she going? Chan Toy nervously wondered. He did not want to be abandoned in the desert. *Why is she leaving me?*

CHAPTER 13 – EL ALACRÁN

1898

Imuris, Mexico

His face felt salty, after being subjected to the blistering desert heat for so long. Chan Toy wanted to drink the water that Ana had left behind. Should he? *She shouldn't have abandoned me! Ana will be back. But why did she leave me?* Chan Toy was still partially delirious from his injuries.

The sun was merciless, and Chan Toy struggled to scoot his butt behind the shale rock. He noticed large black ants scurrying by him carrying white larvae.

Ten more minutes passed. His throat was parched. *Where could Ana have gone? I won't be able to survive without her.* Chan Toy needed to nap. He was weak and readily fell asleep.

He began having a bad dream. *Would he be stranded in the desert?*

Dusk had approached when Ana finally returned. Her arms sagged as they were filled with an assortment of things. Chan Toy was curious about what had happened, but before he could ask, she began to tell a story, breathing rapidly. She was exhausted.

"I went back to the wagon. I wanted to make sure that we didn't leave any evidence that we had been in the wagon. The Mexicans and gringos wouldn't look kindly toward us and would have blamed us for everything."

Chan Toy nodded in agreement. He pointed to the water bag. Ana handed it to him.

"Just a little. We have to save some. We don't know where we are," Ana was settling down. She was now in charge. "But when I got there, the zopilotes were already pecking on pobre Juanito's body. I tried to shoo them away, but they ignored me. I knew that I couldn't bury him. God forgive me!

"I crawled into the back of the wagon. There were no weapons. I'm not sure I could have scared off the buzzards anyway. I scrounged an old horse blanket, some dried fruit, a half-filled water bag, and a few other things."

Ana reached into her sash and pulled out some sort of meat jerky that she gave to Chan Toy. He was starving and chewed it with gusto.

"I used the blanket to force the buzzards back. I took a small knife from Juanito's belt. Then I took some flint steel and strips of flour sacks and started a fire. Soon the wagon was on fire and Juanito was ablaze. The buzzards flew off."

Chan Toy's eyes dilated as Ana told her story. Her voice was shaking.

"This way nobody is going to know what happened and we won't be blamed."

Ana repacked the cloth bag and threw the blanket over her shoulder. It was time to move on.

She motioned for Chan Toy to follow.

They had gone about a mile when Ana exhaled deeply. She had been traumatized and needed to regain control of herself. She saw some cactus pears and cut them up. They scraped out the fruit and sucked out the juice.

"Chan Toy, let's find a place to sleep the night. You must be very tired." She didn't let on that she was drained physically and mentally.

They walked about twenty paces off the road and found some more shale rocks. Ana placed the cloth bag next to Chan

Toy and tossed the blanket over him. She positioned herself about five paces away.

The blackness of night crept in. There were a thousand stars in the sky, but without a moon. The temperatures dipped. An owl hooted in the distance. Some sort of crickets was loudly chirping.

It was almost dawn when Ana woke up and found herself under the blanket. She could feel Chan Toy's body convulsing. It was like he was having a nightmare. She leaped up. Chan Toy was moaning. She saw beads of sweat on his forehead.

She began sprinkling a little water on his temples. Then she noticed movements by his feet. There were dozens of red fire ants zigzagging around his ankles The creatures scurried away when she peeled the blanket back. Ana then pulled up the blanket further and immediately saw dozens of red welts on Chan Toy's leg. A few drops of a crimson liquid could also be seen.

He cried out in pain. He was only semi-conscious.

Ana didn't know what to do. Chan Toy could die from the fire ant bites, and she couldn't save him. *Pouring water on the swelling won't help. Neither will bleeding him out. Maybe there is something in mama Joya's medicine bag. Can't make a tea. No hot water. What other herbs are here?*

Suddenly, the medicine bag started to levitate. It was vibrating and getting hot. She remembered how it had reacted when the bandidos had threatened her. Her tia had said that the turquoise stone would protect them. Could it also cure? A high-pitch clicking sound echoed around the pair. The tone got louder and shriller. Ana reached into the medicine bag. She felt the heat of the turquoise colibrí amulet in her hand. She saw streaks of light emanating from the bird-shaped gem.

She passed the turquoise colibrí over Chan Toy's body several times. Then she rubbed the hummingbird in tiny circles around the welt. More bursts of light radiated. Chan Toy's left leg twitched. Steam seemed to rise from the welts. Ana tried to recall the chants that her tia had sung over Chan Toy back at the pueblo. In a pulsating voice she sang the magical Yaqui words in a staccato cadence.

Ana grabbed some Mexican sage from the medicine bag. She wanted to burn it, but she had no fire. Instead, she held it over Chan Toy's leg and swished it all around. It gave off a sweet smell as she did so.

A short while later Chan Toy finally awoke and was able to take a few sips of water but could not eat. His face was red. His skin was moist. He fell back to sleep.

It was past noon when he stirred. The welts had partially disappeared.

"Chan Toy, how are you feeling?" Ana nervously asked.

He weakly nodded his head and went back to sleep. Ana had scavenged the surroundings and found some long sticks. She devised a simple lean-to with the blanket to keep the sun off Chan Toy. He kept on sleeping.

It was twilight when Chan Toy woke again.

"Ana," he called out in groggy voice. "I'm hungry."

Ana smiled. She was happy that he was conscious and able to talk. She gave him some more jerky and water. She did not drink any of the water so that he could have more.

"How are you feeling?"

"Better," he said. "Something bit me. It was painful."

Ana thought about the turquoise colibrí amulet. *Maybe it did have curative powers. Better to have it, than not.*

Nighttime came and the air was chilly. She took the blanket off the makeshift poles. This time Ana was not shy about slipping under the blanket next to Chan Toy. His body was motionless. She stared up at into the sky. There were a million stars.

The next morning Chan Toy could stand up. He was moving about with ease. It was the best that he had looked in a week.

On the other hand, Ana wanted to keep on sleeping. The last few days had been quite an ordeal for her.

"Ana, I'm ready to go."

The pair went back to the road. For the next three hours they trudged what they thought was westward. The sun was at their back. Chan Toy had to stop and rest often.

Suddenly, they heard a pounding rumble behind them. Two dark-skinned boys in straw hats came running up alongside of them.

Greetings were exchanged as they all stopped to catch their breaths.

"How much further to Imuris?" Ana asked the teens.

"About twenty minutes," replied the round-faced adolescent while the other nodded. "You need any water?"

Both Ana and Chan Toy tried to restrain themselves as they drank heavily.

The two boys soon said their goodbyes and took off running once again.

Twenty minutes later Ana and Chan Toy entered a street with wooden buildings and adobe structures.

"Chan Toy, we're here!"

CHAPTER 14 – STAGECOACH INN

1898

Imuris, Mexico

Ana and Chan Toy found a place to eat and clean up in the little town. Ana was still trying to wipe the blood off her hands and skirt. With some of the few coins they had, the pair indulged on a feast of eggs, potatoes, and bacon. They both inhaled the fresh water. There were five or six Mexican customers in the diner either eating carne asada or drinking beer or both.

The middle-aged waitress, with three yards of coiled black hair on her head corona, started to clear the dirty dishes at Chan Toy's table.

"Señorita, do you know where we can spend the night?" Ana asked innocently. She was not confident about Chan Toy's ability to converse in Spanish.

"For you and your husband?" the waitress said indifferently.

"Sí," Ana replied without pausing. *Why did I just lie?* If people are coming after us, maybe they would only be looking for Chan Toy. She thought it might be safer to appear to be a couple. *On the other hand, if we find a place, we are going to have to stay together. Well, we slept next to each other the other night. Nothing happened.*

The waitress gave them directions to a stagecoach inn at the edge of town, and an hour later Ana and Chan Toy found themselves in a little adobe hut. It was one of three. Transitory passengers and stagecoach drivers usually lodged here.

There was a small bed in the middle of the cozy little room. Chan Toy laid down and started to snore almost immediately. Ana took this opportunity to wash herself and her clothes in the makeshift shower between the huts. The outhouse that was about 100 paces away was literally a shit hole. If the stench didn't kill you, the flies would.

The cold water against her skin invigorated her. She finally felt clean. Returning to their hut, Ana gingerly crawled into the bed next to Chan Toy. He didn't stir.

The next morning Ana and Chan Toy had breakfast. The elderly proprietress had cooked some eggs and refried beans with homemade flour tortillas. The coffee tasted like Sonoran Desert mud, but the pair drank up.

During their breakfast, Ana and Chan Toy started discussing what they were going to do next.

"¿Qué vamos a hacer, Chan Toy?" Ana was nervous. "We can't stay here."

Chan Toy shrugged his shoulders. He knew that he was supposed to take care of her. But heck, he couldn't even look after himself.

"Someone could be after us. For what we did," she whispered. "We need to find out when the next stage goes to Nogales."

Chan Toy nodded. Ana got up and talked to the proprietress who was the innkeeper, manager, and ticket master.

"When is the next stage to Nogales?" Ana asked the older woman.

"Monday. Day after tomorrow."

Ana then asked the fare and was told. Their money was getting tight.

After breakfast, they started back to the hut. After a few steps, Ana stopped and said to him, "You should shower and wash your clothes. I'm going back into town. I'll buy some supplies. Do you need anything?",

If there is a pawnshop, maybe I can trade one of my ring, she thought.

When she returned to the hut, Chan Toy was napping in the bed. He had not showered, and he reeked.

"Okay, cochino, get up and take a shower," Ana ordered. "Otherwise, you're going to be sleeping outside with the other pigs."

Chan Toy stared at her and got up slowly. He went to his cloth bag and grabbed his only other clean clothes. He exited the hut.

His queue was totally wet when he returned. He did not have a towel with which to dry his ponytail. He had hung up his wet clothes next to Ana's on a nearby saguaro cactus. Chan Toy was now wide awake.

"Chan Toy," Ana said in a worried tone. "Do you think they will come and try to catch us? They will do terrible things to us." Ana was talking in the "we" form. She realized that her fate was tied to Chan Toy's.

"I don't know," Chan Toy shook his head.

"Do you think they would follow us to Nogales?"

Chan Toy sat down on the bed. He did not say anything for a few minutes.

Then his brow furrowed. He was speaking deliberately. "If they pursued us, they would naturally assume we would go Nogales and cross the border. That would be the most natural thing for us to do. But I have an idea."

The next day around noon, Chan Toy and Ana climbed onto a stagecoach. The proprietress had given them a few apples and an old cowboy hat.

They headed west. This was a real stagecoach and Ana had traded a silver ring for their passage. The driver had come from Nogales, and they were on their way to Mexicali where Chan Toy had once worked.

The saguaro cacti speckled the Sonoran Desert. Pink, yellow, and white flowers adorned the bushes. The smell of sage wafted through the valley. A road runner scooted by. Squirrels darted to and fro. And an armadillo slogged by. The bird cries brought this wilderness to life.

For almost five days and nights, the stagecoach trekked along the path, stopping only to change horses and for short naps for the driver.

Ana was good about rationing the food and water between them. They were allowed to sleep inside the stagecoach, thus avoiding another expense.

Chan Toy was still recuperating and at times he began conversing with Ana in Spanish. He told her about working in

Mexicali for a few years. He confessed that he had been apprehensive about going to Nogales and the States. He didn't know the language and didn't know how he could find work. He would be outside his safety zone.

"But in Mexicali, there are many Chinese and many Mexicans. They all get along. I should be able to get a job easily."

"But what about me?" Ana asked.

Chan Toy had not stopped to think about her. He had saved her life. He expected nothing in return. But then her mother entrusted Ana to him. He had assumed that responsibility without thinking it through. *What do I know about young girls?* Ana had taken care of him when he was injured and when he was bitten by the fire ants. He had to protect her in return. He owed her. Besides, in most places it would have been very difficult to survive without her.

"Ana, if we are going to survive, we need to be a team," he stated. "We can do this together. But I will understand if you want to leave and go your own way."

"No, Chan Toy, I am staying with you," Ana said tenderly looking into his eyes. "You saved my life and I have destroyed your life."

"Ana, I promised your mother that I would protect you."

"And Chan Toy, I promised my mother that I would look after you."

CHAPTER 15 – NEW MANAGEMENT

1898

Mexicali, Mexico

The stagecoach dropped them off near the center of town. Mexicali had grown a lot since Chan Toy had left six years earlier.

So many people! Chan Toy thought. *Too many horses. Too noisy. Not quiet, anymore. I need to go to the Mexicali Rose. I need to find work.*

In Baja California, the Chinese initially had been recruited by the U.S.-owned Colorado River Land Company from Canton to work on irrigation and land clearing projects. Eventually, many Chinese migrated to La Chinesca section of Mexicali. La Chinesca, an Asian gang of sorts, ran the saloons, casinos, brothels, and opium dens. And if one needed money, there was always the "hui" money lenders.

"There are many more people here then before!" Chan Toy exclaimed as he and Ana walked down the rutted dirt road and gazed from side to side. He vaguely remembered the location. Finally, he saw a big wooden sign over a saloon with the name "Mexicali Rose" and with faded little red roses painted on it.

Chan Toy hesitated before going in. Then he decided that Ana should accompany him. Maybe she could find work too.

He noticed that the place had changed very little. It still stank of rancid tobacco and stale beer. As he stepped forward, he was met by a tall, bulky Mexican wearing a black cowboy hat and silver toed boots. He stepped in front of Chan Toy to block his entry.

"Do you have any money?" the bouncer spouted with a spittle mist. Several of his front teeth were missing.

"No!" Chan Toy said nervously in Spanish. "I'm looking for Hung Far."

"What do you want with him?"

"I used to work for him. Here in this saloon," Chan Toy was talking fast. "I'm looking for work. I was hoping that he could give me my old job back. Or something else."

"He's not here," the Mexican said gruffly.

"When will he come back?'

"Never. He's gone for good."

"Do you know a place where we could spend the night?" Chan Toy was disappointed. He needed to find lodging for Ana and himself.

"Well, there is a boarding house behind us," the Mexican gave a broken smile. "Your lady friend could make some extra money if you play your cards right."

Chan Toy didn't say anything. He turned around. He grabbed Ana by the elbow and escorted her outside.

"Sorry. No good. Old boss gone."

Ana wanted to ask him what they were going to do, but she didn't. She knew that it would put additional stress on him. Besides Chan Toy was not a detail person, but she was.

They wandered over to a brightly painted two story building behind the saloon. A large Mexican flag flew in front of it. There was a large chicken coop to the side with lots of squawking going on. Chan Toy knocked on the door and was greeted by a very attractive full-bodied Mexican woman with lots of black eye makeup and shoulder length hair. She was wearing a long scarlet native dress with a black sash. Her large gold loop earrings contrasted nicely with her black hair.

"Yes? How can I help you?" the woman asked, glancing over the motley arrivals. "Food, lodging, or fun?"

"I used to work here," she stammered. "I mean at the saloon. We need a place to stay until I find work," Chan Toy said in a humble manner.

"I have a room upstairs. I need the money for three nights lodging in advance," the woman said still trying to size up the two visitors.

"I think we can pay," Chan Toy was being circumspect. "Is there a pawnshop in town? I need to sell something." He was being cautious. Once people found out he had money, he'd be a marked man.

She gave him directions.

As Ana and he walked to the pawnshop, he said, "We have to sell something. We don't have any money. I have to find work."

Ana nodded. She understood.

After a little haggling, Chan Toy sold a silver ring with turquoise and coral to a grey bearded old fellow. Chan Toy knew that he was being cheated, but he had no choice. They needed money for lodging, food, and clothes.

On the walk back to the Mexicali Rose, they grabbed a few beef tacos from a street vendor. *The food was good here*, Chan Toy thought.

They reentered the "boarding house." The proprietress had been talking to a broad-shouldered man who had his back to the pair.

Chan Toy handed over some money and the woman gave him the key.

They started toward the stairwell. They weren't carrying very much. Chan Toy and Ana just wanted to clean up and rest.

"Hey, you!" the strange man called out to Chan Toy.

A shiver ran up Chan Toy's spine. He didn't turn around.

"Don't I know you?"

Slowly, Chan Toy turned around.

The man suddenly raced toward him and threw his arms around him. "It's the pinche Chino. I thought you ended up in Copper Mountain." Chan Toy immediately recognized Gonzalo, who had been his boss at the saloon years before.

Gonzalo pushed Chan Toy toward an old sofa, and they sat down. He motioned for Ana to sit down in a straight back chair.

"Paloma, get these two some sarsaparillas."

"What brings you back to these parts?" Gonzalo said with a friendly smile.

"To find work," Chan Toy knew that he had to strike while the iron was hot. "There was not much future at the mine."

"Where did you work when you were here before?" Gonzalo looked up as if he was trying to recall. "In the saloon? In the casino part? I don't remember. It's been too long."

"I worked for Hung Far. Doing a little of this and a little of that," Chan Toy was trying to be evasive. He knew that talking too much would get him and Ana in trouble. "By the way, where is Hung Far?"

Gonzalo's facial expression changed. He looked to his right and then to his left to see if anyone was around. He leaned over toward Chan Toy and whispered, "He was a casualty in an in-house power struggle. Wing Fat is the new boss. We still work for the Ong Association here, but there are a few triads that are trying to take over our business. That's why I'm now working here in Mexicali. I have some Mexicans working with me. The Chinese triads don't want to directly confront the Mexicans. Everybody is related to the mayor or police chief by blood or money. You have to be careful. Very careful."

Just then Paloma brought in a floral painted tray with the two sarsaparillas.

Chan Toy thanked her,

"Paloma, this is my old-time friend, Chan Toy, from many years ago," Gonzalo gave her a big smile. "He is one of us. He will be working at the saloon and casino for me."

Chan Toy was shocked, as was Ana. Paloma nodded and left the room.

"Why thank you, Gonzalo! You are too kind!"

"I only demand one thing," the Mexican became serious. "Loyalty. From time to time, I may ask you to do me a favor."

Chan Toy nodded.

"Paloma runs the entertainment at the boarding house for guests of the saloon or casino who want to blow off steam. Around here it is all business. If your wife wants to make a few bucks, we can arrange that. Our Mexican brothers would like some carne asada." He laughed.

Chan Toy said nothing. He didn't want to correct Gonzalo's impression. He had gotten his foot in the door, and he didn't want to lose this opportunity.

CHAPTER 16 – THE THEFT

1898-99

Mexicali, Mexico

For the next year Chan Toy became a fixture at the Mexicali Rose. He worked long hours, but he never complained. He and Gonzalo became friends and would sometimes stay after work sipping sarsaparillas. Gonzalo would tease him and nicknamed him "El Chino," even though there were hundreds of Asians in the city.

Chan Toy was a slender man without a strong physique. He was accustomed to utilizing his brain to get things done. Little by little his self-confidence was growing. He was not afraid to assert himself if need be. Gonzalo trusted him and let him oversee the bar operation in the saloon.

One day, Chan noticed two young Mexican youths glide into the bar area. He sensed something was amiss. One boy would distract the bartender while the other purloined a bottle or two of liquor from behind the bar. The bartender was, of course, unaware of this little scheme. However, no one ever paid attention to the nondescript Chinese worker in the background. They assumed he was deaf and dumb. Chan Toy informed Gonzalo of the ploy. A week later the boys came into the saloon only to be grabbed by Gonzalo and two bouncers and hauled outside next to the chicken coop. The pair was separated.

"Why did you steal from us?" Gonzalo stood in front of the taller of the two.

"We didn't!" the youth shot back.

"The Chinaman says he saw you."

"You can't believe a Chink."

"Hmm. If you wanted a bottle, all you had to do was ask. Do you want one?" Gonzalo hovered over him.

The youth didn't know what to say. His partner was on the other side of the chicken coop. "I guess so."

With his left hand, Gonzalo slowly pushed a pint liquor bottle into the youth's right hand. The youngster instinctively grabbed it. With the speed of lightning, Gonzalo brought another full bottle down and smashed the youth's hand and the pint flask. The scream of shock and pain awoke the dead.

"That was on the house," Gonzalo quipped. "Bring the other pendejo over here."

The smaller of the two was escorted over. The boy was crying. The front of his trousers was wet.

"We didn't mean any harm, señor! We'll pay you back," the boy sobbed. "Please don't hurt me!"

"I should cut your hand off," Gonzalo said slowly. "That would make sure that you don't steal again."

"No! No!" the youth cried out. "I won't do it again! I promise!"

"Why did you do it?" Gonzalo asked gruffly.

"For the money," the boy sobbed.

"Like I told your friend," Gonzalo gave him a sardonic laugh. "All you had to do was ask. Here, take this." He threw a coin down on the ground in front of him.

The boy looked down and hesitated.

"Go ahead! Pick it up," Gonzalo motioned.

The boy looked up and stared at Gonzalo for a few seconds. His head went back down and reached for the money. No sooner had he done that when Gonzalo's boot came crashing down on the outstretched hand.

There was another blood curdling shriek as the youth rolled from side to side on the ground holding his crushed hand.

"Bring the other one over here."

Minutes later both youths were crying in pain holding their injured hands.

"Did you boys learn your lesson?" Gonzalo roared. "You do not steal from the Mexicali Rose."

The pair's heads gave slight nods.

"Now tell me who put you up to this."

Chan Toy had watched the whole ordeal. He was shocked, but knew Gonzalo was right in dealing out the punishment. But he didn't understand why Gonzalo was pursuing the matter. Did someone put these boys up to something? Why?

"Please don't hurt us anymore," the first boy squealed. "It was the Tsin triad. They paid us. They wanted the Mexicans to be blamed. That's the truth. Please don't hurt us."

The other one shook his head frantically in agreement.

"Okay, get out of here!"

The two staggered away as quickly as they could.

Gonzalo pulled his men close to him. Then he yelled for Chan Toy to join them. They all walked back into the saloon and ended up in Gonzalo's tiny office. A couple bottles of tequila were being passed around.

"We did good work tonight," Gonzalo took a pull of tequila. "Wing Fat will be proud of all of us. He will be especially grateful for the tip from Chan Toy."

The Chinaman looked up in surprise. He was embarrassed. He did not accept a sip of tequila when it was offered to him.

"The Tsins are trying to wage a secret war with us. We must be vigilant and be prepared," Gonzalo stated firmly. "They want to take over our gambling and prostitution businesses. Others have thought about it, but the Tsins are the first to test the waters."

"We should attack them tonight, jefe!" one of the lieutenants shouted out. There was the rumble of agreement among the others.

"Well, that would be an appropriate response," Gonzalo admitted. "But it wouldn't be a smart one."

The men around him look puzzled.

"Let's assume that the mocosos report back to the Tsins," Gonzalo explained. "They would be expecting a frontal attack from us. An all-out war. They would be prepared for it. People would be killed, property would be damaged, and worst of all, we would lose business."

"So, what should we do, jefe? We can't let those pinche putos get away with this," shouted another comrade.

Chan Toy knew that Gonzalo was right. But Wing Fat would lose face if there was not some type of retribution. He piped up. "Señor Gonzalez, I think I have an idea. It is a modest plan."

Chan Toy began to hatch a plot to gather every cockroach, spider, and beetle over the next two weeks. They would be collected and hidden in the underground rooms underneath the Mexicali Rose saloon. Then the creatures would be dumped clandestinely at the rival Hops triad saloon on the other side of town. They would leave plenty of evidence at the scene to cast blame on the Tsins. The Hops would seek revenge against the Tsins, and war would break out between them. In the meantime, Wing Fat's business would prosper.

"Thank you, Chino. It is a good plan," Gonzalo was pleased that he had rehired Chan Toy. He liked Chan Toy's instincts and trustworthiness. "I will talk this over with Master Wing Fat."

Two weeks later the Tsin brothel was burned down and its triad master murdered. The Hops lost half their men in the ensuing war.

Meanwhile, every month thereafter, Wing Fat's enterprises kept prospering. Chan Toy became an informal lieutenant to Gonzalo and enjoyed many benefits, including some gold coins.

CHAPTER 17 – ANA

1899

Mexicali, Mexico

At the same time that Chan Toy was assisting Gonzalo, Ana was working at the brothel. Ana had been assigned to do the housekeeping there. Madam Paloma Blanca would have her strip the sheets off the beds, launder them, and dry them once a week.

Ana and Paloma could not have been more different individuals. Paloma had her hair coiffed in a French styled bun and wore large gold earrings. Tons of makeup scored her eyes, and her lips were glossy with ruby red lipstick. Her clothing always consisted of silk dresses.

Ana, on the other hand, wore Mexican-Yaqui indigenous garb without any makeup.

Within a week of Chan Toy's and her arrival to Mexicali from Imuris, Ana made him buy her a cheap silver wedding band to keep up the appearance that they were married. That night she ordered him to take a shower. He obeyed without protest.

"Chan Toy, you have vowed to protect me," Ana stared at him seriously. "I have made the same vow. We are now telling everybody that we are married. We have a ring to prove it. Now we must act the part."

She pushed him to the narrow bed and lifted the blanket. "Let's make it true!" She took off her shift as she climbed in next to him.

The next morning Ana was taking clean towels upstairs when she ran into Paloma. They exchanged pleasant greetings.

"He sure is a screamer," Paloma said in a stage whisper as she passed.

Well, that objective was met, thought Ana. To reinforce the marital bond with Chan Toy, she had the maids and staff address her as "Señora Toy." With Paloma aka Madam Paloma Blanca, she was now on a first name basis.

Working at the brothel was a challenge. While Gonzalo had a man or two around the premises for protection, it was up to Ana and Paloma to deal quick and efficiently with drunks and abusive customers. Ana knew how to use a knife and a rifle; and if necessary, a bow and arrow. She had hunted small game as a girl at Little Blue Rock.

At the brothel, Ana did not have to do any cooking. Consuelo, the cook, had one of the boys bring over food from the bar's kitchen twice a day. Paloma did not want the girls entering the saloon or going astray.

***

It was in the early spring of 1899, when the dark-skinned criada, Beatriz, ran up to Ana who was folding pillowcases with a young worker.

"Señora Toy! Señora Toy," the maid said, out of breath. "Come quick! Doña Blanca needs you right away!"

Ana put down the bedding. "What happened? Where is she?"

"Follow me!" Beatriz ran in front of her. They hurried to a closet door in the corner of the little kitchen of the boarding house. This area was off limits to everyone. Beatriz opened the door and lit a candle.

What is this? How come I never noticed it before? Ana thought.

The pair carefully walked down some wooden stairs. At the bottom, there was a subterranean crossway where four tunnels fanned out. There was a sconce lit every fifty feet. They took the path to the left. They passed a door where a young mother was nursing her baby.

They made a right turn. The strong smell of ammonia escaped from a large room where emaciated figures were smoking something.

Finally, they arrived in a little room where a dozen candles were configured to give maximum light.

"Thanks for coming, Ana," Paloma was holding a young girl's hand. The youth was lying in a narrow bed with closed eyes. Ana noticed the pallid color of the girl's face and then a pile of red and rust colored rags that were on the floor at the foot of the bed. Every few minutes the girl would convulse, as if in pain.

"What happened?" Ana's eyes bounced from side to side.

"Beatriz, go back to Consuelo, and get some hot water. See if she has some chicken soup or any hot liquid."

The maid obeyed. Paloma spoke in an exasperated tone. She was shaken. The girls, as the prostitutes or putas were called, were a revenue stream for Wing Fat. Fewer girls meant less money.

"This one got pregnant," Paloma shook her head. "And she tried to take care of it herself. She was butchered by a local curandera. She has been bleeding since yesterday. Ana, can you help her out?"

Ana figured out why Paloma had summoned her. The madam did not want to be blamed for losing a money-making asset and she didn't know what to do. Ana had some experience in dealing with injured people, most recently Chan Toy. But nobody knew about that. She would use the herbs in her medicine pouch.

When Consuelo came in with a kettle of hot water, Ana made a tea with some of her herbs from the medicine bag that she always carried on her person. The girl was drifting in and out of consciousness. Ana forced a few ounces of the liquid down the girl's throat over a ten-minute period. While she had been rummaging through her pouch, she found the turquoise hummingbird amulet. She set it aside. She then lifted the girl's stained skirt. There was evidence of vaginal bleeding. She poured hot water over a clean cloth and wiped the girl down. There was still fresh blood oozing out of the girl. *This girl is going to die!* Ana thought.

Instinctively, Ana grabbed the turquoise colibrí and made circles with it over the girl's lower abdomen. Ana's head bobbed as she started chanting some of her mother's Yaqui healing songs.

The hummingbird started to glow. Bursts of blue-white light flashed. A shrill clicking sound got louder. Ana continued the treatment. She felt the amulet's heat. Her heart palpitated. She inhaled deeply, then exhaled. Sparks flew from the turquoise figurine. The sound got shriller and louder.

Beads of sweat ran down Ana's forehead and arms. The seconds drifted into minutes.

"Ana, are you okay?" It was the concerned voice of Paloma. Ana was kneeling next to the girl clasping the hummingbird tightly in her hand.

Gingerly, Ana lifted herself up from the floor. She reached up and touched the girl's neck.

The girl's eyes opened wearily. "I want my mother," she weakly mumbled. The color seemed to be coming back a little in her face.

By evening the girl, who was named Eva as Ana later learned, was drinking hot broth.

An hour later, Ana climbed up the private staircase to return to her lodging. Paloma met her as she exited the closet door.

"Ana, I want to thank you for your help," Paloma put her two hands on Ana's shoulders. "You saved the girl's life." *And your ass,* Ana thought.

“If you could do me one small favor,” Paloma stared directly into Ana’s eyes, “and not tell anybody about this, I would appreciate it.”

Ana understood what this was all about and nodded affirmatively.

“And if you ever need a little extra pleasure,” Paloma gave her a devilish grin. “I can arrange that. Or something for your husband . . . or maybe for both of you at the same time.” She gave a little laugh.

“Paloma, there is another favor you can do for me.”

CHAPTER 18 – MALA SUERTE

1899-1901

Mexicali, Mexico

As a reward for helping her, Ana was given free time to learn how to read and write. Paloma assigned Magdalena to teach Ana. As a young girl, Magdalena had been sent to a convent. She was expelled when the Mother Superior learned that Magdalena had been having carnal relations with a man. The girl admitted that she was in love with him.

"What happened to the man?" Ana asked curiously.

"He's still around, I think"

"Who was he?"

"The parish priest."

Ana met with Magdalena three times a week. In the first week Ana learned the alphabet. Paloma gave her some scrap paper and old pencils. Ana practiced her letters and writing every day.

"Magdalena, I don't understand the difference between an 'ene' and 'eñe.' And 'elle'" Ana would complain.

"It's just the way it is," Magdalena was patient with her new student. She enjoyed being the teacher and feeling empowered.

Every week Ana learned to read a new set of vocabulary words. Fruits, vegetables, numbers, . . . She had to memorize the spellings and write them down ten times. It was difficult for her, but she persevered.

After three months of arduous study, Ana was able to write short sentences and little compositions.

Paloma observed all of this and supplied Ana with old hotel and invoice stationary that had a blank side for Ana to practice her lessons.

Magdalena and Ana developed a great teacher-student relationship. Ana was writing short compositions within six months. Magdalena gave Ana an old, dog-eared book of poems so that Ana could practice her reading out loud. Chan Toy was the recipient of these recitals.

Ana tried to persuade Chan Toy to learn to read and write, but he declined. He said that his job responsibilities did not require reading. He seemed to shrug the whole notion off.

But that was not exactly true. Back at the saloon and casino, Chan Toy had to learn how to count and record numbers in Hanzi (the Chinese math system). He had to weigh the small gold bars that the Wing Fat enterprises brought in and ledger them in Han characters for security reasons. Every night two of Gonzalo's men carried the ingots to a clandestine room in a strong box. It was secretly located in the underground passages underneath the Wing Fat properties. Another small safe was located in Wing Fat's office upstairs as a smoke screen for the real cache.

Chan Toy had proved that he was a loyal and competent employee. The same could be said of Ana.

***

The year was passing by so quickly. Ana's face started to glow. Paloma noticed it. She gave Ana a head-to-toe inspection. Ana's tiny little breasts were starting to swell.

It was early autumn when a trio of Norteamericano cowboys rode into town. They were flush with cash from some recent cattle drive over in Chihuahua. They had no desire to find work. They drank and gambled during the weekdays. They were openly hostile to the patrons of the saloon and casino.

They spent Friday and Saturday nights whooping it up with the girls at the boarding house brothel. Normally the Mexican cowboys would pair up with Mexican putas and the Chinese laborers would engage with the Asian girls. But these gringos were different. They always wanted something different. Something spicy. Something exotic. The tall one, Jim Thompson, wore a bluish grey Stetson cowboy hat. He was a Southerner with an accent as thick as cowhide. The Mexicans grimaced as he slaughtered the Spanish language. At the brothel, his favorite was the cinnamon-skinned Camille who had the blackest eyes. Her smile was not that pretty because of her tiny catlike teeth, but she must have been hot in the sack because Jim nicknamed her his Cayenne pepper.

Then there was the short guy, Dean Klein, who had a Napoleonic complex and a chip on his shoulder. His face was sallow, and it looked like it had been run over by a stampede. He had a quick fuse and was fast to call out people. Most people just ignored him. He liked the young girls who weren't over fourteen years old. He could be a big man with them.

The third cowboy had a clean-shaven face but smelled like a pigsty. He wore brown rawhide gloves on both hands at all times. His name was Willie. He was a real animal with the girls. He favored the young whore Estrellita who was half-witted.

Paloma noticed that this girl had welts and bruises after her sessions with Willie. Paloma believed that the customer was always right, but an incapacitated girl meant less revenue. She had to protect the merchandise.

Six weeks after they arrived, Dean and Jim left and rode northward. It was rumored that they were going to Salt Lake City. Willie remained in Mexicali and moved into the Mexicali Rose boarding house. He settled down, sleeping most of the day and gambling and partying at night. He would have a Saturday bath and a shave.

One day Chan Toy was in the saloon. There was a commotion at one of the tables. The gringo was yelling and calling someone a cheat. Willie put his revolver on the table.

Two of Gonzalo's men came over and warned the gamblers to maintain order or leave. Willie made a weak reply but put his gun away.

Chan Toy's forehead wrinkled. *That cowboy reminds me of someone. Who is he?* Chan Toy couldn't remember. He didn't have a good feeling about him. So, for next few days, he observed the gringo closely.

The next Friday night, Ana was awakened by a blood curdling scream coming from one of the girls' working rooms. Chan Toy was working at the casino as usual. Ana threw a blanket over herself and cautiously went out the door. She went to the left. All of a sudden, another door swung open. A girl came running out. It was Estrellita. She was bent over and bleeding from her neck.

"Get back in here, you little whore!" a gruff voice sounded.

Ana rushed forward, trying to grab the girl.

A naked man appeared behind the girl.

Ana recognized him. She could not forget the man who had tried to rape her back at Cananea. It was that evil Willie Collins. She stopped in her tracks.

Her neck started to feel hot. The medicine pouch around her waist was starting to vibrate.

"Hey, I know you!" the man looked at Ana and bounded over the bleeding girl. "It was your fault!"

Ana turned around and started to run to the end of the hall. *Where is Paloma? Where are Gonzalo's men?*

Little blue streaks of light beamed from the leather pouch.

Ana pounded on Paloma's door but there was no response. The naked man appeared on the stairs. He had a straight razor in this left gloved hand.

"You're the bitch who cost me my finger!"

Ana ran out the door. She had to find Chan Toy. She fell as she tripped over the last step. She was in pain. Her knee throbbed with pain. She struggled to get up. She was gasping for air. She felt abdominal pains.

She felt a tug on her clothes. He had grabbed her.

CHAPTER 19 – LA BRUJA

1901

Mexicali, Mexico

Ana closed her eyes and grabbed her leather pouch. She reached in and touched the turquoise colibrí amulet. A high-pitched clicking sound emitted.

"Ur mine, bitch!" Willie barked.

Instinctively, Ana raised the pouch. She could feel the turquoise hummingbird swirling inside. There were pulses of heat. The bag opened. Streaks of light beamed toward Willie's face. The clicking sound morphed into a continuous hum. Small purple round marks started to appear on Willie's face.

Willie tried to cover his face. His head shook from side to side. The whirring got louder. He writhed in pain. He twisted his body. He raised his razor and wildly slashed through the air. He did not even come close to reaching Ana.

The hummingbird vibrated at a high timbre. The flashes of light increased in size. Welts formed on Willie's neck and arms. He staggered as he groaned in pain.

Ana got to her feet. The hummingbird was now making a high-pitched wailing sound. A flash of lightning from the pouch bolted toward Willie. It knocked him down. He was squirming in agony. Steam started to rise from his head. Willie's cheeks started to redden, and his skin started to shrivel up. Soon the rest of her head followed suit. His head was shrinking! After a few minutes his body stopped moving.

By this time two of Gonzalo's men had arrived. The observed the last few minutes of Willie's life but didn't say a word.

Ana staggered back to the boarding house. She trudged up the stairs. At the end of the hall, she found Paloma standing over Estrellita.

"She's dead!" the madam cried. "The bastard killed her!"

Ana shook her head in sorrow.

Chan Toy rushed into their room an hour later. He had heard about the commotion from one of Gonzalo's men. Ana had cleaned herself up and was lying down on the bed with a blanket over her shoulders, her knees to her chest. She was quivering.

"Are you okay?" Chan Toy asked nervously rubbing Ana's protruding belly. "What happened?"

She regained her composure and started to explain, leaving out the part about the magical intervention of the turquoise hummingbird.

Chan Toy didn't press her.

The next morning Ana barely made it downstairs. She found Paloma sitting with a mug of coffee in her hand. The madam's face had dried streaks of mascara. Paloma asked Ana what had happened and was given the same version of the story that she had shared with Chan Toy.

"I've asked Gonzalo to assign two men here at all times," Paloma was trying to regain her control.

The next day Estrellita was given a Christian burial at the local church and all the girls attended. The priest was very old and did not know in what kind of profession the girl had been involved. The Ong Association made generous monthly contributions to the parish, so no questions were asked.

Some of the prostitutes began to talk among themselves. They had heard that Estrellita had been abused and tortured. Unfortunately, they knew it came with the job. However, no one understood how Ana could have subdued the gringo. One of the explanations was that Ana was some sort of bruja or enchantress who practiced witchcraft.

For the next few days, the girls seemed standoffish to Ana. They didn't greet her and kept their distance from her.

Gonzalo unexpectedly called Chan Toy over one evening. "Wing Fat wants to talk to you."

Chan Toy followed Gonzalo to Wing Fat's office. It was a small decrepit room with three sofas smothered with cushions. It stunk of alcohol and stale tobacco.

"Sit. Sit. Sit," said the big boss in a commanding tone.

Chan Toy looked at Gonzalo who nodded that it was okay to do so. Chan Toy had not had much real contact with Wing Fat.

"How is your woman?" the big boss was trying to make nice. "We have a very risky business."

Chan Toy gave a polite nod. "Fine now."

"I am hearing rumors about your woman," Wing Fat said matter of factly. "They say she is a very powerful witch. She can cast spells and turns people into frogs. I don't know if it's true or not. What I care is about business. If customers are afraid to use our girls, we lose money. If customers don't want to gamble here, we lose more money. If customers don't want to come here and drink, we lose lots of money. You savvy what I'm saying?"

Chan Toy couldn't comprehend why Wing Fat was telling him this.

"I could send you away, but Gonzalo has told me that you have always been a loyal worker. You are part of the family. But unfortunately, you can't be here. I've talked it over with Gonzalo. You and your woman will be moved to one of the underground quarters. You both will no longer be working here."

Chan Toy felt a pain in his chest. He tried to inhale. His hands began to shake.

Wing Fat did not notice any of this. He was deep into his own thought. "But I will give you an important mission. You will have to go back to Guangzhou. You will have to stay there until Beng Ong says you can return. You must take your woman with you. Gonzalo will explain what you have to do."

Fifteen minutes later Chan Toy walked back to the boarding house. He was drenched in sweat. *What did I do wrong to upset the master?* Ana was not in. He could not go back to work at the saloon, so he waited for her. She returned around eight o'clock.

"Ana, we have to get out of here," Chan Toy said quickly.

“What?” her eyes were opened wide. “Why?”

Chan Toy explained the little that he knew. Since they had very few possessions, they made their way to the underground quarters where Gonzalo was waiting for them. It was dark and Gonzalo led them to a dreary room with the aid of a candle.

“I am sorry, my old friend,” Gonzalo patted the Chinaman on the back. “But business is business. The other triads have their mouths watering over our customers. Let me tell you what is going to happen.”

Gonzalo explained that in three weeks’ time, Chan Toy and Ana would be put on a stagecoach to Ensenada. They would be carrying three medium sized ocean steamer trunks. They would be accompanied by two of Wing Fat’s Chinese guards. There would be thirty-three Troy ounces of gold hidden in each trunk. Wing Fat had all his revenues converted into small ingots every week.

Chan Toy and Ana would be put on a steamer bound for Guangzhou. The Chinese guards would guard the trunks on the sea voyage and Chan Toy would monitor them. If everything worked out, the gold would be delivered to Beng Ong in Guangzhou as part of the annual tribute to the Ong Association.

Later that night, Ana was extremely upset and crying. “I will never be able to come back and see my family,” she complained.

"We must do our duty and obey," Chan Toy tried to assuage her. "I promise that we will return here." He was being very gentle with her.

She nodded. "Okay, but now you have to teach me Chinese."

"It's probably too late now," Chan Toy tried to smile. "But I must learn how to read and write."

"Chinese?"

PART III – THE MIDDLE KINGDOM

CHAPTER 20 – BENG ONG

1902

Guangzhou, China

Ana squeezed her eyes and hung on tight to her leather pouch. She had never been aboard a ship before. She needed the turquoise colibrí amulet to protect her. Her abdomen convulsed. She felt nauseous. She had already vomited on the cabin floor three times. The Malay cabin boy grimaced each time he had to clean the mess. Chan Toy was not faring much better, but he procured some hot ginger tea from the ship's galley.

The vessel had left Ensenada under calm seas but had battled stormy seas and high winds for almost four weeks. The three steamer trunks took up half the room. The two guards provided by Wing Fat stood outside the door.

Chan Toy reentered the room and patted her forehead with a damp rag.

"We're halfway there," he spoke softly to her. "Everything will be all right." He didn't know if it would or not, but they had to relax. When they landed in China, she would be in for a big surprise.

It took almost another six weeks for the ship to reach its destination. Chan Toy staggered as his feet hit terra firma. Ana had a splotchy complexion. At the port, Wing Fat's entourage was met by six bare-armed muscular brutes. They did not talk very much. They simply grunted or waved Chan Toy, Ana, and the children on. Upon arrival Chan Toy's family was put into a carriage drawn by four horses. Behind them the guards rode in the carts with the trunks. It was a several-hour ride through the hills. Finally, they reached a white-walled villa. The double wooden gate, guarded by two ceramic lions, opened and they were permitted to enter. There were armed sentries posted everywhere.

At the entry way Chan Toy and Ana were met by several servants, both men and women. Ana was taken to a spacious room upstairs. A young girl drew her bath and motioned Ana to disrobe. Ana sighed in gratitude. She had not bathed properly in almost three months. She knew that she reeked. She felt that her body was contorted and bloated. The food on the boat was barely edible. Her stomach always ached and now her breasts felt swollen, and they ached. Then she remembered that she hadn't had her menstrual cycle for several months. She had been too preoccupied to think about it.

She slipped into the ceramic bathtub. There were aromatic suds floating all around. Ana started to drift into a sleepy trance. *What is going to happen to us? I don't speak Chinese and I don't know anyone.*

One of the handmaidens dried her off, applying fragrant creams to her body. She was given beautiful new clothes. They were green and made of silk. Her old garments disappeared. Another of the staff helped dry her hair and brushed it out.

There was a slight knock at the door. Chan Toy walked in. He had had a similar bathing reception. He had never smelled so good. They were escorted downstairs to a small parlor where small dishes of food were laid out on a table. There were skewered shrimp, rice balls, and bao along with cups of hot tea. Chan Toy inhaled his meal. He had missed the Cantonese food that he had been weaned on. The Mexicali comida chifa was barely passable.

Ana was a bit reluctant to try all the samples. *Where's the meat? Not many vegetables! No fruit! Everything fried and fatty.* Her stomach was not happy with the new cuisine. She had lost several pounds since their departure from Ensenada, yet her body was filling out.

The pair retired to their bedroom. They made love with no one looking over their shoulders. It was an idyllic situation.

The next morning, Ana was looking for her eggs and bacon for breakfast. Instead, she got a bland rice congee. *I would even settle for avena.*

Chan Toy was summoned to see Beng Ong. It had been twenty years since they last met. He found Beng Ong slouched on a pile of dark green cushions. His pot belly protruded through his silk vest. His hair was still scraggly as was his goatee. His fingernails were long and curved.

"Welcome back, my friend," his right hand waved him over. Chan Toy came over and gave a polite bow. Within seconds two cups of tea appeared on a small black lacquered table between them.

"I hope you had a pleasant journey," Beng Ong's smile showed that half of his teeth were missing. "Anyway, let's get down to business." He clapped his hands. Immediately, the Wing Fat guards appeared. They brought in the first steamer trunk that they had guarded on the ship and placed it in front of the triad boss. They repeated this ritual with the other two cases. The two men open the trunks and brought up several sacks of gold bars.

Beng Ong opened the first one and counted out 33 gold ingots, each weighing a Troy ounce. He smiled. "Very good, Chan Toy. Wing Fat did right in trusting you." He repeated the reckoning with the other two bags in the trunk. In front of him were 99 small gold bars. He gave a hearty laugh as he rocked back and forth.

Chan Toy could not believe his eyes. No wonder they had been escorted by two guards. People would kill for such treasures.

The ingots were placed back into the steamer trunk. Over the next twenty minutes, bags were taken from their respective trunks, counted again, and finally all deposited into the first trunk. In his head, Chan Toy quickly calculated the value of the 99 ingots. A small fortune in Guangzhou. Beng Ong clapped his hands again and all three trunks were removed. Then a smallish man dressed all in black approached and handed the boss a silk bag.

"Chan Toy, come closer." He handed the silk bag to Chan Toy. "This is a token of my appreciation for you doing your duty and being loyal."

Chan Toy bowed again, "Thank you."

"I have big plans for our businesses, and you are a part of them. You will have to work very hard. I do not know when you can be sent back to Mexico. That won't be a problem for you, will it?"

Chan Toy nodded no. He would have to inform Ana. But what choice did they have?

"And starting tomorrow you will be my minister of Chinese-Mexican enterprises. You will become an expert in Spanish and Cantonese translations. It would also be good for your wife to be likewise proficient."

I think I'd rather clean ashtrays, he thought. *Ana has been doing fine, but to learn Cantonese?! That is going to be a challenge for her, but she is very capable.*

"In the meantime, you will reside nearby to me. You will have staff and a stipend. I am counting on you. I know you won't let me down."

A few minutes later, Beng Ong was being carried away in a small litter.

In the spacious garden, Ana was waiting for Chan Toy. She was beaming. She entwined her arm with his. A little carriage drove them over to a villa on top of Jade Hill. They were greeted by maids and manservants. It was a gigantic lodging with several halls and gardens.

Mai introduced herself and led the pair into a small casual dining area. The maid had placed little plates of food before them. Ana knew what to expect. She knew that she could not complain. Nobody but Chan Toy would be able to understand her anyway. However, she did have a difficult time using chopsticks.

They had a sumptuous feast. What was missing in taste, was made up for in quantity.

In their bedroom, they found a very large bed with beautiful red silk bedding. There were a dozen cushions.

"This is ours, Ana, during our stay here," he didn't want to tell her how long that could be.

"Chan Toy, I have some important news for you," she put her right hand against the middle of his chest. "I'm pregnant!"

He grabbed her and pulled her close. "A Year of the Tiger baby!"

CHAPTER 21 – CHOPSTICKS

1902

Guangzhou, China

Chan Toy, who was normally not outwardly affectionate, smothered her with kisses. He squeezed her tightly.

"Woman, you have given me prosperity," he beamed. "Hopefully, we'll have a son."

By noon the next day, everybody was aware of the good news.

"Madam, we need to prepare a place for the baby," the main housekeeper Gin greeted Ana in the early morning. "Do you want the baby to have his own room or to be with you?"

Ana knew that the protection of the new arrival was of paramount importance for Chan Toy and her. On the other hand, the baby would need to sleep in a quiet room. "Let's do both. Have baby cribs placed in both places."

A young girl with a round face brought a tray of food to Ana. Her name was Ling, and she was very timid. She was now Ana's personal food server.

For the next few months, different types of food were prepared for Ana. *Ick! These turnips are so plain! These radishes are so bitter! Everything is pickled!* But Ana ate everything. She had been raised to understand that food was important. Taste didn't matter. Survival was. She needed to eat everything to have a healthy baby.

Every day Ana would have an acidy stomach or gas or diarrhea. Chan Toy warned her not to drink the water. Only hot tea. Alcohol was forbidden for her.

Ana struggled learning to eat with chopsticks. Ling cringed when her mistress had a difficult time eating. Finally, Chan Toy with his infinite patience taught her. While Ana struggled to eat the new foods, Chan Toy's mouth watered as he ate the food of his childhood viands. Duck feet. Fried tofu. Lo mein noodles.

While Ana awaited the birth of the child, Qiu arrived every morning to teach her Cantonese. Qiu also tutored Chan Toy in bookkeeping, reading, and writing. Ana was a natural student. She wanted her child to be educated and she knew that in order for that to happen, she, as the mother, would have to be educated first. Chan Toy, on the other hand, struggled, but persevered. He could not disappoint Beng Ong if he wanted to return to Mexico. Besides he could make more money if he knew how to read and write. He would have good joss. He was even allowed to supervise workers and he did it very well. He just treated them like he wanted to be treated.

Little by little, Ana started to learn the Chinese dialect. The names of fruits and vegetables came first. Gradually, she instructed Ling on what foods she wanted. Sweet and sour chicken. Char siu bao. And plenty of rice.

Slowly, numbers and calculations started to make sense to Chan Toy. At first, he had difficulties with multiplication. Qiu used to drill him every day.

"What is nine times eleven?" she would ask him.

He tried to count but always got confused. Then one day when he was working in Beng Ong's counting room, Qiu placed gold ingots in rows of nine, eleven down in front of him. Chan Toy visualized the correct answer. He was so proud of himself.

Each day he waited in joyful anticipation for the next quiz. Beng Ong became aware of Chan Toy's progress.

Chan Toy knew he would be able to support his woman and child. He knew that her stomach was growing, and that she was urinating like a faucet. Her servant Su was emptying out the bedpan a dozen times a day.

But he was worried about her. She had eschewed most foods, especially the staples. Her new cravings were peanuts and watermelon. He didn't understand but made sure that her wants and needs were heeded.

What Ana couldn't control was the weather and the pesky vermin. The weather was perpetually hot, humid, and rainy. Su would wipe Ana down several times a day. Then there were the mosquitos constantly buzzing around her. The netting was imperfect in its protection. Su would burn citronella candles around her bed.

Ana could have complained, but she didn't. She was barely lifting a finger. No more household duties for her. She was almost a lady, with a nice home and servants. Did she really want to give this up and return to Mexico? For what?

As for Chan Toy, he made some forays to the old family shack where he had been raised in Guangzhou. It was on the other side of town. He found the Chan dwelling in the midst of a bamboo copse. It was in great disrepair. Half of the frond roof was missing. A young family lived there now. It looked like they were barely surviving. The place reeked of old garbage and mold.

At the end of the overgrown alley, Chan Toy went up to a mud brick shack with rice plants in front.

"Hello, is anybody home?" he yelled.

There was no answer.

Chan Toy yelled again.

An old woman with buck teeth and squinty eyes shuffled up to the doorway. She didn't say anything. Chan Toy recognized her as his friend Wan Tu's mother.

He bowed politely. "I am Chan Toy, auntie. Your old neighbor," he pointed down the muddy path. "Is Wan Tu around?"

She slowly shook her head. "He's in Beijing."

They conversed for a few moments. He knew that he should have brought a gift or something for the lady. The woman remembered when Chan Toy's mother had passed away. She did not know what had happened to his siblings. Chan Toy figured that everyone that he had known in this village was either dead or had moved away.

Back home, Ana was getting bigger and more demanding. The staff was beside themselves, but nobody complained. Chan Toy wanted a midwife to be available when the time came. He did not fully trust Ling or Su. He made a special inquiry to Beng Ong who said he would investigate it. As a result of the bamboo telegraph, a large boned woman with breasts sagging down to her stomach and big feet came to assist Ana. The woman was Hakka and very hard working. However, she brought eight children with her. There was a lot of yelling and crying and scurrying. The whole household was topsy-turvy. The situation barely lasted two days before the woman was asked to leave.

For the next few weeks, dozens of young women came to the house looking for work. One was only twelve years old. None of them seemed suitable to Ana who was getting larger and larger.

She had started to eat more. Her breasts were aching. Ana liked the local shrimp. She was now proficient in the use of chopsticks and in speaking simple sentences in Cantonese.

Chan Toy would be making a trip to Guilin with Beng Ong in late summer. Beng Ong resembled the sitting Buddha with his belly bulging out. His hair was falling out leaving black tuffs dotting his head. He had lost feeling in the bottom of his feet. He had to be transported by a palanquin supported by six servants. Beng Ong wanted to expand his farm holdings in the region. He also desired to increase his market share in Guangzhou.

It was during their absence that a middle-aged woman appeared at Chan Toy's abode. Her hair was salt and pepper with long bangs. Her clothing was of poor quality and sadly disheveled. She was greeted by Gin, the main housekeeper.

“I am here to see Chan Toy,” she told Gin.

A moment later Ana arrived in the entryway. She asked the woman, “Can you start working tomorrow?” Ana was tired of interviewing nannies. She wanted one now.

The stranger gave her a strange look.

“I don’t know,” she replied. “I’ll have to talk to Chan Toy first.”

“How do you know Chan Toy?” Ana was getting concerned about who the stranger was. *Was this his Chinese wife?*

“Sorry,” the woman became shy. “He’s my brother.”

CHAPTER 22 – HEALING

1902-11

Guangzhou, China

The woman was invited into the parlor where she was served tea and almond cookies. Ana found out that her name was Chan Yun Wu.

"As a child, I was given over [sold] to the local healer, Madam Tong Long," narrated Wu. "I was her caretaker. She taught me about being a healer. I even learned to read and write from her. She passed away four years ago. I live in her old house."

"What do you do for work now?" inquired Ana curiously.

"A little healing and being a midwife."

"Perfect! Would you like to work here?"

Three days later Chan Toy returned from his sojourn. He was exhausted from the extensive travel. However, he did notice a woman shadowing Ana. That evening he asked Ana who the new person was.

"She says that she is your sister. Her name is Chan Yun Wu."

Chan Toy racked his brain. When he was about ten years old, he remembered that a little girl was led away from him and his family. She had departed holding the hand of an old woman. He wondered if his parents had sold their daughter to the village bruja.

The next morning Chan Toy met with the woman. She was indeed his long, lost sister. They spent the entire morning exchanging stories. Chan Toy was overjoyed to hear that Wu would be taking care of Ana during her pregnancy.

In late August, Chan Toy and Ana had a healthy son, that they named Cajemé. There were all sorts of celebrations. It was the Year of the Tiger. People from all over the province sent regards and gifts. Beng Ong sent over a tiny gold ingot.

Thirty days later a Red Egg and Ginger ceremony was held at the local Buddhist temple. Wu convinced Chan Toy that this ritual was necessary to bring luck to the newborn child and restore balance to the mother after childbirth.

Wu was a God send. The baby slept through the night and did not cry. Ana was allowed to sleep and after four weeks she had fully recuperated. Qiu resumed her tutoring of Ana while Wu took care of the baby. Ana breast fed Cajemé, and Wu told the child stories as she held him in her arms.

Ana spoke to the baby in Spanish. When she had something private to say to Chan Toy, they also used Spanish. The new year had arrived and several people in the household were coughing and had runny noses. One morning Wu could not get out of bed. Ana came over to see what was wrong. Ana disappeared and returned with her medicine pouch. She took out the turquoise colibrí amulet. It started to emit short clicks. Then it began to hum. Ana moved the turquoise up and down and all-around Wu. Ana's hand felt hot as she did so. Wu was slightly feverish and did not understand this type of healing.

The next day Wu was well enough to tend to Cajemé. She arrived as Ana was feeding the baby.

"Big sister, thank you," Wu bowed. "I'm feeling fine now. How did you do it? Can you teach me how?"

Ana smiled but said nothing.

Time flew, and in 1905 Mario was born. He was a child of the Year of the Snake. The older brother was now fluent in Cantonese and Spanish.

It was at this time that Beng Ong suffered a stroke. Part of his face and left side were paralyzed. He couldn't walk or speak. Chan Toy requested that Ana be allowed to see him. Despite the protestations of Beng Ong's own physician, Ana came to see him. Again, she took out the turquoise colibrí amulet and waved it over Beng Ong's obese body. More heat radiated from her hand to his body.

"Good morning, little daughter" The following day Beng Ong greeted Ana. Ana was surprised that he could speak. After a week of sessions with Ana and the turquoise colibrí amulet, he regained his ability to walk.

When Ana came back to their household, Wu confronted her.

"How do you do that? I want to learn how to cure people too. Where did you get that magical hummingbird?" Again, Ana did not respond.

***

Life was good for Chan Toy and Ana. They prospered. They both could now read simple Cantonese. However, Wu, Chan Toy's sister, was frustrated by her limited role in the household. Ana was the mistress. Wu couldn't be the healer because Ana was. And besides, Ana had a magical turquoise hummingbird that could heal.

One day Wu asked Ana if she could tutor Cajemé and Mario. Ana informed her that Qiu was still the family's instructor.

After dinner that day, Wu was summoned to a private conversation with her brother. She feared that she had overstepped her bounds.

"Little sister, I hear that you want to utilize your reading and writing skills with the children," Chan Toy began. "That is noble of you, Auntie Wu. But I have a better idea. I need you to chronicle my life. It will be the legacy to my children."

Soon thereafter, Ana dictated to Wu the stories that Chan Toy had shared with her about his life. There was joy, pathos, and adventure. Wu was happier and looked forward to these sessions.

Ana did more healing during some flu epidemics. One day, when Ana was gone from the household, Wu snuck into Ana's room to look for the turquoise colibrí amulet. She the leather pouch found it laying on a little table in the bedroom. As she approached the purse, a shrill noise rang out. It got louder and higher in pitch.

Wu reached for the bag, but the pouch levitated. Wu lurched forward and tried to snatch the hummingbird. Her hand grabbed the top of the bag.

A cry of pain escaped out of Wu's lips. Her right hand was red and steaming. Tears of pain flowed down her cheeks. She ran out of the room and did not speak to anyone for several days. She told everyone that she had burned herself from lifting a huge pot.

In the meantime, China was starting to unravel. The Qing Dynasty had fallen, and the country was caught in a struggle between the old guard and the warlords. Also, the Chinese Communist Party was starting to emerge. People were leaving China, especially the professionals and the rich.

In 1910, a healthy third child was born to Chan Toy and Ana. Their daughter Maya was born in the Year of the Dog.

Flu epidemics were becoming more prevalent. Ana and Wu would make house calls in nearby villages. News from Mexico and the United States was equally grim. Anti-Asian laws were being passed abroad and the Chinese were being constantly attacked.

Additionally, the Wing Fat triad was being targeted by Mexican politicians and other gangs. They were being expelled or killed. Business was suffering.

It was 1911 and the world was looking upside down. Beng Ong summoned Chan Toy. The boss once again was non-ambulatory and he drooled as he spoke.

"Old friend, you have been very loyal to me," the boss said hoarsely. "As you can see, I am struggling to remain a man in my final days. My spirit will be passing on before you know it. Nobody will even notice." He gave a little chuckle, displaying his few yellow teeth.

Chan Toy said nothing. He had known this was coming. He also knew that the nephew, Mao Kee, would be running the operations soon. While Mao and Chan Toy were civil to each other, it was known that the nephew would want to bring in his own men.

"I know that you have worked hard and studied hard," the old man continued. "Next week I am sending you and your family back to Mexico. You will run my Mexico City operation. We will miss you, old friend."

When Ana heard the news, tears of joy streaked down her cheeks. She was finally going home. Bring on the tortillas and beans!

CHAPTER 23 – MEXICAN REVOLUTION

1911

Mexico City

In 1911, President Cardenas nationalized Mexico's foreign-built railroads and signed the first restrictive immigration legislation. The Mexican Revolution was brewing. During this time, the nature of the Chinese population in Mexico drastically changed. These immigrants ranging from laborers to merchants, starting their own small enterprises in a short period of time. By the time of the Mexican Revolution, Chinese merchants had diversified away from railroad and mining economies.

The Chinese workers worked hard and were frugal. Mexico gained by hiring Chinese because they were a cheap source of loyal labor. To further ingratiate themselves, Chinese adopted

Mexican names, learned Spanish, and became naturalized citizens. Chinese men had their choice of marrying Mexican women or contracting with the China Association for a wife from overseas. The Chinese soon became Chinese-Mexicans.

After traveling for almost three months from Guangzhou to Mexico, Chan Toy, Ana, and the three children were exhausted. The sister, Chan Yun Wu, did not come. When the boat had docked in Ensenada, Chan Toy's first inclination was to return to Mexicali and learn more about the tong business before embarking to Mexico City. They had heard rumors of warfare between the triads. Wing Fat's establishments were constantly being attacked and the local police and politicians wanted more money in order to protect them.

Their journey from Ensenada to Mexico City was long, but Ben Ong had arranged for a comfortable carriage that was large enough for the children to lie down and sleep. Everyone rested. The driver of the carriage stopped at Chinese-owned posadas along the way for meals and brief respites.

"Are we in Tiān?" Chan Toy remarked as he stretched his arms and looking upwards when they finally entered the metropolis. "This is Celestial Heaven!"

Ana had never seen so many tall and ornate buildings. This was far different than Guangzhou. It had more people but lacked sophisticated construction.

"What a waste!" Chan Toy saw wide paved roads and parks and houses. "Should be growing crops. Use land! One day they will starve!"

Eventually, they found themselves on Avenida Bucareli where the Chinese Clock tower stood. They walked past Dolores Street and the central part of the Alameda.

"Oh, me!" exclaimed Ana eyeing the Palacio de Bellas Artes. "What a beautiful palace! I wonder who lives there!"

Chan Toy stopped by a café de chinos and asked directions to his new lodging. They proceeded to a hilly district that housed multistoried buildings. Their new home was elegant, especially by Chinese standards. It had three stories, a courtyard, and four bedrooms. It also had running water.

The housekeeper was Albina. She had a Chinese husband and two older children. There were two cooks, Wen Dee and Elvira. The head of security, Raúl Carmona, oversaw six men.

Chan Toy was fortunate. He was able to run his business responsibilities out of his home. He did not have to go downtown most of time. He could also watch out for his family.

Ana tried to read a Mexican newspaper as often as possible. Everyday Ana would share the latest news with Chan Toy who was apolitical. Several months earlier there had been confrontations between Porfirio Díaz and Francisco Madero. The revolutionary Liberal Party accused the Chinese of siding with Díaz, and violence hit the Chinese communities and their properties. Soon thereafter, Madero became president of Mexico.

Ana also was aware of anti-Chinese sentiment growing in the Mexican State of Sonora. The Mexican Revolution was no place for the Chinese. Several Chinese had even been attacked and killed.

Ana needed to protect her three children. Anti-Chinese graffiti was popping up overnight on Chinese businesses. Then came broken doors, torched buildings, and other acts of vandalism. The Mexican police were nowhere to be found even though they had been paid protection money.

One day a short, fat special courier arrived to see Chan Toy at the villa. The messenger had important news. Beng Ong had died back in Guangzhou. His successor was unknown. However, Wing Fat was running the enterprise from Mexicali and was embroiled in internecine warfare with the other triads. Wing Fat wanted to escape to the north, but the gringos were killing Chinese and the potential business interests were limited in the U.S. His prospects to the south were nil. He had no contacts, and Chan Toy was in charge down there.

Two gold shipments to China had been intercepted by unknown parties, so Chan Toy was instructed not to send any more ingots back to Guangzhou.

"What will we do with the profits?" Chan Toy was overwhelmed.

"Mr. Tao will help you," the courier said. "He works for the East-West Bank in Mexico City. He is the bank director and is loyal to our family. He will deal with only you."

For the next hour, Tao tried to explain how an international bank transfer would work. No need to move gold from one place to another. Confirmations could be made by telegraph. Everything was a lot safe and speedier. Chan Toy, however, would have to meet with Tao once a week to make cash deposits, reconcile ledgers, and authorize transfers. Chan Toy didn't like it, but what could he do? Wing Fat would be copied on every transaction as a check and balance.

Chan Toy was unsure of the arrangement but couldn't question the directive. The only person that seemed happy from the chaos was Tao. Chan Toy assumed that he was making a healthy commission for his extraordinary services.

The new year rolled around, and anti-Chinese sentiment seemed to spring to life again. Ana still carried her leather pouch on her person. However, it was tied around the left side of her waist rather than hanging from her neck. She did not want to make it conspicuous.

One morning when Chan Toy was making his weekly trip to the bank in Mexico City, Ana felt a slight movement on her side. Then it was shaking. Heat emitted from the pouch. Ana did not want to look into the medicine bag for fear it would portend badly. Throughout the day she felt the shivers that ebbed and flowed next to her body.

Near dusk, Cajemé came home from school. Shortly thereafter, he noticed there was a commotion at the front gate. The head of security, Raúl Carmona, and three of his guards were engaged in an argument with a group of men.

"You, chinos ricos, are stealing all our money and jobs!" screamed the intruders. "You have to get out of here!"

"Clear out!" barked Carmona.

A bottle was thrown, and it hit one of the guards. There was a barrage of gunfire and at least a dozen of the demonstrators fell. However, the rioters pressed on and overran the guards. Carmona was barely able to make it to the house. He was met at the front door by Ana.

"Señora, we have to go upstairs! Where are the children?"

"Children, upstairs. Hurry up!" Ana yelled in a controlled tone.

"Mamá, what's happening? Where's papá?" Mario cried out.

They could hear glass being broken downstairs. Doors were being opened and closed. Furniture was being dragged and broken to pieces.

The leather pouch on Ana's waist was bouncing from side to side in a frenzy. The pitch was ear splitting.

Carmona motioned the family to hide in a cedar closet. He heard footsteps pounding on the stairs. There was hammering on the bedroom door. Carmona wanted to shoot, but he knew he had to be circumspect. Suddenly, the door swung open, and a dozen of the protesters appeared with clubs and knives.

"Get out or I'll shoot" Carmona stared his attackers straight in the face. He probably could shoot two or three of them before they got him. He didn't have that much ammunition anyway. He feared for Ana and the children.

"Get them!" a short fat man wielding a stick moved forward. He was shot dead before he reached his third step. The others rushed on.

Ana raised her pouch. It was vibrating fiercely. Suddenly, the high-pitched sounds from it turned into lightning bolts, striking the invaders from head to toe. Licks of fire pounced on the intruders. There were screams of pain. Blood spurted out of their bodies. Their torsos were writhing in agony.

"Go back! Go back!" someone at the back of the crowd yelled.

PART IV– ROSETTA STONE

CHAPTER 24 – CHOICES

Saturday, April 13, 2019

Palo Alto

Tina awoke with a start and jerked her head toward the clock radio. It was 8:45 as the early morning sun broke through the east-facing window. *Damn! I've overslept. I missed my yoga class, and I really needed it. Too much stress lately.*

She had been up until two in the morning finishing the first draft of the Chan Toy manuscript. It had been a nightmare. Pages were missing or illegible. There were silhouettes of dead bugs on a few copies. Since Hao Chin Martín had sent only a paper copy of the manuscripts, Tina was unable to cure any defects that she discovered in the documents.

Tina was not in a good space. She had missed her Friday night Happy Hour chill sessions with her colleagues two weeks running. She had no love life. She needed to burn off some steam. And she still didn't have a car. The dealership had said that delivery was running a month behind because of a global electrical battery shortage. She had listened to her father and acted on his advice. She had purchased a new Prius, instead of an overpriced used one.

"No hidden defects," he said. "And a warranty!"

Tina capitulated. Besides, gas prices were always going up due to the greedy oil companies. Better to be green.

She made a small lunch of carrot and celery sticks, a bag of roasted almonds, and a banana. She filled her thermos with matcha tea. She put everything in her backpack She climbed up on her bike. She had no specific route in mind. The coast was too far and too dangerous. Didn't want to go north or south. Every once in a while, she would drive over to the Filoli Mansion in Woodside and do an hour bike spin. The weekends were no-car days on the road there and cyclists could get in some good rides.

Off she went toward Los Altos. By the time she returned home late that afternoon, she was fatigued and tasted like salt. She showered and took a short nap. That evening she once again tackled the Chan Toy manuscript.

***

Tina was antsy again on Sunday. She began to tackle her dissertation again. She reread the last fifty pages. It was a total disaster. Typos, missing words, duplications. She couldn't do two projects at once. She had to choose between making money to pay for a car or finishing her doctorate. She had wanted to finance the car, but her father said that it was a bad idea.

To make matters worse, she received an unusual text from Hao Chin Martín that afternoon:

Dear Cousin,

Now that the project is approved, a quick timeline would be wonderful. Glad that money has been helpful to you. When do you think you will be finished?
Could you also do a translation into English? Lilí does not speak English that good. She is the one funding this project.
May you have good fortune.

I can't believe it! Tina thought. She had only been assigned a Cantonese to Spanish translation. This had almost killed her. It had thrown her schedule off for the spring and maybe the summer. She couldn't make this decision alone. She should probably contact Professor Reynoso on Monday. This was beyond her pay grade.

Well, maybe it is time to revise my dissertation timeline. When will I finish with the writing and the dozen edits? When will I defend my thesis? Looking for jobs afterwards is not a priority. She knew that one of her dissertation committee members, Professor Segreti, was on his way to the University of Bologna on sabbatical. *Rough life!* Professor Reynoso is in Guadalajara. He might be reachable on WhatsApp on Monday. *I'll give him a try. What do I have to lose?*

Tina skipped dinner and went to bed early.

The sound of the local mourning dove woke her up. She had slept like a baby. A little avocado toast and matcha tea gave her a boost.

She was going to wait until 9 o'clock to call Professor Reynoso. Then she remembered that he was two hours ahead of her.

Tina opened the WhatsApp program on her laptop and dialed the professor's University of Guadalajara number.

"Bueno," Juanita promptly answered the phone on the third ring. "La oficina del Profesor Reynoso."

"Buenos días, Juanita," Tina said in Spanish. She would have to recall all her Spanish since the secretary did not speak

English. "Habla Tina Fang. Quisiera hablar con el Profesor Reynoso por favor"

A few minutes later after greetings and pleasantries, Tina was bending Francisco's ear. Every year he would have students ready to crack under the pressure. Francisco always tried to be supportive and also refer them to professional counseling These were stressful situations that could have lifelong consequences. But with Tina, it was a little different. She was a bright and disciplined hard worker. He had more of an avuncular relationship with her.

"Tina, just relax," he knew that she needed someone to talk to. "Tell me everything that you have concerns with."

"Well, the good news is that I did a preliminary draft of the Chan Toy translations," she was speaking calmly. She had a checklist of what she wanted to talk about, and she didn't want to forget anything. "Some of the papers are a mess . . ." She went on to list everything wrong with the documents.

"Tina, you raise some valid points," the professor's mind was racing ahead. "They should have given us the original documents. That should have been a basic requirement for this project because we need to maintain academic standards. I'll contact Hao Chin Martín and say we require the originals."

He could hear a sigh at the other end of the line.

"Hao Chin also texted me and said he wanted an English version of the papers," Tina started to sound exasperated. "I don't have time to do it! I'm slammed. That wasn't part of the deal! That's not fair."

"In the first place, Hao Chin Martín should not be contacting you directly about your work on this project. I am the project manager. Everything must go through me," there was annoyance in the professor's voice. He was not happy about the end-run attempt by Hao Chin Martín. "I'll include that in the letter. In the future, refer his requests to me."

It seemed that Tina had a dozen things on her plate that she wanted to unload.

"Professor, I am worried about not finishing my dissertation on time and not being able to defend it within a year," she was almost whining.

"Tina, Tina, Tina," Reynoso was reaching into his professorial bag of tricks. "You know that there is no magical deadline. Things usually take more time than expected."

"But I also have to take nine more units," she exhaled heavily. "There are no classes this summer that I want to take. I could have taken an Independent Study class from Professor Segreti, but he is on his way to do a sabbatical in Italy." Segreti was also on Tina's doctoral committee.

Francisco was racking his brain about classes she could take. "Maybe you could take one of my classes online in the fall. I'm not teaching this summer. I'm working full time on the Chan Toy project."

Uncharacteristically, Tina then vented about not having her car yet, not having summer employment, and not having mini-summer vacation plans. She was in deep despair. Francisco was exhausted just listening to her. She had some valid concerns, but some of it was just plain whining. And yes, Life was unfair at times.

"Tina, I have to go. I'll keep in touch," Francisco shook his head like a parent with a teenage daughter. "Things will work out."

"Oh, before you go, professor, I just want to mention that the Chan Toy manuscript ends abruptly. It is very old.

"Also, it is full of magical allusions. Reminds me of the Black Pearl manuscripts from last year. Just thought you's like to know. Bye."

Francisco sighed. *¡Así es la vida!*

CHAPTER 25 – SINOMEX MINING

Monday-Tuesday, April 15-16, 2019

Guadalajara

Francisco was dumb struck after Tina's bombastic statement just before she hung up. *She must be under a lot of stress to mention something about the project. It almost seems like a postscript after spending most of the call whining about her troubles.*

On one level Francisco felt sorry for Tina. She was not the first nor would she be the last student to have a meltdown trying to finish a dissertation. He was also pissed at Hao Chin Martín for plotting to do an end-around on the Chan Toy Project. Francisco started to compose a letter to him. But Francisco had to remain cool. The problem was that Hao Chin Martín was the source of very large donations to the University of Guadalajara and Stanford University. Dean Dorothea Chandler of Stanford would counsel him to just play the game and focus on the outcome. Francisco didn't understand why the universities wanted to be involved in this endeavor in the first place. The study of Chinese migration into Mexico seemed like a pretense for something else that Hao Chin wanted. After scratching out the first paragraph of the letter, he paused.

"Juanita, please connect me with Hao Chin Martín at SinoMex Mining, please," he requested of his secretary via the intercom.

A minute later Juanita buzzed back.

"No one is in the office," Juanita informed him. He had forgotten that there was a two-hour time difference with Vancouver, B.C.

"Did you leave a message for him to call me?"

"Yes, but a lady with a strange English accent said that he was in Asia for a few days. She didn't know when he was coming back."

Francisco would just have to chill out. He decided to call Dean Miranda Ríos. He wanted a meeting with her, but he struck out. She was busy today, but she could meet with Francisco the following day at ten. They would be joined by Adjunct Professor Carlos Erandi who was co-teaching Latin-American Studies with Francisco. Erandi was also a curator at the University of Guadalajara. He and Francisco had a great working relationship.

Francisco went home that evening and had a mellow dinner with his wife Alex. Just being with her centered him. *Las cosas saldrán bien*. Things would work out. Tomorrow was another day.

The next day's meeting began with the smell of strong coffee and delicious pan dulce. Dean Ríos knew how to control her staff. Francisco was wearing an olive green guayabera that his wife Alex had recently bought him. He was becoming more Mexican every day (and less pocho).

After the pleasantries, the dean began the meeting. "Here are copies of the agreement between Chinese Dragon Rare Elements Ltd. and the University of Guadalajara and Stanford University. Take a few minutes to read them (ten pages) while you have your coffee (and eat pan dulce)."

Francisco finished first. He had experience with these types of contracts. Each one was unique, but making money was always the first priority.

"Dean, I have a question," Francisco frowned. "I thought that Canada SinoMex Mining was funding the project. It was supposed to be our partner. Hao Chin Martín works for them. Who is Chinese Dragon Rare Elements Ltd.?"

"That's an interesting point," Dean Ríos paused and looked at the agreement. It had been signed by Lilí Song, not Hao Chin Martín. "It's this company that paid us the $5 million. They are out of Shanghai. Lilí Song works out of their Vancouver office."

There were a few minutes of discussion.

"As Program Manager of the Chan Toy Project, I will write to both Hao Chin Martín and Lilí Song asking them to appoint a single contact person," Francisco asserted." We don't care who it is. We just want to clarify the agreement. I will also tell them that I am program director, and everything must go through me. I don't want them to be talking to Tina without my authorization."

"Have they been doing that?" Dean Ríos asked, puzzled.

"Well, yes, Hao Chin Martín wants Tina to also translate Chan Toy's documents into English. Lilí Song does not read Spanish," Reynoso answered.

"We can't have that," the dean said firmly. "The agreement specifically says Cantonese into Spanish. The article on Chinese migration to Mexico will be in Spanish. They can have it translated into English later."

Francisco was happy about Dean Ríos' direction. They were not going to be sycophants just because of the funding.

"Which reminds me," Francisco added. "Tina has done a preliminary draft of the translation but told me that the quality of the manuscripts ranges from passable to really bad. We will need the original documents. I will include that in the letter. Also, she mentioned something interesting about the contents of the manuscripts. She said they end abruptly and talk something about magical properties. While these facts don't directly relate to our contract, we may have to address them at some point."

Carlos and Miranda's curiosity was piqued by this revelation. They took a short break and conjectured about what Tina had related, while the men ate more pan dulce.

"Tentatively, we have up to a million-dollar budget on this project," the dean explained. She was always very transparent in dealing with her colleagues and faculty. She never had a secret agenda. "Any moneys we don't use, go back into the University's general fund and my department. We don't have to run on a shoestring, but we can't splurge. Francisco will have to approve all expenses. Everything must be documented."

"I heard that the project was for three million dollars," Erandi was trying to plan ahead.

"Well, we were wired three million dollars the other day. One million was sent to Stanford and another one million given over to the University of Guadalajara. The remainder is our operating budget."

Erandi's eyes were dilated. He had never seen or heard of so much money.

"And by the way, once the project is completed successfully, each university will receive another million."

Dean Ríos wanted to move on. "Let's talk about the deliverables. The most immediate product will be the Chan Toy manuscripts that Tina is working on. Once she gets the original writings, she'll be in a better position to give insights as to how to write the academic article. Francisco, I want you to take the lead on that."

"Yes, dean. Another reason to have the original documents is for provenance," Francisco remembered the problems they had encountered with a previous project about uncorroborated Mexican journeys to the Molucca Islands in the 16th Century. Most of the information about the journey had to be scrapped from the article.

The dean also added an open-ended question. "What will the focus of the article be and who will be the audience? I'm sure that Rare Elements wants it to be Sinocentric since the Chinese are putting up the money. However, since the topic is more about Chinese migration, Mexico and its total history should be the overlay. Otherwise, I don't see why we are using academic resources. Let's think about it and we can decide when we start drafting the article."

Francisco and Carlos each took another piece of pan dulce. Francisco was only partially successfully in wiping the powdered sugar off his new guayabera. *¡Asi es la vida!*

"The other deliverable of the project is the recovery of a so-called turquoise colibrí amulet with special magical properties. Carlos, with all of your archaeological background and being a curator, I want you to take the lead on its possible recovery."

"Dean, I have been thinking about this turquoise colibrí amulet. I don't think the law will permit us to turn over this Mexican object to a foreign country," Carlos added.

The dean nodded. She knew that Mexico was trying to crack down on the sale of Mexican artifacts to other countries, like China. The trio discussed the topic.

"I will do some research on this," Carlos volunteered. This was really within his expertise as a curator. "I have colleagues at the Museum of Anthropology and at the Mexican Department of Culture. We have worked together before."

They continued to discuss more topics.

"The good news," Dean Ríos was winding the meeting down. "is that we made no guarantees. Chinese Dragon Rare Elements gets whatever we give them. It is very unusual that they did not negotiate this agreement and ask for warranties. Our attorneys were smart in getting the money first."

The two men nodded. The pan dulce was gone. The coffee consumption was creating an urgency to end the meeting.

"One more thing, Francisco," Dean Ríos looked at him. "Let's run the budget and expenses through my Budget Department. It will be cleaner, and I can be on top of the financial portion of the project and share it with Dean Chandler."

"Also, I am going to trust both of you to produce an excellent quality product. I know you are both very capable. If you need resources or staff, let's discuss it, budget it, and then just do it. Francisco, you will be the signatory for all expenses. And if you need staff, go through our Human Resources Department."

She got up from her chair. The meeting was over.

"Thank you both very much. Let's meet again in two weeks."

Dean Ríos caught Francisco as he was about to go out the door.

"Francisco, I sense that you want to talk to me about Tina Fang."

CHAPTER 26 – WELCOME

Saturday, April 27, 2019
Guadalajara

Dean Miranda Ríos was hosting a welcome dinner for the newest member of her department, Tina Fang.

She wanted Tina to experience the best of Mexican hospitality, although it would just be for a short period. But her hidden agenda was to have her daughter be exposed to Tina, the guest of honor for this reception. Tina was the doctoral student that she hoped her daughter would someday be.

As a mother, Miranda Ríos was constantly worried about her daughter. Mirasol had recently turned eighteen and was considered an adult. Like her mother, she was proficient in five languages. She was now awaiting letters of acceptance from the University of Salamanca in Spain and the University of Bologna in Italy. She had already been accepted to the

University of Uppsala in Sweden. As to U.S. schools, she had had been accepted to UCLA, the University of Texas, and the University of Arizona. She was on the waiting lists for Duke University and Smith College. She had not heard from Stanford.

On the one hand, Mirasol thought that she was ready to escape parochial Guadalajara. Her mother was a great role mode who had to excel in an academic world run by men. Miranda being promoted to Dean of the Social Sciences Department at the University of Guadalajara had been an inspiration to Mirasol. Feminism had been part of her DNA since birth. Her mother reaffirmed lessons of life to her on a daily basis.

"Never depend on a man!

"Be self-sufficient!"

"You alone are responsible for your actions."

For his part, Sol, her father, had great faith in his angelic daughter. She would succeed, he knew. Meanwhile, Mirasol was perfectly comfortable being spoiled by her father. Nothing was too good for his little girl, and she knew it.

The table was set with white plates and cardinal red napkins. There was a bouquet of small red and white roses in the middle of the table. Soft classical music played in the background.

Across the table from Mirasol sat a tall stylish young woman with long black hair, brown tortoise shell glasses that framed her marquis-cut emerald green eyes, and alabaster skin.

"Friends and family, please help me welcome the gifted Tina Fang into our home," Miranda said jovially, "She has agreed to assist us this summer on a special collaborative project between the University of Guadalajara and Stanford University. Our own Francisco Reynoso will be in charge. Let's toast to Ms. Tina Fang."

Glasses of sparkling wine clinked together. Miranda sat at the head of the long mahogany table. Tina sat to her right. Mirasol sat on her mother's left, right across from Tina. Sol sat at the other end of the table. Francisco sat next to Tina and Alex sat next to her husband. Carlos Erandi was next to Sol. Normally, he went home to Guanajuato on the weekends, but the dean had made a special request that he attend the dinner at her home this night. He would take Monday off instead.

"When I read her CV (curriculum vitae), I thought we would have to canonize her," Miranda continued. Everybody at the table laughed. Tina's pale skin blushed from head to toe. "Tina was born in the Macau/Hong Kong area. My husband Sol and I went there in 1999. We had just been married."

Miranda could have gone on for another hour. Fortunately, Socorro the cook appeared with the first course. The smells from the kitchen were driving everyone crazy. Mouths were watering.

Socorro served the guest of honor first. It was a salad of heirloom tomatoes, jicama, red onions, and peach slices with Manchego cheese sprinkles and roasted pepitas, dressed with a passion fruit vinaigrette. Alex, Miranda, and Mirasol were served next. Then the men.

A bottle of chilled Albariño was served. Tina made a sign of only wanting a thimbleful. Mirasol received a full portion.

The conversation became very lively at the table. Sol tried to bait poor Carlos into a discussion about the terrible coaches that the Chivas and América teams had. Alex was unable to converse with Tina because her husband Francisco was between them.

"Tina, how long are you staying?" Mirasol was filling the gap in the conversation.

"Until the end of summer," Tina said with her British accent. *So, this is what it would have been like if I had a sibling.*

"She has to get back to school to finish her dissertation," Miranda gave an officious smile. *I can see Mirasol trying to be cool and wanting to show Tina off to her friends. I need to talk to my daughter, and probably warn Tina.*

Francisco just listened to everyone. Then he looked at Alex. They both smiled and gave a little laugh. *Oh, my God, it's going to be a crazy summer.*

The creaky serving cart could be heard again as it rolled over the carpet. Socorro served them dorado (mahi mahi) with pureed broccoli, sliced carrots, and potato pavés. The conversation seemed to become less animated as the guests indulged in the delectable fish dish. Socorro brought out a bottle of a California Grgich Hills Chardonnay that Tina had brought for the Ríos.

Francisco had shared with Miranda that he felt bad about Tina's situation. He knew that the young woman was overwhelmed. She would just have to suck it up, but she was all alone. Francisco had an advantage in dealing with adverse conditions. He often brainstormed his problems and challenges with his wife, Alex, because she was always calm. She had to be, she was a doctor.

The Chan Toy translations were almost done, but Tina still had to edit them and make sure they met stringent academic standards. Francisco also needed more research done. Carlos was good, but he was more of a hands-on type of guy. Francisco had worked with Tina for a few years and knew that she could write an excellent article. Although it was unsaid, he surmised that Tina was struggling financially.

Francisco discussed the matter with Dean Ríos. She had been impressed with Tina's work on the Mexico/Molucca Project and accepted Francisco's recommendation. Consequently, they had offered Tina a paid summer internship. He was astonished when Tina immediately accepted the offer without asking for time to think about it. This was so uncharacteristic of her.

Dean Ríos even offered to put Tina up in her Guadalajara residence. This way Tina would not be alone. Having a Stanford doctoral student around would also be great for Mirasol. Tina could mentor her on university life.

The main meal came to an end. Miranda escorted everyone into the lavish salon where Socorro served dessert. It was a pineapple and tangerine tart with a red grape reduction sauce. Everybody took coffee. Tina asked for tea, green tea, which the cook miraculously came up with.

Alex was finally able to sit next to Tina and chat with her.

"I will be able to afford a fancy trip with all the money that I will be making when I rent out Mirasol's room after she goes away to college," Sol shared with the guests.

"Dad, that's not funny!" Francisco and Carlos laughed anyway. "Besides what's going to happen to all my stuff?"

"We'll probably give it all away."

"Papá!!!"

The night finally came to a close. Everybody said their good nights and gave thanks to the hosts.

Francisco and Alex were exhausted as they were driven home. Fortunately, Alex had no medical appointments scheduled for the following day.

"I was finally able to talk with Tina. I can see why you and she were a good team. She is very bright," Alex shared. "Unfortunately, I think the summer will go by very quickly for her. I hope she gets to experience the culture here. Speaking of that, I invited her to our next Adelita's meeting. Hmm! We need a guest speaker."

"Not again, please," he smiled. His wife and Miranda were deeply involved in the Adelita's, a Mexican professional women's association. "We can always take her to the Ballet Folklórico or something similar."

"Great idea!" Alex replied. "I'm just not sure if Tina wants to be entertained or left alone."

"Well, she tends to work alone. She is very independent."

"Hmm! I overheard my goddaughter. She wants to take Tina on a cultural experience here in Guadalajara."

"Well, that's sounds like a good idea."

"Mi amor, that's code for 'shopping.'"

CHAPTER 27 – FIRST DAYS

Monday, April 29, 2019

Guadalajara

Tina was sharing an office with Professor Erandi at the University of Guadalajara until they could find office space for her. The dean figured that Tina would be able to further improve her Spanish while Carlos could expand his English proficiency.

Dean Ríos had personally given her a tour of the Social Studies Department. Tina was having a challenging time trying to set up her computer. She would have asked Carlos, but he was taking a comp day to spend time with his family in Guanajuato.

Tina had an 11:30 meeting with Francisco. She would ask him for assistance. She arrived a few minutes early at his office and announced herself to Juanita.

"Hola, soy Tina Fang," she gave Francisco's secretary a big, friendly smile. "I have a meeting with Professor Reynoso."

Juanita didn't say anything, but instead marched right into Francisco office.

"This lady sounds just like the woman I talked to in Vancouver," Juanita said in a scornful tone. "I don't like her."

"Juanita, she is not the same person. Tina is very nice and does excellent work." Francisco knew that his secretary was just trying to be protective. "And besides, she speaks Spanish. Please send her in."

Bubbly Tina came in and sat across from the professor's desk. There were no abrazos. She remained his research assistant and everything had to be professional when on the job.

Francisco asked about her parents who lived in Vancouver.

"They are fine. Thank you. And I really like your wife," Tina remarked. "She is high-powered."

They went over the general parameters of the project and Francisco brought her up to speed on the last meeting that he had had with Dean Ríos and Professor Erandi. He was making Tina responsible for all academic research and article writing. He briefly mentioned that the dean had concerns about how the article would be characterized. Ríos wanted it oriented from a Mexican point of view on its Chinese communities rather than on Chinese migration to Mexico. Carlos was in charge of locating and procuring the turquoise "colibrí" amulet if it existed. Tina had given the dean and the two professors the current draft of the Chan Toy papers with the caveat that it was tentative. She had to wait for the original documents before she could proceed further. Tina would work on the ancestry part of her research in the meantime.

Francisco hadn't heard from Hao Chin Martín since he had written to Hao the week before. Francisco was frustrated. Hao Chin Martín wanted the translation as soon as possible but he was dragging his feet on his side of the agreement. Francisco and Tina discussed a strategy to change this stalemate.

"Juanita, can you please call Mr. Hao Chin Martín again in Vancouver," Francisco had buzzed her. He then handed the telephone to Tina.

"Canada SinoMex Mining, Ltd.," the young woman with a British accent answered on the other end of the line. "How may I direct your call?"

"I would like to speak with Mr. Hao Chin Martín please," Tina immediately recognized the Canadian-Chinese accent since she had grown up in Vancouver. “This is Tina Fang with the Chan Toy Project.”

“He’s not in. Would you like to leave a message?”

“When will be back in the office?”

“Don’t know. He is out of the country.”

“What is his cell phone number please?”

There was a long pause. Tina could hear that the other person was consulting with someone else in Mandarin.

“Sorry, can’t give it to you. Private.”

Tina put on her best dragon lady persona. She wasn’t going to let an officious little office person tell her no. Then in her best Mandarin voice, she said, “Listen, Hao Chin Martín has 24 hours to contact Professor Francisco Reynoso. If he doesn’t, we will consider the contract breached and we will keep the money. You will not get the Chan Toy translations. It’s up to you. You have our number.”

The girl started to argue, but Tina quashed it. She could hear the girl starting to whimper.

“I will try to find him.”

“Don’t just try! Do it!” Tina was getting tough.

Both sides hung up.

Francisco looked at her. “I’m never going to piss you off.”

They both laughed. It was a mean thing to do, but it had to be done.

Francisco reiterated that she would be sharing an office with Carlos. He was gone half the time, so it wouldn't be a problem. She was going to take the academic lead and he was going to do the field work. She would improve her Spanish; he would improve his English. It was a win-win, Francisco thought.

Francisco was getting hungry and was thinking of taking a lunch break when Juanita buzzed him.

"Professor, there is a Lilí Song on the line," Juanita informed him.

"Put her through," Francisco put up his right index finger signaling for Tina to hold tight.

"Yes, Ms. Song," Francisco spoke to her in English. He remembered her as the colleague of Hao Chin Martín that had accompanied him to his office six weeks earlier. "How can I help you?" He skipped the formalities. Francisco and Tina had gotten the other side's attention and they had to press their advantage.

"Mr. Martín is so sorry that he hasn't been able to talk to you. He is in China on business. He received your letter. He says that we will overnight the original documents as soon as possible. Will tomorrow morning be acceptable?"

"Thank you very much," Francisco was smiling. "That would be excellent."

"We only ask that you send us a copy of the work that you have already done. We understand that it is not complete. That's okay for now. And we will do the Spanish to English translation here. That will save time."

"No problem. We can do that."

"One more thing," she asserted. "I will be your contact person, but the correspondence must be in English please. My Spanish is not very good. Neither of us wants to have any misunderstandings. I will make sure that Mr. Martín gets copies. His English is good."

There were a few more words and a thousand thank you's before they were done.

"Ready for lunch?" Francisco asked.

"I'm starving. I am still not used to the time change. It seems that I am hungry every two hours. Just like a baby." She smiled.

They started to walk to the Cafetería MUSA. The weather was hot and muggy. As they walked Tina shared that she needed to have Francisco help her set up her computer. She explained to him that her laptop was acting slow and kept falling off the Wi-Fi.

"What kind of computer do you have?"

"An Apple Mac Pro."

He had had similar problems the year before trying to use his Apple on a PC system. He knew that Carlos had a PC.

They arrived at the cafeteria. Tina ordered a salmon bagel and iced chai latte. Francisco wanted chilaquiles verdes with chicken and egg and a jamaica agua fresca.

The two chatted some more. Some work-related. Some not. After lunch they said their goodbyes.

Francisco walked back to his office and went up to Juanita who was diligently sitting at her desk.

"Juanita, please order three iMac Apple computers, 3 Apple iPads, and an HP laser printer. Charge it to the Chan Toy Project." Francisco had made an executive decision to use Apple products because Mac had design simplicity and better integration with other devices. But most importantly, it was more secure and less vulnerable to viruses and malware.

The secretary looked surprised but did not say anything.

"And one more thing, schedule the University IT person to set them up as soon as they arrive, please."

"As you wish, professor."

Francisco paused as he started to go back to his office and then turned around. "Juanita, do you need a new computer?"

CHAPTER 28 – STOLEN DOCS?

Thursday, May 2, 2019

Guadalajara

It had been raining all morning and the sidewalks had zillions of puddles. Francisco was now escorting Tina down the hall to Dean Miranda's office. The old wooden floors squeaked with each step. Carlo Erandi was close behind thumbing on his cellphone. Normally, they would have met with the dean on Tuesday, but the meeting had to be postponed because of the University Council meeting with the faculty.

Francisco pitied poor Dean Ríos because of her numerous meetings where she had to make the day-long speeches about how great the University was, listen to the "crying poor" tales by the Controller who wanted budget reductions and program cuts, and endure lengthy faculty academic recognitions.

Francisco had already attended one faculty meeting that morning which he promised himself would be his last. The main agenda items seemed to be when the next University Council meeting would be and what was for lunch. After the midday all-you-can buffet meal, the Academic Senate President presented a list of questions and resolutions submitted by the faculty:

Why is there an increase in the monthly fee for parking? Do you want us to pay for the privilege of teaching? The Controller responded that they were trying to make the campus greener and encouraged everyone to take public transportation.

Why are the number of cigarette smoking areas reduced? The Dean of Academic Affairs answered that the younger faculty were non-smokers (and didn't have the filthy habit).

Why are faculty teaching loads increasing without commensurate pay increases? This brought on lots of discussion with lots of shouting and fist waving. The timing of this question was perfect since the prior day had been the campus's International Labor Day celebration.

The University Council meeting ended just after 1:30. Francisco ran to his two o'clock meeting with Dean Ríos and the others.

“Good afternoon!” Dean Miranda Ríos greeted her Chan Toy Project team. As usual, there was the mandatory pan dulce. Today it was empanadas de manzana. But in addition to the coffee, there was a teapot of hot water and matcha tea bags. The dean’s cook, Socorro, had advised her that Tina did not drink coffee. How un-Mexican! *Pero así es la vida.*

The dean rattled off the preliminary items on her checklist in quick clipped Spanish. Francisco had been intimidated by her the first few months because of his pocho Spanish. Now he was about 98% proficient. He felt sorry for Tina, but she was a quick study.

“According to the agreement, we only have to provide the translations in Spanish,” the dean was reviewing items so that Carlos and Tina could be brought up to speed. “Lilí Song will be their contact person and Francisco will be ours.”

They took a break, and the guys went after the apple turnovers. Tina didn’t indulge. Francisco asked Tina why she had both an iPad tablet and a paper notebook.

“If there is something I don’t understand, I scribble it down and try to learn the translation afterwards.”

Francisco nodded. Smart idea. He should have done this months ago.

They went back to work.

"Carlos, what did you find out about the Chan Toy manuscripts?" Dean Ríos asked.

"I talked to my friend who works with the Department of Culture in Mexico City," Carlos began. "He thinks that the documents may have been stolen from the Chinese History Special Collections at the Museum of Anthropology. His department has been investigating the exportation of Mexican artifacts to places all over the world, especially China, France, and the U.S. He didn't recognize the name of Hao Chin Martín, but he is going to continue to investigate this."

The other three were shocked at this news.

"Francisco, you said that Hao Chin Martín retrieved the Chan Toy manuscripts from a distant relative. I think the cousin lived in Tucson."

"Yes, dean," Francisco was slightly embarrassed. He hadn't wanted to be involved in this project in the first place. "Hao Chin Martín also represented that he is a distant relative of Tina's."

"That was what I have been told, dean," Tina jumped in. "But honestly, I don't have any recollection of him while I was growing up. I can give my parents a call. They live in Vancouver and know everyone."

"Thank you. That sounds good," the dean took a deep breath. *Why do the simplest projects turn out to be so difficult?* Francisco had been skeptical. All that glitters, is not gold. But the papers must be authentic if somebody was willing to pilfer them, she thought.

"What happens to our project if the papers were stolen?"

"Perhaps, nothing," Francisco bit his lip. "Our job is to do a translation. I don't think there is anything illegal about that." He saw the others nodding their heads in agreement.

"I will need to talk to the university's legal counsel. Legal or not, we can't embarrass the university," the dean was rapidly scribbling notes. "I will contact Dean Chandler and give her a heads up. I don't want her to be blindsided."

Everybody concurred.

"But the second deliverable is the procurement of the turquoise colibrí," Carlos interjected. "Are we going forward with trying to find it if it's related to stolen documents? Or more importantly, if it is potentially going to be sent out of Mexico?"

"Carlos raises a good question," Francisco jumped in. "It was just too easy for them to give us all that money. This project seems to be about more than an academic exercise."

The back and forth got hot. At one point, Carlos suggested stopping the project and giving back the money, or at least part of it. The dean didn't want to be responsible for that decision.

"I will follow up on the legal and ethical parts of the project," the dean stated. "Carlos, follow up with your contacts in Mexico City."

"I can work on the background of Hao Chin Martín. I can track down his ancestry. He says that we are related, so that gives us a lead," Tina volunteered.

"Good idea, Tina," Ríos said.

They started to wrap up.

"One more thing. Francisco, I know that you wanted the project to have new computers, but until we figure this out, we should put a temporary hold on expenditures."

There was a collective groan.

"No! No! I meant future expenditures," the dean was trying to walk back her directive. "The computers and iPads and printer have already been bought, so let's use them."

The meeting ended on a happy note,

"Dean, will you join us for lunch?" Francisco offered. He was starving from all the drama of the meeting.

"Sorry, I must meet with some other department heads. Next time."

The three walked over to the Cafetería MUSA.

"I was afraid there for a minute," Francisco volunteered as they ate their tacos and washed them down with agua fresca.

“The Information Technology department is setting up the computers as we speak, or shall I say as we eat.” They all grinned.

It was Tina’s idea to have a shared server and access to the iCloud and link the iPads. For Francisco, this was just another foreign language.

CHAPTER 29 – IMPRESSIONS

Monday May 6, 2019
Guadalajara

The following week Tina's head was swimming as she and Carlos walked to the bank branch on campus. Her first paycheck with the summer internship on the Chan Toy Project was large by Mexican university standards, but small by U.S. colleges norms. And to be real, miniscule compared to the San Francisco cost of living.

But she was grateful. A few weeks earlier she had been slammed trying to finish up her dissertation, struggling without a car, not having a summer job, and lacking travel plans. To make matters worse she had lost face with her mentor professor, Francisco Reynoso, by making a scene. She owed him. She was sure that he would not have offered her the summer internship in Mexico out of pity. They had worked very well as a team the prior summer on the project to document the Mexico to the Molucca Islands Black Pearl expeditions of the 1520's. She had been given partial credit on the academic journal article. It would be great to work with the professor again. He would be a valuable contact in the future.

All morning she and Carlos had been reconfiguring their new computers and setting up the Internet and Wi-Fi accounts. The initial IT setup had had a few glitches. They decided to take a break and deposit their checks. Now they were dodging students and pedestrians as they zigzagged through campus. The University of Guadalajara was a multi-square mile metropolis.

Dean Miranda Ríos had been super generous in offering free lodging to her. Of course, babysitting Marisol was the cost. Mirasol was a bright young student who would want to show Tina off to her privileged friends. Next year at whatever university she would attend, Mirasol would probably act out, get drunk, and realize that she was just an average student. Tina would model appropriate behavior and not lecture Mirasol. To Tina, Mirasol would be like the little sister she never had (and maybe never wanted).

Fortunately, Professor Reynoso's wife had come to the rescue. The previous Saturday morning Alex's driver, Esteban, had picked up her goddaughter Mirasol and Tina in the luxurious black Lexus SUV. Alex had coordinated and planned the day with Miranda.

Their morning was spent walking about the Historical Center of the city. They took photos of everything: the Palacio del Gobierno, the Orozco paintings at Las Cabañas, and La Catedral. For lunch they drove to Tlaquepaque where they shopped afterwards. Alex knew a little clothing store where everything was elegant with a commensurate price tag.

Tina was mesmerized by the gauze tops that came in a myriad of colors. She didn't have that much money in Mexican pesos, and she didn't want to use her credit card in Mexico. Her account statements would be sent to her home where she wouldn't be for a few months. Besides there were those Russian and North Korean hackers who could steal one's identity with a single computer key stroke. However, a fuchsia gauze top and a white dress wiped her out of most of her cash. Mirasol bought a black tank top with the STARS logo.

They were dead tired when they arrived at Alex's two-story, yellow Moorish mansion surrounded by its tall black wrought iron enclosure. Inside, Alex gave Tina a tour of the historical home previously owned by her grand-aunt Gloria Marín, the famous Mexican actress. Then they went out into the beautiful, fragrant garden. Two canaries were singing in a large black wrought iron cage.

Alex smiled, "These are Chiquita and Manguito."

They strolled into the salon. Alex didn't drink much and neither did Tina. And Mirasol could only imbibe on special occasions with her parents' permission.

"My father died of leukemia. I may have a predisposition for this disease, so, I am careful of what I eat and drink. I am also an endocrinologist. I have to set a good example for my patients." Alex explained. Tina nodded. She liked this woman.

Tina was curious about her but did not want to be impolite and ask questions. Alex preempted the young woman's curiosity.

"I was born in La Paz, in Baja California Sur, Mexico. I moved to Guadalajara to become a nurse. I met my husband, . . . not Francisco, and we were married. He was a doctor. We were together for three years. He died falling down some stairs. We didn't have any children. Then I decided to go to medical school. And here I am. And I still have family back in La Paz. Then last summer I was blessed and met Francisco. And as you know he is wonderful. Enough about me. Tell me a little bit about you."

Tina was a bit embarrassed with Mirasol looking at her.

"As you know, I am a doctoral student in Romance Languages. I was Professor Reynoso's research assistant for a year. I was born in the Macau/Hong Kong region. My family migrated to Vancouver where I graduated with a degree in Spanish from the University of British Columbia. My parents still live there. But I hated the cold weather and left. I got my Master's degree from the University of Valparaiso in Chile. I loved it down there. Then eventually I ended up at Stanford. I hope to finish by dissertation by the end of the year."

"You are very bright woman," Alex beamed. "My husband says wonderful things about you."

"Maybe I want to go to Stanford too," interrupted Mirasol who looked like she had suddenly become alert. "But I haven't heard from them yet."

Vera, the cook, entered the salon and announced that dinner was ready. As usual, she provided them a Michelin star, three course meal.

Since Tina had spent all of her cash shopping, she needed to go to the bank to deposit her paycheck. She and Carlos arrived at the campus bank.

"Señorita, in order to open up a bank account for you, I will need to see your passport, an internship letter, and proof of local residence," said the serious looking bank teller who was wearing a navy-blue nylon business suit.

Tina had checked out all the requirements ahead of time online. She had everything. Twenty minutes later Tina had successfully procured a bank account and had deposited her check. Unfortunately, she had to withdraw all her new income in Mexican pesos because she had almost none. *When is my next paycheck?*

Concurrently, Carlos had also deposited his check. Before going back to their office, they decided to have a snack lunch together. Over lunch she told him about herself, and he shared his background. He was an acting curator for the university and this year he was co-teaching with Professor Reynoso. He also was still working on his doctorate. Tina was awed when he told her that he was fluent in Purépecha as well as Tarascan and Náhuatl. His family lived in Guanajuato, and he went home every weekend. He put three sugars in his coffee. He insisted that Tina should come home with him to sometime visit his family.

Back at the office, Tina thought how brilliant Dean Ríos had been putting her together with Carlos in the same office. They complemented each other with their Spanish and English proficiencies. He was a professor without a Ph.D.; she was a doctoral student on a possible faculty track. She was an expert in academic research, and he was the one with field expertise. A great partnership, especially with Professor Reynoso guiding and grooming them.

Tina was showing Carlos how to do Boolean inquiries with all the databases that he had access to. “You can type in ‘Chan Toy robbery Mexico City’ to start with,” she instructed him. “Then you can add or subtract words to expand or limit your search.”

Professor Reynoso had advised them to use the computers as soon as possible so they could not be confiscated.

It had bothered Tina that Hao Chin Martín had told her that they were related. She was also concerned that Hao had represented to the professor that the Chan Toy papers had come from family in Tucson. Had Hao lied? She decided that she would do an ancestry search on Hao Chin Martín.

CHAPTER 30 – PATRICIO

Thursday, May 9, 2019
Guadalajara

Carlos was like a kid in a candy store. After Tina had given him a tutorial on database searches, he was consumed about the origins of the Chan Toy manuscripts. Having worked the summer before with Professor Reynoso on the Mexico to the Moluccas Sea expeditions project, he knew the importance of accuracy and provenance.

Tina had been out of the office for the last few days reviewing the original Chan Toy manuscripts. She needed to read them and compare them to her current transcription. It had been assumed that the primary sources would be of better quality. But in this case, they were not. The rice paper had absorbed moisture over the years and had diluted the quality of the ink. To make matters worse, bluish-green mold had encrusted itself on several of the pages. These new papers were of only marginal value. The good news was that the translation from Cantonese to Spanish was almost done.

Carlos was surprised when Agent Patricio Gomez returned his call and was volunteering to meet with him in Guadalajara. Carlos knew the 31-year-old from the Department of Culture in the Museum of Anthropology in Mexico City. They had met several years before when Carlos was working with the Mexican Tourist Board to break up a fraudulent tourist company scam at the Pyramid of the Sun at Teotihuacán. They had remained friends, and Patricio spent a week with Carlos and his family in Guanajuato.

"What's been happening with you, cuate?" Patricio began.

"The family is good" Carlos responded. "Gracias a Dios."

They chatted briefly about this and that. Then Patricio got down to business.

"Oye, Carlos, are you trying to find the source of the Chan Toy manuscripts?"

"Yes."

"Are you working on some kind of project or something?" Patricio asked, seemingly innocently.

Carlos explained the Chan Toy Project in general terms. Patricio had helped him before, and Carlos saw no reason not to share what his group was doing. He knew that Patricio's job was to protect archaeological sites and cultural relics.

What Carlos did not know about Patricio Gomez, aka Sean Rangel, was that he also worked as an undercover agent for the Mexican government. He had a Ph.D. in International Cultural Security from the Monterrey Institute of Technology and worked in the Intelligence Department of the Mexican Marines. Patricio's mode of interaction was to answer questions ambivalently but get tons of information from his interviewees.

There had been a lot of internet chatter the last few days about the robbery of Chan Toy's manuscript. Patricio's IT people flagged a hotspot and traced it back to Carlos, which made perfect sense since Carlos had recently reached out to him on the same subject.

"Carlos, I am going to share some confidential information which you can not disclose. Do you understand?"

Carlos said, "¿Sí, cómo no?"

"The robbery allegedly took place in the summer of 2018. We are investigating who was behind the theft and who actually did it. Some of the Mexican cartels have been monopolizing everything from avocados to limes to pieces of fine art. It is one way they can launder money outside the country. However, we have found little evidence to support this. The cartels would rather hide their money in yachts, airplanes, and real estate."

"Another theory is that the Russians are trying to disrupt the Mexican economy. Throw it into chaos by stealing Mexican art. The value of Mexican art is on the increase. Additionally, many countries are vying for petrodollars. Lots of competition. But once again, we don't see any proof of this conspiracy thing."

"The third conjecture is that this is a Chinese ploy. They like to get their hands on unique or scarce items. Sometimes it is the Chinese Communist Party. Other times it is Chinese Army Intelligence."

"Which theory makes the most sense to you, Patricio?"

"Well, until you resurrected this ghost, I would have assumed it was the Russians or North Koreans. But that is what I want to talk to you about. Can we share information? We have a lot of assets, and you are doing the leg work. If you could send us weekly reports, we would appreciate it." That would also keep his supervisors off his case.

"I don't know. This is a special project. I think it is private. Nobody knows what we're doing."

"But we're law enforcement and your cooperation is crucial."

"Just the same, I am not in charge," Carlos didn't want to get sucked in. "Let me talk to the project leader and get back to you."

The next day, a tall, muscular male was waiting outside Dean Rios' office. He was wearing a navy-blue sport coat and a tie. He was definitely out of place at the university. A minute later he was let in and met the dean and Professor Reynoso.

"Welcome, Mr. Gomez, thank you for meeting with us. We know you are busy and are going out of your way to assist us," the dean had her public relations smile. *He should be thanking us. The government will try to get information from us and then take the credit.*

"In the spirit of mutual cooperation, we are trying to find out who stole the Chan Toy manuscripts and why. The Mexican government wants them back," Patricio was making his pitch as the dean and Professor Reynoso nodded their heads. "And hopefully, we can provide you with some information for your project" he added.

Patricio went on and on about what he wanted from Dean Ríos' group.

"That is all very nice, Mr. Gomez, but this is a privately funded project," the dean spoke authoritatively. "You are dealing with two private universities. We've already started our work and are anxious to complete it as soon as possible.'

But Patricio wasn't backing down. "I understand your point, Dean Ríos. But if the Chan Toy manuscripts were stolen and perhaps going to be sold, then the Mexican government has to step in. And that may delay your project. Of course, if there is property involved, the government will get a share and you will get salvage value."

Dean Ríos was getting angry but did not show it. She was not going to be intimidated by this condescending young upstart. "I have talked to the administration, and they do not want to be hampered by government interference. We have a valid contract. We have been paid. We intend to honor our obligations."

"I understand, Dean Ríos," Patricio smiled broadly. "But receiving stolen property is a crime. We have the legal authority to seize the manuscripts when they show up."

Professor Reynoso suddenly realized that Patricio did not know that they already possessed the original documents. The ones that were allegedly stolen. Nor did she want Patricio to know this until Tina was finished with the final translation.

"Patricio, I think that there is a compromise that can be reached where all interests can be protected and furthered," Professor Reynoso intervened trying to break the stalemate. He had been married to a Los Angeles attorney, Maureen Brady, who always appeared reasonable before she cut your throat.

It was after two o'clock when an agreement was reached. Everybody was starving.

Dean Ríos and Professor Reynoso agreed that non-proprietary information would be shared with Patricio. The dean also abdicated her role as lead on the project under the advice of the university's legal counsel. Dean Chandler had decided to do the same. The rationale was to isolate any possible legal liability for the universities. With the allegation of robbery, this also meant being shielded from possible criminal charges.

Reynoso would set out the parameters for information dissemination and sharing. Patricio would be designated a museum artifact consultant and be an ancillary participant of the Chan Toy Project. He would work undercover without the knowledge of Carlos and Tina. The dean and Francisco hated to keep their team in the dark, but too many things could go wrong.

Patricio had a private and confidential memo sent to Dean Ríos protecting them and granting immunity. It was signed by the Ministry of Justice and Ministry of Foreign Affairs.

Everybody was satisfied. The dean had a meeting to attend.

"Patricio, do you want to do lunch?" Francisco asked.

"Sure. I'm starved."

"Do you want to invite Carlos? If Tina is in, you can meet her."

CHAPTER 31 – RUBÍ

Friday, May 10, 2019
Guadalajara

Juanita greeted Francisco when he arrived at his office with a latte in his hand. “There is a package on top of your desk. It arrived first thing this morning,” she advised.

“Thank you, Juanita. I’ll be meeting with Carlos and Tina this morning. Please hold all my calls.” He wanted to debrief them about the status of the Chan Toy Project and future assignments. First of all, he had had to make sure that Tina was coming in today. She had been working from home (the dean’s house), trying to finish the translations. The deadline was May 17, only a week away.

He made a couple of quick phone calls and found that Tina was already in her office with Carlos. Francisco left his office and walked down the few floors to join them.

"Good morning," he said as he walked into his colleagues' cramped office. The greeting was reciprocated. Unlike the Dean Ríos' meetings, there were no coffees, teas, or sweets. His wife Alex was on his case about eating too much sugar anyway.

"You are both now familiar with our agreement with Chinese Dragon Rare Elements Ltd., There are still some loose ends that we are working out. And by the way, since Dean Ríos has abdicated as the director of the project, you now have me." The dean had texted him the night before and thanked him profusely for taking on the role. He hadn't wanted to do it, but what could he do? In exchange, he and Professor Erandi had their teaching loads reduced by one class for the following semester, and Tina was granted a summer internship (that paid).

"Before we can continue, we need to make sure that we follow all academic standards and guidelines with respect to the Chan Toy manuscripts. Originally, we entered into this agreement with the assertion that some distant relative of Chan Toy had given the materials to Hao Chin Martín of the Canada SinoMex Mining, Ltd. But there appears to be a problem."

"Carlos, what have your inquiries revealed?"

"I spoke to Patricio Gomez from the Mexican Ministry of Culture, and he informed me that the Chan Toy manuscripts were misappropriated from the Museum of Anthropology last summer. There are at least three theories behind the ongoing investigations."

Carlos shared about the Mexican cartels, the Russian oligarchs, and the People's Republic of China's global expansion. Patricio shared the same information with the day before with Francisco and Dean Rios. Francisco had asked for copies of any investigative reports, photos, and interviews. Patricio said that he could share all non-confidential materials, but that some of the information was highly sensitive and related to national security. As promised, Patricio had messengered the information overnight. Francisco still had not opened the package in front of him.

"Carlos, I want you to research the origins of the Chan Toy materials and how they landed in the Museum of Anthropology."

"Yes, professor."

"Tina, you are almost done with the Chan Toy translations, correct?"

"Yes, professor."

"When do you think you'll be done?"

"Monday or Tuesday."

"The sooner, the better, please," Francisco was entering tasks and timelines on his tablet. These notes were automatically being shared with Carlos and Tina's apparatuses as well as Dean Ríos' through their tablets.

"Yes, professor."

"And when you are done with the translations, I will send a copy to Lily Song per our agreement."

"Professor, what do I do with the original Chan Toy documents?"

Francisco thought. *What would Dean Ríos do? Probably nothing.* By all rights, the papers probably belonged to the Museum of Anthropology, and he should turn them over to Patricio Gomez who did not know they had the papers. But no arrest or search warrants had been issued. The robbery was only an allegation. They had no obligation to return anything. Besides, they needed to preserve the provenance of these documents. *I sound like my ex-wife.*

"Tina, when you are done, turn the documents over to Carlos. Get a receipt from him. Carlos, because you are a curator here at the university, you have security clearance for safeguarding these types of documents. Please do so. Make sure that you and I are the only signatories."

They talked and assigned big and small tasks with timelines. Tina was going to make the deadline for the translations. That was good.

They took a bathroom break. Everybody checked their emails.

Finally, Francisco tore open the package from Patricio. What he discovered were documents from the investigation of the allegedly stolen documents. Specifically, there were some interviews conducted with the museum staff.

He dug deeper into the notes and stopped when he read the notes of two witness.

Witness #1 July 14, 2017, Museum of Anthropology Library:

> Suspect came into the stacks and inquired about Chinese migration to Mexico. He was described as short and chubby. He was Asian. She thought that he had a scraggly beard. He was accompanied by a tall, slender Asian woman who work purple lipstick, and had some sort of dragon pendant around her neck. She did not speak.

Witness #2 July 17, 2017, Museum of Anthropology Library:

Female Asian gives a desk clerk an envelope. She does not say anything. She is accompanied by a

disheveled chunky man with a goatee. He does not say anything. The Asian woman was wearing deep purple lipstick. She wore a jade necklace.

Francisco then looked through a dozen photos that were included in the envelope. He paused and pulled one aside. He stared at it closely.

"Okay, let's get back to work," Francisco resumed. "Just to let you know, we now have a new liaison working with us from the Ministry of Culture. His name is Patricio Gomez. He has done some work with Carlos. Tina, you will meet him soon."

Francisco had been debating whether to tell Carlos and Tina everything about the project concerning Hao Chin Martín, and Patricio Gomez. The more his team knew, the more likely the project be successful. He understood Patricio's need for secrecy, but he owed his loyalty to his team.

He slid a photo in front of Carlos and Tina.

"Do either one of you know what Hao Chin Martín looks like?"

Both shook their heads no.

"How about Lilí Song?"

"No," replied Carlos again.

But Tina paused before answering. "Wait, is that Rubí's sister?" She looked intently at Francisco.

Francisco slid the photo in front of Tina. "Do they look familiar?"

"I don't know the man, but the woman looks like Rubí."

"Who is Rubí and how do you know her?" the professor pressed.

"I spent last summer in São Paulo studying Chinese and Asian migration to Brazil. I was trying to track down some distant relatives. I met Rubí Song and we hung out together. She was hot and all the guys tried to hit on her. I think she worked for Chinese Dragon Rare Elements in São Paolo. We contact each other about once a month. We found out we are not related. She knew I did research about Mexico, and one day she asked me if I could set up a meeting with her sister and her colleague with Professor Reynoso. I did so, and here we are."

"And you don't know Hao Chin Martín?"

Tina shook her head no again. "He says he is related to me, but I've never seen him before."

"Anything else unusual about Rubí?"

"Yes, she wore purple lipstick."

CHAPTER 32 – DETECTIVE WORK

Friday - Monday, May 10-13, 2019
Guadalajara

Miranda had just taken off her heels when her cell phone rang. It was after six on Friday night and she had just come home from work. Sol had brought her a small sherry glass with some slightly chilled Amontillado. There were little bowls of green olives and almonds on the table next to her.

She was ready for her Friday night retreat with her husband after a long tumultuous week. The phone display showed that the caller was Francisco. She knew that it must be important for him to call after hours.

"Dean," Francisco always called her by her official title, unless it was a social occasion, "sorry to bother you, but I thought this was important. The Chan Toy manuscripts were stolen from the Museum of Anthropology, and we think we know who did . . ."

For the next five minutes he brought her up to speed on the investigative records from Patricio Gomez, witness statements, and the photos of Hao Chin Martín and a female accomplice. He assured her that he would take care of everything.

Miranda thanked him and hung up the phone. She downed her drink.

"Sol, mi amor, another please," she said holding up her empty glass.

Meanwhile, upstairs in the guest bedroom, Tina was working on finishing the Chan Toy translations. She could hear loud Taylor Swift music coming down the hall from Mirasol's room. Tina had compared the originals with the copies and found that there were more than two dozen discrepancies.

What Tina did not understand was why Chan Toy had written what looked like a semi-autobiography. She couldn't believe that it had ended so abruptly, like there was still more to come? *And what happened to the wife and the special turquoise colibrí amulet that seemed to have magical powers?*

The next morning came sooner than Tina wanted. She had stayed up until past one. Professor Reynoso wanted her to contact Rubí Song in São Paolo to clarify a few things. She normally texted Rubí, but for this, she had to talk to her in person. It was eight o'clock Guadalajara time which meant it was 2 o'clock in the afternoon in Brazil. She called but there was no answer. Tina left a voice mail message for Rubí to call back. She also texted her requesting a call back.

She went downstairs and had a simple breakfast of green tea, a small fruit plate with yogurt, and a toasted bolillo with mango jelly. She could get used to this. Miranda came in and sat next to her at the dining room table. They did not talk about work.

"Tina, do you want to go to the Teatro Degollado at the Central Plaza," Miranda was inquiring. "They have the best Ballet Folklórico."

"Oh, thank you so much, Dean," Tina said in an almost whining tone. "I would love to but this weekend I have to finish the Chan Toy translations. I'll be stuck in my room all weekend. Thanks anyway."

"No problem, my dear," Miranda felt sorry for the poor young woman. "Let us know if there is anything you need. I'll keep Mirasol out of your hair this weekend. She's still waiting to hear from Stanford."

After breakfast, Tina took her green tea upstairs and resumed her translation. She wanted to go for a jog or walk but was afraid that Rubí might call.

At about one o'clock in the afternoon, the phone rang. It was Rubí.

"Hey, I was just thinking about you," Rubí said. There was loud music in the background. She spoke Portuguese in a melodious, passionate tone with a lot of Brazilian slang gratuitously tossed in. Tina's Portuguese seemed stilted and monosyllabic. They chatted about this and that.

"Any boyfriends?" Rubí asked.

Tina was embarrassed. Rubí always seemed to have several guys around her. Tina thought that they were more like puppy dogs that followed her everywhere. Rubí was sexy and she knew it. And she loved Brazilian music and even took samba lessons.

Then it was Tina's turn to ask questions.

"Rubí, remember that you wanted me to introduce Hao Chin Martín to my Stanford professor regarding some manuscripts related to Chinese migration to Mexico?"

"Yeah, I think that was the guy that my sister was seeing."

"Hao Chin Martín?"

"Yeah."

"Did you ever meet him?"

"No," Rubí paused. "No, I think my sister met him in Vancouver. My sister works in the Vancouver office of Rare

Elements. I think he works for some Chinese-Mexican mining corporation.

"Rubí, have you ever been to Mexico?"

"No, but that is why I called you back. I am going to meet up with my sister in Mexico for vacation."

Wow! Tina thought. *I'm going to have to share this news with Professor Reynoso.*

***

Monday morning came about, and Tina had finished the translation. She would proofread her work one more time. She loaded the document onto her tablet so that it could be shared. She texted a brief summary of her conversation with Rubí to Professor Reynoso.

An hour later Francisco was ringing up Patricio Gomez.

"Well, first of all, I want to thank you for sending me the packet of information," Francisco knew how the game was played.

"No, problem."

"We think we found a lead for you. In one of the photos, there is a chubby middle-aged man. His name is Hao Chin Martín. Patricio, are you writing this down? I can send you a little memo, but I wanted you to get this information as soon as possible."

"Oh, yes," Patricio's manner had softened into an agreeable tone. "Please continue. I've got the file right here."

"Do you see the photo of an Asian man with an Asian woman?"

"Give me a second, please."

A minute later, Patricio responded, "Okay!"

"That man is Hao Chin Martín. He and the woman came to my office about two months ago. They wanted the Chan Toy manuscripts translated. He said that he was a distant cousin of our summer intern, Tina Fang. I don't think you have met her yet. He told us that another cousin had given him the Chan Toy manuscripts. Anyway, that should help your investigation."

"But who is the woman accomplice?"

"Good question. At first, we thought she was Rubí Song, an acquaintance of Tina Fang, but Rubí was in São Paolo the entire summer of 2018."

"So, who is she?" Patricio pursued.

"The woman who came to see me with Hao Chin Martín was Lilí Song, the sister of Rubí. Lili and Rubí both work for Rare Elements. Lili is headquartered in Shanghai, but Rubí works for the São Paolo subsidiary. Hao Chin Martín works for a Chinese-Mexican mining enterprise in Vancouver. I will send you all the details to you in a memo by late afternoon,"

"Thank you so much, professor. You have almost solved the case," Patricio was trying to make nice now. "It seems that this Tina Fang is in the midst of all of this. I think I should talk to her."

"Then you are invited to our staff meeting in my office at 10 o'clock this Thursday."

CHAPTER 33 – THE DELIVERABLE

Tuesday-Wednesday, May 14-15, 2019

Guadalajara

Tina exhaled as she dropped the translation of the Chan Toy manuscripts on the desk of Professor Reynoso that Tuesday morning.

"Thank you, Tina," the professor knew he was so fortunate to have Tina as an assistant and colleague.

Tina gave him a docile nod.

"Let me have a chance to review it," Francisco always believed in the importance of a second pair of eyes for reviewing important documents. Given the amount of money involved the project and the universities' reputations, he wanted to have the best product possible. "I'll take the original also."

Tina took another manila folder out of her leather satchel bag and laid it next to the other papers. After a few more minutes, she left.

Francisco called in Carlos. He had arranged for Carlos to shadow-check the translation. They worked all morning. There were a minimum number of corrections and questions. Tina had done a stellar job. They took a quick lunch break, before giving Tina the list of errata and areas for clarifications. Fortunately, with the shared applications on their iPads, a secretary was able to immediately make the changes.

By four o'clock Francisco and Carlos had finished their review. Tina and the secretary put on the finishing touches by 5:15.

"Thank you both," Francisco had a big, tired smile on his face. He was exhausted. He knew the other two were at least as tired. He wanted to celebrate, but that would not be fair. He would reward them later.

As they all went their separate ways, each had a head full of unspoken questions. The strange events surrounding the turquoise hummingbird. It read like a science fiction novel.

Francisco went home and had a super cold beer. His wife Alex arrived, and they talked for a while. He skipped dinner and slept like a baby.

***

The next morning, Francisco dictated a letter to Lilí Song:

May 15, 2019

Lilí Song
Chinese Dragon Rare Elements Ltd.,
Vancouver, B.C. Canada

RE: Chan Toy Project

Dear Ms. Song:

We are pleased to send you the Cantonese to Spanish translation as the first deliverable to the Chan Toy Project.
See attached. If you have any questions or concerns, please contact us . . .

He emailed the letter and concurrently sent a hard copy to Lilí Song through the postal service. Electronic copies were submitted to Dean Ríos, Dean Chandler, Carlos, and Tina (the latter two with thank you's and with notice that they would discuss the translations at this Thursday's staff meeting).

"And Juanita, please sent a courtesy copy to Patricio Gomez."

By the late afternoon, Francisco received an acknowledgement from Lilí's office of receipt of the missive. Gratitude came from both deans. Francisco was elated and texted Alex that he was going to take her out for a special dinner. He made 8 p.m. reservations at one of their favorite restaurants.

As he was trying to leave his office early in order to get shaved and dressed for his romantic date, there was a buzz on his office phone. He knew that he shouldn't answer it. It could only mean trouble.

"Patricio Gomez on line 1, professor," Juanita announced over the intercom.

"Thank you, Juanita. I'll take it."

A minute later Patricio Gomez was on the phone. "I received a copy of your letter to a Lilí Song with a translation of the Chan Toy manuscripts."

Francisco was expecting a thank you, but instead he got attitude from Patricio.

"You sent a letter and the translation of the manuscript to the same woman who may have been involved in the robbery of these papers?"

Francisco was surprised at Patricio's tone. "Patricio, as you know, the translation is part of our agreement with Lilí Song."

"But she is a central character in the robbery from the Museum of Anthropology. It looks like you are colluding with her."

Francisco took a deep breath. He was bushed and wanted to get out of his office asap. He wasn't going to put up with this mocoso's hissy fit. "Patricio, you always knew that this was the nature of the project."

"But there was a robbery!"

"Patricio, an alleged robbery," Francisco was glad that he had been married to a prosecuting attorney in a prior life.

"But this is an active investigation."

"And we are cooperating with you and the authorities," Francisco did not want to mention that it was more than "the authorities." had done. "So why are you calling? The translation might give you further clues."

Patricio chose to ignore the question. Instead, he became accusatory, "You never told me that you had a copy of the Chan Toy manuscript."

"You never asked."

"I assume that Lilí Song gave you a copy."

"That is correct."

"I also assume that she has the original."

"That is incorrect."

"What do you mean? If she doesn't have it, do you know who has the original?"

"Yes," Francisco simply replied. "We do. The university has it," No more time for games.

There was a pause. Francisco knew that Patricio was pissed. "Well, we need the original right now. We are in the middle of a criminal investigation."

"As we have stated before, not going to happen. As far as we know, no criminal charges have been filed. The only thing out there are unsupported allegations of a so-called robbery. If and when you present us with a search warrant, we will consider it. Right now, we are working on an academic project that needs original sources."

"Professor, you are making a big mistake," Patricio was steaming.

"We'll see," he knew that Patricio was at a disadvantage. He wanted to say that possession was nine-tenths of the law, but he didn't. Instead, he threw out, "good luck on extradition from Canada on this case."

"I gotta go," Patricio wanted to disconnect.

"You're still invited to our staff meeting tomorrow."

Moments later, Francisco texted his wife that he was on his way home. *Just another day at the office.*

CHAPTER 34 – EPIPHANY

Thursday, May 16, 2019
Guadalajara

Francisco had a smile on his face as he entered his office on Thursday morning. He went to his office and grabbed his materials. He walked over to a small conference meeting room that Juanita has set up for a staff meeting of the Chan Toy Project. There were five chairs around the small table, and a folder in front of each place. A fruit (mango, banana, and watermelon) cup with a plastic fork and napkin sat on top of each folder. Coffee and hot water for tea were set up in the back. A white board was set up in the front.

The professor was reviewing his notes, while Carlos and Tina arrived punctually at nine. They made small talk while they got themselves coffee and tea.

"Please enjoy the fruit," he said in a conspiratorial manner. "The fruit is from Juanita's garden. She made them especially for you."

The other two looked at each other. They knew what to do. Nobody wanted to be on Juanita's bad side.

"Carlos, did you have a chance to review the translation again?"

"Yes, professor, it is very good," Carlos had helped the professor review the document a few days before for form and grammar, but not for substance.

"Okay, let's start. The first section is an executive summary of the agreement between our universities and the third party. It specifies the deliverables and the timelines," Francisco wrote down some salient points on the white board and sent it to print. He passed copies to his colleagues.

Suddenly there was a commotion at the door. A tall, muscular Latino male with a pencil moustache rushed in. "Sorry, I'm late, professor!"

"Welcome, Señor Gomez," Professor Reynoso was feeling gracious this morning. "When did you get in?"

"Last night," Patricio, the new arrival, was harried by the inordinate amount of time it took to get to the meeting. He had taken the last flight from Mexico City and had not slept well. "I wanted to make sure to be on time"

“Patricio, this is Tina Fang,” he motioned to her and continued with a foxlike grin. “Tina, Patricio is on loan to us from the Mexican Ministry of Culture in Mexico City. We have accepted their gracious gesture of assistance. He knows a lot about Mexican relics and artifacts. He will be very useful in our project.” Nothing was mentioned of his undercover agent status.

“There’s a folder in front of each of you,” the professor’s hand pointed toward it. “It’s yours to keep. The information is not technically private, but we are asking you to keep it confidential. Understood?”

Everybody including Patricio nodded yes.

They went on to discuss the logistics of the translations. Francisco had not heard from Lilí Song yet. Patricio kept sneaking glances of Tina who was seated to his left. Francisco wondered if it was curiosity or something more.

“This project, to be candid, is heavily funded. That brings up the question of what is so valuable about this translation?” the professor pointed to Carlos.

“Well, it is a historical document. It is at least a hundred years old,” Carlos answered.

“It is a source document. It’s rare and it is evidence of the Chinese migration to Mexico. It’s an asset for researchers,” Tina speculated.

"It belongs to the Museum of Anthropology," Patricio gave a sharp stare at Professor Reynoso. "It is considered a valuable historical relic."

"But what do you think it is worth?" Professor Francisco Reynoso was in his element. It was like he was teaching one of his seminars. "Forty thousand pesos?" *About two thousand dollars?*

"Fifty thousand pesos!" Carlos blurted out.

"Sixty thousand pesos?" countered Patricio.

"At a maximum we are talking about three thousand U.S. dollars," one of Francisco's great strengths was looking at the big picture and thinking outside the box. "What does this mean? It means the manuscript as a historical document has minimal value."

The three looked at him with incredulity.

"The value has to be in the information contained within. What would be valuable in these documents, Tina?"

"Chan Toy didn't have any money or riches. Just stuff he had brought back to Mexico from China. That was negligible," Tina said.

"It probably had to do something with the mines. Minerals are intrinsically valuable," Carlos added.

"What minerals would be valuable?" continued the professor.

"Copper for sure," Carlos was on a roll. "And maybe turquoise."

Francisco at that moment had an epiphany. It was the item that Hao Chin Martín was trying to obfuscate in their initial dealings.

"I think you have it!" Francisco spoke in an excited tone. "I think it is the turquoise colibrí amulet! Why?"

Tina jumped in, "In the first place, Ana's aunt gave it to her for health and protection. Ana always had it on her person which means that it was treasured."

"I think that this turquoise colibrí had magical properties. It could protect people. It could hurt people. Tina's translations have given us examples of its special powers. This thing could be a boon for the medical field, especially in research and global health," Carlos said.

"It could also be weaponized. Some country could use it to attack another," Patricio had stumbled onto a group of intellectuals who had probably just solved the mystery of the Chan Toy robbery. He had focused his investigation on the theft itself, but not on the rationale for the robbery. He should have analyzed it from the position of the thief. *I owe the professor. I was a complete jerk. And he didn't even have to invite me to this meeting. I would have still been in the dark.*

There was more in-depth discussion. Assignments were given out. Carlos was still trying to find the source of the transfer of the Chan Toy documents to the Museum of Anthropology. Tina would be looking for relatives of Chan Toy and Hao Chin Martín. Patricio said he would redirect his investigation into the robbery with this new information.

"Okay, in appreciation of all your hard work, we're going to have lunch at the Faculty Lounge," Francisco was acting as the gracious host. Actually, the Chan Toy Project was paying for it. Francisco had been told to spend the money in order to look good.

A middle-aged hostess with coiffed black hair sat the small group at a table in the corner. An empty chair was left between Francisco and Carlos. Dean Ríos had a meeting with the French Department and would try to make it if she could. Patricio was seated between Carlos and Tina. A few times Carlos tried to engage with his friend Patricio, but the latter was busy making conversation with Tina. Tina in turn was spellbound looking at Patricio.

That night when Francisco got home, he kicked off his shoes and waited for the arrival of his wife. An hour later Alex was listening to him explain his day while drinking a Taxco mineral water with lime.

“And Tina seemed to be smitten with Patricio,” Francisco explained. “What should I do? She is a grown woman and very smart. I don’t want her to get hurt.”

“Like you said, mi amor, she is an adult and will have to live with any decisions that she makes. You are not responsible for her,” Alex was trying to be empathetic.

“But I should protect her.”

“The best thing you can do is to let her live her own life,” Francisco’s wife counseled. “And give her lots of work to fill up her time.”

“As always, mi amor, you’re right.”

“Now you have to take care of your wife,” she said smoothly taking his hand.

CHAPTER 35 – TRAVELS WITH CARLOS

Saturday - Thursday, May 18-23, 2019

Mexico City, Puebla

Carlos was like a child in a candy store. He was constantly messaging and sending emails with his new iPad.

CARLOS: Professor, arrived safely in Mexico City. The hotel is very nice.

Within five minutes there was a reply.

FRANCISCO: Glad everything is all right. Have a good time. Let's hope we get lucky. Don't forget to keep your receipts.

At the conclusion of the May 16 staff meeting, Patricio had invited the others to visit him in Mexico City where he was headquartered. He surmised that there might be a nexus between the Chan Toy manuscript and Mexico City. Professor Reynoso declined the offer because of a prior commitment. Sol and he were going to watch a soccer match, while the female entourage was taking Tina to see the Ballet Folklorico at the Palacio de Bellas Artes.

Francisco knew that Carlos worked hard and had to commute from Guanajuato during the week. Carlos hadn't had a vacation in years. When Professor Francisco Reynoso offered him an all-expense trip paid to the capital of Mexico with his family, he accepted immediately. He was a favorite of Dean Ríos who had hired him the prior summer to translate documents from Purépecha to Spanish. He had begun his career as high school teacher in Guanajuato and worked summers as a tour guide at Tenochtitlan. He was now a professor (co-teaching with Professor Reynoso) and a Curator at the University of Guadalajara. Like Tina, he was working on his doctorate.

Carlos had married la escuela secundaria principal's daughter, Carmen, when he was 18 and she was 16. They had two children. Gabriel was 13 and Miguel was 11. Carlos had just recently turned 35, although he looked older because his hair was thinning. His family had never been to Mexico City, so this trip would be a rare treat.

The Erandis left early Sunday morning in their beat up grey 2006 Kia SUV from Guanajuato and arrived at the Mexico City Hilton in the afternoon. After checking in, the family explored Chapultepec Park where they snacked on tacos, elotes, and tortas.

The next morning Carlos drove the family to the Museum of Anthropology where they met with Patricio and renewed their acquaintance. Patricio gave Carlos' wife and kids free passes. They were going to explore the museum and take the Metro back to the hotel because Carmen did not drive. Patricio and Carlos had work to do.

Patricio directed Carlos to the Mexican-Chinese Special Collections Department where Carlos spent the next six hours alone going through the logs of documents. It was in the afternoon when Carlos found the sought-after entry:

Author: Chan Toy
Subject: Chinese Immigration in Mexico
Period: late 19th century
Page count: 99 for document 1; 1 for document 2
Source: Nelson Chin Martín, Tucson, Arizona, EUA
Date: April 4, 2009

Carlos took a screen shot of this log entry. He decided to take a lunch break. He and Patricio met in the museum cafeteria. He asked Patricio about documents #1 and #2. Patricio didn't have any information. After they ate, Carlos went to the Miscellaneous Collections stacks. Fortunately, he limited himself to exploring only Chinese documents.

That night, the family went out to dinner at a pizzeria. The boys were overjoyed with the sausage, jalapeño, and black bean toppings. Before he went to bed, Carlos emailed his notes to Professor Reynoso and Tina.

The next morning, Carlos went back to the museum and resumed his search but found nothing more. At the end of the day, he met his family back at the hotel. They had gone to the zoo and the aquarium and were talking a mile a minute about their experiences. They had used their father's old cell phone to take photos.

On Wednesday, the famuli drove to Puebla where they checked into another Hilton hotel. Patricio had recommended the place. Carlos had an appointment with the local historical society. Carlos did not find any information about Chan Toy but did find several old newspaper articles about his wife, Ana. In the article Ana was compared to La China Poblana. The two women were rumored to look alike, and both had special magical healing powers. Carlos took photocopies of these articles with his phone and sent them to the professor and Tina.

In the afternoon he tried went to the location in Puebla where Ana was supposed to have lived at the site. He found dozens and dozens of apartment complexes.

He returned to the hotel where he found two prune-skinned boys who had been in the pool all day. As a special treat, they ate chicken mole at the Meson Sacristía de la Compania with corn tamales for dessert. They returned back to Mexico City late that night.

On Thursday morning, Carlos was having a leisurely breakfast with his family.

"Did you boys have a good time?" he asked.

They both nodded in the affirmative.

"What was your favorite thing?"

Their response was "Everything! We've had so much fun!"

"Mi amor," his wife Carmen asked a question. "What time do we have to leave tomorrow? Do we have time to go to Frida Kahlo's House in Coyoacán?'

Carlos answered almost immediately. "Of course, my dear." She never asked for anything. She was selfless. She devoted herself to the family. They probably wouldn't return to Mexico City for a long time, and this is something that he also wanted to see.

That night Carlos texted Professor Reynoso and Tina with copies of the news articles that he had found. He said that he would be back in the office on Monday.

***

Overall, Professor Reynoso had been pleased with Carlos' progress reports. Focusing on the wife of Chan Toy's wife gave them another avenue of investigation and could lead to more potential relatives. He would assign this new inquiry to Tina. She was already investigating Hao Chin Martín.

In the late afternoon, Francisco received a letter from Lilí Song stating that she had received the translation and was very pleased. However, she did ask what the project's next steps would be in looking for the turquoise colibrí amulet. The colibrí amulet! Aha! His team had guessed correctly. There was potentially valuable information within the Chan Toy manuscripts.

Francisco was dipping his churro in his café de olla when his office phone rang. He had woken up late and hadn't had time for breakfast.

"Patricio Gomez on line one," Juanita said in a neutral tone.

"Hello, Patricio, how are you?" the professor said amicably.

"Fine, professor," Patricio was being more respectful. "Just called to say thank you for your cooperation."

"No problem. You're welcome. Anything in particular?"

"After our meeting last week . . . by the way, 'thanks for inviting me . . . we reviewed the museum videotapes. In them the Asian woman is seen slipping an envelope to one of the museum's staff. We looked at some other tapes. We think this staff person has been selling museum documents. She has been arrested. We think that she has sold more than the Chan Toy papers. We're going to question her this afternoon."

"Wow! That's quite a breakthrough!" *So Lilí Song is somehow involved in this theft*, Francisco thought. "Congratulations!"

They talked for a few more minutes promising to keep each other apprised of further developments.

"By the way, professor, is Tina married or seeing anyone?"

CHAPTER 36 – NELSON

Monday - Friday, May 20- 24, 2019
Guadalajara

Tina wiped her forehead with the small white towel. Now that she had cranked out the Chan Toy translations, she was trying to get back into her weekly exercise routine. She had encouraged Mirasol to jog with her, but the young girl disliked running intensely. Tina showered and dressed. She was the only one at the Ríos breakfast table; everyone had left. By 9:30, she was in her university office, nursing her green tea latte.

She checked her texts and emails. Tina had spent all week trying to track down the six generations of Chan Toy descendants. She had made inquiries of census data from Mexico, the U.S., and Canada. The Chinese information was "unavailable." The most hits came from Arizona in the U.S., and Baja California and Sonora in Mexico. She even had a few names from the Philippines. She then entered the “Martín,” “Toy,” and “Chin” into an Excel database. Lots of “cuts and pastes.” She had hundreds of names. Her second source was the Mormon Genealogy Library. The University IT tech tried to tutor her on how to simplify the building of a database, but that was slow going. Finally, a few YouTube videos solved the problems. Some wildcard asterisks, question marks, and tildes worked miracles. She found some databases of immigration records that proved productive, but for the most part the information banks proved futile.

When Tina finally finished the data entry, she decided to focus on the most promising prospects. She reduced the thousands of probabilities to several dozen. Professor Reynoso had approved her request for a private search service that provided mailing addresses, email addresses, and phone numbers.

On Thursday she sent out a generic email in English, Spanish, and Cantonese to the 37 names on the list that were still seemed viable:

To: Descendants of Chan Toy
Subject: Chinese Immigration in Mexico
Period: late 19th century

Hi, my name is Tina Fang. I am a doctoral student doing research for Stanford University and the University of Guadalajara on Chinese migration to Mexico starting in 1862.

I am looking for the descendants of Chan Toy, originally from Guangzhou, China . . .

Within minutes, six emails came back with error messages: "Incorrect address," "Addressee no longer available," and "Server not responding." Tina created another column in the database and made these a second priority.

By the end of the day, she had two email responses. She was just about to call it a day, when she saw the text from Carlos that he had sent her a few days earlier. Tina hadn't paid much attention to it the first time. Then she saw the copy of the document stating that a "Nelson Chin Martín" was the source of the Chan Toy manuscripts that had been turned over to the Museum of Anthropology. *Just twenty more minutes!* She checked the list of the last group of names in her database. Sure enough, "Nelson Chin Martín" was on it. But to her surprise "Hao Chin Martín" was on the selective list also. She was now excited and couldn't wait. Her finger ran down the list until she found Hao Chin Martín. It was a Tucson, Arizona number. She dialed and the phone rang six times, but no one answered. No answering machine picked up.

Then she decided to call Nelson Chin Martín. She was surprised to find that he had the same phone number as Hao Chin Martín. She was now tired and hungry. She would go home and fight another day. She left the office. After dinner, she stayed up and watched a Mexican telenovela with Mirasol. The young girl was growing on her. Mirasol was like a little sister.

The next morning after her jog and a minimalist breakfast, Tina was back in the office catching up with emails and texts. She was always interested in Carlos' progress reports.

At 10 a.m. she decided to call the Hao/Nelson Chin Martín phone number again.

"Hello," a voice quietly answered in English with a Spanish accent. The voice sounded like the person was older.

"Hello, my name is Tina Fang. I am doing research for two universities. I'm looking for Mr. Hao Chin Martín. Is he available?"

There was a pause. "Who is this?"

"I'm Tina Fang. I wrote Mr. Hao Chin Martín an email. I'm working on a research project, and I would like to talk to him. Is he around?"

"No, he die ten years ago."

"I'm so sorry. May I speak to Mr. Nelson Chin Martín?"

"No, he die too."

"I'm sorry again," Tina took in a deep breath. She felt sadness. "Do you know who I could talk to about Chan Toy? I'm involved in a research project about him."

"Don't know. You give me phone number. My daughter call you when she get back work"

"Do you have an email address?" Tina didn't want the woman to have to make a long-distance call. "I can email you." It sounded like English was not the woman's first language and she was getting a little frustrated. Tina switched into Spanish.

"Señora, what would be a good time for me to call you and your daughter back?"

Suddenly, the woman responded in Spanish in a more relaxed manner. "Seven o'clock. Maybe 6:30. We'll be having dinner at 7. She will help you."

At 7:30 Guadalajara time, Tina called back. A young woman answered in English.

"Hello, this is Leti."

Tina went into the whole spiel about who she was and what she wanted. She found out that the daughter was named Leticia "Leti" Ronstadt.

"My Uncle Hao died about ten or eleven years ago. Around 2009, I think. He had cancer. He lived a block away and we took care of him."

"Was he married, or did he have any children?" Tina drilled in a bit.

"No, he was my dad's only brother. My uncle died of leukemia. He had no sisters or other relatives as far as we know. Then my dad died last year. So, it is only my mother Hortencia 'Tencha' and my son, Victor, left."

"Leti, do you know any of your Chinese relatives?"

"Not really. I think they all used to live in Mexico. Some of them moved to Arizona but I think they have all passed away."

The two kept talking about Chan Toy and possible relatives.

"Tina, have you ever called us before?"

"Not before today. I just got this number recently," Tina was perplexed. "Why do you ask?"

"My mother says that you sound like a lady who called last year. She said you spoke English with a funny accent. Like an English lady."

"No, it wasn't me. When was this?"

"It was a year ago. My mother and I were cleaning up my Uncle Hao's room where he stored all of his belonging. Most of the writings were in Chinese. We don't know Chinese. A friend of ours put us in contact with a museum in Mexico City. We sent the papers there. Along with Hao Chin Martín's skull cap and other things. We told the English lady all of that."

Tina was now getting suspicious. Could the strange caller have been one of the Song twins? To the untrained ear, a British Columbian or Macau accent could have sounded English. *Do I really have a discernible accent?* Tina wondered about herself. And it looked like the Chan Toy papers did come from Tucson. *I need to run this by the professor.*

"But, Tina, we still have more papers here. We found them under some other things. Too much junk! Would you like us to send them to you?" Leti offered. "They are in Spanish."

"Leti, could you take a photo of them with your phone and email them to me please?" Tina knew it would be burdensome for the woman, but she wanted to see these documents. They could prove to be valuable.

"No problem. One page looks like a map."

Tina's head snapped back. Her curiosity was really piqued.

"Could you also overnight mail the papers to me here in Mexico please? I'll give you my address. I'm going to send you $200 to cover the costs."

CHAPTER 37 – MORE DOCS

Monday - Wednesday, May 27- 29, 2019
Guadalajara

Francisco was exiting his office early Monday morning when Tina intercepted him. “Professor, do you have a minute?”

“Yes, but just a minute.” He had a nine o’clock meeting with the Human Resources Department that he had to keep. Nobody dared make problems with HR. He stopped in his tracks.

“It looks like we caught a break, professor,” Tina was jubilant. “As I mentioned in my email, I talked to the niece of Hao Chin Martín . . .”

Tina recounted in detail her conversations with Hao Chin Martín’s sister-in-law, Hortensia “Tencha,” and her daughter “Leti.”

"The bottom line is that Hao Chin Martín is dead," Tina spoke emphatically. "And someone had been plotting to get the Chan Toy manuscripts away from the family. The original Chan Toy papers came from Tucson. Fortunately for us and Leti, they had already sent the documents to the Museum of Anthropology in Mexico City."

"But subsequently, the papers were stolen," Francisco nodded his head. "And fortunately, we have them now."

"Right, professor," she was rushing to finish. "But Leti found other papers after the original ones. They looked like some kind of diary in Spanish. She took photos of them and sent them to me. She is going to FedEx the originals to us."

They both knew that overnight mail to Mexico took at least two days.

Francisco started to pull away. He was going to be late to his meeting.

"I think there is also a map with the papers."

The professor turned his head. "Oh, my god! Let me run this by Dean Ríos. We need to have a project meeting as soon as possible. I'll bring Dean Ríos up to speed. Thank you for your quick thinking on this matter. Have Carlos take a look at the map."

Francisco's internal alert system had gone off. He knew that this Chan Toy Project could be a ticking time bomb. He also knew that the next decisions were above his pay grade.

The next morning Tina had received the papers via FedEx from the niece, Leti Ronstadt. After she sorted the documents, she gave a parchment depicting a map to Carlos.

Tina started reading the papers that Leti had sent. A few hours later Carlos appeared in front of her. "Hey, Tina, was there another map?"

"I haven't seen any. Why do ask?"

Carlos walked over to her and placed the map document in front of her. He pulled out a magnifying glass and ran it over the left border of the page. He performed the same procedure on the right side. He took out his iPhone and turned on the Measures application. He then measured the length and width of the map, recording both.

"See the ragged edge over here. It has been torn. This is part of a larger document. It could a diptych (double paneled drawing). There is at least one more part to the map."

An hour later Professor Reynoso was calling Lilí Song in Vancouver after emailing her. A secretary patched him through to Lilí.

"Hi, Ms. Song, this is Professor Reynoso in Guadalajara," he was calling her under a pretense. "How are you?"

"Fine, professor. Good to hear from you," said the woman in a cautious voice.

"How is Hao Chin Martín?" He wanted to see if she was sticking to their ploy.

"He is still in Asia."

"We're still trying to locate the turquoise hummingbird," Francisco threw out the bait. "Do you have any more documents?"

"No. What kind of documents?"

"Like a map."

"No."

The superficial discussion went on for a few more minutes. Francisco was convinced that Lilí did not have any part of Ana and Chan Toy's map. *Who could have it?*

***

On Wednesday morning the small conference room smelled of fresh coffee and pan dulce. Dean Ríos was joined by Professors Reynoso and Erandi, along with Tina and Patricio from the Mexican Department of Culture. Patricio had been invited in case there were illegal dealings going on.

"Welcome, everyone," Dean Ríos began. "We're here to follow up on the Chan Toy Project. Let's begin by everyone giving an update on what they have been doing. I'll start." The dean talked about the administrivia of the undertaking but did not mention the budget or expenditures.

Next came Tina. She explained that she had learned that Hao Chin Martín was dead and that his niece had sent them more manuscripts. "I made copies of the new documents for you all. Carlos will do some research on the map."

Carlos high fived her. Patricio leaned over to his colleague and whispered. "I can help you if you want."

"When will you start the new translations?" Reynoso was scribbling notes on his spread sheet. "Do you need Carlos to help you?"

"Not right now," Tina was starting to understand office politics. "But I would like him to review the translations once I finish."

"When do you think you can have them done?"

"Maybe one week. Two weeks at the most."

"Sounds good."

Carlos and Professor Reynoso talked about the missing part of the Ana and Chan Toy map and Lili Song's denial that she possessed it.

Patricio's big news was that the arrest of the museum employee involved in the theft of the Chan Toy documents was imminent.

At around 11 o'clock Dean Ríos decided to delve into the belly of the beast. "Tina has told us that Hao Chin Martín is dead. Yet, two months ago, someone by the same name approached Professor Reynoso and wanted to contract a Cantonese to Spanish translation of these papers. We did that. We were paid handsomely by Ms. Song of the Chinese Dragon Rare Elements Ltd, Vancouver."

"Our next deliverable is the procurement of Ana's and Chan Toy's turquoise colibrí amulet. It is said to have magical powers. We believe that Ms. Song and the man posing as Hao Chin Martín are trying to retrieve this turquoise colibrí amulet, and they are using us to locate this object."

The others had had the same thought but somehow it was startling to hear it put into words. "The problem we face now is both legal and ethical. If the turquoise hummingbird is a Mexican artifact, it can't leave the country legally. Stanford University and the University of Guadalajara will have to forego the additional moneys if there is any illegality involved. This is where Patricio comes in. He is here to help us find the magical totem and have it delivered to its rightful owner which we believe is the Museum of Anthropology. The importance of cultural patrimony may outweigh the academic importance of this particular study of Chinese migration to Mexico." For the first time Patricio looked happy.

In the afternoon Tina cleared her desk and began the Spanish translations. The quality of the documents was different compared to Chan Toy papers. The paper was parchment and the writing seemed cruder. The level of Spanish was rudimentary. Tina assumed that Ana was the author of these logs.

Suddenly, Carlos stuck his head into her little cubicle. "Guess what?"

Tina looked puzzled. "What?"

"We're going back to the Museum of Anthropology in Mexico City," he was smiling from ear to ear. "Patricio tells me that they have a whole section devoted to maps. He wants to help us find the turquoise totem."

"Okay," she did not know what to say.

"Oh, us means us," Carlos grinned. "You and me. I've already cleared it with Professor Reynoso. Go home and start packing. Our flight leaves tomorrow morning at 7:10."

CHAPTER 38 –THE CHART ROOM

Thursday, May 30, 2019

Mexico City

At five past eight Patricio met Carlos and Tina outside of the domestic terminal baggage claim area at the Mexico City International Airport. Both travelers had retrieved their duffel bags with rollers.

"How was your flight?" inquired Patricio politely after shaking Carlos' hand. He did the same with Tina but added a peck on the cheek. He was wearing a lightweight blue blazer with an open collared white shirt and tan chinos. He grabbed Tina's duffel and rolled it out to the parking lot. Carlos was in his usual professorial chocolate brown sport coat, and Tina wore a white silk embroidered blouse and a long black skirt.

Patricio inquired if they had had breakfast. Both replied they were fine. They knew that Mexican breakfasts lasted at least two hours. Patricio loaded the two duffels into his black KIA Seltos SUV. Tina sat in the front seat, Carlos in the back.

It was a quarter to ten when Carlos and Tina checked into the Museum of Anthropology and received their identification badges.

The trio had taken the elevator and soon found themselves in the Cartography Department. They were greeted by the department's head director, Doctor Manuel Pinteiro. He had a heavy accent. The small-statured, elderly gentleman sported a long grey beard and round glasses. His worn-out sport coat looked two sizes too big.

Patricio and Tina left the other two. They all had agreed to meet at the cafeteria at noon. Patricio was going to show Tina copies of the recent arrest report of Augustina Rojas, who was a research assistant at the museum. Sra. Rojas had been shown in film footage receiving an envelope from an Asian couple the previous summer. An internal investigation had been conducted with Patricio coordinating the task.

At first the suspect denied that she involved. Tina read the transcript:

"I didn't do anything."

"We have photographs."

"It wasn't me."

The holdout lasted about twenty minutes. The accused was shown photos and records of missing documents.

"It must be someone else."

"We have looked at your bank records. You have had some big deposits over the last two years. Far more than your salary."

"I was a saving for a new car."

"You already have a new car!"

The suspect remained silent.

"Well, we know that you are lying. We have no choice but to arrest you. Your two children will be taken to Social Services."

"No, wait! I'll tell you everything. You can't take my children! My husband left me. I didn't know what to do!"

When Tina finished reviewing the transcript, her face showed that she was in shock. She looked over to Patricio.

“What will happen now?” Tina asked.

“We’re in the process of trying to find out what other artifacts are missing. The semi-good news is that her contacts seemed to be with only one couple. However, the money transfers came from a varieties of sources. We have enough evidence to be able to deduce that the ultimate consumers are overseas markets. Oligarchs and money laundering.”

Meanwhile, Carlos was two floors away examining the original Chan Toy map that Leti Ronstadt had sent Tina. Doctor Pinteiro had placed the document on an examining table with a bright light and a large magnifier. He made the same measurements that Carlos had made. He carefully examined the parchment and the ink.

“My initial conclusion is that this parchment was the type that was commonly used on Pacific Ocean voyages. It is made from sheep skin and resists moisture. The ink . . .”

The director went on as if he were conducting an autopsy on a body.

“Carlos, I think you and I are done for now. Thank you for letting an old man bend your ear,” Dr. Pinteiro smiled. “This has been exciting for me.”

“Doctor Pinteiro, this has been a rare treat for me as well.”

“With your permission, I will turn this document over to our Forensics Department for further examination.”

Everybody was excited about their experiences at the museum when they reconvened in the cafeteria for lunch. Dr. Pinteiro had been invited but he respectfully declined. Carlos and Patricio both ordered the enchiladas suizas backed by cold Coronas. Tina ordered the shrimp tacos with cold mint tea.

"I can't believe that that woman stole and sold all those treasures as if they were her own. What will happen to her now, Patricio?" Tina was sitting next to him.

"She will have to make restitution and probably spend some time in jail. Not going to be fun. The worst part is that her kids will end up in Social Services if they can't find relatives or a suitable place of them."

The food came and the chatter ceased. Carlos gulped his lunch and fought the urge to order a second beer.

"Doctor Pinteiro was simply magical. I swear the map was speaking to him. His department is doing all these forensic tests as we speak."

"Do we know what the map is of?" asked Patricio.

"Not yet," Carlos was hedging his bets. "But the good news, hermano, is that after this Chan Toy Project over, we will return all the original manuscripts to the museum. Please advise Professor Reynoso's office how to proceed and what papers must be signed and notarized. You will also get a copy of our provenance to show the chain of custody. If you need anything for a criminal prosecution, I am sure we can work things out."

"Thanks, carnal. I think the woman is going to plead out."

They talked more about the project and the museum.

"What are you two doing for dinner tonight?" Patricio was looking at Tina. She in turn blushed.

"We are taking you out for dinner," Carlos interrupted. "Per Professor Reynoso's directive. He wants to thank you for your assistance."

"What kind of food would you like?" Patricio asked.

***

It was eight o'clock when the trio met at the restaurant. Patricio and Carlos wore the same clothes they had on during the day. Tina had changed into a light green silk dress offset by a green jade bracelet and earrings.

The Villa María was a tony restaurant in the upscale Colonia Polanco. The first round of passion fruit margaritas put the threesome at ease. The guacamole and queso fundido tempted their palates. It was really the first time they had had an opportunity to relax together. To encourage gaiety, there was humorous signage everywhere including the bathrooms. The smells from the kitchen were overwhelming, causing all three to salivate.

At 8:30, handsome mariachis in black charro outfits with silver braiding began serenading the guests. Carlos and Patricio ordered the chicken mole that tasted liked a chocolate sundae; Tina ordered the turkey mole that had a citrus tang.

They split a tres leches cake, and the two men ordered coffee. Patricio's hand grazed Tina's every time he reached over for bite.

CHAPTER 39 – DIM SUM

Friday, May 31, 2019
Mexico City

The next morning the black KIA SUV pulled up in front of the boutique Hotel Vienna. Carlos and Tina had been waiting outside and climbed into the vehicle.

“Thanks for the great dinner last night,” Patricio made circular motions over his stomach with his right hand. “I am still full.”

“You can thank Professor Reynoso for the eats,” Carlos laughed. “This Chan Toy Project has given us some resources we have never had before.”

An hour later, Patricio was acting as a docent of the Museum of Anthropology. He was escorting Carlos and Tina through the diorama exhibits of the State of Sonora gallery. There were indigenous people figures with adobe housing in the middle of a saguaro cactus landscape, and a jaguar atop a rock and a scorpion resting in the desert sand. Carlos was taking photos with his cellphone.

"Can you take our photo, please?" Carlos had grabbed a young visitor's attention. A minute later the trio had been captured in a photo.

"I'll email you both copies," Carlos offered.

At about eleven o'clock the threesome made their way to Doctor Pinteiro's office. Patricio had received a text earlier that morning asking for the meeting.

Patricio reintroduced the elderly man to Tina. "A pleasure to meet you," he bowed as he shook her hand.

"Muito prazer, você," Tina responded in Portuguese since she was fluent, having been born in Macau. She had detected his Lusitanian accent.

He gave her the biggest smile. "Would you like coffee? How rude of me not to offer you some."

For the next few minutes, they made chit chat. Finally, Pinteiro looked at the three. "Carlos has told me of your herculean efforts to return the Chan Toy documents. Thank you," he paused and grabbed a document that looked like a map. "Carlos shared this map with me yesterday. Our staff has been conducting some visual examinations along with some spectrophotometric and electrostatic detective procedures."

The three visitors gave no indication that they didn't know what the doctor was talking about. They just nodded affirmatively.

"We have measured and inspected the parchment paper and analyzed the ink. The preliminary finding is that this is an authentic document, that is, the original. It has not been altered and is typical of a Spanish ship's log. The handwriting is in nonnative, rudimentary, common Spanish. And remember I said these were preliminary results. We will need to do more examinations."

The four discussed the forensic procedure for document investigations.

"The momentous discovery on this map, however, was the microscopic detection of a word etched onto the bottom of the page. It was barely discernible to the naked eye. It was found by an instrumental optical magnifier." He went on in superfluous detail about the process. The threesome seemed overwhelmed.

"Doctor, what was the word?" asked Carlos impatiently.

"***Devolver***," he answered manner of factly.

"To return?" mouthed Tina.

"I don't think so," Carlos inserted himself. He knew that although Tina was fluent in Spanish, she might not realize that this verb, although similar to "volver," meant something different. "Devolver means to return an object."

Tina nodded that she understood.

"And all this leads to the highpoint of today's meeting. Our procedure upon receiving archival documents is to catalog them into the museum's database. Dates, descriptions, distinguishing marks. We have been using comparative testing with this map against our archives and other databases. It seems that when the Chan Toy papers were received here, one of the documents was separated from the rest and sent to the Chart Room. Yesterday afternoon when we catalogued this map, we found another related map. It appears to be part of a triptych. We pulled it and sent it through the forensic process. There were similar results and the correlation with the other map is very high. Additionally, the word '***Volver***' is thinly scratched on the bottom of this document." He pulled out the new map and passed it around the room.

"Not 'devolver.'" This word is different. It is 'volver' and means to return or go back," Tina tried to reassert herself.

There was a frenzy of excitement as they discussed the ramifications of these discoveries. *Are we going to be able to find the turquoise colibrí amulet?* Each of the three had the same thought. *How does this all fit together?*

It was almost noon when the meeting ended. It was agreed that Doctor Pinteiro and his team would maintain custody of the maps to conduct further investigations. The threesome was given paper copies. Carlos took a photo of the new map with his phone and sent a copy to Professor Reynoso.

They thanked Doctor Pinteiro. Everyone was in a good mood.

“Hey, I’m hungry again,” voiced Patricio. The other two rolled their eyes. “Where do you want to go to lunch?”

“Patricio, if you could do me a favor and drop me off at the hotel,” Carlos seemed anxious. “I’m going to try to catch an earlier flight to Guanajuato. I can take the hotel shuttle to the airport.”

“No problem,” responded Patricio. “I can drop you off at the airport, if you like.”

“No thanks. That won’t be necessary.”

“And how about you? Are you leaving early too?” Patricio was looking hopefully at Tina.

“Oh, no,” Tina said with a slightly nervous edge. “I’m staying until tomorrow.”

Twenty minutes later Carlos stepped out of the SUV. He got goodbye hugs from his colleagues.

“Okay, Tina,” Patricio grinned. “It’s just you and me. Where do you want to go for lunch?”

"Chinatown," she said firmly.

"El Dragón Rojo, here we come!" Patricio shouted happily.

"It seems that you have some Chinese friends in town," Tina gave him a tease.

"Actually, I don't have any Chinese friends," he said smugly. "I have 'friends' who are Chinese or who are actually Mexican-Chinese. Mexican and Chinese at the same time."

They walked into a slightly rundown restaurant with red window frames. Tina was missing her Chinese comfort food. A large and long dragon was painted on the front window.

After they were seated at a rickety table, a disheveled waiter brought them hot tea. A very young girl with long black ponytails pushed a cart with several small plated items by them.

"You order," Patricio said.

Tina ordered siu mai dumplings, sweet and sour pork, and lo mein noodles. She did not laugh when Patricio struggled using his chopsticks.

They giggled between bites. Patricio purposely let slip that he was not married. Tina countered that she was going back to Palo Alto in September to finish her doctoral dissertation. The waiter came and Tina grabbed the bill.

"You should let me pay," Patricio said, his male pride being challenged.

"Chan Toy is paying for it." They both laughed.

They left the restaurant.

"What now?" asked Patricio.

"I know there is an Asian Historical Center here in Chinatown. Let's go find it," she showed him the address on her phone.

Three blocks later they were at a Mexican-Chinese community center. One of the buildings was the historical center. They entered. Tina spoke Cantonese to an elderly lady volunteer with two ivory front teeth, who in turn whispered to another lady. The two staffers spent at least twenty minutes looking at yellowed three by five cards in old wooden card catalogs cabinets. They were searching for Chan Toy.

The two volunteer ladies shook their heads no. They hadn't found anything.

Patricio then jumped in. "Ask her if she has any information about Chan Toy's wife, Ana." Tina did so. A quarter of an hour later, the lady said no.

Tina and Patricio thanked the staff. Tina slipped two five-hundred-peso notes into a little charity box as they were leaving the building. "The community should really set this place up with computers. Look at all the archives they have. That way people could research their families and relatives," Tina sighed.

Tina stopped in her tracks. “Wait! Let’s go back!” The next thing Patricio knew Tina was asking the volunteer to make another search.

Five minutes later Tina was taking photos of documents with her cellphone regarding Cajemé, the son of Chan Toy and Ana. There were records of Ana taking her three children Cajemé, Mario, and Rubí to Puebla. There was also a forwarding address in Tucson, Arizona.

The historical center closed, and Tina was emailing the documents to Professor Reynoso and Carlos, copying Patricio.

“What a day!” Patricio exhaled. “A lot was accomplished!”

“Thank you for your help. I couldn’t have done it without you.”

“I have an idea. Let’s celebrate,” Patricio had a devious smile. “You don’t have to work tomorrow. You bought lunch. Let me buy dinner.”

Tina knew that she had been outmaneuvered. “Where are we going?”

“Be patient. You’ll see.”

They found his SUV and drove down Cinco de Mayo Street and parked.

“This is Sanborn’s. It’s kind of a coffee shop restaurant chain.”

"But look at all the beautiful tiles covering this place. It looks like a palace," Tina was impressed.

"This is La Casa de Los Azulejos," Patricio put on his Mexican artifacts expert hat, "officially known as the Palacio de los Condes." He went on to explain its elaborate history. The blue and white Talavera tiles are from Puebla . . ."

Tina was enthralled. Patricio stopped and smiled at her. He looked her right in the eyes. He paused and then reached over and gently kissed her on the lips. She did not resist.

She stopped and put her hands on his strong chest. "I'm not sure this is a good idea."

He came closer and kissed her again.

CHAPTER 40 – PEKING DUCK

Friday, May 31, 2019

Vancouver, B.C.

"Boss lady," the panicky voice on the phone said in Mandarin. "Augustina is caught. We think that she is going to talk."

"What else do you know?" the Chinese woman demanded in a very curt manner.

"Cho says that police are questioning everyone and looking for missing documents. He thinks that Augustina is afraid and will tell them everything."

The Chinese woman was quiet for a moment. "I don't think they can trace it back to us. Give Cho a thousand pesos." She did not want to give out too much money for intelligence. Too much and the informants would make things up. Too little and no information was forthcoming.

"Yes, boss lady."

Seconds later the caller from Mexico City hung up. Lilí Song texted Hao Chin Martín and told him to meet her for dinner at the Golden Rabbit in Vancouver's Chinatown.

They met at the entry way and embraced. She was wearing an emerald-green wool business suit that contrasted with her bright red lipstick. He had on a checkered polyester sport coat and an open collared white shirt.

After they were seated, she ordered a glass of chardonnay and he a gin Martini, neat. “You seemed stressed, my bao bei,” he said.

“Nothing. It’s nothing,” then she told him about the afternoon’s phone call regarding Augustina’s arrest.

“They have no evidence.” He and Lilí had planned the theft. Lilí was upset but showed no outward signs of her fear. *Nothing was supposed to go wrong. They had levels of protection. He was the one who talked to Augustina! He’s a loser! He’s an idiot! Èyùn!*

“Well, we’ll have to stop doing business at the museum for a while,” he continued glibly. “Nobody can blame us.”

A nicely dressed waiter came over and was ready to take their order. Lilí ordered the lobster since Martín was going to pick up the tab and later that night, she would have to give him sex. She knew she was a whore.

Lilí Song’s long black hair hung over her very expensive clothes. She had been born in Shanghai 28 years earlier. She had a twin sister named Rubí who was ten minutes older. Her parents were very strict with the girls. They enrolled Rubí in ballet school. Lilí wanted to join her but wasn’t allowed. The parents could only afford to support one daughter. However, Lilí was born a math prodigy. She could multiply three numbers by three numbers almost instantaneously. For this reason, her parents forced Lilí to take business classes. She was always at the top of her class.

But the tragedy was that Rubí had fractured her ankle while practicing for Giselle. The medical team put in metal pins and told the parents that their daughter could no longer be a prima ballerina. However, the one who cried the most over this tragedy was Lilí. Life as a ballerina would have suited her. At first, she hated her twin sister for her own second-class status, but later realized it was really her parents' fault. Now the family would lose face and they would all be disgraced.

In college Lilí excelled in math and business. As a college junior, she began an internship in the Arbitrage Division of Shanghai Bank. A year after graduation, she was transferred to the Vancouver branch of the bank to work in its Antique Art Collections Section. She then worked with rare currencies. By the time she was 25, she was a second vice-president for Chinese Dragon Rare Elements Ltd. in Vancouver, B.C. She was fluent in Shanghainese and Mandarin, but not Cantonese. Her latter transfer and promotion were initiated by the PRC's Army Intelligence. She was now in charge of finding rare gems and elements.

She wolfed down the lobster. Lilí really had no allegiance to the People's Republic of China (PRC). Her only loyalty was to make money. Lots of it. Sure, she would deliver the turquoise colibrí amulet to Chinese Intelligence. Supposedly, it had magical powers. Okay. *Who cares anyway?* She wanted to flee the friggin' cold winters and rainy weather to move in with her sister in São Paolo.

"Hey, did I tell you my sister is coming up here in a few weeks? You and I need to reassess our plan and talk strategy. We need the professor and his group to find the turquoise hummingbird as soon as possible and give it to us. Then we can leave."

Hao Chin Martín may not have been the smartest guy, but he knew that Lilí was exploiting him. The thought of getting laid every once in a while and making lots of money intrigued him. The PRC had arranged a meeting with him and Lilí 18 months prior and directed them to procure the turquoise hummingbird amulet. For her, it was the money, but for him it was something else.

Hao Chin Martín was born in Beijing in 1981. His real name was Way Oh and his father had been in Chinese Army Intelligence for the PRC. His mother was a Buddhist monk. He had a yin and yang personality and was always following the latest trend. Neither parent approved of his behavior and beliefs.

He was a metallurgy engineering student at the University of Beijing when he decided to travel to Hong Kong in 1997 to join a mass protest strike against the Chinese government annexation. He was arrested and bludgeoned by the local police. The local magistrate had recommended ten years in prison. Way broke down and started to cry. He reached out to his father who had contacts within the PRC. A plea bargain was reached. Way would serve one year in a reeducation camp near the Mongolian border. Afterwards, he would work as a spy for Army Intelligence. By this time, Way was broken in spirit and ideology. After a year of starvation and deprivation, he was ready for the better things in life. If Way complied, his parents would no longer be subjected to shame and loss of prestige and privileges. Way wanted all of it to go away and so he agreed to the espionage.

The PRC was always looking for ways to corner the global markets on rare elements. One of their projects was to find the magical turquoise hummingbird amulet of the Chan Toy legends. There could be a multitude of possible uses in medical procedures, military weaponry, and parapsychology. All could bring in more economic growth, revenues, and prestige for the PRC.

A plan was concocted that involved appropriating the deceased Hao Chin Martín's name, and placing Way as the District Manager of Canada SinoMex Mining, Ltd. in

Vancouver, B.C. He was teamed up with Lilí Song of Chinese Dragon Rare Elements Ltd. also in Vancouver. For the sake of expediency, they became an item. Nothing special.

The strategy fell into place when Tina Fang spent the prior summer in São Paolo, Brazil, and befriended the twin sister, Rubí. Rubí had always told her sister everything, although Lili did not reciprocate. After discovering that Tina worked with historical artifacts and her professor's connections, Way and Lili plotted to co-opt the professor into finding the turquoise hummingbird amulet. Hao Chin Martín pretended to be a descendant of Chan Toy and a distant relative of Tina Fang. Tina was so gullible that she easily fell into the trap. Months later Professor Reynoso and two major universities were sucked into the conspiracy. The potential $5 million payoff was negligible compared to the potential rewards of recovering the turquoise hummingbird.

"We need to encourage Tina and the professor to expedite the search for the hummingbird," Way stated.

"Let me text the professor. He won't respond to any threats," Lilí was getting antsy. "I'll text him tonight and ask him what progress they are making."

"Are you going to offer them more money?" Way inquired. *How greedy are they?*

"Not yet," Lilí's forehead squinted. "The effect might be counterproductive. Let's proceed as if everything is normal."

They left the restaurant. Lilí pulled out a cigarette from her gold case and lit up.

"Don't forget to take a shower before we go to bed tonight," she frowned. She didn't know who or what smelled worse: Way or the durian fruit dessert?

PART V – PUEBLA

CHAPTER 41 – MISSING

Monday, June 3, 2019

Guadalajara

"How was your weekend?" Carlos asked. He set down a cup of coffee on Tina's desk. She whiffed the caffeinated fumes. She had traveler's fatigue from her work in Mexico City, not to mention Patricio's persistence that she should stay a little longer. And the night before had been Sunday dinner with the Ríos family, Professor Reynoso, and his wife. Before dinner, Mirasol was being needy and kept pestering Tina who just wanted to take a nap.

"Fine," she said noncommittedly, avoiding his perceptive stare. "I like Mexico City. Maybe I'll spend some time there before I go back home."

"Patricio likes you," Carlos added as he left the room.

Tina wondered what he knew but decided to put it out of her mind. She needed to focus on the new diaries that Leti had sent. Professor Reynoso had assigned the translations to her. They were in Spanish and were quite different from the original Chan Toy documents. Carlos, in turn, was to follow up on the maps, liaise with Patricio, and do a site visit to Puebla where Ana Chan and her children supposedly went after they fled Mexico City.

As she reviewed the documents, Tina took notes. She knew this was a different author, not Chan Yun Wu. For the moment, she presumed the new documents were written by Chan Toy's wife, Ana. The Spanish was basic and mostly phonetic. The spelling and punctuation were elementary. "Yo" was spelled out as "llo" and "señora" as "senyora." It would be slow going, but Tina was persistent.

***

1912

Mexico City

There was smoke and flames emanating from the downstairs portion of the Chan Toy mansion. The sound of footsteps was fading as the intruders fled.

"We need to seek refuge, señora," Ana's security captain Raúl Carmona strongly advised. He had come up to her room to warn her. "They may return. We were fortunate this time."

"We have to wait for my husband," Ana said in a plaintive tone. "I'll have the children start packing."

"Señora, we'll need to travel light." Raúl was trying to exercise tact and remain calm. He did not want his mistress to panic. "Which of the staff do you want to accompany us?"

"Everyone."

"But señora, we only have one carriage."

"For right now then, you and a few guards. Both cooks. I don't know who else."

"That seems sufficient. Let's limit the baggage to two each for you and the children; and one small suitcase for everyone else. That still may be too heavy for our carriage."

"Let's have two of the guards drive the wagon. One to ride along."

"Good idea."

"We should leave as soon as possible."

"Raúl, we will wait until my husband arrives. Make sure the cooks pack food and some wine."

"Yes, señora."

Ana packed her most expensive silk clothes that she had transported from Guangzhou. She also grabbed her jewelry.

She went into the children's room and inspected their suitcases. "Only one toy! Each of you must bring three books."

"Oh, mom!" there was communal whining.

She made sure they had enough socks and underwear.

"Mario, not those shoes. The black ones."

"But, mom!"

Ana went downstairs and talked to the two cooks. They were grateful for being brought along.

The smell of burnt wood was acrid and overwhelming. Her eyes were burning. Furniture was strewn everywhere. Wall hangings had been torn down. The house was virtually uninhabitable. They had no choice but to leave.

Ana walked back upstairs. She paused and exhaled. Her heart was racing. "Raúl, please come with me."

The two walked into her bedroom and proceeded to the back of her closet. She moved some hat boxes and behind them was a small Asian motif chest with a rectangular base of thirty by forty centimeters. She pointed to the strong box.

"We'll need to bring this," Ana directed. "Guard this with your life. This is all we have. Our survival, . . . and yours, depend on it."

Raúl nodded and bowed. He hoisted it up on his shoulder.

Ana tried to go back down to the parlor, but the wreckage was overwhelming. She would wait for her husband Chan Toy. Everybody was on standby. She laid on her bed fully clothed. Ana had to be ready. She had her children do likewise. They would have very little time to escape the unknown dangers.

About an hour later, there was a loud knocking on the front door, or what was left of it. One of the servants answered and soon ran up the stairs to awaken Ana. Minutes later Ana came downstairs with a greyish shawl draped over her traveling clothes. In the foyer stood a young Mexican man. Actually, he was more of a boy.

"Excuse me for intruding, Señora Toy," he politely addressed. "But I'm sorry to bring you bad news. Our bank was attacked last night. I work closely with Señor Toy . . ." He didn't mention in what capacity.

This can only be tragic, Ana pressed one hand into the other.

"There was blood everywhere, but no bodies were found. Your husband is missing. But we did find this. We think it is his because he is the only one that ever wears this type of hat."

Ana recognized Chan Toy's skull cap. Her eyes started to moisten. She inhaled. *What am I going to do now?* She was descended from a line of strong women. She would survive. She would overcome. Mexican-Yaqui blood ran through her veins!

Raúl came through the front door. “Señora?” he said with quizzical eyes.

Ana dismissed the messenger and then addressed her guardsman. “We are leaving as soon as possible. Get the last-minute things packed.”

“Yes, señora.”

“And you have the . . . box safely put away?”

“Yes, señora.”

Ana started to walk away when Raúl called after her. “And your husband? Are we going to wait for him?”

“Unfortunately, he’s gone missing. “I will leave a note on the kitchen table and let him know that we have left and where we are going.”

“Very good, señora,” Raúl replied. “And where are we going?”

CHAPTER 42 – NEW ARRIVALS

1912

Puebla, Mexico

Ana stared at the slip of paper in her hand. It had the address of a friend of Chan Toy's. Doña Filomena Antuñano lived in the Puebla area. The trek had been miserable for Ana and her entourage. No one had been able to sleep except the children. Ten-year-old Cajemé leaned against his mother's shoulder while his younger brother Mario was balled up in a corner of the carriage. Baby Maya's hair was being stroked by her buxom nanny Berta Pacheco.

It was late afternoon when the carriage pulled up in front of the cathedral facing the plaza in Puebla. One of Raúl Carmona's guardsmen found the directions to the Antuñano residence after a few inquiries to the very polite local citizenry. The pace of life here seemed relaxed. Men and women were elegantly dressed as they walked up and down the streets. Seeing the colorful buildings mixed with Baroque and Spanish colonial styled architecture was like strolling through an art gallery. Minutes later the tired travelers made their way out of town toward the 17th century church of Nuestra Señora de Los Remedios in Cholula and the Popocatépetl Volcano. At a pine tree copse, the lone guardsman turned right; the coach followed him. The narrow, red lava rock path zigzagged up a hill. At the top was a walled, pinkish palatial mansion. Ana thought they had crossed into a foreign country. The estate was enormous.

An hour later Ana and her three children were in an elaborate waiting room parlor eating fruits, breads, and cheeses. The walls were covered with decorative tapestries. As there was no tea, Ana imbibed on strong coffee with lots of cream.

"Is there anything you need, Señora Toy?" the ebony-skinned ama de casa with a big derriere, Salomé, politely asked in her coastal accent. "Madame Antuñano should be coming home shortly. Please make yourself comfortable. We'll figure out everything when she gets here."

"And Raúl and the others?" Ana inquired. She was concerned about her staff. They were part of her family.

"The guards are in the horse stable quarters, señora. Your other staff are staying with the household servants. I think they are eating," Salomé smiled. She wanted to put the young woman at ease.

It was almost nine o'clock when a short, full-bodied woman entered the parlor. The 67-year-old-woman with cloudy hazel eyes was dressed in a long black dress with a red scarf around her neck. The woman had long silver, grey hair all in ringlets. Her face was smothered in makeup. The children had been sent upstairs to clean up and retire to bed. Ana remained in the parlor.

"I had heard that you were coming. I know something of what happened to Chan Toy, but I don't know the details," the older woman smiled and held out her hand for Ana to shake. "I'm Filomena Antuñano and you've met Salomé. Welcome to our humble abode. We'll make sure that you are comfortable."

Ana smiled. "Doña Antuñano, thank you for your gracious hospitality. We were given your name . . ."

Ana explained the recent events in Mexico City and the presumed death of her husband Chan Toy. "And here we are. How do you know my husband?" Ana was talking in the present tense. She didn't want to believe that her husband was dead.

"Please call me Filomena, my dear," the old woman said. "Señor Toy and I both did business with Señor Tao at the East-West Bank. I was one of your husband's clients."

The two shared short personal histories. Ana was very guarded in what she revealed. She was sure that Filomena had done the same.

"For now, your family and staff will stay with us," the older woman smiled. "We will see how things work out."

"You are very kind, Doña Filomena."

"Huh! If you only knew what people around here say about me behind my back, my child" the elderly woman chortled. "One thing though. Where did you get that exquisite blouse?"

Ana was wearing a white silk blouse with tiny peony flowers embroidered on the bottom right-hand corner of the garment.

"Guangzhou," Ana replied. "China." She had packed all of her silk blouses and other pieces of clothing in their escape.

"I'm in the textile business," Filomena understated. She owned the largest cloth enterprise in the valley, manufacturing everything from simple women's wear to haute couture. "And I love your outfit. Maybe we can talk more about it tomorrow. You probably should rest and get things in order. We have plenty of time."

With that, Filomena took her leave and Salomé escorted Ana up to a guest bedroom. It smelled of lavender. Ana checked on the three children and Berta, the nanny. Everybody was asleep. Ana came back to her room and cleaned up. The next thing Ana heard was the sound of a rooster crowing as the morning light lit up her face. She could have slept on for days. The escape to Puebla had physically and emotionally drained her.

Ana's children were in three separate bedrooms. The mansion seemed to have dozens and dozens of rooms. Portraits of whiskered gentlemen and ruddy cheeked ladies were conspicuous everywhere. The carpets looked like they had been part of the Alhambra.

"Hurry up and get dressed!" she ordered her children.

She felt a presence behind her. "Señora, please follow me," announced one of servants dressed in a black dress uniform.

"And my children?"

"Salomé will look after them."

Ana remembered the very serious ama de casa. The large black woman seemed to have a stern disposition. Her own housekeeper was nowhere to be found, and she had only seen the nanny, Berta, minutes earlier with Maya.

Ana had only superficially made her toilet but had managed to change her clothes. As the pair walked down the stairs, they exited to a courtyard with a fountain in the middle. Several of the walls were tiled from floor to ceiling.

"Good morning, my dear," Doña was seated under a gazebo dipping her bolillo into her ornate cup filled with steaming hot coffee. Ana stared a second too long.

"I'm from Veracruz," she laughed. Ana observed that half this woman's teeth were missing and severely were discolored. Ana gave a courteous chuckle.

"How did you sleep?" There was an awkward smile.

For the next half hour, the pair made small talk and got to know each other better, while Ana nibbled on breakfast foods brought to the table. The food was very different from what she was used to. Similarly, Filomena barely ate anything. Part of a banana, some soft cheese, and a hard-boiled egg.

"We are so grateful for your hospitality and kindness," Ana said again softly. Doña Filomena Antuñano had offered Ana and her household an indefinite stay.

"In a little while, I will go the textile factory. I want you to take a few days and rest. We'll see if we hear anything more about Chan Toy.

***

A few days later, Doña Filomena again had breakfast with Ana,

“Ana, I have been thinking. I am a businesswoman. I inherited this textile enterprise from my late husband. I think I could use your help.”

Ana looked bewildered. *What can I possibly offer to this rich business magnate?*

“My haute couture line has been faltering lately. With the threat of the Mexican Revolution and cheap French imports, sales have dropped off. My designs are stale. That’s why I need you to assist me.”

Ana was shocked.

“You have been wearing beautiful white silk blouses with subtle designs on the hem line. Simple, but chic. Silk would be too expensive to use. But we have lots and lots of high-quality cotton. We could combine your designs with our materials.”

At the textile factory, they talked with the designers and production managers. They decided to make a limited run for the local market.

The following weeks brought the project to fruition. Cajemé and Mario were being tutored by a local professor five days a week. Baby Maya was being cared for by Berta and spoiled by Salomé. Life was good for Ana.

“Ana, why do always wear that pouch?” Filomena asked Ana one day. “It looks so plain.”

“It’s for protection and healing.” Ana made a mental note to keep the medicine bag under her blouse. Too many curious eyes.

Ana’s domestic staff from Mexico City had very little to do. She and Doña Filomena Antuñano found them employment in other local households. As for her security team, Ana gave Raúl, the three other guards, and Albina several gold coins as they left the mansion to return to Mexico City.

“Thank you, Raúl,” there was a tear in her eye as she bade him goodbye. She wanted to ask him to try to find out what happened to her husband, Chan Toy, but she didn’t. She wanted to grieve but didn’t want to give up hope. Chan Toy had been her protector, friend, and spouse. She owed him a lot. She would keep his memory alive.

It was at this moment that she decided to start writing her diary.

CHAPTER 43 – HAUTE COUTURE

1912

Puebla

Ana nervously smiled as she was introduced to la crème de la crème of the Puebla upper classes. She wore her latest Colibri outfit. In the beginning the signature design was a blue colibrí with some embroidered red flowers. This outfit was easy to manufacture because it was made from cotton that was cheaper and more available than silk. The machinery at the textile factory was set up for this kind of production. It allowed for greater efficiencies for the garment workers who did not have to learn a new technique.

"Señora Toy, I would like you to meet the mayor's wife."

"I simply love your new outfit. So indigenous and yet so elegant."

"Were you a fashion model in China?"

The social events happened at least twice a week. If the get togethers were scheduled Monday through Thursday, Filomena and Ana would go to all of them. Locals thought Ana was Mexican. Others wondered if she was Chinese. There were so many incongruous things about her. Filomena knew everyone and, moreover, everyone knew her. However, women tried to emulate her. Men tried to give her a wide berth. A simple whisper by her could lead to a person's social demise. On the weekends Filomena went to her casino and hotel to oversee her businesses.

During the week a coach drove Ana to the textile factory at the edge of town. Her children stayed at the mansion. The boys were being educated in proper Spanish. Cajemé still retained his basic Cantonese proficiency, but Mario did not. And as far as Maya was concerned, Ana had caught Salomé dancing with the baby in her arms in the parlor on several occasions. Ana always made it a point to converse with her children in Spanish or Cantonese at least an hour per day. Sometimes right after breakfast or at bedtime if she didn't have to go out.

The workers in the plant were all young women. But upon close observation, they looked older and worn out. The hours of operation were long but not very difficult. They all wore white smocks. Even though the place was well-ventilated, there seemed to be a lot of wheezing within.

One evening when Ann and Filomena were in the parlor talking about what to name the latest line of clothing, Filomena leaned forward and started to go into a coughing fit. Ana reached over and tried to slap her back. That didn't work. The older woman's tongue was sticking out.

Underneath Ana's blouse, there was a pulsating. It was coming from her pouch. The skin on her chest touching the bag started to get warm. There was a sharp shrieking sound.

"Salomé! Come quick!" Ana cried out.

Filomena's face was turning red. Her body was convulsing.

Instinctively, Ana reached under her blouse and pulled out the turquoise colibrí amulet that was radiating heat. She whispered some words and holding the stone bird in her hand, made circles over Filomena's nose and lungs.

The coughing did not cease.

Salomé ran into the room and was shocked at the sight.

"Do you know what is happening to her?" Ann asked loudly.

"No. Not really."

"Has she had this coughing fit before?"

"Yes," Salomé was answering nervously. "What should we do?"

"Call her doctor!"

"Okay."

"And make her some chamomile tea."

"Okay."

"With honey and lemon."

An hour later Doctor Ojeda found Doña Antuñano sitting up in her large bed propped up by pillows. She was sipping hot tea.

"Doña Antuñano, are you all right now?" the doctor had rushed to her side and did some preliminary examinations. "You seemed to have recovered."

"Thanks to my loyal companion Ana."

"I just want you to relax, Doña," the doctor said softly. He knew better than to confront her. It would be futile. Instead, he pulled Ana outside the bedroom.

"Señora, thank you for saving her life. I hate to say this, but she could have choked to death but for your quick reactions."

Ana did not care to explain the curative powers of the turquoise colibrí.

"Doctor, what exactly is the matter?"

"She has bynninosis," the doctor adjusted his wire-rimmed glasses. "The locals call it brown lung disease. It's caused by inhaling cotton dust."

"Do some of the girls at the factory have it?"

"Unfortunately, yes."

"We didn't know."

Ana took her leave of the doctor.

In the morning Filomena was soaking her bolillo into her strong coffee.

"It was nothing to be concerned about, but thank you for helping me," she said to Ana.

"Doña, with your permission, I would like to talk to some of the girls at the factory. The ones who cough a lot. Maybe I can help them."

"Sure. Go right ahead. Healthy workers mean more production and that means more profits," the older woman grinned.

For the next few months, Ana visited the workplace and tried to identify the worst cases among the women workers. At their limited meal breaks, Ana would ask them some questions, examine them, and undertake the turquoise colibrí healing process. Over the course of a short period of time, the results were mixed. For some, the wheezing stopped completely; for others there was no change.

However, word of Ana's healing powers spread near and far. She would be met at the factory's door as she was leaving, by dozens of townspeople begging for her assistance.

"My hands are swollen, and I am in pain all the time."

"I'm bleeding all the time. It won't stop," the youngish woman pointed to her lower abdomen.

"My stomach always hurts. I can't take a shit."

Finally, Ana decided to take the bull by the horns and talk to Doña Filomena.

"Doña, I need a room by the factory to see sick people. I want to help them," Ana was not asking, but almost demanding.

The elderly woman was silent. "How can I deny you? You cured me. It would be cruel and unfair to deny others. Whatever you need, we will provide."

Thus, Ana began her clinic in one of the storage buildings of the factory. A woman was hired to do scheduling. It was only open on Mondays. A few assistants were also brought in.

The nature of Ana's interaction with high society changed drastically. Instead of having to explain the different types of embroidery, the town leaders wanted to know about contagious diseases (e.g., syphilis) and influenzas. Inexplicably, the sales of the Colibri haute couture doubled. Both Ana and Filomena were happy.

The people who were not so pleased were the local doctors who called Ana a quack and the parish priests who characterized Ana as a witch.

CHAPTER 44 – PUTAS

1913

Puebla

The months were flying by. There had been sporadic correspondence between Ana and her former security captain, Raúl Carmona. The Chan Toy mansion had been gutted and quartered by the revolutionists. Raúl and his men were now providing security for Mr. Tao and the East-West Bank because of daily acts of vandalism. With the assistance of local federal troops, Raúl had been so far successful against the onslaught. He also reported that the body of Chan Toy had never been found and was presumed dead. After the second letter, Ana resigned herself. Chan Toy was gone.

Ana spent the next day isolated in her bedroom. She cried. She grieved. One of her children knocked on her door. She couldn't open it. After a while she inhaled deeply. She had to regain her strength and talents. She was responsible for her family, just like her mother and grandmother before her. They were all tough women, seasoned to survive. *Mexican-Yaqui blood!*

Things started to get better. Ana was enjoying her freedom and independence from the male-dominated world. Doña Filomena and her textile factory were doing well. She was making money. A new line of blouses and skirts in red, blue, and green colors was successful. Not so much locally because the market was small and the women did not want to be seen wearing the same outfit as a friend, but there was high demand from Mexico City. Her textile factory manager, Ysidro Mondragon, discussed trying to expand their distribution to Guadalajara, but they already owed too much money to the East-West Bank.

It was a Monday morning when Ana and Filomena pulled up in their carriage in front of the textile factory. All the workers were inside working. Ana's makeshift clinic was in a separate building at one end of the property. Today she saw a dozen people or so waiting for her in front of the building. *Going to be a busy day!* she thought, clutching the medicine pouch underneath her blouse.

Ana walked toward the clinic. The small crowd stared at her as she approached. They did not look like potential clients to her. As she got closer, she noticed that some of them were gazing at some writing on the building wall. The letters were large and in black print. They spelled, "PUTAS." Human or dog feces were also splattered around the graffiti.

Ana grabbed a handkerchief from her skirt and covered her mouth. Tears flowed down her cheeks. Instinctively, Filomena had the driver ride over to the front of the clinic. From afar she observed the handiwork of the hooligans.

"Bastards!" Filomena said aloud.

While she was not shocked at the Doña's language, she was surprised that her companion had said it so vocally.

"Do you know who did this, Filomena?" the two had resorted to talking informally between themselves."

"I have a good idea," Doña had a scowl on her wrinkled face. "Probably some of Father Gallegos' boys."

Ana knew that there were rumblings throughout Mexico about limiting the powers of the Catholic Church. There was intense conflict between the government and the church about who should govern the people. Los Cristeros had been organizing.

"Father Gallegos was a nemesis to my husband, Próspero. Always threatening to excommunicate him for this or that. But my husband was never intimidated. He supported me and my work."

Ana walked back to the factory entrance trying to gather her thoughts. She ran into Ysidro, the middle-aged plant manager, who was broad shouldered and wore a dress shirt with a leather vest.

"Ysidro, have some of your boys clean up this mess," barked Filomena. "And repaint the wall. Those bastards. They will pay."

"Yes, Doña."

"Ysidro, have guards posted. I'm sorry it has come to this. If you catch anybody, make sure you teach them a lesson before turning them over to the authorities."

An hour later Ana was tending to her patients in a waiting room of the main building. There was little privacy, but everyone understood the situation. The patients were all factory women anyway.

Filomena was furious. She wouldn't let it go. She pouted and yelled for the next few days. Nobody dared talk to her.

A week later pairs of federal soldiers were also patrolling the perimeter of the cotton textile factory. The daily newspaper reported that three young men had been apprehended. They resisted arrest and were restrained by the authorities. Each of the trio suffered a broken right arm. They were purportedly part of a group called the Cristeros who were strong supporters of the Catholic Church.

The next day, two of the municipal council members called upon Father Gallegos.

They warned him to cease these demonstrations against Doña Filomena. If there was more vandalism, even he would be thrown in jail.

"You're protecting this harlot and her whores over me, a holy man," the priest raged with spittle coming from the corners of his mouth.

"She brings money into the pueblo. And jobs. And Señora Ana cures people. What do you do? You leech off the poor to buy gold for your false idols!"

Despite the bluster, the priest got the message. Things got back to normal.

Then groups of foreigners from other countries started coming into town. There were more federal soldiers. Sales started to slow down again.

"What is happening, Doña?" Ana asked her one day.

"The Mexican Revolution has everyone frightened. Nobody wants to buy anything. My hotel business is doing very well," Filomena grinned sheepishly. "There seem to be a lot of German tourists and investors moving here."

Ana had heard similar things in her last letter from Raúl who was still in Mexico City.

***

By December, her family had settled in. Christmas and the New Year's found Ana and her children content and grateful. El Día de Los Reyes came and Ana went to the clinic. She brought some special baked treats for her patients.

When Ana arrived home, there was a pall of gloom over the house. Salomé was downstairs in the parlor sobbing. The children were with her.

"What happened? What's wrong?" Ana's eyes were searching Salomé's face.

The housekeeper took her hand and the two slowly walked up the stairs. Standing inside Filomena's bedroom was Doctor Alvarez, her physician.

"She passed late this afternoon," the doctor sad sadly. "There was no pain."

Salomé took Ana into a side parlor. The latter was in shock.

"She was a good lady. She was very noble and charitable," Salomé sniffled. "She took care of us. I owe her everything."

Ana nodded.

"Unfortunately, she died of syphilis."

Ana was surprised but did not react.

"Doña Filomena was courageous. She was born in Córdoba and was sold to a brothel in Veracruz. We worked together in a brothel that serviced a lot of sailors and soldiers. She was a rare beauty and men were always selecting her for a night of pleasure. One of the soldiers from the fort became overly possessive and was always trying to spend time with her. Unfortunately, Filomena was also the favorite of Capitán Antuñano of the fort."

"In Veracruz?"

"Yes. One night the soldier beat her and slashed her face with a razor. The captain found out and had the soldier apprehended by two hired thugs. They beat the soldier and castrated him. He was put on a ship bound for who knows where. The doctors did what they could. She had always been self-conscious about the scar on her face. She was in pain and in despair."

"How old was she when this happened?"

"About 15 or 16, I think. Captain Próspero Antuñano was soon thereafter ordered to Puebla. Being a man of honor, he married Filomena. He fought at the first Battle of Puebla and was promoted to general for his bravery. Afterwards, he started the cotton textile factory that we have now. All the workers were prostitutes, like me. The Doña saved us. She gave us a better life."

For the next few weeks, Filomena's household was in disarray. Nobody knew what to do. It was as if the queen bee of the hive had died.

The textile factory manager, Ysidro Mondragon, was doing the best he could without direction. There was talk of several companies, both domestic and foreign, wanting to buy the enterprise.

The speculation was quashed when Próspero's nephew arrived from Monterrey. Ernest Antuñano had a wooden leg and walked with a cane. He was pudgy and had salt and pepper whiskers and a handlebar moustache.

"Who is in charge here?" he asked gruffly as he entered the textile factory. Ysidro was intimidated. He wanted to keep his job, and he didn't want foreign investors to take over. He thought he would make the best of it. There had been indications that the war in Europe was going spread around the globe. There was increased German investment from abroad in Mexico. Germany was trying to backdoor its way into North American via Mexico. Mexico had a tenuous relationship with the United States, because the latter always trying to pilfer oil from its southern neighbor. But Mexico need the hard currency and did not want to bite the hand that fed it. Therefore, Mexico decided to take advantage of the situation, both politically and economically. The Mexican Revolution had impacted its financial solvency. Within weeks, the new Antuñano company was making uniforms for Great Britain.

As for Ana, she disliked Ernesto Antuñano from their first encounter.

"Who are you and what are you doing here?" he demanded as he waltzed in the front door of the mansion without knocking.

Ana had never seen such behavior and was not going to tolerate it. "We were wards of your late aunt Doña Filomena. She was a very charitable woman."

"Well, I didn't know who you were," Ernesto blustered. "You understand."

"With your permission, we will pack and depart from here in a few days," Ana said in a neutral tone. "We are going to need a carriage and horses. We will send them back, of course, once we reach our destination.

"Take whatever time you need," he said dismissively. "The carriage, go ahead and take it. I have my own anyway."

Two days later Ana was saying goodbye to Salomé. "Are you sure you don't want to come with us. The kids will miss you."

Salomé nodded no. There were big tears running down those jet cheeks. She reached under her shawl and pulled out a brown leather purse. “Doña Filomena wanted you to have this. I will miss all of you.”

A stable hand from the household was driving them to their destination.

“Mom,” Cajemé asked as he leaned against his mother inside the carriage. “Where are we going?”

“Vamos a volver a nuestra tierra.” As she said that, she felt a warmth emitting from the pouch with the turquoise colibrí.

PART VI – THE PURSUIT

CHAPTER 45 – STAFF MEETING

Tuesday, June 11, 2019

Guadalajara

It had rained all morning. Francisco let his driver Esteban drop him off at the Social Studies Building at the U of G. Tina and Carlos would be in attendance at the prearranged meeting and Patricio would join them by teleconference since he was unable to fly up Guadalajara in time.

They would be meeting in a board room that had three dozen chairs rather than three, and a large video monitor hung on the front wall. On the long, light-colored conference table, there was strong coffee and green tea. As a rare treat, Carlos had brought some mango slices sprinkled with chile. The trio devoured the fruit like it was candy.

At around ten o'clock they tried to start the meeting. The video portion of the screen did not work, but the sound did. The AV person tried for about fifteen minutes but was unsuccessful.

"Patricio, are you okay going with just the audio."

"No problem, professor. Just don't talk about me. I'll be able to hear you."

The four laughed. This was a good group, Francisco thought. It was a dream team. He even liked Patricio, because Patricio reminded him of a younger version of himself.

"Okay, Tina, let's begin with you," Francisco began to orchestrate the session in the large room that echoed his voice.

"You all received my text," Tina started. "You should have copies of my latest translations of the new documents. They most likely were written as diaries by Ana Azuleta Toy. As you may recall, Ana was the young daughter of Joya Azuleta. Ana became the very young bride of Chan Toy, when they fled Mexico and eventually ended up in China."

"They're in Spanish?" Patricio asked over the static of the teleconference call.

"The documents are in Spanish . . . rudimentary language," Tina added. She was not looking at Francisco whose face reddened slightly for being a pocho and not totally proficiently in Spanish. "I did these translations from Spanish into English."

Tina went on to summarize the life of Ana with Chan Toy and their three children in China and later when they returned Mexico.

"The logs start when Ana and her children escaped Mexico City and went to Puebla during the Mexican Revolution. Her husband Chan Toy went missing and was never found. They suspected he was murdered by some revolutionaries. Ana's writing style is very basic. The diaries only covered her stay in Puebla. Unfortunately, the writings end when Ana and her children leave Puebla. There is no mention of where they went after that."

"Thank you, Tina," Francisco frowned. *What's going to be our next step?* "Carlos, you're up next."

"I am meeting with Doctor Pinteiro at the museum," Carlos said in an upbeat tone. "He thinks that he knows what Map #1 depicts. He is between 95 and 98 percent certain. As to Map #2, he thinks he has narrowed it down to some mines in northern Mexico.

A voice squawked from the spider shaped speaker in the middle of the conference table. "Carlos, I suggest you and I visit the sites," said Patricio in a static-laden voice.

“Sounds like a good idea,” Francisco quickly responded. He knew that Patricio had gone to some sort of mining school in Monterrey.

Carlos concurred.

Next, Patricio reported on the progress of the investigation of the international theft ring. The museum employee was singing like a canary.

“Okay, gang, what’s our next step? How are we going to find the turquoise hummingbird?” the professor asked.

“Do we have a deadline?” Tina asked. She knew that she had to go back to school in late August. She didn’t want to leave the professor and Carlos hanging.

“I’ll need to contact Ms. Song and give her a progress report soon,” the professor needed to communicate with the project’s client.

“Lilí Song. . . You mean Lilí Song?” Tina voiced.

“Yes. Sure!” Professor Reynoso was surprised by her interruption. “Are you concerned about something?”

“Well, no. I mean, yes,” Tina’s spoke nervously. “It’s only that her sister, Rubí, is coming to visit me.”

“Lilí Song’s sister?” Patricio burst out suddenly in an overly loud voice. “When?”

“Friday,” Tina was surprised at Patricio’s reaction. “Why? Is there something wrong?”

Professor Reynoso had not seen this coming. He needed to control the situation before unintended consequences blew up in their face. “Let’s take a ten-minute break.”

The professor hurried out the door and ran into the men’s restroom. He looked around. There was no one else in there. He took out this cellphone and dialed Patricio’s direct line.

“I’m sorry, professor,” Patricio had calmed down. “But Lilí is a person of interest in all of these thefts. We can’t let Tina get involved. Things may go sideways.”

“Patricio, I agree with you,” Francisco was trying to take control. “There is a high probability that Lilí Song is up to her eyes in these crimes. You probably have enough evidence to arrest her. At this point Rubí’s involvement is unknown. But you can’t arrest Lilí unless she is on Mexican soil. Maybe Rubí can lure her down to Mexico.”

The two talked for a few minutes.

“Neither one of us wants to deceive Tina,” the professor spoke. “We can’t lie to her. But we can’t tell her everything.”

Five minutes later the group was back at it. Patricio was quiet.

“Okay, where were we?” Reynoso pivoted to the next agenda item. “So, we think the trail is cold. What do we do?”

"Keep looking for more clues," Patricio contributed. "That's what we do with our investigations. That's why they take so long." There was a little laughter.

"I'll talk more with Doctor Pinteiro on Friday and try to get some additional insight from him. The maps must have clues."

"And I think I should reread Chan Toy's papers and Ana's diaries," Tina was pensive. "This is like a puzzle with many pieces missing."

"Well, let's make this a game. We are trying to find the turquoise hummingbird amulet and we are given the Rosetta Stone."

"Every person contained in the papers is dead," Carlos remarked. "I think we should concentrate on places. And prioritize them."

The professor stood up and moved the whiteboard closer to the table. He started writing as comments began flowing.

"All the sites mentioned in Ana's diaries . . . Mexicali, México City, Puebla, . . ."

"Probably China and Mexicali are the least likely."

"And we don't know where she went after Mexico City."

"We have never found out where she died. That would be a logical place to look."

Lunch time was approaching, and they were all hungry. But the discussion was dynamic and productive.

“Let’s select some sites,” Francisco flipped the whiteboard. “Let’s use one-week timelines that we can always adjust. Carlos, since you are going to be in Mexico City, you can do research there.”

“Puebla seems to be important. I’ll do that one,” Reynoso smiled. “I had a visiting professorship there a million years ago.”

“Tina, your time is committed, and Rubí is coming to visit you,” Reynoso did not want to exclude her. “In addition to rereading Chan Toy’s papers and Ana’s diaries, I want you to research Mexicali. See if Ana ever returned there. Better yet, try to find out where she died. And see what became of her children.”

Tina nodded. She was going to pull her weight. As she had been brought up, her personal life was secondary to her work.

CHAPTER 46 – HORSEMEAT

Friday, June 14, 2019

Mexico City

"You missed a spot, mi amor," Alex softly brushed the back of her hand up Francisco's cheek. Francisco randomly alternated between three-days beard growth and clean shaven. It seemed counterintuitive, but trimming the growth was more difficult than the clean cut.

Alex, as an endocrinologist, was used to getting up at 4 a.m. a few days a week for performing thyroid and pancreatic procedures. And today, Francisco was catching an early morning flight to Mexico City. This pre-dawn coffee between the spouses was a rare treat.

"What time is your operation?" Francisco sipped his decaffeinated latte.

"Six," she looked beautiful with her hair uncombed and dressed only in her semi-open night gown. "Don't forget about our celebration dinner Sunday night with Miranda and Sol. Mirasol will have a fit if we don't show up." Mirasol had just received a letter of acceptance from Duke University. She was now waiting for Stanford. However, she was mentally crossing the University of Bologna off her list.

Twenty minutes later they kissed goodbye.

"See you tomorrow," she said in a soft voice.

Francisco met Carlos at the airport. They were both toting overnight bags. They grabbed some breakfast burritos and boarded the plane to Mexico City in jovial spirits.

At the Mexico City Airport, Francisco went to the car rental office. He had rented a car to drive to Puebla. Meanwhile, Carlos waited outside of baggage claim and was picked up by Patricio. They found a little hole in the wall dining spot and Carlos had his second breakfast of the day. *Nothing like huevos rancheros!* They chatted about the Chan Toy Project and the likelihood of finding the turquoise hummingbird.

"Doctor Pinteiro said he has some good stuff for me," Carlos rubbed his hands together and wiggled excitedly on the hard wood chair. "We'll see."

They were talking some more when Patricio suddenly blurted out, "Is Tina seeing someone? Is she serious about anyone?"

"I don't know," Carlos did not want to give his friend the green light. Tina was his friend and colleague. "You should ask her."

"What if she breaks my heart?" Patricio was being earnest.

"Then we'll sacrifice you to the gods."

The museum opened at nine o'clock. Doctor Pinteiro offered them coffee as they sat in his paper stacked office. Carlos politely declined. His bladder was ready to explode.

After some social chit chat, Doctor Pinteiro brought out Map #1. He had a paper copy of it for both Carlos and Patricio.

He began to describe the document. "This was written on paper consistent with record keeping on Spanish ships in the nineteenth century. The cartographer was right-handed and mostly likely a native Spanish speaker. Notice the bold strokes . . ." For the next quarter hour Pinteiro droned on. Carlos and Patricio tuned out.

"So, doctor, what is Map #1 of?" Carlos finally said.

"I can say with about 95% assurance is that it is the shipping route of a Spanish ship between Mexico and China. Let's compare it to a Google map." They did so and it was reasonably close. By the end of the nineteenth century world maps were fairly accurate. However, satellite photos have since filled in the gaps."

"So, doctor, if someone who was not a real cartographer drew a map like this, what was the reason?"

"The most obvious motive, Carlos, is to preserve a memory or an event."

Patricio inserted himself, "Doctor, was this a trans-Pacific journey from Mexico to China, China to Mexico, or round trip?"

"That's a good question," Pinteiro laughed. "During these times ships were carrying hundreds of Chinese workers from China to the New World. On the other hand, goods were being shipped from Mexico to the Orient."

They ruminated on the topic for another half hour. Then Carlos sprang to life.

"¡Mierda!" Carlos called out. "How could I be so pendejo? According to all the manuscripts, Chan Toy, Ana, and the children were coming back to Mexico from China. The map had to be drawn by Ana. She wrote the word "Volver" on the bottom of the map. They were returning! I don't see any other possible explanation."

"I think that is a good hypothesis," Doctor Pinteiro calmly said trying to mollify Carlos's excitement. "However, unless

Ana was a cartographer, she had to have copied a map that someone on board had made."

"Let's look at Map #2. But let's take a break first. Old man's disease."

Carlos jetted out of the room ahead of Pinteiro and went straight to the men's room. He had thought that he was going to die. When he came back, there was a plate filled with pumpkin quinoa protein bars. Patricio was already gobbling his second one.

"Now, as to Map #2, we used Google satellite map overlays," Pinteiro handed out several topographical depictions. "I think we have narrowed it to an area more specifically around the State of Sonora. We think that the black spot marked on the map is in the vicinity of the Cananea mining region."

"Where's that?" Carlos asked.

"It's in the northern, southern, eastern, or western part of the State of Sonora region. Choose one!" Patricio asserted himself. "I worked there one summer when I was taking mining classes. We labored in the high desert and dry climate when we were not crawling down some dang tunnel that went who knew where. This was Yaqui and Apache land, so you know that the living is tough. Lots of copper mining. Mexicans, gringos, and chinos have poured in there throughout the years."

"I've never heard of it," Carlos admitted.

“The land was taken from the Apaches by the Spanish. ‘Cananea’ is the Apache word for ‘horsemeat,” Pinteiro continued. “The Spanish called it the ‘city of copper.’ They later sold off the mines to a U.S. conglomerate. It played an integral part in the Mexican Revolution with strikes and federalist intervention. Local government had a hands-off policy which allowed the copper company to act with impunity. It became a mining town and controlled the local business practices.”

“Why didn’t Mexico do something about this?” Carlos was stirred by the exploitation of the local people.

“It did!” Pinteiro said sarcastically. “They sought more foreign investors. They sold themselves to the devil.”

The discussion went on for a few more hours. Doctor Pinteiro had a luncheon appointment, so, the meeting was over by one o’clock

Carlos had several hours to kill before his flight home back to Guanajuato. He and Patricio decided to grab a beer or two at Max’s Cantina. It was the start of Happy Hour, so the two were all in. They started with a few ice-cold Coronas and an overpriced order of guacamole. Then they went to shots of mezcal and street tacos.

“That was a very interesting meeting,” Carlos was shaking his head. “Doctor Pinteiro is one smart dude. I think we may have picked up a clue or two.”

“I will try to hit up a buddy to get more information about the Cananea mines. It might be a lead to finding the turquoise colibrí amulet.”

“One thing I don’t understand, Patricio. What does a turquoise specimen have to do with a copper mine?”

Patricio smiled. It was gentle smile, not a malignant one. “The simple answer is that turquoise is derived from a form of copper. The technical explanation is that it comes from a hydrated phosphate of copper and aluminum. “

“Holy mierda! I didn’t know that. And all this time I thought it came from horsemeat.” They both laughed and clinked glasses.

Carlos eventually segued into a discussion of the Yaqui populations around Cananea. “Ana was part Yaqui, wasn’t she?”

“Yeah.”

“Crap, I think we may have found the Rosetta Stone.”

CHAPTER 47 – BLAS

Friday, June 14, 2019

Cholula

After separating from Carlos at the Mexico City airport, Francisco had wandered over to the Avis car rental office where he had a car reserved. There were only two employees behind the counter, one of whom was in a deep contentious conversation with a client.

When Francisco's turn came, he showed the necessary paperwork to the young reservationist who wore a white shirt and a company logo tie.

"Mr. Reynoso, we have your reservation, but unfortunately we don't have any more mid-sized vehicles. We can give you an SUV or a smaller car at no extra charge."

Francisco knew he would have to pay for gas and that the SUV was a gas guzzler. It was also too wide a vehicle to have to negotiate narrow and curvy mountainous roads.

"What kind of small car do you have?"

The agent turned a booklet on the counter toward him and started to list them. Francisco selected a white Honda Civic. He opted for full coverage with zero deductible. It was more expensive, but it was chargeable to the Chan Toy Project. After getting the car key, he made a restroom stop. He knew that he had a two and a half hour challenging drive ahead of him. He had purchased the GPS, and so it was full speed ahead. Unfortunately, the traffic leading out of Mexico was very slow.

At a quarter to twelve, Francisco was walking through the Roman arches of the three-story administration building of the Universidad de las Américas Puebla in Cholula. In a back corner office, he was greeted by a devilishly handsome, slender older gentleman with a salt and pepper goatee and a full head of hair.

They embraced. "Francisco, you are looking good, hijo mijo," Provost Blas DeSoto grinned.

"And you, congratulations on your promotions," Francisco said. He had met Blas in 2004 when he was here in Puebla. Blas was a history professor who took a liking to the Stanford professor and acted as his mentor.

"You must be tired from the long drive," the provost said. "Let's grab a coffee. We can catch up."

Francisco found out that Blas was widowed. His wife had died from breast cancer three years prior. He had two children. His son lived in Madrid with a wife and child. The daughter worked at the United Nations as an interpreter. Reynoso shared about his recent marriage and invited Blas to Guadalajara. Francisco had a double expresso and a ham and cheese croqueta. They talked about academia in Mexico. Blas had met Dean Ríos once before and had been impressed with her.

Blas had a gigantic office with a scenic picture window. The walls were strewn with plaques, photos, and certificates. It looked like a museum.

"I think there is a photo of you and me somewhere over there in the corner," the provost pointed. "I should make a copy for you. Now, tell me why you needed to see me."

Francisco spent the next twenty-five minutes recounting the journals of Chan Toy and his wife Ana. "We trying to gather information about Ana Chan and Filomena Antuñano around 1913." Reynoso chose not to mention the quest for the turquoise hummingbird amulet.

"Well, the history of the Antuñano dynasty is very rich. Most of what I am going to share with you is common knowledge, but some is new. I was born and raised in Puebla. My parents came here from Spain. The Spanish sold their textile interests to the Antuñanos in the 1850's. General Próspero Antuñano was a famous local citizen. He was very popular. However, since he was a Freemason, he had problems with the local Catholic church."

"He was a Mason?" Francisco interrupted.

"Yes, and so were many of the members of the Poblano high society. While Próspero was not anti-clerical, his libertine views and federalist partisanship made him a constant target of the local church and the Cristeros. Próspero had aligned himself with the Mexican federalists and thus became an enemy of many of the Catholics in the pueblo. He was also very progressive in terms of women's rights. He gave his wife, Filomena, free rein in hiring former prostitutes into their textile factory. They were given decent working and living conditions. They had access to health care. Ana Chan played an important role as healer for these women, despite the opposition from the Catholics."

"I know that Benito Juarez was a Mason. But I don't know about Porfirio Diaz."

DeSoto gave out a little laugh. "Diaz was the consummate politician. Yes, he was a Mason, but also supported the Catholic Church . . ."

“What happened after Filomena died?” Francisco was trying to get back on script.

“The nephew took over. Ernesto Antuñano was a real puto. While he posed as a Mason, behind the scenes he was forcing the textile workers to work in a brothel. No more haute couture. He turned the textile factory into a military uniform production complex. While he was known for his support of Great Britain, he was within a half-step of selling out to the Germans. Germany wanted to establish a presence in Mexico to offset the Yankee influence. They were buying up properties and businesses at a premium. Only the intervention by President Huerta stopped that. He was also a Mason.”

“The usurper of the Madera presidency!”

“The Catholic Church, Freemasonry, the federales, and the Mexican Revolution. Women’s rights, Communism, and U.S. Imperialism. That’s the history of Mexico. Not perfect, but rich in culture.”

“But at least Mexico was neutral in World War I,” Francisco stated.

“Officially, yes,” Provost DeSoto was shaking his head with a big grin. “You remember that President Huerta was forced to resign. He fled to Spain. Later he was arrested for colluding with German spies. He was arrested and died in U.S. custody.”

They discussed the historical context of Mexican presidents and Europe for the next quarter hour.

"And don't forget the Zimmermann Telegram, in World War I," DeSoto reminded Reynoso. It was Germany's plot to support Mexico's claim to recapture California and other U.S. States if they attacked the United States.

Gradually, the conversation started to wind down.

"One last thing, Blas, do you know anything about Ana Chan? It seems that she left the Antuñano estate, either voluntarily or forced out by Ernesto."

"Very little," Blas admitted. "I understand that you want to track down her history. She was revered as the reincarnation of the China Poblana. Especially for her healing powers."

"Interesting," Francisco was getting tired. "Was there ever any mention of a turquoise healing stone?"

"Not to my knowledge, but let's try this," Blas was still going strong. "When she left Puebla, she wouldn't have gone south or west. She had originally fled Mexico City, so she wouldn't have gone back there. The Revolution was still going on strong there, and the Chinese probably wanted their money back from what they thought Chan Toy owed them. That route seems improbable. A better option may have been Veracruz. She might have had contacts from Filomena's associates."

Later that night, after Francisco called his wife Alex, he laid in bed. So much information. The provost had provided so much reliable background, but the real meat was in the projections of where Ana could have traveled after Puebla. She had written “Volver” on Map #1. To go back. That would probably eliminate Veracruz. Could it mean back to China?

CHAPTER 48 – UNEXPECTED GUEST

Sunday – Monday, June 16-17, 2019

Guadalajara

They slept in late that Sunday morning after Francisco returned from his short trip to Puebla. He brought Alex a sampler of different mole poblano sauces.

The cook, Vera, prepared the sesame one for their Saturday night dinner.

"It's very good," commented Alex nonchalantly making sure that the cook could hear her, "but not as good as Vera's." Both Alex and Francisco smiled.

"I also brought some chocolate sauce from Puebla," Francisco gave a lascivious grin at his wife. "We'll need to try it."

Sunday morning, they got ready to start the day. Francisco wanted to get his clothes ready for that night's dinner with Miranda and her family.

"Mi amor, what should I wear tonight?" Francisco asked his wife.

"You always look good in that burgundy guayabera," she smiled. "I'll have Mercedes get one of the maids to iron it for you. And the tan slacks."

That evening Esteban drove them to Alex's compadres' home. Ostensibly, it was to celebrate her goddaughter's acceptance letters to several colleges. In a few short months, Mirasol would be leaving the nest and studying in a foreign country. Despite the bravado, Alex knew that her godchild was scared and nervous. Having Tina living with the Ríos had been a great idea. Mirasol had a big sister for the summer. Things would work out.

Alex wore a black cocktail dress with a low neckline and spaghetti straps. As always, she wore her omnipresent black pearl earrings and necklace.

Upon arrival, they were greeted by Miranda and her husband Sol with hugs and kisses. Francisco saw Miranda give him a head gesture like she wanted to talk to him. He broke away from Alex while Sol put on his bubbly persona for Alex.

"Francisco, I didn't have time to warn you," she put her hand to her mouth with her index finger craftily pointing to the salon.

Francisco looked puzzled. A minute later he understood.

"Professor, I want you to meet my friend from São Paolo, Rubí Song. I think you've met her sister, Lilí," Tina was all smiles. It was like "show and tell."

"It's a pleasure to meet you," Francisco was shocked beyond belief. *What the heck is she doing here?*

"Igualmente," Rubí's Spanish was very basic. It was certainly not as good as Tina's. She looked like an innocent siren with her purple lipstick and white Suzie Wong dress.

"How long are you visiting?" Francisco was trying to think quickly. He would have to speak with Tina. And especially to Patricio! *Will this spoil our plans regarding the procurement of the turquoise hummingbird?*

"I don't know. I just finished seeing my sister in Vancouver," Rubí had a disarming smile. "Maybe one more week. Tina has been showing me around Guadalajara. Nice weather. Not as cold or rainy as Vancouver," she giggled. "And food tastes better."

Before they could continue, Alex came in and was introduced to Rubí. Vera had set a small, but elegant, hors d'oeuvre platter on the reddish-brown mahogany coffee table.

Mango margaritas rimmed with Tajín were de rigueur for welcoming drinks at the Ríos house. Guacamole and queso fundido with totopos were the complements. Everybody was noshing, drinking, and conversing when Mirasol made her regal appearance. She had twin pigtails sticking up, braided with green and red ribbons. She wore a gold sequined top with tight black jeans and red Converse sneakers. She didn't wear any makeup or jewelry.

Mirasol went around the room, giving everyone pecks on the cheek. She sat down next to her father on the couch.

"Okay, what's the latest on colleges?" Alex grinned. "I don't remember all the colleges she applied to."

Mirasol responded, half-girl, half-young woman. She was the center of attention. "I haven't made up my mind yet. I'm not sure I want to spend four years in the snow. Maybe I'll go where the boys are the cutest." She threw a glance at her father who growled. "I did get admitted to Smith, papá. It's 98% female."

"The two per cent men makes it even worse!" snarled Sol.

Moments later dinner was served. Socorro had prepared a demi-glace coated cochinita pibil roast with grilled chayote and mixed peppers. Francisco was tuned out throughout. *Why is*

Rubí here? It's too much of a coincidence! She wants something. She is probably spying on us!

After dinner they left the dining room. Socorro was serving coffee, tea, and brandy back in the salon. Everybody inhaled her scrumptious tres leches torta.

On the way back from the bathroom, Francisco ran into Miranda who pulled him into the library.

"I'm so sorry, Francisco. I just met Rubí this weekend when Tina asked if Rubí could be invited to Mirasol's dinner," Miranda spoke fast in an exasperated tone. "I knew that I couldn't refuse to include her."

"No worries," Francisco, of course, didn't believe what he had just uttered. "I'll talk to Patricio tomorrow and figure this out."

On their way home, Alex put her hand on Francisco's leg. "Mi amor, all night you looked like something was bothering you. You didn't seem quite yourself tonight."

Francisco wanted to say nothing was wrong, but Alex read him like a book. They had a good marriage based on honesty and communication. In the end he told her the whole Chan Toy story.

"Tina is smart and she's your most loyal follower. You have to give her some credit for knowing what she is doing," Alex counseled.

"You're right," Francisco exhaled. "But on the other hand, I need to protect the universities' interests and I can't let Mexican artifacts leave this country."

"Okay, worry about what is right for the universities and Tina. Let Patricio deal with the Mexican specimens. That is his job and responsibility."

Francisco realized she was correct. "You're so good. Thanks, mi amor."

***

The next morning, Francisco called Patricio and told him about the debacle they were in with Rubí's surprise visit.

"I agree with you, compadre," Patricio was on track. "It can't be a coincidence that Rubí is here. What can she want? Information?"

"Let's not tell Tina about our suspicions. I think that might be the best way to protect her and prevent her from blurting out something that is sensitive," Francisco suggested.

"Francisco, as I see it, your job is to find the turquoise hummingbird. I have been doing some research and sharing it with Carlos. My responsibility is to make sure that no more Mexican artifacts leave our country and that Lilí and Hao Chin Martín, or whatever his name is, are arrested for their thefts."

"I agree. But in order to arrest them, they have to be on Mexican soil. Isn't that correct?"

"Sí, señor."

"So, we need some sort of a trap to lure them here."

"Sí, señor."

"But Tina can't be the bait."

"Sí, señor."

"Patricio, I think I have an idea."

CHAPTER 49 – THE SNARE

Tuesday, June 18, 2019

Guadalajara

Francisco liked the way Patricio's mind worked. Together they made a formidable team, at least on paper. Batman and Robin. He had cancelled the staff meeting that was scheduled for that morning. Patricio couldn't have made it anyway.

With a free morning, Francisco cleaned up his emails and caught up on his correspondence. Francisco sent Lilí Song an email in English along with a hard copy registered letter through Correos de Mexico, the Mexican postal service.

June 18, 2019

Lilí Song
Chinese Dragon Rare Elements Ltd.

Vancouver, B.C. Canada

RE: Chan Toy Project - Update

Dear Ms. Song:

We hope all is well with you. Just a note to keep you up to date on our project. We have been doing our due diligence in trying to locate and procure the turquoise hummingbird amulet. We will not bore you will the details.

As you know, the Chan Toy chronicles tragically end in Mexico City around 1912. However, we may have a lead or two about what happened to the artifact afterwards. Assuming we are successful, we will need specific delivery instructions from you . . .

If you have any questions or concerns, please contact us . . .

He emailed the letter to Lilí Song and concurrently sent a hard copy mailed through the postal service. Electronic copies were submitted to Dean Ríos, Dean Chandler, Carlos, Tina, and Patricio.

Two hours later there was an email response from Lilí.

June 18, 2019

Professor Francisco Reynoso
University of Guadalajara

RE: Chan Toy Project - Update

Dear Professor Reynoso:

So good to hear from you. Glad you are making progress.

When you find the turquoise hummingbird, please send it to us by FedEx International. Upon receipt, we will release the remaining funds to the University of Guadalajara and Stanford University . . .

Cc: Chinese Dragon Rare Elements Ltd.

Upon receiving Lilí response, Francisco immediately texted a copy of Lilí's email to Patricio. "We've piqued her interest, I think," Francisco wrote.

"Yes, sir," Patricio was in agreement. "By the way, I told Carlos about the ploy in broad terms. He knows he has to protect Tina foremost."

The breadcrumbs had been dropped. He sent a second email to Lilí Song.

Dear Ms. Song:

Thank you for your prompt reply. Unfortunately, upon further investigations of protocols and pursuant to our agreement with you and per the policies of the two universities, you or your legal representative must take physical possession of the artifact.

Receipts and releases must be duly attested and notarized in accordance with Mexican laws. You are responsible for any Customs clearances for Canada or anywhere else . . .

This latter language had been the brainchild of Patricio. He needed Lilí physically present on Mexican soil to apprehend her.

In the late afternoon there was a second response from Lilí.

Dear Professor Reynoso:

We understand. No problem. Attached is a Power of Attorney giving my sister Rubí Song the authority to receive any and all artifacts on our behalf. See attached.

She says that you have been very kind to her. Thank you very much . . .

This time Francisco phoned Patricio after forwarding Lilí's email and the power of attorney to him.

"So, we now know why Rubí came to visit," Patricio stated. "While I think I would prefer to snag Lilí, a twin sister should give us some leverage. Now that Rubí is in Mexico, the federales can run traces on her travel and expenses."

"How about tapping her phone or text messages?"

"Not at this point. That's about five levels above me and it gets into a lot of politics. Besides, to minimize leaks we need to keep this close."

In the late afternoon, Professor Reynoso called Carlos and Tina into his office. He gave them each a copy of a summary of his visitation notes to Puebla the prior Friday.

"I think one possibility is that Ana went to Veracruz when she left Puebla. Filomena had worked there, as well as some of her workers. This would make sense. So, we need to find out more about Filomena Antuñano's early life and if Ana ever lived in Veracruz."

There were only a few questions, and then Francisco said to Carlos and Tina, "I'm sending you both to Veracruz. Is that going to create a problem for either of you?"

Tina was about to say something but stopped herself.

"Oh, Tina, you can invite Rubí Song to join you too. We received a power of attorney from Rare Elements. She is now an official observer of the Chan Toy Project, representing Rare Elements. Her expenses, however, will be her own responsibility. Remember to keep receipts and document everything."

"Is she an observer like Patricio?"

"No, Patricio works for the Ministry of Justice and is our liaison with the Mexican government. Rubí is like an overnight guest. Nothing official."

CHAPTER 50 – GIRL TALK

Thursday, June 20, 2019

Veracruz

Carlos had arrived in Veracruz the night before, rented a medium-sized Honda sedan, and checked into the Hotel El Tajín. The next morning, he was wearing a light lime green guayabera when he picked up Tina and Rubí at the Veracruz Airport. The Volaris flight had been a quarter of an hour delayed, but both women had brought only carryon luggage, so Carlos did not have to wait very long.

Tina introduced Rubí to Carlos.

"She's going to be our official observer," Tina laughed.

Carlos gave her a nice smile, remembering what Patricio had warned him about.

"Welcome to the place where Mexico began."

They stopped by the hotel and the two women checked in. Twenty minutes later Tina met Carlos in the hotel lobby and the pair was ready to go. Rubí was on her own to explore the city. She was not allowed to be an official participant in the Chan Toy Project. Professor Reynoso had told her that it was for legal liability reasons. There had been no push back.

Carlos and Tina decided to do their investigative research on foot. Parking scarcities and traffic jams were endemic in this port town.

The duo began at the San Juan de Ulúa Fortress a few blocks away. Carlos slipped into his tour guy mode with Tina. Prior to becoming an assistant professor at the University of Guadalajara, he had been a high school teacher in Guanajuato and supplemented his meager income by being a guide at Tenochtitlan and other historical locations in Mexico.

"Hernán Cortés came here in 1519, and with only a small army conquered Moctezuma and the Aztec empire. He claimed all these lands in the name of Spain . . ."

They arrived at the entrance to the fortress. Carlos stopped at the ticket booth but kept talking.

"Veracruz, or as it was originally named, La Rica de la Vera Cruz or Heroica Veracruz, had become an important port to Spain. Throughout its history it has been the target of pirates and countries like France, and the United States. After Mexico's

Independence, it was the major gateway for trade with Europe. It also played a vital role in the Mexican Revolution . . ."

Carlos and Tina showed their university credentials at the entryway. They had an appointment to meet with the chief historian of the fortress, Dr. José Adán, who had white hair parted on the side and a white moustache.

"Welcome. Welcome," the distinguished gentleman greeted them. "I hope we can assist you today."

Adán led them to a small room that had a large wooden table where scholars used to do their research there.

Carlos explained that they were involved in a project on Chinese migration in Mexico. He made it sound innocuous. They were trying to track down the movements of two individuals, Filomena Antuñano and Ana Chan. Dr. Adán asked some clarifying questions and then said, "You may use this room for your research. Some of the information will be available by computer. I assume you brought yours."

Tina and Carlos nodded.

"Anything not stored in the electronic archives, will be brought to you from the stacks. These are very fragile documents. We ask that you utilize the utmost care."

The pair assented. They were given special usernames and passwords to access the fortress' proprietary information.

Tina looked for Ana under various names but found nothing.

Carlos found several dozen articles on Filomena Antuñano, documenting her contributions to various charities, women's suffrage, and the cotton textile industry. Tina assisted him in reviewing the documents.

Around three o'clock they decided to take a break and go to the cafeteria. Carlos had two fish tacos and Tina had a seafood salad.

"I can't believe how fresh the fish is!" exclaimed Tina.

Carlos just grinned as he took another bite of the dorado.

When they returned to the research room, there was a six-inch thick pile of documents. These were records of Próspero Antuñano that highlighted his heroism against the French in Veracruz and Puebla. There were also newspaper clippings about how Captain Antuñano had throttled a young soldier, but no disciplinary proceedings were ever carried out. The documents also talked about his cotton textile empire.

The fortress closed at six and so the pair slowly walked back to the hotel. Carlos then pointed to the Hilton Doubletree that was about a block away.

"That is the brothel that the young Filomena worked at was located. That's where Próspero Antuñano found her and rescued her."

By seven-thirty, Carlos, Tina, and Rubí walked into the Gran Café de la Parroquía.

"This place has the best coffee in Mexico," Carlos bragged.

"Carlos, you know we only drink tea," Tina said.

"Oh!"

A dark-skinned young woman with brown kinky hair and dressed in indigenous clothing took their order. Tina ordered the Spanish tortilla, Rubí the enchiladas suizas, and Carlos the steak arrachera.

Rubí shared her day. She had walked around the historical part of the city and then the malecón pier walk.

For dessert they split a torta de elote. A delicious corn cake with vanilla ice cream. Carlos had a double cortado espresso.

They returned to the hotel and Carlos said good night.

Tina and Rubí were sharing a junior suite. Nobody thought it would be fair if Rubi spent the night alone and so Professor Reynoso had preapproved it.

The ladies got ready for bed and were in their pajamas.

Tina was exhausted and did not want to watch television. The phone rang and Tina walked to the far wall for privacy. After five minutes, she hung up and came back to her own bed.

"Tina, how long have you been in Mexico?" Rubí suddenly asked in Mandarin. They had been speaking English all day because Rubí's Spanish was not very good.

"About a month."

"Do you have a boyfriend?"

"Well, I've met someone. I'm not sure if he considers himself my boyfriend."

"The one on the phone? Is he a professor too?"

"No, he works for Mexican law enforcement," she answered as if she was embarrassed.

There was the slightest pause. The expression on Rubí's face did not give away her sudden apprehension.

"Do you have a picture of him?"

Tina pulled out her cell phone and scrolled down some photo albums.

"Here he is," Tina held it up for Rubí to see.

"He very handsome," Rubí gave a crafty smile. "Text it to me. Maybe he has a brother."

Tina naively complied.

Rubí started to call it a night and crawled into bed.

"Rubí, one thing that has been bothering me," Tina had been wondering about this for several weeks. "Who is Hao Chin Martín?"

"He's my sister's boyfriend."

“How did they meet?”

“They work in similar fields. They both work in Vancouver,” the pitch in Rubí’s voice increased. “Why do you ask?”

Tina paused for a moment and looked like she was thinking.

“Well, in the course of our research we found out that Hao Chin Martín died many years ago. That means this person is not a relative of Chan Toy. What does your sister know about him?”

“Oh, I didn’t know. I don’t think my sister knows about this,” Rubí acted panicky. “I will have to tell her. She needs to be careful.”

After a few more minutes of drama, they both turned off their lights. Rubí suddenly got up and went into the bathroom. She pulled out her cellphone and texted her sister:

DANGER! DO NOT COME TO VERACRUZ!

I THINK THEY KNOW ABOUT WAY OH!

She attached the photo of Tina and Patricio to the text.

CHAPTER 51 – PLAN B

Friday, June 21, 2019

Veracruz

There were ten text messages from Lilí asking what was happening. Rubi was not able to respond until the next morning when Tina had left the hotel with Carlos to continue their investigation into Ana's travels post-Puebla.

Rubí decided to call even though Lilí was apprehensive about using the public airways.

She dialed a private number on her cellphone and Lilí picked up immediately.

"Sister, I've been texting you all night," Lilí was speaking in a very sharp Mandarin tone. "What is happening?"

"I think we have been discovered. They know that the real Martín is dead. They know that Way Oh can't be a relative of Chan Toy!"

"That shouldn't be a problem. He could be a cousin or nephew with the same name."

Rubí knew that probably wouldn't work, but she never wanted to contradict her sister. It would be a loss of face. "And I think Tina's boyfriend is a policeman. Somehow, he is involved."

"I'm glad you found out. We have to be very careful. As long as we dangle the money in front of them, we will be okay. They are greedy! What's your next step?"

"We fly back to Guadalajara tonight. I don't know what is next for Tina. So far they haven't found anything here in Veracruz. And I prefer Hong Kong and Macau fish."

A minute later Rubí hung up. Way Oh (who had been impersonating Hao Chin Martín) asked what was happening. Lilí told him.

"Maybe we should go down there, snatch the turquoise hummingbird and flee to São Paulo."

"Don't be so stupid. They are waiting for us. This is a trap." Lilí had sent the photo of Tina and Patricio to one of Augustina's coworkers. The colleague confirmed that the male in the photo was the same person who had interrogated Augustina for the theft of the Chan Toy documents. Lilí found out that the man, Patricio, worked for the Museum of Anthropology and the Ministry of Justice in Mexico City.

"But our bosses want the turquoise hummingbird amulet as soon as possible," Way Oh complained to Lili. "They have paid a lot of money to get this far. They are powerful! They could make trouble for us!"

"Don't worry. We'll deliver," Lilí did not feel the same political pressure from their bosses (the People's Republic of China) that Way Oh did because of his youthful transgressions. All she cared about was the money and how to escape to São Paulo.

"And what if we can't deliver?" he questioned her.

She gave him an icy stare and walked away.

Around the same time, Francisco had received a text from Carlos and Tina. They had discovered a lot about the Antuñano family, and they would be returning home tonight.

For Professor Reynoso, the choices were getting slimmer and slimmer. Veracruz was a bust. *What is our next step? Cananea? Mexicali? No way could it be China!*

Reynoso called Patricio. He wasn't in. He left a message, and just before lunch they connected.

"Just as we suspected, nothing in Veracruz. You didn't miss anything. The sister has been innocuous, according to Carlos and Tina."

"And judging from Tina's research, there is nothing in Mexico City. The speculation that Ana went back there after her husband was killed seems very remote."

"How is your research on Cananea coming along, Patricio?"

"Don't know why Ana would return to Cananea, Professor. She left with Chan Toy to escape the Yankee pendejos"

"I think you're right."

"As for the investigation, there is too much territory to cover. There were dozens and dozens of mines in Cananea and in the State of Sonora. Gold, silver, and copper mining. Not to mention the U.S. mining companies exploiting the Mexican miners who called a nationwide strike in 1906 Too many mines!"

"But according to the Chan Toy's papers, Ana grew up in one of these mining towns. And her mother worked at one. She escaped from there around 1898 and left Puebla in 1914. That's a sixteen-year gap. Could her mother still have been alive?" asked Francisco."

"There's a good chance," Patricio concurred.

"Okay, I guess next week we're going to check out Cananea," Francisco said.

"Am I included in the 'we'?"

"Naturally. With all the research you've done and expertise in the mining field you have to go. Do you want to start on Monday or Tuesday?"

"I don't know."

"Let's split the difference. Get there Monday afternoon. Check in and get a lay of the land and then you can hit it hard on Tuesday."

"Sounds good," Patricio then added, "I'd like Carlos and Tina to be part of the team."

Francisco had been waiting for the time when Patricio might attempt to spend time with Tina under the pretense (and expense) of the project. *That's not going to happen,* Francisco smiled to himself.

"Carlos would be fine. You two make a great team. Tina is best suited to do the computer searches in Guadalajara. Besides she needs to babysit Rubí. The twin is still an integral part of the plan."

"You're right," Patricio said weakly.

Later that afternoon, Francisco called Carlos who was still in Veracruz. He was on his way to leave the rental car at the airport. There was a 4:30 flight to Guanajuato. He would be home in time to have dinner with his family.

Carlos reported that he had done more digging that morning on Ana Chan, but still nothing. He shared that Tina and Rubí were taking a later flight to Guadalajara.

"Carlos, I need you to rest up this weekend. You are going to spend next week in Cananea with Patricio. He is responsible for making your lodging arrangements. You just need to get there by Monday afternoon. I don't know the airline schedules, but you'll probably have at least one connecting flight."

"No problem. I'll check in with Juanita and Patricio for any final changes. I'm assuming that I won't arrive in Cananea until late afternoon."

They talked for a few more minutes. Francisco asked Carlos if Tina was nearby. Carlos said no. Francisco dialed Tina who picked up and repeated what Carlos had said about how Veracruz had been a bust.

Francisco informed her that Carlos and Patricio would be going to Cananea to follow up on Ana Chan.

"Patricio wasn't sure why Ana would go back to Cananea, especially after the bad experiences she had encountered," opined the professor.

"The answer may simple," replied Tina. With her husband gone, Ana had to raise her three children. Although the kids were Chinese-Mexicans, Ana's knowledge of the Chinese culture and language was limited. From the documents, there was no mention of her having any Chinese friends, only Mexican ones. "It would have been much easier to raise her children in the Mexican culture in a place she was familiar with."

"I see your point. I need you to get as much information as possible on Joya Azuleta."

"Ana's mother?"

"Yes," Francisco's mind was racing. He was thinking. "And check out the husband-and-wife team who were the suppliers to the mines. I don't remember their names. I think some of this information is in Chan Toy's papers."

"How did Rubí survive Veracruz?" Francisco switched gears.

"Fine," Tina was perky. "She will be leaving us soon."

Crap! Francisco thought to himself. *She is the one who has to take delivery of the turquoise hummingbird amulet. Otherwise, things will fall apart. How do we keep her here?*

CHAPTER 52 – CASA LLENA

Saturday- Sunday, June 22 -23, 2019

Guadalajara

There was a slight southwesterly breeze blowing through the house after the early morning rain. The scent of the garden's flowers permeated the air. The purple and white bougainvilleas were in full bloom. Francisco was connecting his iPod to the household sound system. Stan Getz would keep it mellow.

Francisco brought his soy latte over to the overstuffed sofa where Alex was sitting sideways. She was wearing rosa-colored silk pajamas. Her toes touched Francisco's as she sat sideways on the couch supported by two multichromatic cotton pillows. He was casually dressed in navy and white nightwear pj's that Alex described as his prison garb. He began playing footsies with her.

They hadn't had a free day together for weeks. Alex with her endocrinology practice and Francisco with the Chan Toy Project. They gave each other casual and brief summaries of their recent activities, making sure not to complain or cause negative vibes.

"Mi amor, have you thought anymore about the Netza Project?" she asked. They wanted to make a significant financial donation to a literacy program for indigenous children in Zihuatanejo.

"Let's do it," Francisco had a token say in their financial affairs. Alex had all the money, and he really didn't care that much about it.

They also tossed around the idea of sending the Netza Project boxes of books. Since most its students were non-native Spanish speakers, they decided that the books would probably have to be in Spanish. They would leave the book titles up to the teachers in the project.

They were interrupted when Vera called them for a light breakfast. Francisco kept seeing his weight slowly creep up. He tried smaller food portions during the week but compensated for the workday fasting on the weekends.

"Portion control," was the mantra of Alex who neither ate too much sugar nor drank in excess.

"Mi amor, what are you plans for today?" she inquired.

"Do you want to take a little walk in the park? We haven't done that in a while. We could buy some mangos en palos from the vendors."

"Sounds good," she then gave him a devilish smile. "And how about doing the hot tub when we get back?"

***

The next day came too quickly. Francisco spent the whole morning trying to wake up. When he finally did, he found himself seated next to Sol on dark green plastic seats in the third row near third base at the Charros baseball stadium. The humidity was rising, and Francisco already wanted to take a shower. Black clouds started to form in the western skies.

Sol had scored some free baseball tickets from one of his business associates who supplied him with electrical converters and battery backups for his solar business. Today the local team, Los Charros, were hosting the Bandidos of Chihuahua.

"Oye, amigo, the catcher looks like he is almost fifteen years old," Sol sipped his red-cupped beer. "Maybe next year he'll start shaving."

Francisco had the good fortune of being available while their wives were at a Latinx/Chicana Leadership Conference. The ladies had invited Tina, but she said that she had to take Rubí shopping because she was going to be leaving in a few days. Mirasol latched on to this opportunity to tag along. The adults were boring but hanging out with Tina and Rubí was cool.

The Charros struck first, scoring two runs in the bottom of the second inning. The score lead changed several times. Lots of walks, very few hits up until the bottom of the sixth.

"¡La casa está llena!" Sol sipping his third beer. The bases were loaded, and the Charros were threatening to blow the game wide open.

The wind suddenly picked up. The first baseman's hat flew off his head. *¡El pinche viento!* The crowd got noisier.

Francisco found a hot dog stand and purchased a pair. Half the fun of the games was watching Sol yelling this and that. Sol maligned every coach in baseball (and every other sport). The other half was eating hot dogs and drinking beer.

The next batter hit a slow roller up the third base line that was miraculously scooped up by the third baseman who threw to home to force an out at the plate. The subsequent throw to first was too late.

Bases were still loaded. The best hitter for the Charros was now up.

The count was one and one when Francisco felt the first drop of rain on his cheek.

Five minutes later it was a full count, three and two. "Cuenta completa!" Sol cried out in desperation.

Francisco's head jerked back. It was like someone had shot him with a pea shooter. Then suddenly he was being pelted by hail. Sol put up his hands to cover his head.

"Let's get out of here!" Francisco yelled

Sol paused. "Wait a second." He sat in his seat getting deluged.

Then there was a public announcement over the loudspeakers. "There is a rain delay. We will inform you if and when we'll continue the game."

"Pinche granizo!" Sol barked as he got up.

Traffic was a mess trying to exit the stadium. They were listening to the radio. "I don't see why they let Valenzuela pitch today. No vale madre." Sol kept on grousing all the way to his favorite cantina. They were both soaking wet. There he found out that the game was called because of rain and that the Charros won 6-5.

"Well, at least, we won," Francisco really didn't care.

"I still think they need a new coach," Sol complained.

They were semi-dry when they made it back to the Ríos' home. Sol went upstairs to change.

Mirasol, Tina, and Rubí had come home earlier because they had also been caught in the rain. Rubí left to go back to her lodging and Tina went to her room.

There was a little fire going in fireplace. A rarity in that home. Francisco was scanning the newspaper when Mirasol plopped herself in the chair next to him.

"How was your shopping, Mirasol?" Francisco asked.

"It was alright." She went on for several minute describing the stores they went to. Francisco was bored but did not want to show it.

"Tio, may I ask you a question?" Mirasol called Francisco uncle because her actual uncle and godfather had died of prostate cancer. He was Sol's oldest brother.

"Sure."

"Why do people still treat me like a child?" Mirasol was engaging in a self-pity party. "I'm eighteen years old!"

"Who are we talking about?"

"Well, Tina and her friend."

"I don't think it's about you," Francisco knew nothing about teenage girls, but he knew that his female students could be very sensitive. "It's more about them. They are over ten years older than you. They are different than you. They do different things than you do. It's like you have very little in common with a ten-year-old. Right?"

She nodded.

"It's going to get worse. In August you will a freshman. Or freshwoman. Whatever you prefer," he gave her an avuncular smile. "You're going to be lower than pond scum. The juniors and seniors won't even give you the time of day."

They talked for a long time. Mirasol would rather listen to him than her parents, he thought. *That's the way young people are wired.*

At 6:30 Miranda and Alex arrived from their women's leadership conference.

"Did you boys behave while we were gone?" Miranda asked grinning.

They settled down in the living room where they imbibed all in some margaritas and guacamole. Dinner came and Francisco was starting to nod off. His clothes were still wrinkled from the rain.

On the drive home, Francisco told his wife about his conversation with Mirasol. Alex sighed.

"I've noticed a change in her, mi amor," Alex said. "I think part of it is that she wants to be independent. Or thinks she does. The other part of her is afraid to grow up. We protect her. We spoil her. And going to a university in a foreign country will not be easy for her."

"I was hoping that having Tina around would help."

"I'm sure it has. But not everyone can be a super student like Tina."

PART VII – TREASURE HUNT

CHAPTER 53 – THE APPEARANCE

Monday - Thursday, June 24 - 27, 2019

Cananea

Carlos was starving as the plane landed at the Cananea Airport. He rented a subcompact car and drove to the Posada Exprés where he was supposed to meet Patricio in the lobby by ten. Francisco's secretary Juanita had made all the arrangements, making sure all the essentials were met. Since Patricio was not officially a member of the Chan Toy Project, he had to fend for himself. Fortunately, his agency was picking up his tab. Equally lucky was Carlos. Francisco was covering his classes for the week.

The air was hot and dry. There was a grit in the air.

"Oye, carnal, we are in the middle of a dump," Carlos described the impoverished city with more bars than stores.

"I did an internship here when I was going to school. Nothing but mining, and everything associated with mining," Patricio replied

"Hey, dude, I'm hungry. Haven't eaten anything all morning." Carlos' stomach was growling.

"I know a place about two blocks from here."

At the Mission Restaurant, Carlos ordered chilaquiles with chicken and salsa verde; Patricio was having huevos divorciados. The coffee was acidy but plentiful.

They started to plan out the whole week. Carlos was officially in charge, but this was Patricio's turf. They had a twelve o'clock meeting with Buzz Halow, the president of the Cananea Mining Association. Buzz had been raised in Colorado and had come to Cananea as part of a U.S. mining syndicate. While most North Americans went home after making some money, Buzz stayed. He married a local Mexican woman and had risen as a community leader. They had three children.

Patricio slurped up some sauce with a flour tortilla. "We need to find the mine where Chan Toy worked. Unfortunately, I think it might take a month to do that."

"We need a way to pare the number of mines down," Carlos bit into more chips. "I think we can cut the total in half by eliminating the open pit mines. There were very few of them a hundred years ago."

Carlos picked up the check because Francisco had put him on a very generous per diem. They walked a few blocks to the Cananea Mining Association that was situated in a two-story brick building.

Patricio introduced Carlos to Buzz Halow and the two shook hands. The trio retired to a small conference room. The walls were decorated with dozens of photos of mines.

"What are you boys here for?" said the crusty elderly man with white lamb chop sideburns. His cheeks were ruddy and puffy and matched his portly figure.

Carlos explained that they were looking for the lodging locations for mining camps in the late nineteenth century, especially those that had Chinese workers.

Buzz caressed his chin with his right hand. "This is what I know . . ."

"Cananea was founded by the Spanish in 1760. The Jesuits enslaved the indigenous people to work the Cananea mines, but subsequently abandoned the operations. Mexican General Pesqueira rediscovered them and sold them to a mining company. The population of the Cananea site was one half Mexican, a quarter Chinese, and the rest gringo. Mining operations resumed but were stopped by Apache raids.

Pesqueira reclaimed the mines and then sold them to the Cananea Consolidated Copper Company.

"Working conditions were atrocious and in 1906 the workers went out on strike. The federal army was called in to intimidate the miners. People were killed. Shortly, thereafter, the Mexican Revolution began.

"Mining camps survived off and on. There were significant U.S. and British investments here. The companies bypassed local governments and were protected by the Mexican governors. In fact, Cananea had a strong American influence with the support of Mexican President Porfirio Diaz.

"The mining problems were exacerbated by low water tables and clashes with the Yaquis and Apaches . . ."

Buzz Halow was interrupted by a young brunette dressed in a long granny dress who served them watermelon-flavored agua fresca and salted peanuts powdered with chile.

"Señor Halow, can you guess where there was a copper mine that had Chinese workers a century ago?" Carlos asked.

"Well, I probably could give you fifty, but let me show you some of the places," he pointed to a map that was marked with a couple hundred red tipped pins.

Carlos and Patricio wrote down the most probable candidates and their locations.

"Buzz, do you have any records on the Heinz's? Günther and Hilda? I think they were suppliers for a mine."

He checked his computer and then said no.

"Just remember that times have changed. Most of those places don't exist. Many have been converted to strip malls, gas stations, and apartment buildings," Halow waved his hand dismissively. "Land is cheap."

An hour later the pair were in Carlos' hotel room sitting st a small coffee table. They were setting up a visitation schedule for the next three days. They would bunch the mines closest to each other. They would have to do between four and six per day. It was a rough and ambitious schedule for them.

At six-thirty they met in the lobby, ready to go out for dinner. Carlos went over to the middle-aged man with a dark blue checkered bowtie who sat at the receptionist desk and asked a question.

They left the hotel and walked a block to the Red Lantern Chinese restaurant. Carlos pigged out on sweet and sour pork. Patricio had the moo goo gai pan. Carlos asked the tall, slender Mexican waiter for more rice and then asked a question.

"Do you know where there were old mines that Chinese lived at?"

"Yo no soy chino. No sé nada," the waiter seemed agitated. "You go Celestial Phoenix. Ask there."

Later, Patricio laughed. "You, sly dog. That was a clever trick."

"Tomorrow. Celestial Phoenix."

For the next two days they slowly visited mining sites at Minas Prietas, Sleeping Beauty, and Silverado. They talked to the owners who knew very little of what had happened a century earlier. For them, the Chinese were not on the radar. They were advised to go to Mexicali if they wanted to see Chinese.

Thursday afternoon was upon them, and the pair were tired.

"I think we are finished, my friend," Patricio put a hand on Carlos' shoulder. "Mala suerte. Sixteen mines and three Chinese restaurants later and we found very little. I'm going to text Professor Reynoso."

An hour later Francisco sent an email telling the pair to come back the next day with a copy of their report for Tina.

That night, a few thousand miles away, Tina was getting ready for bed. She had just read the professor's email. She was feeling discouraged. However, Rubí would soon be leaving, and Tina could get back to work full-time. She read for a while and then turned off the light.

She closed her eyes. Her body felt hot. She threw off the cotton sheet. She rolled over on her stomach. Her breathing got more shallow. Her eyes felt heavy. Then a long yawn.

Flashes of light pulsated throughout the room. Her bed began to shake. Waves of heat floated through the air.

Tina moaned. She could not open her eyes, but she saw a muscular masculine figure in front of her. He had a blue body and feathers on his arms and legs. He wore a colibrí helmet. He carried a serpentine staff in one hand and an eagle-feathered shield in the other.

"Go to my sanctuary!" a deep telepathic command was uttered by the blue figure. "I need my tributes!"

Tina was walking on a high desert plain. The sun was guiding her.

"Follow me!"

Tina saw an old hogan abandoned on the mountain slope. She stepped toward the shack.

"Obey!" the form gnashed its teeth. "Pay attention!"

Tina passed into the little hut. There was very little furniture. An old coffee cup was turned over on a small table. There was something tacked to the wall. She knew this place.

"Go to my sanctuary now!"

CHAPTER 54 – DECISIONS

Friday, June 28, 2019

Guadalajara

At five o'clock in the morning Tina woke up in a panic. She frantically called Professor Reynoso. Groggily, he picked up and took his cellphone into the hallway so Alex could keep on sleeping.

"Sorry, professor," Tina was panting. "I think I know where it is."

"Where what is?"

"The turquoise colibrí amulet." She frantically proceeded to tell him about her vision that night.

Francisco was very skeptical. *Is Tina working too hard? Is she stressed or getting burned out?* "Tina, what do you suggest that we should do now?"

"I don't know. I know that Carlos wants to go home today. And probably Patricio does too. This vision was just too real."

Francisco wanted to go back to bed.

"But it all makes sense, professor," Tina was trying to assert herself. "We have been looking at Ana's departure from Puebla as an escape. After Doña Filomena died, she had to find a way to raise her family. She couldn't raise the children as Chinese because Chan Toy was dead and she didn't know the culture or language well enough. The Chinese-Mexicans barrios in Mexicali were too dangerous. The Mexican government was in flux. It would be only natural for her to go back to her Mexican-Yaqui roots."

"Assuming I agree, where do you think it is?" Francisco was circumspect.

"According to the Chan Toy papers, Ana's aunt Teta Chi'ila gave Ana the turquoise colibrí amulet at the Little Blue Rock pueblo. For protection. My recollection is that her mother Joya had kept it in her home village."

"We need to check with Patricio to see if there were any turquoise quarries in Cananea or any other place close," Francisco added with a frown on his face.

"Professor, have him for sure check out Little Blue Rock. That was the Yaqui village where Joya was raised."

"Tina, we have a small logistical problem. I gave Carlos permission to go home today. He has a family."

"Well, that leaves Patricio. Can he stay an extra day?"

"Well, that might be a bit unfair, don't you think?" Francisco wanted them to work as a team. It was as important as the outcome. "I want there to be two persons around for corroboration and safety."

They talked for a few minutes and Tina was beginning to agree with him, when she said, "Oh, Rubí is leaving tomorrow."

"Oh, crap!" Francisco blurted out. "We need her to take possession of the turquoise colibrí amulet if we find it. That's the deal with Lilí and Rare Elements."

"Professor, I can talk to her and see if she can delay her departure."

"In the meantime, I will email Lilí and ask if Rubí can stay longer. It's in their best interests," the professor put another task on his To Do List.

"Professor, I probably shouldn't say this, but I talked to my father the other day. We were talking about my work. I asked him if he knew anything about Rare Elements, Inc. He railed that the mainland Chinese were driving up housing prices in Vancouver and were trying to gain control of Canadian mining."

Francisco knew that there was discord between mainland Chinese immigrants to Canada and the ABCs/CBCs (American and Canadian-born Chinese). It was common knowledge that Beijing was harassing and interrogating Canadian Chinese, especially those who had supported an independent Taiwan. And that Beijing was investing billions in high tech spying in Canada and the U.S.

"Let me talk to Carlos and Patricio about staying an extra day or two. I'll also ask Lilí to let Rubí stay a few more days. You can also ask Rubí to stay. Can you meet me in my office at 10 a.m.?"

They hung up. It was too late to go back to bed. He had an early breakfast with Alex. He briefed her on the latest developments of the Chan Toy Project. He arrived at his office an hour earlier than usual.

The first text he sent was to Carlos and Patricio apprising them of a possible change in plans. He asked them if they would be willing to stay a few extra days to verify the possible location of the turquoise hummingbird amulet. The decision would be entirely up to them. It was their days, and he didn't want to force them to work extra.

Then he sent a text to Lilí:

June 28, 2019

Lilí Song
Chinese Dragon Rare Elements Ltd.,
Vancouver, B.C. Canada

RE: Chan Toy Project

Dear Ms. Song:

We are making progress in locating the turquoise hummingbird amulet that we have agreed to procure for you. We have a strong lead and will be investigating it within the next few days.

As we have discussed, Rubí Song has your authorization and power of attorney to receive the turquoise hummingbird. However, we understand that she is planning to return home tomorrow. Is it possible for her to stay a few more days?

If this is not case, should we assume that we can transfer the turquoise hummingbird amulet directly to you in Guadalajara at a mutually agreed upon time.

If you have any questions or concerns, please contact us.

By nine-thirty, he had heard from Carlos and Patricio They agreed to do one more overnight if they had a specific place to go. They did not want to do any more random exploration. Francisco wrote back and thanked them. He would let them know if he would actually need them to do the extra work.

Francisco then got a text from Tina asking if they could delay their meeting for an hour, to 11 a.m. She was working on something. What could Francisco say?

Tina caught the professor yawning as she waltzed into his office. Her hair was a mess, and she wore a loose fitting cotton sweater. Francisco had never seen her so casual.

"Professor, you won't believe this!" she offered some sheets of paper. "I think I really found the place!"

She explained to him that they had been too myopic in their investigation. They had been looking for linear solutions and making inaccurate generalizations. They had not been following the clues. "Volver" and "Devolver."

Tina had been researching the children of Ana and Chan Toy all morning. She finally found a copy of property tax records for Cajemé Chan. There was a purchase of property in Little Blue Rock. She got the address.

Francisco was shocked. He shook his head in disbelief. He immediately texted Carlos and Patricio. Were they going to be in for a surprise!

CHAPTER 55 – SASHEEN

Friday, June 28, 2019

Little Blue Rock

"Wow! It looks like Tina may have figured it out!" Carlos was shaking his head in approval. He was driving his rental car down the dusty road. It was scorching hot. They bought some bottled waters at the first OXXO convenience store they passed.

"It makes more sense. Very few turquoise mines in Cananea. Mostly gold and copper," Patricio commented.

The serpentine road wound up and down the foothills north of Sierra de Cananea. While the GPS showed the location of the Cajemé Chan property, it did not show any roads leading into it. The Google map said it was between 12 and 15 minutes from Cananea, but it took Carlos and Patricio an hour to reach it. Dead end roads and deep ditches challenged their drive, not to mention that the rental SUV did not have four-wheel drive. Eventually, they came to a fork in the road. To the right going uphill was stationed a pine tree with three ribbons wrapped around it. It was probably a sign. There were also acres of barrel cactus. The vehicle bounced and bounced and twice the oil pan scraped bottom but finally they saw a plot of almost flat land. Corn was growing in one section. The hogan nearest the front had a dilapidated porch.

Carlos stopped and got out of the car. He yelled out as he approached the shack, “anybody home?” No answer. He went up to the screen door that was tattered and torn, and tried to look in. Nobody seemed to be home. He returned to the car. Carlos and Patricio snacked on pumpkin seeds and bottled water while they waited. There were no bars showing on their cellphones, so they couldn’t call anyone. Carlos closed his eyes to take a nap. Almost an hour later, there was the sound of a dog yapping. The pair saw a squat old woman dressed in indigenous garb and wearing a medicine pouch around her bulk. She was walking slowly accompanied by two young boys.

“Buenas tardes, señora,” Carlos was trying to be friendly. “We are looking for the Chan property.”

One of the boys who had dark skin and thick black hair yelled out, “She doesn’t speak much Spanish!”

Carlos knew only a handful of words of Yaqui, so he tried talking to her in Purépecha and Nahuatl. The next five minutes were torturous. Patricio was not much help, so he stayed out of it. The two boys did speak Spanish but were very young. They tried to assist.

The old woman was stout and had a million beautiful wrinkles etched on her face. There was also a string of white dots tattooed across her cheeks. She motioned with her two forefingers back and forth from her mouth. She seemed to want a cigarette.

"Sorry, we don't smoke."

Patricio quickly got up and went to the car where he retrieved some of their food provisions. The boys loved the chips. The woman had almost no teeth but scooped up the peanut butter with her fingers.

"Where is the girl?" the old woman asked through her two young interpreters.

"What girl?" Carlos responded. She did not pursue it.

She invited them into her hogan. She started to boil a kettle of water on a butane stove in the back. The shack had two twin beds at one end and a table at the other. In place of chairs, there were cushions on the wood planked floor. The walls were hung with multicolored weavings.

After a long series of linguistic trials and tribulations, the men discovered that the woman was named Sasheen, and that she was the pueblo healer. When they asked her questions about Ana Chan or Joya Azuleta, she muttered something incomprehensible and pointed uphill. She served them some type of herbal tea in mismatched terra cotta cups. It was bitter.

Carlos and Patricio were feeling frustrated. They were ready to call it a day, when the dog named Chuu'u barked. The old woman got up and started up the hill. The path was dusty and smelled of Mexican sage. Everyone followed her. The old woman swayed as she walked up the incline. They passed a copse of barrel cactus and watched Chuu'u chase after a roadrunner. He gave up after about twenty seconds.

They stopped at a graveyard that had about a dozen wooden crosses peppered through it. Patricio tried to study the wooden markers, but there were no visible names or dates. *Could Ana or Joya be buried here?* wondered Carlos.

Sasheen led them to another hogan. The two boys were constantly by her side. In the middle of a dark room was a weaving wheel. The shack also had its walls covered with weavings.

The woman turned around and poked her finger into Carlos's chest. He jumped back in surprise.

"You buy!" she said in Spanish pointing to the weavings hanging on the walls.

Carlos and Patricio looked at each other. "Okay." He made a gesture like he wanted to look around for something he liked. The two men walked to the back of the shack. There were piles of rocks, bottles, and leather items everywhere. There were some large leather bags and Patricio asked if he could look inside. The boys translated and the woman nodded. There were loose lavender boughs in the bags.

In the second bag they found men's black silk pants. They were all dusty and faded out and moth eaten.

"To whom did these belong?" Patricio asked slowly.

The old woman shook her head and said something. One of the boys said, "Ancestor. She said ancestor."

They found stained and dirty silk blouses with embroidered designs. *Could these have been Ana's? The ones she wore in Puebla? The ones she brought from Guangzhou.* Carlos' mind was racing.

Carlos made a sign to the woman that he wanted to buy the black pants and the silk tops. All of them. If she was surprised, she did not show it. He offered her a one thousand peso note and she nodded. He would expense it when he got back. Maybe they were valuable for their own sake.

Patricio was moving to the front entrance. Suddenly, he was blocked by Sasheen.

"You buy too!" she voiced sternly. Her face said that she wasn't going to take no for an answer.

Patricio looked apprehensively at Carlos.

His friend chuckled in a soft tone, "Don't worry. We'll expense it. The professor won't mind. If he does it, you'll just have an expensive souvenir."

Patricio exhaled and started to scan the weavings on the walls. One that depicted three women with different colored long veils caught his eye. Then he looked at another in various shades of red with dozens of patterned shapes of squares, triangles, and straight lines. Suddenly he felt as if something touched his skin and he shivered. There was a smaller wall hanging that was not made of cloth. It looked like parchment. It was tacked to the corner and didn't receive much light.

"Carlos, come here," there was excitement in his voice. "Look at this!"

Carlos frowned. *What is it?* He approached Patricio and peered over this shoulder. The drawing seemed familiar. Then it hit him. "This resembles the other two maps. The ones that Ana drew. This is part of her triptych!" The two fist bumped each other as their grins stretched from ear to ear."

Patricio said to Sasheen in a pleasant tone. "I take this one."

The older woman shook her head no.

"But you wanted me to buy something!"

She shook her head no again.

After fifteen minutes of haggling, Sasheen was four thousand pesos richer, and Carlos and Patricio seemed to have Ana's Map #3.

As they were leaving, one of the boys came up to them. "You have to come back here in five days."

"Why?" Patricio replied.

"Abuela. She go to the mountain and speak with Lios."

"Who is Lios?" Patricio asked.

The boy shrugged.

"I think he is the Yaqui Sun god." Carlos explained to Patricio and turned to the boy. "Okay, we'll try."

"And bring cigarettes," the youngster demanded. "And wooden matches."

It was getting close to dusk, and they wanted to get down the mountain side before it got dark and dangerous.

Carlos and Patricio debriefed and decided that they had time to catch flights back home. At the airport they grabbed a quick beer and some spicy beef enchiladas.

"Why do we have to come back in five days?" Patricio asked. His flight to Mexico City was being announced for departure.

"From what little I understood," Carlos said. "She is going on a vision quest. She wants to talk to Lios."

"The Sun god?"

CHAPTER 56 – MAP #3

Saturday - Monday, June 29 – July 1, 2019

Guadalajara

Francisco was elated when he heard from Carlos and Patricio from Cananea the night before. With a copy of Map 3 in their possession they were one step closer. The authenticity and accuracy of the third part of the triptych would have to be verified before they could proceed, but they planned out several scenarios. They had sent a copy to Francisco by text message.

Carlos related the story about Sasheen, the Little Blue Rock pueblo healer.

"She certainly made some money off of you guys."

"It's all reimbursable, right?" Carlos was frugal with his money. "Otherwise, Patricio owns the third map."

"Of course," Francisco didn't care, and besides, the third map was invaluable if it led them to the turquoise hummingbird amulet.

"Professor, what is our next step?"

"I'll apprise Dean Ríos and Dean Chandler of our progress. If everything checks out, we'll go back to Cananea and see Señora Sasheen."

Francisco could not see the look of terror on Carlos' face over the phone.

That afternoon Alex and Francisco took a walk in their favorite park. Since it was Saturday, they had some time together. Children were playing ball, vendors were selling balloons, and teens were sitting on benches smooching. Lunch was a chicken taco for each of them with a fruit cup to split.

Back at the house, Francisco poured over the map. It looked like a drawing of a mine with its various shafts and tunnels. *What is its significance? Where is this?* He was fortunate that Patricio was part of the team. He needed to call him.

But before he could, the phone rang. It was Tina. She was excited about finding a new piece of the puzzle.

"Well, it was thanks to you and your dreams," Francisco said pleasantly. "Any more supernatural experiences?"

Tina did not know if the professor was being serious or humorous. “No. But the vision was so real. You must think I’m crazy.”

“Tina, I know you. I’m certain that you visualized or dreamed what you described. The information turned out to be true. I don’t believe in coincidences of this sort.”

She gave him an update on Cajemé Chan and his property holdings in Little Blue Rock. There was nothing about his siblings.

“How is Rubí doing?” the professor was afraid to ask. Francisco had screwed up her departure plans.

“On again, off again,” Tina commented. “She had wanted to leave today. For the last few days, she hasn’t seemed very happy.”

“How so?”

“Well, I’m not sure. I haven’t spent as much time with her as I would have liked. My time has been taking up working on this project, hanging around Mirasol, and talking to Patricio. I don’t think she has a boyfriend. She seems lonely.”

“Do you think she is jealous?”

“No, probably just bored. I know that she has been in contact with her sister a lot lately. I even heard Rubí get angry during one of their conversations.”

"How long will she be staying on?"

"I don't know."

"Tina, I need you to clear your calendar," Francisco thought he better tie Tina down now. "I want you to calendar a trip to Cananea this coming week. Probably from Wednesday through Friday."

"Do you want Rubí to stick around that long?"

"Probably so. If we do find the turquoise hummingbird, we have to turn it over to her. We will have to document the entire chain of title. There is big money involved and the universities do not want to lose it. We need to think about the best way to do this."

***

Mexico City

Earlier that Saturday morning, Patricio had called Doctor Manuel Pinteiro, the Director of Cartography at the Museum of Anthropology.

"Doctor, we think we found the third part of the Chan Toy triptych. We'll need your assistance again."

They met in Pinteiro's office where Patricio handed over the document (map #3) to the director.

The older man turned the document around several times in his hand. He brought out a loupe and examined the map inch by inch.

He looked up. “It looks consistent with the sea log parchment and ink of the other two documents. We will need to do further tests.”

“Thank you, doctor.”

“One more thing, Patricio,” Doctor Pinteiro added. “There is a word etched on the bottom. It looks like the word, ‘Revolver.’ I don’t know its significance.”

Patricio shook his head. He had no notion either.

Patricio left Doctor Pinteiro’s office and went to the Textiles Department that catalogued and inventoried thousands of items of clothing. He gave them the black silk pants he had purchased from Sasheen as well as the dirty Chinese silk blouses. He kept one out for himself.

***

The following Monday morning, Patricio was soaking a piece of a cinnamon sugar pretzel into his coffee. His cellphone rang. It was Doctor Pinteiro.

“There between

is a 95% and 98% chance that this was from Ana Chan . . .” They talked for another ten minutes.

Patricio immediately called Professor Reynoso. "Professor, I think we caught a break. Map #3 is from Ana Chan."

"Do we know what this is a map of?"

"No, not yet. But with your permission, we can send a copy of it to Buzz Halow over at the Cananea Mining Association. If anybody would know, it would be him. He's a friend of mine and will be discreet."

"So, Patricio, Señora Sasheen is expecting a visit from us on Wednesday?" Francisco asked. "She probably has a lot more information. I want us to fly out to Cananea on Wednesday. You, Carlos, and me. Oh, wait, and Tina also. I'll have Juanita make the arrangements. I hope you and Carlos found some decent restaurants for us."

For the next half hour, they discussed timelines, travel logistics, and equipment needs. They hit a brick wall when the subject of Rubí came up.

"She is anxious to get out of here. It could be for a variety of reasons," Francisco stated. "I still have not heard from Lilí."

"What if we simply invite her along. She could travel with Tina," Patricio offered. "We need to catch her leaving with the hummingbird amulet."

"Patricio, exiting the country with a Mexican artifact is your department," Francisco knew that their ultimate objectives were different, but they could cooperate when possible. Patricio had already been an asset to the project. “Mine is documenting the handout to comply with our contract with Rare Elements,” Francisco added.

They went back and forth, and in the end decided that Rubí coming along could simplify their plan. If Rubí took possession of the turquoise colibrí amulet, she could be apprehended once she checked in at the airport. She would be easy to spot.

“One more thing, Patricio, could you please do me a favor? Find us someone who will be able to speak Yaqui and the other local dialects with Señora Sasheen.”

CHAPTER 57 – CIGARETTES

Wednesday, July 3, 2019

Little Blue Rock

Rubí's face sagged with a sour scowl as she shuffled toward the Guadalajara Airport terminal gate. Tina was walking between her and Professor Reynoso. She had made it known to everyone that she did not want to go to Little Blue Rock. She just wanted to leave Guadalajara and go home. Her sister Lilí beat her into submission and here she was. Not happy.

"Oh, I see you're wearing red lipstick today," Tina was in a good mood. Rubí normally wore purple lipstick. Rubí didn't respond. In a few hours Tina would get to see Patricio, her new beau.

On the short flight, Francisco washed down the little airline cookies with his coffee. Tina and Rubí drank their tea. There were only three other passengers on the small plane. They would meet Carlos at the Cananea Airport. He was flying in earlier and would rent a car. Then they would rendezvous with Patricio at the Mission Restaurant.

Carlos met them at baggage claim, and they all drove in his silver-grey SUV to the Mission Restaurant for breakfast. He texted Patricio to advise him that they were on their way.

They grabbed a table in the corner. "Rubí, as you know, this is Carlos. He is a fellow professor at the university and has a widespread expertise with Mexican and pre-Columbian artifacts," he paused a minute while the young cinnamon-skinned waitress with long braids took their order. "And this is Patricio. He works with the Museum of Anthropology in Mexico City and has an extensive background in mining."

Rubí nodded politely as she gave Patricio the once over. Twice. She thought that he looked better in person than in the photo Tina had shown her.

The coffee was acidic, but the men guzzled it down black. Francisco tried not to do dairy products based on Alex's counsel, and had to endure his coffee black because there was no soy milk within a hundred miles. The ladies had mint tea.

Francisco gave an overview of the next three days.

"Most of us will visit the medicine woman," he said. "We'll see why she wanted us to come back. Carlos, I hope you didn't forget her cigarettes."

"¡Diablos!" was heard from the across the table.

"If we get a lead, we'll follow up on it tomorrow. We are going to take this slowly. We are running out of options in locating the turquoise hummingbird."

Francisco picked up the tab and they all ended up at La Posada Exprés to check in to their lodging. Rubí didn't want to go to see the medicine woman. So, she was allowed to stay in her hotel room.

The remaining four jumped into Carlos' rental silver-grey SUV and started toward Little Blue Rock. At the OXXO convenience store at the edge of town, they stocked up on bottled water, chocolate bars, chips, sunflower seeds, wooden matches, and of course, cigarettes. No alcohol!

They resumed their drive and then stopped in front of La Cantina de Cobre.

"You're not serious," Tina blurted out. She was surprised that they were going to a bar before their encounter. This was crazy, she thought.

Her concerns were allayed when a skinny young man with long black hair, wearing a red bandana tied around his head, emerged from the cantina. He was wearing scuffed up cowboy boots and sported a scraggly black moustache. He walked toward the SUV and Patricio opened the door for him.

"This is Prócoro," Patricio announced. "He is going to be our Yaqui interpreter today. He works for Buzz at the Cananea Mining Association."

Hellos were exchanged and the SUV resumed its trek. Fortunately, Carlos had rented a four-wheel drive this time and it was easier to climb the rutted gravel road up the mountain.

Finally, they reached the pine tree with the three ribbons and drove right up to the hogan. They were greeted by the barking Chihuahua, Chuu'u.

Carlos parked and they waited. After twenty minutes, Sasheen the medicine woman slowly exited her shack. She walked about ten paces in her leather moccasins and then motioned for the visitors to come forward.

She looked straight at Carlos and said, "cigarettes!"

Carlos pulled out a big paper sack. He pulled out a carton of Winstons. She took them and nodded. He handed over another grocery bag to her and showed her the stash of goodies.

Carlos pushed Prócoro toward her and made motions to introduce him. After a few moments Sasheen and Prócoro were having an animated conversation. He translated her words to the group and vice-versa. Sasheen had opened a pack of cigarettes and lit one. Prócoro joined her. Nobody else smoked.

They were invited inside her hogan, and everyone sat on the splintery wooden planked floors covered with small woven rugs.

She lit some sage and circled it over the heads of her visitors. The sweet smell made everyone relax. And then she made some kerosene-tasting tea and everybody smiled as they drank it.

"Girl here now!" Prócoro translated for Sasheen looking at Tina. "She good girl. She belongs." Everybody stared at Tina who had a puzzled look on her face.

Sasheen began to spin her tale, and everybody carefully listened as Prócoro translated. Sasheen had just returned from the mountains where she had fasted for the last two days before making the vision quest to the Sun god Lios. She was looking for some answers.

Lios spoke to Sasheen in tongues of fire. He told her that greedy people were trying to kidnap the turquoise colibrí amulet. The girl had to protect it from the evildoers. Human sacrifice would be the price for evildoers' trespasses.

After a long twenty-five minutes of elaborating and repeating herself many times, Sasheen motioned them outside. She walked toward the SUV and motioned for Carlos to open the door for her. Since there wasn't enough room for everyone, Tina stayed behind. She was trying to piece this all together.

With great difficulty, Prócoro directed them up a steep incline following a barely discernible road. Sasheen pointed to a saguaro cactus and motioned for them to stop. Patricio got out first and opened the door for Sasheen. Everyone else followed as he held her arm going up an incline. They stopped by some large granite boulders. She went behind them and snaked her way to a hole in the mountain. It looked like the entrance of a mine shaft. She pointed to the dark interior and then turned around.

"You must go there. You must save him."

They studied the exterior. No one had a flashlight. Patricio used his cell phone and entered the cave. A minute later he came out and shook his head.

Without flashlights they could not see. So they decided to return to Sasheen's shack. Tina was patiently waiting for them. She had been curious about Sasheen's place and had treated herself to an unofficial tour.

The group began to ask Sasheen questions.

"Who owns the mine? Who made it?"

"What was the significance of the word 'revolver' that was etched onto the map?" They were referring to Map #3.

"Who were the last people to enter the mine?"

It was almost seven o'clock when they left Sasheen.

"You bring chocolate," Sasheen sternly told Carlos.

On the way back, everybody was full of energy and took turns reciting what they thought they heard and threw out ideas and theories.

"This god Lios is Huitzilopochtli, the god of the sun and war. He probably wants a human sacrifice!"

"That mine was not commercial. It looks like the Yaqui tribe excavated it. Not sure if was to mine for minerals or to bury ancestors."

"The old woman sensed evil. That's not a good sign." Francisco and Patricio exchanged furtive glances.

Francisco looked at his watch. "Tina, please do me a favor and call Rubí. Tell her to join us in thirty minutes at the restaurant."

On the way back, they stopped and dropped Prócoro off at the cantina. Francisco slipped him two one-thousand-peso notes.

"We should have our dinner here," Patricio commented. "I could use a cold one. Especially after drinking that horse piss tea." Everyone laughed.

“I don’t think that’s a good idea,” Francisco regained control. “Tomorrow we are going to attack the mine bright and early. It’s our best shot for finding the turquoise colibrí.”

“Excuse me, professor, but we’re going to need a lot of equipment if we are going to explore that mine. Lanterns, ropes, compass . . .” Patricio inserted. “And there is no cell service.”

“You’re right. Good call,” Francisco agreed. “Can you get all this equipment?”

“No problem. The mining supply store opens at 7:30. I also suggest that we bring two bottles of water for each person, some protein bars, and premade sandwiches.”

“Carlos, can you take care of that please?”

“I’ll steal a roll of toilet paper from the room,” Tina chimed in.

CHAPTER 58 – DOUBLE CROSS

Thursday, July 4, 2019

Little Blue Rock

The dawn had diffused its reds and oranges and yellows. Carlos was taking his time driving back to the hotel. The morning air was cool, but he knew it would heat up. He had made the grocery run for today's mine exploration. He didn't feel the slightness twinge of guilt sneaking a piece of freshly baked pan dulce. Slippage.

He noticed that Patricio's green SUV was not in the parking lot. Carlos was supposed to have acquired all the mining equipment, and had left very early to make the equipment purchases. Maybe he went to buy gas, Carlos thought. He was ready for the day's adventure.

Carlos knocked on Patricio's door. No answer. He then moved two doors down and rapped on Professor Reynoso's room. No answer. *That's really weird,* he thought. They were supposed to meet in the lobby at eight. He was there. Nobody else was. *What's going on?* He had the young indigenous receptionist call Tina's room. No answer. The same result with Rubí's room. *Maybe someone was sick and they went to the hospital!* Most likely Rubí. He walked up to Rubi's floor and knocked. No answer. The housekeeping person was close by. His first inclination was to ask her to open the door to Rubí's room to find any clues about the disappearance of his colleagues. He then decided to ask the housekeeper to let him enter Tina's room. He had made nice with the maid on his prior visit, and she figured he could be trusted. She used her white plastic electronic access key card and let him in. He slipped her a hundred pesos.

Tina's computer was still on the bedside table. He called out and when he didn't hear an answer, he went to her bedroom. Her few clothes and suitcase were still in the closet. He walked into the bathroom and her toiletries surrounded the sink. Carlos knew that this was such an invasion of privacy. How embarrassing it would be if she walked in on him right now! He went over to her computer. It was in sleep mode. He noticed Tina's cell phone close by. *She is never without it.*

With some hesitation, he picked up the cell phone and opened her messenger application. He looked at the latest text. It was from Rubí. It was in Portuguese.

Adjud! Venha ao meu quarto! Eles me pegaram! Vamos para a mina.

Carlos didn't know Portuguese, but with his linguistic acumen he guessed that Rubí was in trouble and needed Tina's help. He took out his cell phone and did a Google translation. "Adjud" meant help. Somebody was in trouble. He rushed out the door and located the housekeeper. He asked her to open Rubí's room which she did. A quick search revealed that all her belongings were gone. Had she run away?

He then caught sight of a copy of Map #3 on her table. There were markings on it from a red ink pen. *What gives?* Carlos rushed back downstairs and went to the receptionist's desk and asked if Rubí or anyone of his party had checked out. The woman said no.

Had Buzz taken them to the mine? Someone should have waited for me, or at least, left a message. None of this made sense. He had the receptionist call the police and explain the situation. They replied that they need more details before they could act.

A half hour later Carlos was parked in front of Sasheen's shack. He was sweating and his body was shaking. He remembered to give Sasheen her chocolate protein bars. The two struggled to communicate with each other. She pointed up the mountain. He understood that to mean the mine. As he was leaving, she gave him a handful of small round turquoise stones.

"You take Chuu'u," She handed him the Chihuahua. So he did. He was rewarded with a lick.

Fifteen minutes later he was at the entrance of the Revolver Mine. That's what Sasheen called it, and that confirmed what was on Map #3. Carlos saw Patricio's green car parked next to a big, black SUV about fifty meters away. Carlos got out of his vehicle and Chuu'u ran toward the larger vehicle, barking all the way. He saw a figure in the car. The door opened. It was Rubí. She looked scared.

This was a good sign, he thought. *The others are probably around.* "Rubí, are you okay? Where is everyone?"

She nodded yes and pointed to the mine entrance. Chuu'u stopped in front of her and growled.

Carlos went back to his car and retrieved some bottled waters and snacks for Rubí. "Are you going to be okay if I leave you alone for a while? I'm going to try to find them. Is there a flashlight around here somewhere?"

She gave him an empty look. He examined all three vehicles but could not find a flashlight. There was no mining equipment in Patricio's car. Carlos decided to chance it. He entered the mine that had a low ceiling. The air smelled like a sewer line. It was moldy and moist. He took a few steps in and turned on the light function on his phone. It did not give off much light, but it was better than nothing. The uneven walls were rough and jagged. He proceeded very slowly. He didn't have a hard hat or any other proper clothing or equipment. Patricio had been in charge of all of that. The ground was a gravelly mixture and was very hard to walk on. No footprints. Luckily, Carlos always wore hiking boots.

"Is anybody there?" He yelled out. No answer. A mild echo.

The light from the cell phone was minimal. He took each step carefully avoiding potholes. After about fifty meters in, it was pitch black, and Carlos couldn't see. He turned off his phone light and waited five minutes. His eyes adjusted to the darkness somewhat, but after walking another ten meters he decided it was too risky to continue. His colleagues would come out eventually and then he would find out what was happening.

***

Earlier that morning Tina had heard her phone ping. It was a text from Rubí. It was an urgent request for help from her. It was in Portuguese. Her friend was in trouble and had used Portuguese to disguise the distress message.

Tina ran out her room and banged on Rubí's room. No answer. She tried the door. It was unlocked. As she entered, she saw Rubí on the couch. There were two young muscular tattooed Asian men pointing handguns at their prisoner.

"Call the others!" one of the kidnappers shouted at Tina in Mandarin. "Tell them to come down to their car immediately. It's an emergency!"

Tina hesitated, trying to collect her wits.

"Hurry up! Or someone gets hurt!"

Tina had left her phone in her room. She grabbed Rubí's phone that was on the table close by. She opened the Text app and forwarded Rubí's note to the professor with her own:

> **Please come down to our car immediately. It's an emergency! Bring Patricio.**

Francisco was in his room working on his emails when Tina's text came through. He opened it and first saw Rubí's text in Portuguese. He didn't speak Portuguese but knew something was wrong. Then he read Tina's note. She was in a predicament.

He called Patricio who picked up immediately.

"Patricio, we got an SOS message from Tina," the words jetted out of his mouth. "We have to get down to your car!"

"When?" Patricio responded.

"Right now!"

They met in the hallway and ran down the stairs.

As they approached Patricio's green car, a young Asian youth popped out from behind a black SUV that was parked next to it. He had a gun and pointed it at the two of them.

Francisco blurted out, "where is Tina!"

The young man pointed for Patricio to get into his green SUV. The driver's seat.

The door of the black SUV opened and Rubí got out. She got into Patricio's vehicle.

The youth suddenly grabbed Francisco's wrists and put plastic zip tie handcuffs on him. Francisco knew better than to struggle. Too much risk. He was forced into the backseat of the black SUV next to Tina, with his tied hands on his lap. She was also cuffed in the same manner. Next to her was another young henchman.

From the front passenger seat, a woman turned around and looked directly at Francisco. She had a cigarette in her right hand and inhaled deeply.

“Professor, please direct us to the mine,” the red lipsticked twin said in a sultry voice. “The fate of your colleagues is in your hands.”

CHAPTER 59 – THE CHAMBER

Thursday, July 4, 2019

Revolver Mine, Little Blue Rock

After they arrived at the mine, everybody except Rubí had been forced to exit the two vehicles. Patricio was immediately handcuffed with the plastic ties. He was pushed toward Tina and Francisco who were now facing Lilí and Way Oh (aka Hao Chin Martín). Lilí lit up a cigarette. The two Chinese thugs still had their handguns out.

"Ah, Professor Reynoso, you have done such an excellent job. We have been pleased with your work," Lilí inhaled deeply on her cigarette. She spoked in her drawn out British accented English. She exhaled.

"Ms. Song, what is this all about?" Francisco asked. "I thought we had a deal. There is no need for any of this."

“Unfortunately, your Mister Gomez would disagree. According to certain sources, he wants to arrest us. Huh!” She kicked her hiking boots into the ground. “This mine visit was a ruse to lure us here and lock us up.” She walked up and got into Patricio’s face and gave him a malevolent smirk.

“What does this have to do with Tina and me?” Francisco tried to reason with his captor.

“Nothing and everything,” she pursed her red lipsticked lips as she again kicked the ground with her hiking boots like an angry bull. “If you follow instructions, you will be allowed to live. If not, the consequences may prove fatal.”

Lilí spoke to Way Oh and the two armed thugs in Mandarin. Minutes later Francisco and Patricio were carrying backpacks. They could not reach behind themselves since they were still handcuffed in the front.

“We will go in single file. Follow the light on my hard hat,” Lili directed.

Francisco observed that Lili’s team was equipped with hard hats, boots, ropes, and carbide lamps. His group had nothing.

“If there are problems, we will tie you all together with a rope,” she did a head count. Seven, including herself.

Rubí stared anxiously from the black SUV. She was not going. She checked her watch as the group entered the mine entrance. It was 8:30. Right on schedule.

The initial portion of the mine's entrance was relatively straight. Lilí led the parade, followed by Francisco and Way Oh, and then a guard, then Tina, Patricio, and finally the other guard. The path was pocked like the lunar surface. Pieces of sizeable gravel were strewn everywhere. Tina tripped over a protruding rock. "Diu!" she let escape. Her toe ached. One of the guards picked her up. Nobody said anything.

After about ten minutes of walking, there was a sudden "STOP!" Everybody complied. Lilí called one of the guards up to the front. A large hole about two and a half meters in diameter was emitting a little draft of sulfuric rotten egg smell. There seemed to be no way around it. Then one of guards cried out, "Next to the wall!"

Lilí spotted three splintered wooden planks measuring about three meters long. Carefully, they were laid across the aperture.

"Way Oh, you go first," Lilí Way Oh in Mandarin.

"Why me?" he replied in a fearful tone. "How about one of guards? Or better yet one of the prisoners?"

"Suck it up! We need the prisoners for the moment," she was stern with him. "Our government is counting on us. It's our patriotic duty."

A minute later Way Oh was slowly inching his way on the planks. His weight made the boards bend and creak. His lamp was aimed directly in front of him. Everybody waited in anticipation. No one knew how deep the hole was and they didn't want to find out.

Tina was pushed to the front of the line, limping slightly. "Please cut off these cuffs!" she pleaded.

"It will help you concentrate with them on," Lilí responded harshly, nodding her head no.

Tina felt like she had to go to the bathroom. She inhaled deeply and passed over the abyss without incident. For the next few minutes, the group went across one by one. The last one was the second guard. His boot caught on a splintered edge of one the planks. He fell on the remaining two boards as the culprit plank and his gun plunged down the hole. It took about four seconds to hear a rebounding sound at the bottom. The guard righted himself and ran across the remaining distance.

"Clumsy idiot!" Lili blurted out.

They continued onward. After traipsing past a rusty bucket, broken bottles, and pieces of wood for a while, they came to a fork in the road. It went in three directions.

"Professor, which way does your map say the turquoise hummingbird is?" Lilí asked. She had a copy of Map #3 and had her head lamp illuminating it.

Francisco's eyes blinked as he looked at the chart. His eyes were overwhelmed by the bright light.

"I don't know," Francisco answered. "Nothing seems to correspond."

"You, Gomez," Lilí barked. "What do you think?"

Patricio had been trying to gather clues and intelligence ever since the moment they were abducted. He surmised that Lilí did not speak Spanish well and the guards didn't at all. They had been communicating in Mandarin. However, Way Oh knew some Spanish. It was going to be risky to try to covertly communicate with Francisco and Tina.

"If you are asking me which way we should go, I think the middle one would have been the path most taken. Or the most practical." Patricio's English was passable. "But as an explorer, I would go from the left to the right. It makes sure everything is covered."

Lilí spoke to Way Oh. They were jabbering for a minute. "Okay, we go straight."

The path was wider and level. As they walked, they started hearing crunching sounds under their feet. They finally reached a large room with a vaulted ceiling. It was very dark, but it looked like there were drawings on the surrounding walls.

All of sudden one of the guards screamed as he jumped into the air. He cried out and pointed to the ground. The lights went downward and peered around. There were hundreds of skulls on the floor. The group retreated. The frightened guard was forced to make a thorough search of the area before he was allowed to rejoin the group.

A minute later there was another scream. Tina was on the ground. "My ankle" she cried out. "Get these damn cuffs off of me." Nobody moved to help her until Lilí gave an instruction to the thug to cut Tina's ties which de did.

Tina rubbed her wrists for a bit and then her right ankle. Finally, she got up and hobbled over to the professor. He tried to support her as they walked back to the fork in the path.

"I feel like I've been playing soccer," she said lightly, squeezing the professor's shoulder. "If Sol could only see me now."

"No more talking!" shouted Lilí.

When they finally reached the fork, Lilí sent everyone except Tina to explore the left fork.

"If you have to go to the toilet, this is a good time to do so," she said to Tina.

Tina did not have to think twice and staggered down the incoming path. She did her business sans toilet paper. *This is one way to mark your territory,* she thought. She went back toward the light of Lilí's head lamp.

"Lilí, why are you doing this? We were looking for the turquoise hummingbird amulet for you. Lots of work. We were going to hand over the object when we got it. That is why we kept Rubí with us."

Lili lit a cigarette and took a few puffs before she extinguished it.

"Too slow. Government wants it now. Too dangerous. Your boyfriend will arrest us. We pay lot of money. It is ours."

They argued for a few minutes and then remained silent until the group returned.

"Well, what did you find?" Way Oh was interrogated by Lilí.

"Very steep. Very long. Lots of bat guano on the rocks. Very slippery. We climb high but impossible to go further."

The guards corroborated his story, mostly out of fear of contradicting their boss.

Francisco would have added, if asked., how much stinky bat shit had accumulated there over the decades. Patricio thoughts were on the methane gas produced by the bat guano.

They took a five-minute break. Unfortunately, they hadn't brought any food or water.

"Okay. Let's go."

They next took the path to the right. It went downwards in a serpentine direction. After about 150 meters, they were blocked by a walled-off entry way.

"Look!" Way Oh shouted as he pointed to a double-headed snake over the portal. It looked like it was made of turquoise.

"Inside. We have to get inside," Lilí yelled at the two guards. They took out a pickax and a short shovel from one of the backpacks. They started attacking the dried mud that blocked the entry. Whack! Slash! Grab! This noisy excavation went on and on, until there was a small opening large enough to crawl through.

"¡Finta!" a high voice whispered in Francisco's direction during the demolition. *Where did it come from? What does it mean?*

Way Oh and a guard went in first and cautiously flashed their lights around the chamber. In the middle of the back wall there was a form. The guard carefully crept closer and then stopped in front of it. It was the skeleton of a small person. Its clothes had dissolved and all that remained was a leather pouch near the left hip.

CHAPTER 60 – THE EXPLOSION

Thursday, July 4, 2019

Revolver Mine, Little Blue Rock

“Could this be Ana?” everybody silently asked. The four headlamps were focused on the human form at the other end of the chamber. The chamber’s ceiling was about four meters high and twelve meters in diameter. The lights of the headlights reflected on thin lines of copper veined in the walls of the cave. The walls seemed to be decorated with pictographs that were indiscernible. In the middle of the chamber was a circle of rocks that had served as a fireplace. The air smelled stale and moldy.

One by one everyone stepped through the enclosure. Suddenly, the gravely floor trembled. Everyone started to panic. There was rumbling outside. All the lights flickered and then went out.

"¡Finta!" someone yelled out. Then it came to Francisco. It was a soccer term that Sol used. It was some type of trick play, but he didn't remember what it was.

A small light came on. It was Lilí's lighter. Carefully, she moved her arm from side to side checking out everyone. She stopped. Tina was now sitting in front of the skeletal figure.

There was a second shaking of the chamber. This time it was more powerful, and rocks fell from the ceiling. Then the lights came back on.

"Okay, Tina, show us what you found!" Lilí demanded.

At first Tina pretended not to know what she was talking about. She then inhaled. The feint had not succeeded. Lilí was too well trained and had anticipated the diversion. Slowly, Tina put the leather pouch that she had pinched from the skeleton on the ground in front of her. She turned it over and started to pour out the contents. Some old brittle twigs, a copper penny, and several buttons, and finally the smudged turquoise hummingbird amulet.

There was a collective gasp. "Well, finally, we found you," Lilí said to the turquoise talisman. "You're coming with us."

All of a sudden, a soft high-pitched buzzing sound emitted from the artifact. The ground shook again. The turquoise hummingbird seemed to glow.

"Take the thing!" Francisco yelled. "And just let us go."

"It's not that simple, professor," Lilí reacted. "Your friend Patricio wants to arrest us as soon as we leave. We can't let that happen. Our government won't allow it."

"But you have what you wanted. We fulfilled our end of the agreement!" Francisco implored. "You promised to let us go!"

"No, professor, I promised to let you alive," Lilí said mockingly. "In fact, you can keep Ana company. I'm sure you will have some great conversations."

Way Oh laughed.

Lilí gave him a dirty look. "Grab the lead apron and put the hummingbird in it! Be careful with it."

In a split-second, Tina snatched the turquoise amulet and twisted her body as she lunged sideways.

"Get it!" screamed Lilí to the two thugs.

The pitch of the buzzing increased. It got louder and louder.

The turquoise hummingbird continued to glow. It was getting hot. Tina dropped it because it was burning her hands.

One of the guards grabbed her. The other thug tried to snatch the hummingbird amulet.

Little bursts of fire and light flew out of the hummingbird. Tina thought she sensed the presence of the black headed, blue bodied warrior beside her.

The first guard held Tina more tightly. Tina screamed out in pain and fear.

Then comets of fire flew from the hummingbird figure into the faces of both thugs. Puffs of smoke emanated from their sockets. Then the thugs' faces turned bright red. Their bodies shook convulsively. Their eyes started to shrivel. Their heads seemed to get bigger and bigger. The chirping noise increased. Unexpectedly, the heads of the two guards exploded into hundreds of pieces. Nothing was left of them, including the head lamps.

A cry of horror came from the others.

"Grab the hummingbird and let's get out of here," Lilí barked at Way Oh.

Way Oh threw the lead apron over the amulet and scooped it up. The object was hot and shaking, but the lead apron dampened its vibrations.

"Come on! Let's go!" Lilí yelled as she started out of the enclosure.

"What about us?" Tina cried out.

"Shall I tie her up?" Way Oh yelled out.

Lilí ignored him and retorted toward Tina. "What about you? You are all spoiled and privileged. It's our turn to be rich and serve our country!"

Lilí and Way Oh rushed outside the chamber.

“Shall we reseal it up, my dear?” Way Oh asked submissively.

“Yes! No! Just a little bit. Just enough to make them think they are trapped,” she said malevolently. “Hurry up. Let’s get out of here!”

Way Oh sloppily threw rocks and mud toward the entry to the chambers. After a few moments of huffing and puffing, he stopped. “This thing sure is very heavy,” Way Oh was struggling to carry the turquoise hummingbird amulet in its lead apron plus the backpack.

“Suck it up! I just want to get out of here,” Lilí complained. “I want it all to be over.”

The pair tried to retrace their steps out of the cave as quickly as they could.

“Aiyah!” Way Oh screamed suddenly.

Lili turned her lamp on him. “What?”

“Something grabbed me,” he was shaking with fear. “Maybe it’s a snake or some creature.”

Lili approached him and shined her light all over him, going from top to bottom. “You, idiot, it’s just cobwebs.”

“I feel spiders crawling on me!”

“Shut the fuck up!”

After about twenty-five minutes the pair reached the chasm. Way Oh was still whimpering. They paused. The two boards spanning the cavity were still intact.

"You go first," Lilí ordered Way Oh. "Be careful. Don't drop the amulet! Leave your pack!"

"Don't worry," he took off his pack and cautiously took small steps on the planks. Deep breaths. He had done it before, and he could do it again. He was going to be rich in some foreign paradise. He reached the other side safely.

A minute later Lilí confidently followed. She got over also.

"Give me the hummingbird!" she said in a loud voice. "Go back and get your backpack!"

"Do we really need it? I could just leave it," he cringed.

"Can't leave any clues."

He handed her the turquoise hummingbird amulet wrapped in the lead apron.

Reluctantly, he repeated his steps and retrieved his backpack. He was exhausted from lugging the lead apron. Beads of sweat dotted his forehead. Way Oh was halfway back across when he heard a click. Then he heard the first shot but not the second one as he plunged down into the void.

"Did you really think I was going to waste my life with you and give you my money? You were such a fool!"

She sat down and lit a cigarette. She was drained. *Too much work and worry! This step is almost over,* she thought. By tonight, she and Rubí would be flying to São Paolo. They would be rich beyond their dreams.

A cold breeze toward wafted her. She thought she heard footprints approaching. She grabbed her headlamp and quickly peered from left to right and back again.

The iron apron opened. There was a high-pitched humming sound. Lilí's ears were ringing.

A large figure loomed in front of her. She got up quickly and tried to grab the hummingbird amulet, carelessly throwing her cigarette butt down the abyss.

The gossamer figure pressed forward toward her. Flames radiated from the lead apron as she tried to recover the amulet.

Then there were a series of powerful seismic tremors, and Lili and the hummingbird were thrown into the air. Rocks, dust, and debris flew everywhere. Lili was lying on the ground, choking until finally she recovered. With her left hand, she felt the edge of the abyss in front of her. She stretched out her right arm and felt around desperately trying to find the amulet. There was no light except for little patches of flame. Her eyes strained. Then she saws a small bluish glowing object. She tried to reach for the object with her right hand as she clutched the side of the hole with her left. Inch by inch her fingers got nearer to the shimmering artifact She was closing in on it. Finally, she lunged for it and grabbed it. She had seized it! *Gotcha!*

Suddenly she shrieked and jerked upward from the burning heat of the turquoise as it exploded. The edge of the pit crumbled, casting Lili into the depths of the abyss. There were several seismic explosions. The floor and the walls quivered. The roof of the tunnel started to collapse.

It took several minutes for the tremors to cease and the dust to settle. The turquoise hummingbird was now at rest.

CHAPTER 61 – SMOKE

Thursday, July 4, 2019

Revolver Mine, Little Blue Rock

Carlos and Rubí were leaning on his silver-grey SUV talking. He was trying to find out from Rubí what was going on. He didn't understand her Portuguese, but it seemed that Rubí didn't know anything. Suddenly, the earth shook. Was it an earthquake? Rubí seemed nervous. For the next hour, there were continuous aftershocks. He decided to explore the mine again, but the air was dense with smoke and debris. He retreated again.

"Rubí, I think there has been a terrible accident! I don't think it looks good. We have no phone service here," Carlos was trying to remain calm. "I think we need help. I think we need to contact Buzz and get a search and rescue team up here. Can you go do that?"

She nodded affirmatively. He hoped that she understood him. Carlos gave her Buzz's phone number. Chuu'u began barking and snarling. Minutes later Rubí drove away in the black SUV.

***

Surges of dusty air slowly penetrated the chamber with each tremor. Francisco was reaching for the guard's backpack that had been dropped during the tussle. He had covertly sat on it to avoid detection. He pulled it out from underneath and felt around with his still bound hands. He then carefully turned the mochila over. He found a head lamp and immediately turned it on. He spotted Tina by the skeleton; she was forced to squint because of the light. He swung the lamp around and found Patricio close to him. They were all covered with dark blood splotches.

"How are you both?" Francisco asked.

"Fine!" They both responded.

"At least we have a light," he said slowly aa he clumsily tried to inventory the knapsack cache: one length of nylon rope, one compass, but no knife. *¡Demonios!*

Francisco cautiously scooted next to Patricio.

"Do you want to look around?" he struggled to push the light toward Patricio.

After a minute of searching his surroundings, Patricio yelled out, "I found a gun!" *Too late now,* he thought. *For all the good it would have done.*

"Hey, guys, shine the light over here," Tina shouted. The lamp showed her bent over the strewn items from the medicine pouch. She picked up a flint that was very sharp.

Minutes later with a slight casualty, Francisco's and Patricio's ties had been cut. They rubbed their chafed wrists. They were free!

"I think we are trapped inside here," Francisco said. "I didn't see another way out."

"But maybe we can dig ourselves out," Patricio suggested. "Let me give it a shot." He trudged over to where they had originally entered the chamber. A foul-smelling air was wafting in.

Handful by handful, Patricio scooped out the loosely-packed dirt. More dust came in with each effort.

Suddenly, he stopped. He had discovered something. It was the shovel.

Moments later he resumed digging and found the pickax.

Francisco came over and spelled him. Soon the aperture was big enough for all three to exit. They slowly crawled through. The problem was the dirty air. Cautiously, they proceeded forward. After quite a while, they arrived at the fork in the tunnel.

"Stay here!" Patricio called out. "Let me scout out the path." He left with the head lamp. Francisco and Tina remained in the dark.

"Good call!" Francisco looked in Tina's direction and said as he attempted to laugh and then coughed. "Sol would have been proud of you!" He was talking about the "Finta" warning Tina had used to distract Lili and Way.

Minutes later, the sounds of footsteps approached. Patricio had returned. He was hacking. "The roof collapsed! We can't pass!"

Francisco was thinking. "Let's look at Map #3 . . . Just need that section," he grabbed the lamp.

All three looked and looked at the rough sketch of the mine. *Hopefully, this is the right mine*. They rotated the map. All three were confused and couldn't agree.

"Well, I think we are left with only two choices. Bats or skulls?" Francisco offered in an indifferent tone.

"My recollection is that the skull cavern was a closed system. The air was stale," Patricio posed. "On the other hand, the cauldron probably has an opening. The bats have to leave every night to forage for food. But it's very steep and rocky and slippery with all the bat guano. Really dangerous!"

"It would mean big trouble if one of us fell and got hurt," Tina said nervously.

After a brief pros and cons discussion, they decided to risk the perilous route. They tied the rope from the backpack around their waists, about seven meters apart from each other. Patricio led the trio. He had the head lamp. He would take four steps forward and then turn around to illuminate the path for the others. The air was still dusty from the explosion; and rank from the bat excrement.

They needed their hands to climb over some of the rocks. Patricio told everyone to stop and take off their socks. Francisco and Tina complied.

"Put them over your hands," Patricio directed. "Don't touch your face. Tina, you should pull your hair up."

They continued on. The path was getting steeper and craggier. It seemed to spiral upwards. Another tremor. They all stopped dead in their tracks. They were unsettled. They did not want to be buried alive in a heap of bat poop. *¡Qué asco!*

***

It had been at least an hour since the last big explosion. More and more smoke poured out of the entrance of the mine after each tremor.

"Where's Rubí?" Carlos was half way between being frustrated and being angry. *"She should have been back here by now!"* Chuu'u barked in agreement.

The ground below him shook again. On cue, Chuu'u, barked again. Carlos hadn't been paying much attention to him. The Chihuahua ran around Carlos several times and then started up a little path to the right of the mine entrance. He kept barking.

It was then that Carlos saw a billow of black smoke coming from the top of the hillside up ahead. Carlos stared at it. *Was there a back way into the mine?* He thought for a second and decided he wasn't going to stand around and do nothing. Forget Rubí and any help! He went back to his car and Patricio's and started to load his backpack. Four waters. Ropes, Face masks. Quinoa peanut bars. What else?

He started up the hill with Chuu'u leading the way, constantly yapping. The path zigzagged with saguaro cactus dotting the rugged terrain. Halfway up the hill, Patricio noticed that what he thought was black smoke was really hundreds of birds in flight. He paused and rested for a minute. The view of the valley behind him was spectacular.

Carlos and Chuu'u continued climbing. There was a slight pine scent all around them. They were only about thirty meters from the aperture when Chuu'u darted forward barking. To Carlos' astonishment, he realized that what he saw were not black birds, but a steady stream of bats flying out from an opening in the hill!

Chuu'u peered into a narrow fissure in the ground snapping at the bats as they were escaping. Chuu'u barked louder.

A few seconds later a reverberation from deep within the hole echoed, "Help!"

"Professor?!" Carlos yelled back.

"Help!"

"Be calm!" Carlos opened his backpack. "I'm going to throw down a rope. Pull on it when you get it."

Slowly, Carlos let out the rope. Ten meters . . . twenty meters . . . thirty meters. Arm over arm. Then he felt a tug.

"Can I pull one of you up?" Carlos yelled down.

There was another tug on the rope.

Minutes later Tina miraculously slipped out of the opening. She had the mine's placenta dripping from her. She was exhausted and looked and smelled like a drowned rat. Carlos guessed that the rope had gone down about 50 meters. Chuu'u barked as he ran around her in circles.

"Water!" she said hoarsely as she coughed and coughed. Her elbows were scraped and bleeding.

Carlos handed her a bottle. She gulped it down.

"Who all is down there?" Carlos looked over into the opening. "How many?"

"Just the professor and Patricio," she gasped as she answered showing two fingers.

"Are they okay?" Carlos was thinking about his next steps. "Anybody bleeding or in critical condition?"

She shook her head no.

A minute later Carlos was again dropping the rope down the aperture. "Rope coming down!" he yelled. "Send the professor up next!"

He motioned for Tina to help him. "Grab the other end."

"There are some really tight spots," she said.

About five minutes later the professor climbed out, clinging to the narrow rim of the hole. He was gasping to catch his breath.

"How are you, professor?" Carlos grabbed him under the armpits.

"Okay," Francisco groaned in a subdued tone.

Tina gave him a water bottle.

"How's Patricio?" Carlos asked.

"Surviving. He fell. I think he might have broken something."

"Do you think he can drag himself up the rope?"

"Don't know."

"Anybody else?" Carlos asked again.

"They abandoned us," the professor responded exasperatedly. Carlos did not understand what Francisco had meant.

Carlos and the other two continued with the rescue. The rope was lowered again. With Patricio injured it was especially problematic, and because of his muscular build, he was not that flexible. At times Patricio was being pulled up by all three of his colleagues. On more than one occasion, he got stuck on a crag and had to twist and turn to break loose or use the pickax to break away some of the stone to escape. As he ascended, he could feel warm liquid seeping through his shirt.

One last tug and Patricio was finally out. Chuu'u barked. Tina gave Patricio a bottle of water which he guzzled. She pulled up his torn shirt and dabbed at the blood with some water and a piece of her own blouse.

"Is anything broken?"

"I don't think so. Just bruised."

The three survivors discarded their socks and shoes, and tried to wipe off as much of the mud and guano as they possibly could.

There was another tremor.

“Let’s get out of here,” yelled Carlos. “I’m glad you’re safe, but you all smell like shit.”

Chuu’u barked.

CHAPTER 62 – SEARCH AND RESCUE

Thursday-Friday, July 4-5, 2019

Cananea

Carlos rolled down his window as he and Francisco hopped into the silver-grey SUV. The miasma was overwhelming. Chuu'u had the whole back seat to himself.

"Where's Rubí?" the professor asked.

"Good question," Carlos explained that he had instructed her to call for assistance from Buzz, but she had never returned.

"And Lilí and Way Oh?"

"Never saw them exit." Now it was Carlos' turn to ask questions. "So, did you find the turquoise colibrí?" Carlos was trying to get to the bottom line.

"Yes, but Lilí and Way Oh ran off with it when they abandoned us in the cave to die," Francisco was starting to get angry again. He explained to Carlos the whole sequestration from the hotel and the trek where they found to the skeletal remains of Ana Chan Azuleta.

Carlos took his cellphone from the car charger and saw that he now had some reception. He quickly dialed Buzz. It was past nine o'clock. The latter picked up.

"Buzz, this is Carlos with the Chan Toy Project. Patricio's colleague. Did Rubí or anyone else try to contact you today?"

Buzz said no, and then Carlos gave him an abbreviated version of what had happened at the mine.

"Is anyone hurt" Buzz inquired.

"Some superficial cuts and bruises," Carlos replied. "And they're covered in bat shit."

"Better get them some medical attention, just to be on the safe side," Buzz gave him directions to the Cananea Search and Rescue location. He got some personal information about the three survivors. "Meet you there in about twenty minutes."

Patricio was following Carlos and Francisco in his green SUV. Gripping the steering wheel with his slimy hands was a challenge. His bruised ribs were throbbing with pain. "I didn't understand the interchange between you and the professor in the tunnel. What does 'la finta' mean?" he said to Tina who was riding with him.

"Obviously you're not a real futbolista," Tina taunted him. "It's a fake play. It's a distraction. I grabbed the medicine bag when the lights went out knowing that Lilí was keeping a sharp eye on me. Meanwhile, Francisco stole one of the guard's backpacks while he was digging."

"And you learned this term how?" Patricio was incredulous. He was not into sports.

"From Dean Ríos' husband. He lives soccer 24/7."

They chatted for a few minutes. Then Tina reached for a cell phone that she had borrowed from Professor Reynoso. She dialed Rubí's number but there was no answer.

Then the ring tone of her cell sounded. She answered. Francisco was directing them to meet them at the Search and Rescue. "Just follow us."

***

The Search and Rescue Center was 3 kilometers from the OXXO convenience store. Buzz Halow was waiting for them when they arrived and took them in to be processed.

Each was given a private room where they stripped. Their clothes and shoes were put in hazmat refuse bags. Medical technicians escorted each into their own wide shower stall; and with a shower hose and antiseptic soap washed them off. Tina's hair had to be washed and rinsed three times. Then they were escorted to examination tables and underwent rigorous visual and tactile inspections. Patricio had bruised ribs and a broken right pinkie finger. Bat bites and scratched were treated with a special disinfectant ointment that had a strong eucalyptus scent. They all received antibiotic shots.

An hour later all three were wearing unfashionable orange miners' overalls with white tee shirts underneath. They all wore boxer underwear (including Tina), and socks and flip flops.

While he was waiting for his colleagues to receive medical attention, Carlos called Dean Ríos and apprised her of the situation. She was deeply concerned about the physical well-being of her team. She would give Francisco's wife a heads up. Carlos also fed Chuu'u some food Buzz had scrounged from the facility's kitchen.

Buzz had directed two of the Search and Rescue staff volunteers to clean and sanitize the two SUVs and to put some protective paper coverings on the car seats.

When they were finally discharged, the head doctor gave each a bottle of antibiotics that had to be taken over the next three days. Patricio read the instructions. No being out in the sun. No alcohol. *This sucks*, Patricio thought.

In the end, they all thanked Buzz and said their goodbyes. From there, they drove back to their lodgings.

“Anybody up for some food?” Carlos asked when they arrived at the hotel. There were no takers.

Francisco told everyone to sleep in. Since Carlos was the only one hungry, he snuck over to a bar for tacos and beers. The team, minus Carlos, was going to get together at the restaurant at ten o’clock for breakfast the following morning.

Loyal Chuu’u slept at the foot of Carlos’ bed that night.

***

Carlos met Buzz and his crew at the mine scene around 10:30 the next morning. Buzz’s men had done some preliminary investigation into the mine’s entrance and had determined that it was completely blocked off.

Carlos repeated what had happened the day before to Buzz. Afterwards, Buzz, Carlos, and one of the workers hiked up the hill to the aperture from where the three survivors had escaped.

“Do you think there are other exits, Buzz?”

“Don’t really know. All I really know is that it was a Yaqui mine that was converted into a native burial ground. It was called the Revolver Mine a long time ago.”

At around noon, Carlos left the mine with Chuu’u faithfully in tow. He drove down the hill to Sasheen’s hogan and took out a big paper bag filled with groceries. It included more cigarettes and chocolates. He walked toward the shack and yelled out.

A young Yaqui woman came out with the two boys he had seen on a previous occasion. Chuu'u ran toward her. Carlos talked to the kids and pulled two chocolate bars out. The boys were elated. The young woman, named Katrina, was Sasheen's grandniece. She invited Carlos inside. Carlos handed the bag of groceries to Katrina. He was given a compulsory cup of tea. Ick!

He told Sasheen what had happened at the mine, with Katrina acting as interpreter. Katrina was fluent in Spanish.

"We don't know what happened to two of the people, Lilí and Way Oh. They disappeared without leaving a trace."

Sasheen looked downward and spoke to Katrina. "Auntie says that they are with the four godfathers of death."

Carlos had expertise in indigenous cultures and beliefs. He knew that this meant that Lilí and Way Oh were dead. "What happened to the turquoise colibrí?"

"Revolver!" Sasheen spoke.

At first Carlos did not comprehend what this meant. Then it hit him! *That was old name of the mine. That was the meaning of Map #3!*

"The turquoise colibrí went home and became part of the mountain again," Katrina explained. "You know 'revolver', to mix. To become one."

Carlos nodded.

As he was about to leave, Katrina said that Sasheen wanted to tell him something. He walked over and shook her hand.

She said something and Katrina smiled.

"What did she say?" Carlos asked.

"When you come back, bring more chocolate and peanuts. And cigarettes."

CHAPTER 63 – AFTERMATH

Saturday - Friday, July 6 - 12, 2019
Guadalajara

Francisco had a long week of recovery after returning from Cananea. His wife took him under her care.

Dr. Alejandra "Alex" Mora had been widowed in her early twenties. She knew about psychological pain. As an endocrinologist, she also understood the physical pain and sufferings of others. When her comadre Miranda Ríos had told her about the phone call from Carlos, she got very anxious.

Francisco had barely been married to Alex for six months but he knew her penchant to know all the facts. When he had returned home from Cananea the prior Saturday, he had given her an abbreviated version of the events, not mentioning any dangers or risks. After giving him a bath and a neti pot nasal treatment, she went to a private website and pulled up the recent medical records and histories of Francisco, Tina, and Patricio from the Cananea Rescue Center. Francisco had understated the risks and their conditions. She frowned.

Alex forced Francisco to stay home on both Sunday and Monday. She recommended that he text Tina and Patricio to advise them to recuperate at home. Francisco also canceled their Tuesday staff meeting.

Tina was only too glad not to come into the office. Instead, she and Patricio recovered in his hotel room in Guadalajara. He had convinced his boss that he could not work with bruised ribs and was under a doctor's care for possible bat bites.

Alex finally gave Francisco permission to return to work on Wednesday because he had behaved, and he had finished the cycle of antibiotics. She gave him some additional tests which came back within the normal range.

Francisco had lunch with Dean Ríos at the Faculty Club. He started with a glass of Tempranillo and leapt into the tri-tip luncheon special with a picante salsa roja.

"I'm glad you're safe, Francisco. The things we do for money," She lamented.

He related the full version of the events. And then Francisco asked, "are we going after the additional two million?"

"Certainly, we delivered the turquoise hummingbird to them per the agreement."

"Technically they stole it from us, but it was in our custody even if it was only for a minute or two."

"I am assuming that all three of you will sign affidavits to that effect."

"Yes, dean."

"This really is no longer our problem. It now belongs to the administrations of both universities and their legal teams. I understand we have a staff meeting next Tuesday to debrief. Is Carlos going to write the final report?"

"Yes, dean."

"He has come a long way."

"And technically, I think he saved our lives," Francisco said sincerely. "Please don't share this with Alex. She might freak out."

"No problem. By the way, you and Alex are invited to the house on Saturday to celebrate some good news. I took the liberty of inviting Tina, Patricio, Carlos and his wife, and some surprise guests."

Do the Chivas have a new coach? Francisco wondered.

The next day Francisco had lunch with Tina and Patricio at a Mediterranean restaurant. The men had beef kabobs and Tina had a Greek horiatiki salad with chicken. Tina looked different.

She had her hair cut to shoulder length and had her fingernails manicured. The thought of bats crawling all over her body and muck underneath her fingernails made her cringe.

"No problem with your boss about taking some rest and relaxation?" Francisco asked Patricio. "You really deserve it."

"No. I did file my report. I should have sent you a copy."

They discussed the Cananea incident. "I talked to Carlos this week, professor. Buzz has thoroughly investigated the Revolver Mine. No survivors. They sent special cameras and listening devices down the bat hole but didn't discover anything."

Tina hesitated but finally said, "I think Lili and Way Oh got trapped in the mine and died during the explosion."

"I guess we'll never know for sure," Francisco rubbed his chin. "Where does that leave you, Patricio?"

"We had arrest warrants for Lilí and Way Oh for their thefts and for out of country transfers. But if they are dead, the point is moot. Likewise, with the turquoise colibrí amulet. Neither of the suspects are alive and the object in question can't be found. My report will be dumped in the dead files," Patricio smiled. He knew bureaucracy. "We'll see if anyone fills the vacuum for stealing and illegally transporting Mexican artifacts."

"The universities are still going after the extra two million," Francisco added.

"Good luck," Tina jumped in. "Remember that Lilí let on that the Chinese military was behind the attempt to obtain the turquoise colibrí amulet. It would be valuable for their medical and military industries."

Francisco thought that any possible resolution would not come from the courts, but from foreign diplomacy. The Chinese would not admit to anything but would be more than happy to excavate the Revolver Mine.

"What about Rubí?" Francisco continued.

"No sign of her. She was not seen exiting the Guadalajara Airport," Patricio said. "But here is what we did find. A black SUV was found abandoned in a private airfield in Tucson. Video cameras show an Asian woman in a car with Arizona license plates stopping at the Nogales Border Station. The name on a rental agreement is listed as Lilí Song."

Francisco's head snapped back. "The sisters were going to switch identities with Rubí coming back down to Guadalajara as a decoy! Crap! What about Way Oh?"

"No sign of him," Patricio continued. "You haven't heard the best part. There was a private jet chartered for Lilí Song and Way Oh. Guess where it was going."

"Back to Vancouver?"

"To China?"

"No and no," Patricio had their attention. "São Paolo!"

The other two gasped.

They kept talking.

"Unless you object, Tina, I'm going to have Carlos write up the final report. You will be leaving in a few days and still have to finish your dissertation"

"No problem, professor. I have a question about the third triptych though," Tina had been consumed with an open question. "The word 'Revolver' was etched on Map #3. What does it mean?

"Good question, Tina. Carlos said that the mine was originally called the Revolver Mine before it became sacred Yaqui burial grounds. It makes sense and it seems an appropriate place for the turquoise colibrí amulet to be returned."

"You all are the scholars, but let me give you, my take.," Patricio was self-deprecating. "Revolver in mining terminology can also mean mixing or remixing substances together. The elements of the turquoise colibrí amulet became part of the mountain again."

"And since it was a burial ground, Ana and Joya were also reunited in the mountain!" Francisco was in awe. "Full circle!"

"Holy bat shit!"

CHAPTER 64 – CELEBRATIONS

Saturday - Saturday, July 13 - 20, 2019

Guadalajara

"Well, you passed your physical, mi amor," Alex said as she fluffed up her large pillow on the bed. "With flying colors!"

"It's your doctor's bedside manner that does it."

They leisurely went downstairs, and Vera served them the customary soy lattes. Later, they breakfasted on fresh fruits, nuts, seeds, and yogurt.

"What are you wearing tonight, mi amor?" Alex asked her husband. She always wanted to make sure that he looked his best. They were going to a surprise party hosted by Miranda and Sol Ríos. It was going to be a special event.

"That navy-blue guayabera and tan slacks."

“May I suggest that you wear a red guayabera and white slacks,” Alex softly suggested, which meant he needed to heed her advice. Red? Really?

“Okay,” he gave her a puzzled look.

Before he could continue the conversation, his cellphone rang. It was Dean Ríos. After a “brief” dialogue, he hung up the phone.

“I have to go over to Miranda’s, Alex,” Francisco was not happy about command performances on Saturdays (unless it was with Alex).

“Hopefully, it won’t take too long,” Alex was trying to reassure him. “And you’ll have enough time to get ready for tonight.”

Twenty minutes later he was at the Ríos’ residence. Francisco received two pecks on the cheeks from Miranda and was led into the living room. To his surprise Dean Chandler was sitting on a chair drinking coffee. They exchanged abrazos.

“Long time no see, Francisco.”

The pleasantries went on for a few minutes while Francisco grabbed a coffee and one of Socorro’s famous cinnamon churros.

“We can talk privately here. Sol took the young ladies and Lena out shopping before they leave for college.” Francisco knew that Lena Zoltar DeAlba was Dean Chandler’s partner.

Lena had been born in Lviv, Ukraine and had been a concert violinist for the Krakow Philharmonic Orchestra and the San Francisco Symphony.

"Francisco, Dean Chandler and I have been discussing the Chan Toy Project for months. We were probably a bit overly ambitious in chasing the money. Unfortunately, we put you all at risk. We would like to make it up to you."

"First, Francisco, you did a miraculous job marshalling this undertaking," Dean Chandler jumped in. As such we would like to promote you to Associate Dean of the Social Science Department for both Stanford and the University of Guadalajara. Details to be worked out later."

"I'm honored. Thank you," Francisco was humbled. "Details will include more money and benefits, I hope." Normally, leaving the faculty meant forfeiting ones Due Process and other rights. But he wasn't concerned. This would mean that he would be in Guadalajara for a long time. Alex would be happy.

"Great, now as a dean, we must make some decisions regarding your team. First, we want to have Tina Fang teach a class at Stanford," Chandler continued. "It will be on the Asian influence in Mexico and Latin America. It'll run parallel to her dissertation. It'll give her a little boost when she starts looking for professorships."

"I think that is a fantastic idea, dean, thank you," Francisco was exuberant. "If I may, I would also like to have her be the Faculty Advisor for the Latino Club. I heard there was a vacancy, and she is more Latinx than most."

"Done!"

"We know that you and Carlos have been team teaching for a while," Dean Ríos stated. "His quick thinking saved this project . . . and probably, your lives. We are going to accelerate his doctoral track. Probably to study the Yaqui influence in Mexico."

"Wow! You two have really done some extraordinary planning!"

"There's more. Carlos probably won't be teaching with you anymore. He is going to be Director and Curator of the Ana and Joya Azuleta Cultural Center in Little Blue Rock. He'll be still working here but going out there a couple of times a month. How does all this sound?"

"Fabulous!" Francisco's eyes were as big as saucers.

Right on cue, Socorro came into the salon with three distinctive Talavera glasses filled with añejo tequila.

Francisco was slightly buzzed when he rushed home to change. He told Alex the good news and she was happy.

"One more thing, my dear, we need to celebrate," he hugged her tightly. "Next weekend we are going to Zihuatanejo to celebrate our anniversary."

"But that's not until January."

"But it's the time when we first got together," he smiled. "Let's not forget to bring the chocolate."

Despite the temptation to be late, Francisco and Alex arrived at the Ríos' home on time.

The entire entryway and interior of the house were strewn with cardinal red and white balloons.

"She was accepted!" Miranda threw her arms around Alex and Miranda. "And she's going! Stanford here she comes!"

EPILOGUE

2019

Guadalajara, Little Blue Rock

The remainder of the year was feverish. Mirasol was having the time of her life being a student at Stanford. She was leaning toward being a Spanish Literature or maybe a Comparative Literature major. She was already planning to do a Junior Year Abroad in Barcelona. Mirasol met some awesome Latinas who were going to set the world on fire. And the Latinx Club provided her opportunities to meet cute boys who were smart. She loved having Tina as the Faculty Advisor of the club.

Tina was always around if Mirasol needed something. Tina had only two speeds: Work hard or work harder. She was putting the finishing touches on her dissertation, but always wanted to add another chapter or two. Her casual summer romance with Patricio fizzled but she wasn't too disappointed.

He had been reassigned as Mexico's representative to Interpol and would be traveling the world. Maybe one day they would hook up again.

Francisco and Alex were enjoying married life. Francisco loved his new role as Associate Dean, in spite of more meetings, endless circular discussions, lunches, and planning the dates and places for the next meeting.

The good news was that Francisco and Alex could go on an official honeymoon. They were going on a two-week tryst to Verona, Lake Garda, and the Dolomites in northern Italy. Plenty of red wine, risotto, and tiramisu were in their future.

As for Carlos, he was driving over to the Yaqui Cultural Center in Little Blue Rock at least twice a month. The University of Guadalajara had built a cultural center and a bilingual education elementary school there. Spanish and Yaqui and other indigenous languages were being taught. Carlos had hired Prócoro from the Cananea Mining Association to coordinate with the local teachers. Carlos was also the curator and spent a lot of time inventorying Mexican and indigenous artifacts.

During every trip, Carlos would visit with Sasheen. He would take along Prócoro to translate the conversations.

Sasheen would always ask for something sweet, which Carlos would always bring. Chuu'u would get his treats too.

On the Day of the Dead, Sasheen asked Carlos to drive her up to the mine. Chuu'u and the grandniece Katrina came along. Near the entrance Sasheen lit three candles and a bouquet of sage. The air became sweet and fragrant. She took out pieces of chocolate and laid them by the candles, except one which she ate. She poured out some jamaica (hibiscus) agua fresca into a small cup, and then dropped three small turquoise stones into it,

Sasheen stretched out her skinny, sagging arms and called out to the spirits of Ana and Joya.

Suddenly, there was a click! click! click! sound fluttering above them. Chuu'u barked as a blue colibrí swooped down upon them.

ABOUT THE AUTHOR

Rocky Barilla lives in the San Francisco Bay Area with his wife, Dolores, and the dozens of avian friends who visit their back yard daily, ranging from hummingbirds (one is named Taquito) to red-tailed hawks. The couple spend part of the year in the paradise of Zihuatanejo, Mexico.

Rocky was formally educated at the University of Southern California and Stanford University. He also spent two academic quarters in Vienna, Austria. His passions are 19th century French literary fiction, Mexican history, global traveling, studying foreign languages, ceramic painting, and cooking.

Rocky has been actively involved in human rights, social justice, immigration, and multicultural issues, especially those involving Latinos and other people of color. As a state legislator, he was directly responsible for the Oregon State Sanctuary movement in the 1980's.

Currently, he and his wife are researching literacy programs for pre-teen Latinas.

His books have won numerous International Latino Book Awards (ILBA) and Latino Books into Movie Awards.

Rocky's mantras are "Life is Good," "Do Good Deeds," and "Do No Harm."

Made in the USA
Columbia, SC
23 November 2024

46710603R00270